THE EXAMINATION

MALCOLM BOSSE

The Examination

FARRAR STRAUS GIROUX

NEW YORK

For Mark Elliot

AGAINST ALL ODDS

Pinyin is the generally accepted phonetic script for modern Mandarin, but because other transliterations of Chinese are familiar to
us—especially Wade-Giles and Yale—I have sometimes used
those alternative spellings for the sake of recognition at the sacrifice of consistency: Taoism, for example, instead of Daoism.

Text copyright © 1994 by Laura Mack
Map copyright © 1994 by Susan Clair
All rights reserved
Published simultaneously in Canada by HarperCollins*CanadaLtd*
Printed in the United States of America
Designed by Lilian Rosenstreich and Amy Samson
First edition, 1994

Library of Congress Cataloging-in-Publication Data
Bosse, Malcolm (Malcolm J.)
The examination / Malcolm Bosse.—1st ed.
    p.   cm.
    1. China—History—Ming dynasty, 1368–1644—Juvenile fiction.
[1. China—History—Ming dynasty, 1368–1644—Fiction.   2. Brothers—
Fiction.]   I. Title.
PZ7.B6494Ex   1994   [Fic]—dc20   93-50955   CIP   AC

Learning without thought is labor lost;
thought without learning is perilous.
—CONFUCIUS

A journey of a thousand miles
must begin with a single step.
—LAO TZU

A NOTE TO MY READERS

My representation of the Ming Dynasty is based on research, my own experiences in China, and ideas I have shared with others about the country and its people.

Kings and queens have always had their documented place in history, but their subjects, most of them toiling in villages, left only scarce or unprovable facts to account for their existence. When we look back at the past, we want to see more than the pomp and circumstance. Although there is much we will never know about the daily lives of those who lived centuries ago, what we do know is enough to lead us into past and distant worlds, where people like Hong and Chen aspired to more than they were meant to have and sometimes lost and sometimes won, just as you and I do, in our own time.

Part One

Lao Hong was born under the sign of the Tiger, so he ought to be strong, if reckless; loyal, but hot-tempered; compassionate, though with little respect for authority. People declared that in every respect young Hong was true to his birth sign.

At least, he was going to be true to it by being loyal. He had decided to give up a happy life in the village for the sake of his older brother, Chen. Lao Chen, Two Brother (One Brother died years ago in a flood) was born under the sign of the Ox, which should make him patient and stubborn, with a gift for language, and skillful hands. One thing brother Chen didn't have was skillful hands. He couldn't untangle a kite string if his life depended on it. But by the time he could walk, Chen had demonstrated a wonderful gift for language. At the age of two he could read the first twenty-five characters usually taught to bright children of five. When read vertically from right to left, the characters spelled out a poem:

> *Let us show our work to Father.*
> *At our age Confucius knew three thousand characters.*
> *Capable gentlemen at our age know seventy.*
> *We know more than eight or nine!*
> *Work hard to learn*
> *And you will know right from wrong.*

Whether he knew right from wrong, Chen at two could recite this poem and write each character without error; at four years of age he memorized the entire 250 lines of the *Primer of One Thousand Characters*. At five he had a vocabulary larger than that of most villagers when they died. But now Chen's gift of language from the Ox was challenging Hong's trait of loyalty from the Tiger.

Surely Hong's mission this morning would prove his commitment to Two Brother. If he accomplished this, then probably he could keep Chen out of harm's way. Hong carried two small lacquered gourds, each shut with a lid of bamboo. If he had saved money, Hong thought gloomily, he could have replaced these bamboo lids with ivory ones. Ivory was used by city people for all their cages, whether or not they had anything of value to put inside them. It's what rich country people did who had insects of real value. Surely his own were of value equal to theirs: Fire Star and Dragon Legs were the most renowned fighting crickets in the region. Each had dispatched more than a dozen opponents. Every owner of crickets hereabouts feared them. And yet the last time Hong made money on a fight, dutifully he gave it to his father, who spent it drinking and gambling.

Hong had too much on his mind to notice this early June day. It was typical for the province of Sichuan: clouds lowering for a brief shower, followed by mists that settled like the smoldering aftermath of brush fires. Mist and fog helped to make this a green, wet land. It was said that Sichuan dogs barked at the sun as if at a stranger. Fifteen hundred miles inland from the China coast, the region was isolated by mountains, with deep valleys ideal for crops of both rice and wheat, for the planting of barley and broad beans. Hong didn't want to leave a home so prodigally rich in good food. Though short in stature for a boy of fifteen, he was broad-shouldered and thick-limbed and had the appetite of a goat. How he'd miss cold noodles in chili sauce and twice-cooked pork!

But there was no sense in feeling self-pity. When a decision was made, it was made. He meant to sacrifice his own comfort for a brother who could never get by without him. Hong quickened his pace through the narrow muddy streets; rustic houses lined the way with rammed-earth walls pierced here

and there by wooden doors leading back into hidden courtyards.

Stopping at one such doorway, he stared a moment at the fierce image of a guardian spirit pasted on the lintel to repel demons. Opening the heavy door, he walked only a few steps before confronting a spirit screen. This hardwood obstacle was positioned to block the path of demons. Since they traveled only in straight lines, they couldn't pass around the screen into the compound. The screen was painted red—yet another way of warding off demons, because red thwarted evil. Red meant virtue and sincerity. It symbolized heavenly blessings. A bride wore red on her wedding day. Gifts of New Year money were wrapped in red envelopes. *And* Hong's name meant "red," a fact of which he was inordinately proud.

Walking around the spirit screen, he entered the main court- yard of the Ma residence, second largest in the village, with upswept eaves on each of the tiled roofs, wooden tracery at the windows, tall vases and heavy black furniture inside the dozen stone buildings that made up the compound. It was the home of Ma Wujiang, his best friend. Hong never came here without recalling that his own family had once lived in a house nearly as grand; that was before his mother's death had turned his grieving father into a drunkard and a gambler.

A black-gowned, white-bearded servant hurried across the courtyard, waving dismissively at Hong. "Isn't here! Isn't here!" the old man shouted in a high voice, meaning that Wujiang was not home.

"Where is he, then?" Hong asked.

"Isn't here!" The man gave Hong a sneering grimace over his shoulder.

"What's the hurry?" Hong shouted back. "Looking for some- one? Don't you know your own father?"

Halting at this insult, the old man turned with both hands on his hips. "You're a disgrace to your brother! But you are definitely your father's son!"

Hong bowed low and replied sarcastically, "May ten thousand good things come your illustrious way." With satisfaction he watched the old man huff off angrily and enter one of the stone buildings. Two young maids came along, both carrying piles of cotton blankets stacked so high that Hong couldn't see their faces. But one of the maids called out, "He's at the kite field!"

When he returned to the street, Hong did not head directly for the outlying field, but turned instead down a path that was lined by tiny food stalls. For a copper coin he bought a leaf-dish of pickled vegetables and some slices of duck skin. Bolting the vegetables and munching on duck skin as he went along, Hong came to the end of this lane, where an umbrella mender had a shop. There were piles of rolled oil-paper umbrellas everywhere. Others were suspended by their struts like laundry from overhead lines. The shop seemed to bristle with black sea-urchin spines; some of the spindly frames were half-covered by blue paper made from the bark of mulberry trees; other frames stood bare. The mender, a skinny little man, sat cross-legged, gluing paper on a frame.

"There he is," the mender said with a smile. "How is Ququ today?"

Hong was known by many villagers as Ququ—the word for "fighting cricket."

"I have decided to do it," Hong declared, holding up the small gourds.

The mender shook his head, either in sympathy or in disapproval. "Does your brother know?"

"Ha! When did he ever know anything that wasn't written down?"

"I hope he appreciates it," said the mender, returning to the umbrella frame. "It's not every brother who would do so much."

"He won't even realize it. Or he'll soon forget."

"Then why do it?" asked the mender with a frown. "After all, he may be a big fish here, but he'll probably fail at the county seat. His chances of success are this much ..." The mender held finger and thumb together so there was only a tiny space between them.

Hong gulped down the last of the duck skin and hurried away. He criticized Two Brother all the time, despite the four years' difference in their ages. Hong grimaced at his older brother's perceived foolishness and even scolded him publicly—scandalizing the elders of the village by this breach of fraternal piety—but if anyone else so much as suggested that Chen was ungrateful or not really talented, Hong grew restive and sometimes downright angry. It was a measure of his liking for the umbrella mender that he simply walked away. In defense of his older brother, Hong was quite prepared to take on anyone. In fact, people for miles around had heard about him standing in the street and yelling at Magistrate Peng.

That had been two years ago, just before Chen competed in the district examination. When people told the visiting magistrate about the village wonder, Peng had scoffed at the idea of a seventeen-year-old coming in first. A day later, Hong had scurried across the street and blocked the magistrate's path. "You are wrong!" Hong had shouted. "You don't know anything! My brother will win first place!" His recklessness and lack of respect for authority had been the talk of the region. "That boy is true to his sign," people affirmed wearily. They also suggested that if Hong's father had been a respected citizen, Magistrate Peng would have admonished him for having such an impudent son. As it was, talking to Lao Lu would have had no effect; the man was always drunk.

Hong set out for the field, unsown this season to give it a rest. Above it, a dozen kites were swirling through the air in the shape of birds, centipedes, dragons. There was a low whistling sound from bamboo strips fixed to some of the kites. Approaching the field, Hong watched four boys about his age trying to launch a giant dragon kite. Beyond them he saw Wujiang tugging on the string of a caterpillar to stabilize its

8   circular segments, which were jerking erratically in gusts of wind.

Hong sat on the ground and patiently waited, holding both gourds in his lap. His friend Wujiang, much taller and thinner than himself, tugged too hard on the kite string and the long caterpillar dove earthward, crashing near a pine tree standing beside the field. Shaking his head with disapproval, Hong got up and walked toward his friend, who was gloomily reeling in the string.

Wujiang glanced sideways and let out a whoop of welcome.

Hong liked his friend's enthusiasm; it went with generosity and good humor and a certain recklessness that matched his own, even though Wujiang was born under the Sheep, which should have made him calm and shy. In fact, Wujiang was the only person Hong knew who was more capricious than himself.

"I thought you were giving up kites," Hong declared severely as he came up alongside the other boy.

"I was, but an uncle brought me this new one." He stood up and stared at the four boys tugging at the giant dragon kite. "They want me to fight next week, but maybe I won't do it. I hate all the work." He meant smearing glue on the last section of string near his kite, then dusting it with powdered glass in order to sever an opponent's line in flight. Not much work to it, but then Wujiang was impatient with such things.

"You shouldn't fight kites if you're going to fight crickets," Hong warned dryly as he watched his friend fold and pack up the kite. Hong rarely agreed with Two Brother, but on the subject of concentration he did. To do anything well you had to give yourself completely. That was why he had become a first-class fighter of crickets. But Wujiang here played chess or flew kites or collected birds along with trying to fight crickets. You couldn't do that with crickets. You had to concentrate on them. All of Wujiang's crickets—more than a dozen, a few of them costly—had died last winter. That was around the time when he entered a chess tournament and got beat in the first

round. If you had crickets, you paid them attention. Fire Star
and Dragon Legs had survived last winter—not an easy thing
for crickets. Hong had kept them in a small urn lined with
cloth like a chicken incubator; this sat on top of a small tank
of warm water. All day long he had checked the water's temperature. Having slept late one cold morning, he'd looked into
the urn to see Fire Star lying there, legs up, near death. He'd
put the insect in his hair under his hat and walked for hours
until at last, revived by the warmth, Fire Star began crawling
around up there. You could never relax your vigilance in the
cold months.

When Wujiang finished securing the kite, they walked across
the field together.

"I see you brought them." Wujiang glanced solemnly at the
two gourds. "So you mean to do it?"

"I do. Will you still buy them?" They had discussed a price
of one silver qian—three hundred copper coins, or the average
farmhand's wage for three months—for both Fire Star and
Dragon Legs. It was more money than anyone else in the village
could pay for them, celebrated though they were.

"Maybe I know of something better," said Wujiang.

They both looked up at the mournful sound of a hawk lute—
seven strings fixed across a gourd-shaped frame on a kite. It
was a large frog kite striding high above them, across the blue
belly of a swollen rain cloud.

Wujiang explained that a business associate of his father had
come for a visit, bringing with him a half-dozen fighting crickets. Landlord Meng had heard of Fire Star and Dragon Legs.
He'd like to match two of his best fighters against them. Wujiang
laid a restraining hand on Hong's shoulder. "Be careful. This
man has been fighting crickets for years. It's his passion. If he
brought them all this way, he means to win."

"Let me think," Hong said. They walked in silence awhile
before he halted and faced his friend. "You sure he doesn't
fancy guoguo?" Guoguo were singing crickets, big fat lazy crea-
tures who rubbed their back legs together and made noises

that some people called music. Someone who fought ququ had contempt for collectors of guoguo.

Wujiang shook his head. "I've seen his fighters. They're small, black, fast. He means to win."

"What about the money?"

"He didn't say, but then I told him I wasn't sure you would want to fight."

Hong was through thinking. "I'll match Fire Star and Dragon Legs against his best," he announced boldly. "I don't have money to lose, so if he wins, he just gains reputation for his fighters. But if I win either fight, I want one silver tael. If I win both, I want two tael." One silver tael equaled a thousand copper coins, or the wages of a field hand for nine or ten months. When his friend hesitated, Hong added, "A rich land-lord would do it."

"Yes, I suppose so."

"If he really believed in his fighters. He'd do it to gain honor."

Wujiang smiled; he had a long narrow whitish face. "Yes, I think you're right. He'd agree." Then he walked forward with head down, thoughtfully. "Are you sure?" he asked, turning to Hong. "I know how much they mean to you. If I bought them I'd only fight them against weak opponents, so you'd never worry about their getting killed. But Meng will match his best against them. I tell you, he wants to win."

"Will you set up the match?"

Wujiang nodded glumly. "Do you want spectators?"

"Of course. I have faith in my fighters. Let people come and watch."

"A lot more will want to see this match than we can crowd around the arena."

"Let them pay well for the privilege." Hong tapped the lacquered surface of one gourd lightly against the other. "To provide for Two Brother, I need all the money I can get."

The next night Wujiang's younger brother brought word that everything was set for noon tomorrow, that Landlord Meng had agreed to terms, that Wujiang would bring the weighing scale, that cricket fanciers throughout the neighborhood would be notified.

That night Hong didn't sleep at all, but lay brooding over the chances of Fire Star and Dragon Legs. Fire Star was quicker, but Dragon Legs had the more powerful jaws. Once he had ripped the foreleg off an opponent as easily as if tearing paper. Dragon Legs had the better chance of surviving, even if his leaping ability was less than average.

In the morning, when Hong went to inspect his fighters, he appraised their cages first. These gourds were his own work. He had selected the two best in his tiny backyard garden, waited until their blossoms withered, then covered them with clay molds in which they continued to grow. They remained there, assuming the contours of an hourglass, until he broke off the clay, removed the gourds from the soil, scooped out the meaty insides, and carved the names FIRE STAR and DRAGON LEGS on them. Then he lacquered them with the help of the village pottery maker. To keep the insects from jumping out, he fitted little brass springs inside, with release catches. Hong himself designed the bamboo lids, perforating each of them with four holes.

What sort of urns would Landlord Meng bring? Surely they'd have lids of ivory or tortoiseshell or rosewood.

This morning Hong didn't feed his crickets their usual mixture of boiled chestnuts, lettuce, bone meal, and mosquitoes. He wanted hunger to sharpen their fighting instinct. Removing each lid, first critically and then proudly he studied his fighters: their large heads and long antennae, their flattened cylindrical bodies and the knees of their powerful hind legs, with enlarged femurs for jumping, raised higher than their black abdomens.

As if in anticipation of performing today, Fire Star was clean-
ing himself with meticulous care. He ran his flexible threadlike
antennae through his mouth and washed his face by moisten-
ing it with saliva, then wiping the wet shell-like skin against
the gourd's side.

Although they were not guoguo singers, they often
chirped—more than most fighters—and this morning was no
exception. Dragon Legs rubbed a tiny scraper at the base of
his right wing over a small ridge on the underside of his left
wing, creating a high pure sound that seemed to hang in the
air like a dewdrop. Because it was a warm day, the chirps came
rapidly, resonating in the sound chamber of the gourd. Often
in winter, if the crickets sang at all, the sound they made was
a low sluggish rattle.

Putting the lids back on, Hong sighed with anticipation and
dread. Then, taking his favorite cricket tickler from a long box,
he inspected it thoroughly. Inserted in a reed handle, each of
the mouse whiskers was intact, springy, ready for use. He
would bet anything that the tickler brought by Landlord Meng
had an ivory handle.

Prepared to leave for the arena, Hong wondered if his fighters would be up against bigger opponents. Usually insects
were matched by size and by weight determined on the tiny
weighing scale designed solely for this purpose, but since
the contest was a challenge, no matter how big or little the
opponents proved to be, four crickets were going to fight to
the death.

Cricket contests took place in a shed behind the old Buddhist
temple. As Hong approached the temple's crumbling walls and
roof that had caved in long ago—long before his father or
even his grandfather was born—he saw Wujiang come around
the corner and rush toward him.

"The shed's crowded with people! Most won't see a thing,
but they've come just to say they were here."

"Have they paid?"

Wujiang nodded. "Meng had his best cages brought from

home. A servant traveled by wagon last night from Meng's village, holding the cages in his lap. One's made of coral. Can you imagine that? Coral!"

"Last night, what did you have for dinner?" Hong asked suddenly. He had eaten rice gruel for breakfast. His friend's family ate better than any in the village, and with a guest in the house, they must have had a feast last night.

"Dinner?" Plainly it didn't interest Wujiang, but he checked off each course on his fingers. "Minced squab and pancakes. Honey-braised ham. Eel cooked in garlic sauce—"

Hong interrupted impatiently. "What was best?"

"The eel."

"Why?" Hong persisted.

"Well, the sauce. It was garlicky and filled with the taste of ginger and hot pepper."

"Yes," Hong said thoughtfully, "the sauce sounds good. Your younger brother said you'd bring scales, but since it's a challenge we don't need them."

"Landlord Meng said the same thing. I saw his crickets again." Wujiang looked away from his friend as they walked the last few yards to the shed. "They're bigger than Fire Star and Dragon Legs."

Hong shrugged bravely. "I thought as much. It doesn't matter."

At least two dozen men had crowded inside the shed, including cricket fanciers well known to Hong: a retired soldier, a shoemaker, a carpenter, a basketmaker, a medicine dealer, a wheat miller. They stood shoulder to shoulder, packed tight in the hot room lit by torches. They jostled for position closer to the arena, which sat on a tabletop.

The arena was actually a bamboo box two inches high, eight inches long, four inches wide—about the size of a counting abacus—with a latticed top set on a polished frame. At each end was a sliding door, and in its middle another sliding door that would separate the combatants after they were placed into the box at opposite ends.

Hong hadn't reached the arena before a fat man plowed

through the crowd to block his way. No taller than Hong, the man wore a black silk gown and held a cricket cage.

It was made of porcelain.

Wujiang introduced Hong with great deference to Landlord Meng, following his words with a low bow. Meng responded with a faint smile of satisfaction, but failed to acknowledge Hong except for a disdainful glance at the two plain gourds. A boy about Hong's age stood beside the corpulent landlord; clearly, from his air of arrogance, this was Meng's son. When the landlord held out the porcelain cage to be relieved of it, the boy snatched it away and cradled it protectively in his arms.

Then Lao Hong did something daring.

In a voice loud enough for everyone to hear, he spelled out the agreement between himself and the visiting landlord. Implied was his suspicion that if the landlord lost, there might be a refusal to pay according to terms.

"How dare you speak so publicly of our agreement!" Meng bellowed.

"This is a challenge match," Hong said coolly. "All these citizens have paid to be here, so they deserve to know what we agree to."

That explanation had the spectators smiling. When Meng glanced around, he saw to his dismay that everyone there was against him. Turning, he pushed through the crowd to the arena.

"I have two fighters and you have two fighters. Here's what I propose," said Hong, emboldened by the reaction of the villagers. "We pick the opponents sight unseen."

Glaring, the landlord nodded in assent and snapped his fingers. His boy stepped up with a padded case, which enclosed another cage. Removing the case, Meng held high for display a cricket urn of blue jade. Onlookers gasped. That cage was surely worth much more than the combined yearly income of all the men in the shed.

Hong chose Dragon Legs to fight the initial bout. If only one of his fighters did well, better to have it the one who went first. Opening the door at his end of the arena, then removing the lid and releasing the brass spring, Hong tapped hard on the gourd bottom. Dragon Legs leaped from the cage into the arena.

Landlord Meng did the same from his end, simultaneously. His tickler was mounted in an ivory handle, just as Hong expected.

Hong stared at Dragon Legs's adversary. He was a very big cricket for a ququ—nearly as big as a guoguo singer—and from the rapid sweep of his antennae Hong could see he was also very alert. Taking out his tickler, Hong inserted it through the arena's latticed top of bamboo strips and touched the mouse whiskers against Dragon Legs's left antenna.

The cricket jumped instantly.

Following his movements through the lattice, Hong expertly touched first one antenna, then the other, each time agitating the insect into short quick leaps.

At the other end Landlord Meng was tormenting his fighter into a frenzy.

Dragon Legs, after a few minutes of teasing, clapped his hind legs together, producing a sharp metallic sound. Then he drummed on the arena floor with his abdomen. He was worked up into a murderous excitement. Hong called out, "Ready!"

"Ready!" answered Landlord Meng.

Wujiang, acting as referee, lifted the sliding door in the middle of the arena. Both crickets lunged forward. Meng's Great Leaper (for that was the fighter's name) sprang high and landed on Dragon Legs's back, clacking mandibles and snapping off the left antenna. It was a bold swift move, presaging worse to come. Hong backed a step away from the arena, wincing for his beloved fighter.

The contest didn't last long. Great Leaper was much too quick, to say nothing of too powerful, for Hong's fighter. First the left antenna, then a slender front leg went, then a middle leg, leaving Dragon Legs crippled and squirming. Great Leaper circled leisurely, as if taunting his opponent, then moved forward and slowly, with deliberation, gripped Dragon Legs's head in his black jaws, turning them forcibly until it came off. He walked off, unscathed by the conflict, with Dragon Legs's head held in his mandibles.

There was complete silence in the shed. Then, with a triumphant guffaw, the landlord reached in and grabbed the victor, lifting Great Leaper out and holding him high for all to see. He followed this flamboyant gesture by putting the cricket back into his jade cage, held out to him by the grinning son.

Hong didn't waste time in brooding over his loss, but scooped his beloved dead fighter from the arena, returned Dragon Legs's corpse to the gourd, and took the other gourd from the retired soldier, who was holding it for him. Fire Star entered the arena, as did the landlord's fighter from the porcelain cage.

Again the tickling took place. Again the calls of "Ready!" And again Wujiang lifted the door that separated the combatants.

Bull Jaw was the larger of Meng's two fighters, but much slower—Hong saw that right away; instead of lunging forward, Bull Jaw lumbered across the dividing line, his long antennae waving back and forth as if searching an empty space.

Fire Star didn't lunge either, but backed away. This did not surprise Hong, who regarded Fire Star as the cleverest fighter he had ever seen. What gave Hong sudden hope was the clumsiness of Bull Jaw, who kept marching forward while Fire Star kept backing away, just out of reach of the probing antennae.

The crowd strained to see what was happening in the small arena. The only sound in the shed was of humans breathing expectantly.

Abruptly Fire Star sprang forward. Then, in a series of blindingly fast moves, he had chewed through a membranous front wing and nearly dismembered a middle leg. Bull Jaw turned laboriously, trying to shake off the smaller assailant, until of his own accord Fire Star backed off once again. And once again Bull Jaw bumbled forward, antennae twitching stolidly.

Hong's hope soared. But then, leaping high and landing on Bull Jaw's back, Fire Star made a mistake; he let one front leg

dangle over the bigger insect's head, so that when Bull Jaw
turned violently, he took Fire Star's leg in his big jaws.

Bull Jaw crunched down and snapped the leg off.

A groan of dismay filled the shed, while the visiting landlord smiled broadly.

Fire Star managed to get away without further damage; with five other legs intact, he could still maneuver without much loss of speed or skill. The match lengthened, as each of the combatants, perhaps sensing the strength of the other, thrust and parried and turned and never launched an attack. Hong feared that a prolonged combat would favor the bulkier fighter, who depended on power more than quickness.

But Hong was mistaken.

After at least ten minutes of feigning and dodging, Fire Star leaped higher than before and landed on the bigger insect's back, turning instantly to chew through Bull Jaw's left eye. Hong yelled triumphantly, for this had been Fire Star's strategy during an earlier fight. Jumping off, Fire Star backed far into his own side of the arena, leaving his one-eyed opponent disoriented, turning in circles. But this didn't last long. Once again they went into a slow wary dance, which continued until Fire Star leaped suddenly and attacked the other eye.

Bull Jaw was blind. The fight was surely over. The shed was filled with whoops and yells of triumph, as men leaned forward to watch Fire Star finish the job. But when the insect sprang again, he miscalculated, landing in such a way that his left hind leg grazed the mouthparts of his opponent. Bull Jaw didn't need to see; he merely turned his massive head and clamped down on the tibia, breaking it off like a twig.

Without both hind legs Fire Star could no longer jump, so the outcome was once more in doubt. The shed grew quiet again.

Fire Star limped beyond the clacking mandibles of his opponent and stood motionless, nothing but his antennae gently moving. The fighters remained apart for a few minutes, adding to the tension in the crowded room. Then, bravely (so Hong thought), Fire Star hopped forward to nip at the bigger insect's left hind leg. When Fire Star's mandibles closed down on it, Bull Jaw turned and pulled free. This action was repeated and repeated and repeated, until some of the spectators grew restless.

At last Fire Star succeeded in gripping one of the hind legs and munching through it. Bull Jaw fell over on his back, legs waving emptily in the air. Crippled badly himself, Fire Star nevertheless had the energy and strength left to bite through each of the remaining four legs, then sink his mandibles into the soft belly of his opponent and chew. After a minute or so, Bull Jaw stopped moving.

Despite his mortal wounds, Fire Star raised his wings almost perpendicular to his body, nearly vertical. A song of victory poured from the rasping of one wing against the other.

Wujiang craned his long thin neck toward Hong and exclaimed, as they walked through the village, "Do you think Fire Star will live?"

"No, he'll die before nightfall."

"But he won! And you have the money."

Not without a fight, Hong thought, but didn't make this wry comment to his friend, who, after all, was responsible for his getting such desperately needed funds—funds obtained, however, at the cost of his beloved fighters. But he had meant to sell them anyway; they went out fighting with honor, as ququ should!

His own fight had been with Landlord Meng, who proved to be a bad loser and a shifty man in the bargain. First he tried to pay in flying money—kuan made of paper.

"I'm no fool," Hong declared. "Even the government won't accept that stuff. I want silver."

His village audience murmured, a few calling out, "That's right, boy, take only silver!"

Finally, signaling his morose son to come forward, the landlord waited for three small bars of silver to appear from a leather pouch the boy grudgingly opened. Each bar was stamped QIAN on one side. Meng's son also produced copper coins of fen denomination. Altogether the ingots of qian and the fen equaled one tael. Hong was no expert about money, but he had watched merchants throw coins on a table to ascertain from their ring if they were counterfeit. Walking over to the table where the arena still sat, Hong dropped each ingot and every coin, cocking his head as if listening for a false ring. The watching crowd smiled with satisfaction.

"Are you suggesting, boy," said Landlord Meng angrily, "I am cheating you?"

"A man who has such honorable fighters must be honorable himself," Hong stated grandly, but kept dropping coins and listening for the dull thud of lead.

"I have a mind to take you before the magistrate," Meng threatened.

"What? Why? Who do you think you are!" chorused the villagers, who stepped toward him, forming a wall of angry faces.

Meng muttered, "Never mind. It was a good match. We both won. Let's let it be."

Now as Hong walked homeward with his friend, he fingered the valuable weight that filled a leather pouch swinging from his belt.

Wujiang was saying that Meng would give his dead crickets a royal burial. A few years ago, the landlord had put a good fighter to rest in a little gold coffin.

Hong wasn't listening. In his mind he was counting a thousand copper coins, arranging them in groups of one hundred; then he'd scatter them about and start again. There was money enough for their journey to Sichuan's capital city and for the bribery surely needed to ensure Chen's success in the examination.

He had toyed with the idea of giving something to their father, but decided against it, although upon waking this morning he'd recalled the story of the Gaos.

Once upon a time there was a couple named Gao. Mr. Gao's father was very sick, as was their infant boy. They realized there was money enough to buy medicine for only one of the afflicted. "You have only one father," reasoned Mrs. Gao as they discussed whom to save. "But we can always have another child." So they gave medicine to Mr. Gao's father and let their child die. When Mr. Gao started digging a grave to bury their dead infant, he struck gold and became rich. The gods had rewarded Mr. Gao for showing filial piety. The moral was clear. Of all debts owed in this life by a man, the greatest was to his parents. Everlasting shame to anyone who neglected his father or mother!

Even so, Hong was firmly resolved to give none of this money to his father. It was his to give or withhold. If he must choose between Two Brother and Father, he'd choose the one who could benefit from its use. Give money to Father, within a day it would be wasted on cards and jiu lu, the distilled spirits that often transformed this humble, frightened man into a boastful fool.

As usual, before reaching his home, of which he was ashamed, Hong bade his friend goodbye and walked the final steps alone. This was the poorest area of the village, a clutter of huts of wattle and plaster, sagging doorways, mangy dogs, children with heads covered by boils. He was glad that his dead mother couldn't see the squalor her family now lived in. Sometimes at night he wondered if her ghost wandered nearby and witnessed it. He imagined her ghost crying bitterly. These were the worst times of his life.

Before going inside the hut that he, his brother, and his father occupied, Hong went around back to the tiny garden, where he meant to bury Dragon Legs today: not in a gold coffin but in the gourd that this honorable insect had lived in. Tomorrow, surely, he would have to bury Fire Star, too. They were great heroes, Hong thought. Tears filled his eyes when he passed through an opening in the broken fence and looked at the small graveyard where previously he'd buried other noble fighters, but none more noble than the two that had fought today.

Lao Chen had just returned from a week's stay in the town of Tianquan at the invitation of a retired official who wished the young scholar to inspect his extensive library. Chen hadn't visited that town since taking first place in the district examination held there two years ago.

Now, entering his village in a donkey-drawn cart, Chen wore the dark blue robe of a scholar for having succeeded in the county examination last year in Mingshan. On his head perched the winged cap worn by such scholars, fitted with an ornament of gold foil on red paper. The Director of Examinations himself had placed the cap on Chen's head. Everyone Chen passed on the road, seeing this distinctive costume, though worn by a very young man, either bowed to him or moved off the road as a sign of respect.

Chen stared at but failed to see his village as the cart entered it: the wattle and plaster walls, a pond green and fecund with slime, the sagging door on a weathered old hut, shoes drying on hooks after an early morning rain, a pile of sodden straw. He saw none of these things. His mind was filled with a book he had lovingly held in the official's library. It was an old commentary on Confucius by Chu Hsi, a great philosopher. In the year 1148, Chu Hsi had placed only number ninety in the fifth group of the final examination at the palace. That had been three hundred years ago, when examinations were less competitive than today. Chen was asking himself the strangest questions. Was it possible that he, too, would someday take the palace examination? Could he pass? Rank higher than ninety? Do better than the great Chu Hsi?

Momentarily his attention shifted to something moving in the sky. It was a dragon kite writhing in swift currents of air. He recalled that Taoists, in their search for truth, used to believe that kite flying was a kind of meditation. Imaginary flights of the mind were associated with the air. Altering tension on a kite string to compensate for changes in the wind resembled the need for a human mind to adjust for changes in thought. This comparison so intrigued him that he didn't notice a straw basket, more than twenty feet long, being hauled down the muddy street by dray horses. Later in the year it would be filled with harvested field beans.

Will I, too, go to Beijing and sit for the examination in the Forbidden City before the Emperor? A boy from an isolated village in a remote province? With nothing to my name? No money, no status? His attention was diverted again, this time by a familiar figure hobbling down the street. It was Old Shen on his daily walk through the village. As usual, he swung a hooded bamboo cage that contained one of his songbirds. To keep its balance in the swinging cage, the bird had to exercise. Such a bird needed to flex its muscles to maintain the strength for singing. The swinging cage simulated the effect of a brisk wind.

Seeing the young scholar in the cart, Old Shen smiled broadly and bowed low. Old Shen had been a close friend of Chen's mother's father. Chen bowed from the waist in response.

"Flowering Talent, good morning," said the old man, using the title bestowed on Chen for passing the county examination.

"Good morning, uncle."

In deference to the aged man and the young scholar, the cart driver drew up his reins and stopped so they could talk.

"When do you leave for the provincial examination?" the old man asked, without ceasing to swing the cage gently.

"I'm afraid there's no money to get me to Chengdu."

"Oh well, as to that, I think your younger brother must help you. Now that he's rich."

"Younger Brother rich?"

Old Shen regarded the young scholar skeptically. Then he sighed and let the cage hang motionless at his side. "They say you live in a world of your own. I surely believe it if you don't know how rich your brother is."

"Three Brother Hong?" Bemused, the young scholar shook

his head slowly. "What's happened here? I'm just coming back from Tianquan."

"Ah, that explains it." Old Shen gave a long, detailed report of the match between Hong's fighting crickets and those of the visiting landlord. His version was vividly dramatic though secondhand. In fact, when the story got around, everything became exaggerated. People believed that Hong won not one but ten silver taels. It was said he was rich enough to buy up half the village.

Having regaled Chen with this tale, the old man, weary of carrying the cage so long, bade him goodbye and went away.

The cart rumbled on over the rutted street, until Chen instructed the driver to turn into the narrow lane where his house stood. A humpbacked pig grunted by. A woman sat against the wall of her house at a rude spinning wheel. In a wooden cradle near her feet a baby lay asleep. She was too intent on her work to notice the skinny boy of nineteen in the rattling cart.

Chen tapped the farmer on the shoulder. "Here," he said. When the farmer halted, Chen thanked him for the ride. "I have no money," Chen said apologetically.

"Never mind that. I am honored. I will tell my family you were in my cart, Flowering Talent."

Chen eased his long, lean body out of the cart and stood in front of the small house that he and Three Brother and Father called home. The wooden shutter at the single front window was open. A large earthenware pot of yellow flowers sat next to the entrance. A heavy leather bag on his shoulder (heavy from books he'd taken along), Chen pushed on the wooden door, which creaked as it swung inward into a small, dimly lit room. Two candles lit the ancestral shrine that sat on a high brass-nailed mahogany trunk—one of the last possessions of value left to the Lao family. Two small cheap paintings of Shang Ti, the Supreme God, and Kuan Yin, the Goddess of Mercy, stood on either side of a copper bowl filled with sand and bristling with used joss sticks. On a long strip of framed paper were written the names of ancestors for five generations. Five

years ago, at the death of their mother, the Lao sons and daughter burned the old genealogy paper. Chen wrote out a new
one with their mother's name at the bottom. Aside from three
chairs lined up along one wall, there was nothing else in the
room.

When Chen entered and threw down the heavy sack, a broad-
shouldered woman, with strands of gray in her hair, came
through the far doorway, wiping her hands on a rag.

This was Big Sister Bao, who, though married with a family
of her own, had taken over the task of ministering to her father
and brothers. Her drawn face suggested a weary life of constant
labor. She didn't waste time in exchanging amenities with her
brother but motioned him into the next room, where she had
a meal ready for him.

"You're later than I expected," she grumbled, then glanced
at him with a smile. "Was it a difficult trip?"

"Not at all, jiejie." He called her the affectionate word for
"big sister."

"Then Three Brother was wrong. He told everyone you
would have a terrible time without him to look after you. I've
cooked something special for your homecoming."

Chen sat down at the table, regarding the stone chimney and
the stove with pots bubbling on it and his sister stirring a wok
with a long wooden spoon. He wouldn't tell her he lacked
appetite; for two days his stomach had been sour. Even at the
best of times Chen didn't have much interest in food, not the
way Big Sister and Three Brother did.

So it was hard pretending that he liked the bowl of beans
and goat braised in sesame paste that she'd prepared especially
for him. Working his chopsticks diligently, Chen hoped to get
away with only one helping.

Meanwhile, standing at the stove, Big Sister Bao told him
what had been happening in his absence. Her eagerness to
relate news was always proportional to its nature: bad news
usually elicited more enthusiasm than good. Today she spoke
rapidly, throwing her hands up to emphasize certain points.

Their brother was the subject of gossip throughout the village, she declared. Quite enough was his rude treatment of a visitor; Hong had tricked a poor man into betting a lot of money on a cricket fight, when anyone who knew anything knew that Hong's crickets were the finest to be found. Not that he won both bouts. And the cricket that did win died the next morning. Both crickets were buried in the garden.

Bao flung one arm out to indicate the garden, as if Chen didn't know where it was.

"Last night there was another fight, only this," she said with a deep sigh, "was not between insects. Three Brother and Father argued terribly over money. Father wanted some of the fight money, but Three Brother refused him." Bao threw up her hands in horror. "Hong is a disgrace to the family name! Refused his own father money!"

"Why did he refuse?" asked Chen, shocked.

"He claimed Father would spend it on cards and drink."

"Well, of course, that's true."

"Speak to him, persuade him to hand over *something*. The whole village knows. I'm so ashamed." She put her head in her hands and began crying. "I can't go to market without people staring at me. I know what they're saying: she's the sister of the boy who turns his back on their father. Father can be an awful man," Bao sobbed, "but he's father to us and to Hong and we must all respect him. Isn't that so?"

"Yes," Chen said.

Enheartened by his emphatic reply, Bao dropped her hands and wiped her wet eyes on a sleeve. "If he'll listen to anyone, he'll listen to you."

"He won't listen to me or anyone," Chen said, putting his chopsticks down, though his plate was still half-full. "Where is Father?"

"He went to see friends."

That meant he went to play cards and drink millet beer.

"I must go home and cook for my own family," Bao said with a sigh, picking up his plate and regarding it sadly. "You didn't like the goat."

"I have a bad stomach."

"That's because you never eat well," she countered briskly. "Our mother wouldn't be pleased if she saw how thin you are. I'll light a joss stick and pray that her ghost doesn't see you until you gain weight. Will you talk to our brother?"

"I will, though it won't help."

After his sister left, Chen sat at the table without moving. He watched a ribbon of noon sunshine unroll against the floor and reach the tabletop, throwing a streamer of gold across the pine boards. He was thinking of the great poet Tu Fu, who tried many times to pass the examinations and never succeeded. If Tu Fu failed, how could he presume to succeed?

Such hapless questions were still drilling into Chen's mind when his short husky brother appeared suddenly in the doorway. Chen smiled at the square face and the small but cunning eyes that seemed to take in everything at once. Although often at odds with his brother, Chen felt closer to him than to anyone else in the world.

Hong was sniffing the air. "That smells good. Was Big Sister here?" he asked without even welcoming Chen home. Nor did he wait for a reply. "When it's only Father and me, she cooks rice and any kind of vegetable in vinegar. Or she makes gruel. But you come home and it's delicious goat." He was sampling it from the wok with a wooden spoon. After heaping a large portion on a plate, Hong sat opposite his brother and dug in.

Chen watched him eat awhile, knowing he'd get nothing from Hong until hunger was appeased. When Hong went back for seconds, this time adding beans, Chen felt it was time to talk.

"I hear you fought your crickets and won."

Hong nodded while eating.

"And they both died."

Hong nodded.

"That must hurt you."

Hong nodded.

"I hear you won ten taels."

Hong held up one finger.

"Well, I suspected as much from such gossip. Even so, that's a great deal of money."

Hong nodded.

"Enough to give some to Father."

Hong slammed down his chopsticks and glared at his brother. "For drink and cards?"

"He is our father," Chen reminded his brother stiffly.

"Don't lecture me. I know what Confucius says about respect for parents." Ever since Hong could remember, his older brother had lectured him about Confucius. According to Chen, everything in life depended on the ideas of that great sage. Confucius argued that respect for parents was the source of all virtue, so Chen took it to heart. "Look at you," Hong scolded. "You're so thin and weak because you won't exercise, and you won't exercise because you're afraid to harm yourself, and you're afraid to harm yourself because that would show lack of gratitude to your parents for giving you a body." With a sigh, Hong shook his head.

"Thinner than ever," he added glumly.

"One silver tael is more than enough money for yourself."

"But it's not for myself. It's for you. I have to get you to the provincial exam. You'll need lodging in Chengdu for some time. And then there's the bribes."

Chen raised his eyebrows. "What bribes?"

"Do you think a candidate's successful on merit?" Hong laughed cynically.

"I will bribe no one."

"Then fail!"

They sat awhile in silence, Hong shifting restlessly, Chen as motionless as stone.

Finally Hong said, "We must leave for Chengdu soon. There could be flooding or something else could go wrong on the way. You must be there early enough to settle in, relax, adjust your mind."

Chen smiled. Three Brother talked more like a father than Father ever did. "I do want to try," he confessed.

"Then let's get ready!"

Chen's narrow face took on a determined, thin-lipped expression only too familiar to his brother.

Hong sighed. "What's wrong?"

"Father must have something before we go."

After a long morose pause, Hong agreed. "Something," he said. "But only enough to keep him in drink and gambling money for a few days."

That night, when Father staggered in drunk, the brothers confronted him with the news that they were leaving soon for Chengdu.

Lao Lu rubbed his stubbled chin and coughed briefly. His bloodshot eyes and shaky hands contributed to a general look of dissipation. Long ago he had been the well-to-do son of a landlord. Marriage had only enhanced his good fortune, as his bride, also of good family, soon proved to be a lively wife and talented mother. But perhaps her virtues contributed to his downfall. Never a strong man, never someone of mature judgment, Lao Lu fell apart when his wife died of fever. Or he used her death as an excuse for indulging his love of drinking and gambling. Within two years he had lost the house, along with his other ancestral lands, to gambling debts, then drank away any chance of recouping his fortune.

"So my sons are deserting me," Lao Lu muttered, resting his chin in his hands.

"Only for a time, Father," Chen claimed. "Just long enough for me to take the examination."

"That isn't so. He"—Lao Lu turned to look at his younger son—"told me as much. He'll encourage you never to come back."

"But I will come back, Father," Chen declared earnestly.

Lao Lu shook his head. "I'd bet on him coming back before you do. You'll go on to other successes. You'll forget about your father soon enough." Turning again to his younger son, he said with a sneer, "Isn't that right, boy? You know more about the world than your brother does. Tell him. Tell your brother he'll never see this village again once he's seen Cheng-du and, who knows, maybe even Beijing. And when people fawn over him, he'll forget the name of his father."

"Never!" cried Chen.

"He won't forget you, Father," said Hong. "But why should he come back here? A scholar like him in a village like this? What can be here for him? He only reads. He knows nothing else. He's worthless among farmers. I hope he never comes back!"

Father and sons looked warily at one another in the deepening silence. Lao Lu shoved his chair back and stumbled out of the house, bound for cards and millet beer. Chen went into his room with a candle and read from the *Analects*, though he scarcely needed to read, having memorized the entire Confucian classic long ago.

Hong went into the backyard and by moonlight stared down at the little graves, marked by stones on which he had laboriously scratched the names of Fire Star and Dragon Legs.

He had questions of his own. Was Two Brother worth sacrificing his own life for? What made a scholar so important anyway? Why was he doing this? Two Brother was a fool. If not controlled, he'd give everything away, first to Father and then probably to anyone who came along with enough wits to see how gullible he was. He'd waste his time on girls. For it hadn't escaped Hong that the only real thing about his brother was a growing interest in girls. It was a weakness, Hong decided gloomily, that might cost them a great deal of trouble in days to come.

How had Lao Chen become a Flowering Talent?

It began at four years of age with his mastery of the *Primer of One Thousand Characters*. He went on to the history book called *Ming Chiu—The Beginner's Search*—and then, with his well-educated mother tutoring him, young Chen proceeded to

the standard texts based on Confucian philosophy. By the time
he entered the village school at seven years of age, Chen could
recite two of the Four Books and three of the Five Classics by
heart and was known throughout the region as a prodigy. That
made his attendance at school more difficult than it was for
other boys, because the schoolmaster was an embittered old
man who had failed the provincial examination five times. The
blue gown and winged cap he wore as a Flowering Talent—
earned many years ago in the county exam—were faded, and
the gold foil on his cap was so torn that students snickered
behind his back.

Chen's schoolmaster was deeply jealous of gifted students,
but he was also a natural tyrant who made every boy in the
cramped little classroom quake with fear. A boy placed his
books on the schoolmaster's desk when his turn came to recite
the rote-learned assignment. He faced his eight or nine classmates and loudly recited what he'd memorized the night before. If he did a poor job, the schoolmaster would slap him
hard in the palm of the hand with a rosewood ruler. An outcry
merely encouraged the schoolmaster to add an extra blow.
Students were given twenty to thirty characters a day to memo-
rize from a passage of the Classics. After a few years the daily
workload increased to a hundred characters, then two hundred, so by the time the students were fifteen or sixteen the
brightest of them had learned by heart an amount of textual
material totaling almost a half-million characters.

The schoolmaster discounted Chen's remarkable prowess,
made jokes about the boy's long, skinny look (sarcasm relished
by classmates who hated his composure as much as his talent),
and often struck him brutally with the ruler for daydreaming
or smiling at the wrong time or ignoring a nicety of dignified
behavior. What enraged the schoolmaster most was Chen's
inner life, which was so isolated from the outer world that
the boy seemed truly indifferent to humiliation and physical
punishment. Chen sailed through the curricula with mad-
dening ease.

Rich boys preparing for the district examination were usually
taken out of school at fourteen or fifteen. This was because the
schools had nothing to offer a bright boy after that age. Although the Ming government believed wholeheartedly in the
examinations and counted on them to supply talented young
men for the civil service, no public interest was taken in the
schools. Only the civil service exams counted. Schools existed
for the purpose of giving employment to retired minor officials
or aging teachers who had failed the examinations many times.
Rarely did the staff give lectures. Never did they test their
students, most of whom were enrolled in name only as a way
of claiming to be scholars.

Rich boys were taught by tutors at home, usually in an elegant study detached from the main compound. Chen did not
have that luxury, nor was his mother around anymore to give
him the benefit of her knowledge. Like other poor candidates,
he had to educate himself. Fortunately, Chen was capable of
it. He did not find repetitive study a bore, nor did he have
any hobby or interest to compete with daily toil at books.
Fortunately, too, the examinations were based upon a limited
number of classics, so that his field of study was clearly set for
him whether he was ten years old or fifty.

And then along came a retired official, Yang Zuolin.

Or rather his servant came along—appearing at the Lao
house with an invitation for "the young scholar" to have tea
with Honorable Ex-Commissioner Yang.

Chen was fifteen.

One unsettling trait of the boy was his casual demeanor
when in the presence of a superior. Unlike his younger
brother, Chen respected authority. It was a measure of his
full acceptance of Confucian ideals. But he seemed not to
comprehend the reality of power—of the status and experience and wealth that set one man above another. He treated
everyone equally in a world of rigid social distinctions.

His first meeting with the retired administrator was a case
in point. For twenty years Commissioner Yang Zuolin had

served with honor under four governors of the province of Sichuan. In distinguished retirement he lived outside the village in a rambling villa with a garden famed throughout the region. Its beauty and sophistication reminded people (those wealthy enough to have traveled) of the great gardens of Suzhou.

When the elderly man took the fifteen-year-old on a tour of the garden—its pebble-mosaic paths, airy pavilions, and covered galleries, its fishponds and half-moon bridges—the boy appeared neither restless nor overwhelmed but merely curious.

Once he stopped in front of a pile of limestone rocks and, after staring awhile, turned to his host and asked, "What is this garden for?"

"To look at," said Yang Zuolin with a faint smile. "This is a controlled space for the mind to play in. Do you understand?"

"No," Chen said honestly.

"Surely you understand Taoist thought. They tell me no other boy of such brilliance has come out of this province in many years."

"I read and understand some of what I read. But not all."

Such candor brought a nod of approval from the retired official. "A controlled space for the mind to play in—I mean in the sense of the mind wandering without restriction, enjoying the freedom of a child at play. The idea of such a garden is to encourage in the onlooker a deep but simple communion with the universe. The garden strengthens one's familiarity with the Tao, the underlying principle of everything. What I look for here in the garden is always hidden behind what my eyes see. I often watch the shifting light of day, how the shadows fall and how the walls by changing color become different walls at sunset from what they were at sunrise. Just as everything becomes different, just as the Tao flows and changes and remains the same. I walk along these paths as though I were walking through an unrolling scroll, through a painted landscape. See that wall behind us? It's the color of ivory right now.

It's like silk in a Sung painting. But as the day flows on, the color will change into the earthen brown typical of a Han painting. Now do you understand?"

"I understand the words you're saying. But since I don't know about paintings, I don't understand your feeling about them."

"Well, a good answer. Tell me, I'm curious about this. How do you remember characters so easily?"

"I have a method."

"Yes, go on."

"I've never told anyone."

"Because you don't want them to copy your method?" Yang laughed.

"Yes. I don't want that. But I'll tell you."

"Why?"

"Because you're only curious. You don't want anything. You won't use the idea against me."

Yang studied the lanky boy. "They told me you live in another world. I see now you live very much in this one. Why do you study so hard?"

"To know more," Chen said instantly.

"Come now. Is that all? The Sung Emperor Chen Tsung wrote a poem about the rewards of scholarship. Do you know the poem?"

"I know it."

"So, according to it, what are those rewards?"

"Riches and beautiful women."

"Are they what you want?"

After a thoughtful pause, Chen said, "Perhaps someday. I'm not yet old enough to think of wealth. Right now I just want to know more. And to"—he hesitated—"to test myself against others. I want to know how much I know."

"Tell me about your method of remembering."

"I have rooms in my mind. In these rooms I keep characters as you might keep chairs or tables or kitchen utensils in a house. Similar chairs are kept in one room, similar tables in another, similar kitchen knives in another. Instead of furniture I put the characters I learn into different rooms. I think of the room furnishings in terms of the lines, angles, sweeps, and hooks needed to write characters." He paused. "It is complicated."

"I imagine so," Yang said.

"One room contains characters with at least three horizontal lines. Another stores the characters with more than three curved hooks, and another room holds those with at least three long sweeps, another with three short sweeps. Each room is a storeroom of similar characters."

"Wouldn't it be easier," Yang suggested, "just to look hard at a passage and then write it a hundred times and remember it that way?"

Chen shook his head somberly. "Not for me. I have my rooms, and I move around in them very quickly."

"I believe you do move around them quickly." Yang was so impressed by Lao Chen that he took the boy under his wing. They met three times a week for study, and Yang began to regale Chen with stories of his own examination days. He had passed the provincial examination, but had never gone on to Beijing for the final tests.

"I felt I had gone as far as I could go," Yang Zuolin admitted. "To go on for the municipal and palace examinations, you must be the best of the best. And the journey from our province to the capital is so long, so arduous, so fraught with danger, that I decided to count my blessings for having gone this far. I haven't regretted it. I've had a wonderful life." Glancing at the boy as they walked in the garden, Yang said, "If you passed the provincial examination, would you go on to Beijing?"

"There wouldn't be enough money."

"But assume there was. Would you go on?"

"Yes, I would."

"To make a name for yourself?"

"To test myself and find out how much I know."

Unluckily for Chen, this man, who intended to provide money for such a journey, would not live to see his protégé

take any of the examinations. Commissioner Yang died of the
same kind of mountain fever that had taken the life of Chen's
mother.

But like a cork on the sea, Chen had managed to overcome
bad luck and keep himself afloat in the struggle to know. Alone,
the boy continued to practice his calligraphy until he could
hold his brush vertical against a page and fill it with quick,
confident strokes without blotting the ink once. He labored
hard at composing essays and poems. Mastering the technique
of writing essays was his most difficult task. Each form of essay
involved special rules. A rule governed the number of words
in a paragraph, the number of paragraphs and their length, the
type of language used—either highly formal or conversational.
A dozen rules determined the stages of argument to be developed according to patterns of debate a thousand years old.
Chen understood that not only must a young scholar have a
splendid memory but his handwriting must be elegant in five
different styles; his essays must follow a labyrinthine set of
rules; and his poetry had to display competence in the use of
three modern and two ancient rhyme schemes.

Because science and math were not required for the examinations, Chen hardly learned to count. Buying something in
the market, he was unsure of how much change to get back.
Merchants tittered openly, but he went on counting with his
fingers, unashamed of his ignorance of numbers.

At seventeen he was ready for the first hurdle on his quest:
the district examination, held in the town of Tianquan. On his
application Chen had to indicate his height and weight, his age
and address, and whether he wore a beard. That was all except
for one thing more. He must supply a guarantee from someone
of established reputation that no one in his family was a bandit,
an actor, a policeman, a prostitute, or a drunkard. For a boy of
his age with a father widely known as a drunkard, such a
guarantee of good family seemed like an obstacle that would
end his scholarly career before it began.

This is where Three Brother first asserted himself in Two

Brother's life. Barely thirteen and heartily disliked by the schoolmaster for both his impudent behavior and his poor scholarship, Hong went directly to Master Fei Qun, kowtowed to show he was serious, and explained his brother's plight. Would the schoolmaster write a recommendation for Lao Chen and disregard their father's unfortunate condition?

Surely Chen would have stopped his younger brother from making such a bold request. Enraged, the schoolmaster would probably inform the district authorities of the Lao brothers' attempt to corrupt him. When Chen heard of his brother's action, he told himself his dream of competing in the examination was shattered.

So he was amazed when the schoolmaster came to the Lao house, bearing in hand a document which stated that he guaranteed the good name of the Lao clan without reservation.

The stout old teacher guffawed at the young scholar's stunned expression. Master Fei Qun had the big-boned physique of a carter and the red face of a brawler, so that people stayed clear of him in the village. "I took the provincial exam years ago with your uncle, who failed, too. That made us friends. And what you don't know either is this: through him I met your mother before she married. Few women have the chance to study as she did. And she took advantage of it. She was better at calligraphy and composition than her brother. She would have passed the county, I'm sure. Maybe even the provincial. Now listen to me. I think your brother Hong is a devil who'll end up a bandit or worse. I think your father is a weak man, a complainer, and a drunkard. But I liked your uncle and respected your mother, and though I have no faith in your ability to pass the exams, at least not beyond the district, I have decided to falsify the truth. I've not mentioned your father's drinking in this statement. I've claimed the Lao family is without flaw—as pure as Confucius himself would desire."

Chen bowed low in relief.

Master Fei Qun glowered at the young man. "Don't be smug and proud. I confess I dislike you. Your ease of learning is the

trouble. It's prevented you from struggling to perfect virtue.
You don't emulate the Confucian ideal of a gentleman. You're
disdainful, aloof, indifferent. You're terribly bad-mannered,
and what is worse, you've never taken the trouble to know
precisely when you're rude or thoughtless. It just doesn't occur
to you—the worst possible thing to say about a follower of the
Great Man. So why have I debased myself by lying about your
family? To help *you*? Not at all. I've merely paid my respects
to dead members of your family. But more than that, I've lied
in this statement because it gives me comfort to know that
those officials who stand in judgment of men better than themselves, who kept me from success because they were too ignorant to read an essay properly, who call themselves examiners
and upholders of academic excellence when they're actually
turtle-headed and greedy—what was I saying? Ah yes, indeed!
They're nothing but fools. Fools, fools, fools, so easily hood-
winked that on the basis of my false statement they'll accept a
candidate unqualified by their own rules to compete in the
examinations!" Breathing hard after saying so much so rapidly,
his red face even redder, the brawny old teacher smiled until
his uneven teeth showed yellowly, just as if he had finished
slapping the hand of a poor student with his rosewood ruler.

Armed with the guarantee, Chen applied for the district
examination. He traveled alone to Tianquan because the town,
only fifteen miles from the village, was easy to reach by a
wagon ride. He stayed on the edge of town with a family
whose patriarch had once served Chen's mother's father as a
stablehand. The family was impressed by having a scholar stay
in their modest hut, though when he fell sound asleep without
the slightest show of nerves on the eve of the examination,
they decided he wasn't serious enough to compete successfully. They had expected him to toss and turn all night.

At four in the morning the primer powder of a cast-iron
cannon was lit. The following bang was accompanied by a shot
of roundstone flying through the air, signaling the students,

hundreds of them lodging in town, to rise and prepare for the examination.

The old stablehand had to shake Chen awake. The young scholar rose with a deep yawn, washed his face unhurriedly, and accepted a cup of tea, while a half-dozen scruffy children gathered around to have a curious look at him. From his knapsack he took a small wicker basket and filled it with an ink stone, sticks of ink, three brushes, a water pouch, and some fruit for lunch. He strolled out into the darkness, hearing another cannon report. Students, their families, and well-wishers were funneling toward the town hall from every direction. At the sound of a third cannon shot, the great doors of the district yamen swung open and everyone surged inside, searching frantically for assigned desks, each candidate's name indicated by a tally stick. Friends and relatives were then ordered to leave, and the couple of hundred candidates waited at their desks until the town magistrate in ceremonial gown appeared at the dais. He had assistants give out answer sheets in the form of a folded book of plain white paper with ruled vertical lines in red. Then he himself locked the hall and affixed a seal to the lock.

By then it was six in the morning. While others looked curiously around at their rivals, Chen inspected his brushes, gently touching the bristles and testing them for firmness.

The magistrate read the first question out loud. Then it was written on a large piece of paper and carried by an assistant around the hall on a placard so everyone could see. There was a quote from Confucius: THERE ARE THREE THINGS A MAN SHOULD FEAR. The candidate's task was to quote the next passage from the *Analects*, then add a commentary by another philosopher and end with his own opinion.

While others stroked their chins and fiddled with their ink brushes and tried to recall the next passage, Chen wrote instantly, "He fears the will of heaven, he fears great men, he fears the words of the sages." Having quoted it exactly, he then provided a commentary by Chang Tsai; for good measure he included a commentary by Chu Hsi on Chang Tsai's commentary—quoting both philosophers with meticulous accuracy. He had nothing revolutionary to offer as his own opinion, but warily discussed the strengths and weaknesses of both thinkers and humbly submitted the idea that their work was of equal value.

In two hours the proctors went around and stamped each answer sheet at the final written word, so nothing could be added later to the answer. The exam went on to part two, also about Confucius. The final task of the day was to compose a poem in the old ku-shih style, using five words to the line, on a set scheme of even-numbered lines rhyming, and alliteration appearing in the odd-numbered lines. Chen wrote a poem that imitated a ku-shih composed fifteen centuries before, the first lines being

> *I bathe in orchid water,*
> *wash my hair with scents,*
> *put on colored robes,*
> *flower-figured.*

He created a forty-line poem in this ancient song style, put away his writing materials (he ate only one pear for lunch), handed in his work to a proctor, and waited at the front door until an assistant broke the seal and let him out. Chen was gone more than two hours before anyone else turned in an answer sheet. The majority of candidates finished still later, around sunset.

That was the first day. There were three more days, which followed the same pattern, only sometimes an essay about an historical event or the working of government was substituted for a poem.

All these papers were graded by the District Magistrate and local teachers. Names on the answer sheets were covered, so only the seat number was visible. This prevented favoritism. Once graded, the successful candidates were listed on a large

sheet of paper for posting on the yamen gate. About one candidate in twenty made the list. The name of the candidate ranked
first was placed at the top and the others were written counter-
clockwise in descending order.

Chen was first.

The next year he took the county examination at Mingshan,
where there was a permanent hall for this purpose, with a
director appointed by the Emperor to preside over the four-
day test, which followed the same pattern as the district
exam.

This time Chen stayed until the end and worked on his
composition. Even so, he did not rank first. He did, however,
receive the title of Flowering Talent, along with the blue gown
and winged cap of an officially recognized scholar. This time,
when the list was posted, the ranking was written clockwise in
descending order; he came third.

So at the tender age of eighteen Lao Chen was a member of
the Ninth Grade of the civil service (though he had no job),
was exempt from taxation, and deserved a seat of honor wherever he went, even though it was the last thing he cared about.
What did he, as a Flowering Talent, care about?

What do I know? he asked himself, tossing restlessly in the
silent darkness. How does my knowledge compare with that
of others? Two candidates at the county exam beat me. What
do they know that I don't? What can they write that I can't?
There are five counties in the province of Sichuan. That makes
five places in which people took the exam. How many did
better than I? And there are so many provinces in the empire,
more than twenty-five. How many scholars in all the counties
of all the provinces in all this vast empire have done better?
There must be dozens. What do they know? How do they write?
Where am I in all of this?

What else, he wondered, can there be to care about?

When the retired soldier came to see him, Hong was squatting in front of the little garden where he'd raised gourds for cricket cages. Would he ever grow anything in the garden again, Hong wondered. Chengdu, where he and his brother were going tomorrow, was called the City of Hibiscus. Because the hibiscus flowered in autumn, its old name was jushuang: "resists frost." His mother used to call it jushuang; she had taught Hong to grow things. So autumn was the season for jushuang; it was also the best season for cricket fighting. It was said that in the far western parts of the province, local magistrates allowed farmers to pay their harvest taxes in a strange currency: fighting crickets. That was why in such a region the magistrate often had the best ququ: he accepted them in lieu of silver.

Hong would not fight his insects this fall; he'd be off with his brother, chasing fame, and anyway his best fighters were dead. Would he ever see the like of Fire Star and Dragon Legs again?

This gloomy train of thought was interrupted by Zhu Tong. The retired soldier farmed six acres of land given to him by the government; it was just enough land to support him and a wife. In his spare time he raised crickets, but rarely did one of his insects defeat a fighter owned by Lao Hong. Their rivalry had brought them together, so that the old ex-soldier felt no embarrassment in coming to see a boy. Zhu Tong entered the house as if visiting an equal.

He was a short wiry man with a gray mustache whose ends curved around his mouth like the claws of a crab. Bowlegged, he swayed when he walked. Entering the backyard garden, Zhu Tong saw immediately that his young friend was grim and unhappy. He knew the reason.

"You don't want to leave," Zhu Tong declared bluntly, "because you don't think you'll return. Well, maybe you won't.

Your brother might pass the provincial and go all the way to the palace examination."

"I think he will."

"Take comfort in this. Most people expect him to fail the provincial. No one from this village has ever passed it. They say your brother is very smart, but once he sees the big city of Chengdu and all the other candidates, many of them rich, he'll be so humbled he'll forget what he knows. Then you'll be home in a month. You know what they say about the provincial."

Hong knew. To pass it, a man needed the spiritual strength of a dragon, the power of a donkey, the insensitivity of a wood louse, and the endurance of a camel. It also helped to have bribery money.

Hong was squatting at the edge of the garden patch, so the old soldier squatted beside him like another boy, like an equal. "Here." Zhu Tong gave a sealed scroll to his young friend, explaining that the local scribe had written a letter for him. It was addressed to his former commander in the infantry. "If you do go all the way to Beijing with your brother, you could stop at Suzhou. The Fifth Army Group is there, so Commander Ma, if he's still alive, will be there, too. In this letter I pay my respects to a great warrior. I fought as a lancer and a crossbowman under his command." Because Zhu Tong rarely spoke of his military service, Hong looked curiously at the weathered little man. Zhu Tong took this occasion to recall a tour of duty in Burma with the Third Army Group of the Southwest. That was where he had first served with Battalion Commander Ma. They had seen action against the Maw Shan and besieged the walls of Ava, a Burman city on the border, finally destroying the city by tearing down a river dike and flooding the whole region. Later the battalion had been sent to the Second Group when the Kalmuck Mongols were threatening to break through the Great Wall. The battalion had learned to divert the reckless charges of the Mongol cavalry by using a square formation and allowing their own cavalry to pour through it as through a sieve and closing up against the

Mongols at the last moment, spraying their mounts with shot
from battle wagons.

Suddenly, fired by a vision of the past, Zhu Tong rose to his feet and drew back an imaginary string of horse gut, set a square-headed arrow in the wooden groove of the stock, lifted the crossbow, and pulled the bronze trigger. He made a whirring sound between his teeth in imitation of a bolt sailing through the air to its target—Burman, Mongol, Japanese. "They have repeating crossbows now," he said dreamily, as if speaking to himself. "They fire eleven bolts one after another. I haven't seen them, though. Anyway, I prefer the old infantry squad. We had two shield carriers to the front, then two bamboo-tree carriers, then four lancers—usually I fought as a lancer—and two rear guards with three-pronged spears. At times we had two crossbowmen. I did that, too. Our formation was called the Mandarin Duck, an old formation. Our squad fought as one. We were rewarded and punished as one. Commander Ma believed the peasant was the best of fighters because he got up close to the enemy. So we fought that way, like peasants, as close as possible. Commander Ma believed in infantry, in weapons that reached the enemy an arm's length away. Never had faith in the new weapons like guns, because sometimes a fuse didn't ignite and a gun was the devil to load and sometimes blew up in a soldier's hands before he could fire it. In my day we liked the rattan shield, the spear, and the crossbow, and especially a tree of bamboo shoved in the enemy's face. You had to be brawny for that—to carry a whole bamboo tree! But I knew men who could wield one like a stick. Soldiers today aren't what they were in my time."

Poking Hong's arm to emphasize certain points of argument, Zhu Tong criticized the new army. There was low pay for soldiers, desertions, too much time spent at labor other than military training, and corruption among officers who stole from their own troops. He shook his head sadly. "For twenty copper coins a month, I hear a soldier today can get out of drill and other duties. In my time, when a soldier disobeyed, he was beaten with a hard wooden pole as thick as four fingers.

The first blow took the skin away. Each blow after that would tear out lumps of flesh. I've seen men die from such beatings. I've seen it happen after ten blows; only the very strongest could survive thirty. And officers who acted the fool had their noses cut off, or their upper lips, and sometimes even a hand or a foot. In my day there was discipline."

After a long ensuing silence, Zhu Tong sighed. "I hope, boy, you come back, because your crickets are the best opponents I know of hereabouts, but if you don't return I wish you ten thousand good things wherever you go. If you reach Suzhou, give the commander this letter. He'll be grateful, believe me, as we served together sixteen years, and I saved his life three times, and it was he who saw to it I got my retirement land."

Because there was no postal service, anyone traveling abroad was expected to accept letters for delivery elsewhere. The ruggedly built old schoolteacher sought out Lao Chen and handed him an ornately sealed letter for delivery in Chengdu. "I'm putting you under this obligation," Master Fei Qun said haughtily, "because of my report in your family's favor. You owe it, so be so kind as to discharge your debt. I'll be blunt. Officials would not like this letter if they intercepted it."

"Not like it?"

"If you were stopped and searched and this letter found, what would you say?"

"Well, that I got it from you."

"I see. After I just told you they might not like the letter?"

Chen smiled uncertainly.

"Would you consider lying about it?"

"Why?"

"To save yourself," Master Fei Qun declared, fisting one hand against the other, as if missing the rosewood ruler that threatened slow-witted students.

"And the person I was to give it to?"

"What about him?"

"Must I save him, too?"

"Don't worry about him. Saving himself is his problem. Just worry about yourself. And what about me?"

"You, Master?"

"Would you mention *my* name? Ah, I can see by your face that's exactly what you'd do. But you mustn't, hear? If anything happens, you don't know me, never heard of me!" Gruffly the thickset old man continued, "Now listen carefully. You say that someone you met along the way, perhaps at an inn, gave you the letter. That's all you know about it. Are you clear on this point? Do you comprehend what I'm telling you?"

"I lie."

The corpulent old man smiled bitterly. "So that at least is clear."

"What if they don't believe me?" Chen asked sensibly.

"Don't worry if they believe you or not. You're a Flowering Talent. They don't want to give honored people like you any trouble, so almost any lie will do. You're in a most enviable position. I'm sending it with you because a Flowering Talent's as safe as a prince."

Having a Confucian duty to respect a teacher's wishes, along with being indebted to his schoolmaster for the favorable reference that got him through the district exam, Chen put aside his misgivings and accepted the undertaking.

Even then Master Fei Qun did not seem grateful. "Let's forget the letter now and talk about your conduct at the examination. Remember the old saying: 'Tall trees are struck down.' Don't be arrogant, don't be conspicuous, don't preen and show off. And consider this. Like most people around here, I regard your chance of passing the examination as very remote. It's one thing to have a good memory; it's quite another to use your mind cleverly under duress. And you'll know what duress is when they lock you up for three days and two nights in a tiny cubicle with a few brushes, an ink stone, and some ink sticks and paper. Then we'll see how vain and boastful you are."

When Chen opened his mouth to protest his humility, the schoolmaster waved both hands as if warding off bees. "I won't have students disobeying. I won't have excuses! Say no more!" he bellowed. Turning to go—but before moving a step—Fei Qun blurted out a saying of the great Confucius: "Men of true breeding are ashamed for their words to go beyond their deeds." Then at the doorway he turned for a parting shot. "So keep your mouth shut. Save yourself for an ordeal worse than any you expect. Do you hear? Say no more! No more excuses! Deliver the letter, please. I regret putting it in your hands, but there's no other way. Think for once! Don't quote poetry if anyone asks you about the letter. Don't babble the truth just because you study Confucius! For one time in your life show a bit of cunning! All around you, you see peasants, don't you? Think like them. They're shifty and dishonest, but they survive. Oh, and yes, may ten thousand good things come your way," Master Fei Qun mumbled rapidly as he departed.

On a path some distance from the Lao neighborhood the schoolmaster came upon Chen's younger brother. When the boy turned sharply and walked alongside the opposite wall to avoid a meeting, Master Fei Qun hurried to intercept him. The stout old man towered over him. "I just saw that fool you call your brother!" Fei Qun declared loudly. When Hong brazenly returned his stare, the schoolmaster jutted his chin forward angrily and shouted, "I fear his stupidity! So I'm telling you. Make sure he delivers a letter I gave him or your family will know more trouble than your father brings to it!"

The threat didn't humble young Hong. Instead of averting his eyes after such an outburst from a superior, he stared openly at Fei Qun.

In response to the boy's insolence and to his own fear of having made a mistake by entrusting Lao Chen with the letter, Master Fei Qun stamped on the ground childishly. "Ah! Ah!" His big body quaked; his red face turned a purple color. Then from narrowed eyes, while catching his breath, the old school-master studied the boy. That calmed him for a moment. "I have knowledge of one thing you do well. I've seen it in the classroom. You know how to lie. If there's a choice between telling the truth and lying, you lie. Isn't that so? Isn't that why you're smiling now? You know it's true! Insolent turtle!" For an instant an odd look came over the schoolmaster's face, as if he felt grudging admiration of the boy. But then his ruddy face became sullen again, the big loose mouth curving down in disapproval. "Well, well, here's a chance to put such a gift to good use. Teach that fool brother of yours how to lie, or if you can't do that, lie for him." Fei Qun regarded the boy with interest. "The fact is, I admire your brother. He's by far the most gifted student I ever had. If only he knew something of the world. Anyway, I want to help you help your brother." His voice now was low and cajoling. "Do, please, get that letter to its destination. Believe me, you'll be rewarded."

"Who'll reward me?"

"The man who receives the letter. But if questioned before getting to Chengdu, your brother must never say where he got the letter. They'd think him some kind of conspirator. Do you understand?"

"Of course. You're up to something and this letter proves it. We can't say where we got it. We play innocent. If we deliver the letter, we'll be paid something. The question is how much?"

"Insolent—!" With effort Fei Qun got hold of himself, cleared his throat, and continued, "Never mind that now. Get the letter where it belongs." The schoolmaster actually smiled, the yellow stubs in his mouth showing. "I must admit to something extraordinary. I feel better for having talked to you. Between you and your brother, it's you I trust if there's trouble."

"If there's a reward," Hong said loftily as he went around Master Fei Qun with a scornful smile, "I promise you the letter will get where it belongs."

Being so intent on his decision to put a dangerous letter in the hands of Lao Chen, the schoolmaster hadn't noticed the large woven basket carried by Lao Hong.

Within it were the five gourds that held the last of Hong's crickets. He had been on his way with them to find his friend Wujiang when his path crossed that of Master Fei Qun. Not at home, Wujiang was either playing chess near the village pond under an old chestnut tree or flying kites in the open field outside of town.

Hong found him in the field, maneuvering a large dragon kite over a stand of poplars. Will I ever see him again, Hong wondered as he called out his friend's name.

Helping Wujiang bring the kite in, Hong then handed over the wicker basket.

Wujiang took it with a frown. "I'll keep them until you get back."

"No, they're yours."

"When you come back, you get them back," Wujiang persisted, as they sat at high noon under a shade tree beyond the field.

"I won't be coming back."

"How can you say that? What if Two Brother fails at Chengdu? You'll come back, won't you?"

"Ah, but he won't fail. Not at something that has to do with books. Of course, if the examination was for driving a wagon or selling something in the market or planting cucumbers, then I'd say we'd be back soon enough. He won't fail at the books. We'll end up traveling thousands of miles from this place and probably never see it again."

Wujiang acknowledged that possibility by looking away. "I won't ever leave here," he declared softly. "Father owns good land, and when he dies, I'll own it, and when I die, my children will own it, and when they die, theirs will, and on and on. I don't ever expect to go even as far as Chengdu in my lifetime."

"I envy you," Hong declared with feeling.

Wujiang looked at him in surprise.

"I like it here. Everything I need is right here. Good food, crickets, my garden. You."

"Then why leave at all? Your brother can get to Chengdu by himself. He's four years older. He ought to take care of his own life."

"Gege can't." Hong was using the affectionate term for a brother. "Gege needs me."

"If he needs you so much," Wujiang said bluntly, "let him

stay here and have you take care of him where you want to be."

"No. Mother would have wanted him to take the exams, to go as far as he can go."

"Then you're doing this for your mother?"

Hong nodded. "And for our family name. Father has ruined it. Now we must restore it, gege and me."

Wujiang laughed ruefully. "Your brother studies Confucius, but you're the one who lives by his rules."

When Hong shrugged and got to his feet, Wujiang called out, "Walk slowly, friend."

Turning, his lips trembling, Hong said, "You too. Walk slowly."

Lady Kuo had gone to school with Lao Chen's mother; rare in this area of the province, they had both learned to read and write. This special merit bound them in friendship. When Lao Chen showed early promise as a scholar, the Kuo family often invited him to their villa, where he was allowed to converse with their daughter Daiyun. The two had known each other since the early days of the girl's foot-binding. Aside from the big toes, the toes on both feet were forced down and wrapped in thick cloth under the arch. On one visit Chen heard the seven-year-old girl cry out in pain; later on he helped Daiyun walk after discarding her crutches. He knew the old saying: Every pair of small feet costs a bath of tears. Through the rest of Daiyun's childhood her toes had remained curled in hard casings like the retracted claws of dying birds. She minced along in a pigeon-toed gait that nearly pitched her forward into a fall. Now she possessed "lily feet," along with a fingernail two inches long on the small finger of her left hand—both signifying her status as a young lady who never did manual labor.

When Chen came for his visit that day, she was sitting in the courtyard, doing embroidery on a silk jacket. In the heat of the afternoon, she wore pale blue trousers and a pink blouse. Her black hair was tied severely back from a pretty but morose little face. Seeing him, she pouted and looked away. For years they had teased each other; on Chen's last visit before leaving for the examination, they would not do otherwise. Daiyun shifted in her chair, ostentatiously displaying her lily feet in satin shoes only three inches long.

"I didn't think you would have time for me today," Daiyun declared petulantly. She threw down the jacket and picked up a silk fan, which she spread with a skillful flick of her wrist.

"I was just passing this way, which is why I thought of you," teased Chen, "and so I came in."

"How honorable and considerate of you to remember me," she commented dryly. Though only fourteen years old, she had been taught the coy social banter of an older girl by her nanny and her mother.

"You, of course, will soon forget me," Chen said. "Once I'm on the road to Chengdu, I'll be gone from your mind."

To show that his cynical remark annoyed her, Daiyun briskly shook her fan. "You want nothing more than to be gone and never see me again."

"I'll return in a month."

Her eyes flashed. "You? You'll be on your way to Beijing and the imperial palace."

"Oh, I won't pass." He sat down on the edge of a large tub of chrysanthemums. Within the larger garden was a small enclosed rock garden with a moss-covered piece of granite rising up, pitted and scarred, in imitation of an old mountain.

"You will definitely pass," snapped Daiyun.

Chen shrugged. "What does it matter? Things bring misery, it says in the *Tao Te Ching*. Things bring misery, and so does success. I have no need of either."

"What do you have need of, then?"

Pursing his lips, Chen said thoughtfully, "Freedom to follow the Tao. It is said if you open yourself to the Tao and trust your natural responses, everything will fall into place."

"You talk in riddles sometimes," Daiyun grumbled. "Always about the Tao, the Tao, the Tao."

" 'Since before time and space were, the Tao is,' " Chen

quoted mellifluously, so that the listening girl gawked at him.
" 'It is beyond *is* and *is not*. How do I know this is true? I look
inside myself and see.' " The awe in her look gratified him.
" 'It flows through all things, inside and outside, and returns
to the origin of all things.' " Chen clapped both knees with his
hands, finishing the quotation. " 'We can do without rules in a
life devoted to following the Tao.' "

Daiyun giggled and rattled the fan. "You are such a devil."
She thrust the fan at him as if it were a sword. "All the time
studying Confucius. But when you see me, you preach the wild
ideas of the Taoists."

"Who told you that?"

"Nanny."

"What does your nanny know about philosophy?"

"Enough to know when boys tell the truth and when they
lie." Abruptly Daiyun became solemn, and in her grave new
mood put the fan down and sat with folded hands. The one
long fingernail, encased in a protective sheath of gold, lay on
the right hand like a peeled twig. "Will you come back?"

"Of course," Chen told her easily.

"Mother says I must think about marriage soon. I'll be fifteen
in only four months."

Chen said nothing.

"If I marry, will you remain my friend?"

"Of course. Always."

She didn't like his quick and nonchalant answer, so, turning
away, not allowing him to see her expression, Daiyun said,
"Well, then, go. Go to Chengdu and your examinations. Write
your poetry and essays and prove how clever you are. Go,"
she commanded with her back toward him.

Pausing, unsure if she was still teasing, Chen finally got to
his feet. "When I return—"

"Go!" Her rising voice had lost its firmness. Her left hand was
raised, next to her cheek, the long fingernail sheath flashing in
the sunlight. "Go!" she demanded, her back still toward him.
Hearing his footsteps click against the courtyard flagstones,
Daiyun waited a long time after they had faded away. Then she

turned, unable to see clearly through the tears that filled her eyes.

As Chen walked home, there came from over a wall the whacking sound of women beating clothes against rocks in a nearby stream. But he scarcely heard them at their laundry work. It was true, he realized: whenever he talked to a girl, his mind was filled with Taoist thoughts of naturalness and spontaneity and freedom, not the rational order of a Confucian universe. Master Fei Qun was wrong about his being arrogant and boastful. Chen prided himself on behaving with the discretion and humility of a Confucian gentleman. Yet around Daiyun he did posture, he did try to seem mysterious and wise and superior, and for this purpose often quoted lines from the *Tao Te Ching* that he didn't understand.

Why had Daiyun become so angry? Had she wanted him to say "Don't marry"? How could he stop the Kuo family from seeking a bridegroom for her? Unless he offered himself! One thing was certain: though at nineteen he was of marriageable age, he had no wish for a wife. What he wished for was the road tomorrow, the long journey to Chengdu, and a tiny cubicle where he might sit alone at a bench and write his examination.

By midmorning they were on the road, each carrying on his back a bedroll attached to a wooden frame. For the two-hundred-mile journey to Chengdu—about two weeks—they stowed extra clothes and sandals in the bedrolls, along with Chen's scholarly paraphernalia: a coarse linen cloth for drying brushes, a half-dozen fox-hair brushes, a dozen rectangular ink sticks, three oblong ink stones, two rolls of mulberry-bark paper, and four long commentaries on the Classics of Confucius. Shoved inside each of their sheepskin belts was a set of chopsticks and a utility knife. A money pouch dangled from

Hong's belt, as he insisted on handling their funds—a responsibility unwanted by his older brother.

Their departure for the provincial capital was without fanfare, notwithstanding the fact that Lao Chen would bring honor to the village simply by taking the provincial examination. No one saw them off, though unknown to Hong his friend Wujiang, hidden behind a tree, pensively watched them stride out of the village. As they trudged eastward on the dusty road toward a mass of lowering clouds, Hong brought up the subject of their unacknowledged departure.

"Not that I care, but I expected people to line the road for a little way, to wave and wish you success."

"Oh well. Perhaps it's better they did nothing," Chen said with a little shrug of tolerance. "You know what happens to the child of proud parents."

It was an old superstition. If parents praised a child too much, the gods in heaven would overhear and from jealousy bring disaster down on the child's head. But Hong had another explanation (kept to himself) for the village's disregard of their young scholar. People would not publicly commend someone whose father had lost a fortune gambling. For himself Hong didn't care what they thought. In the communal mind he was already linked by his rebellious behavior in school to the disgraced Lao Lu. He knew what people said: "All that boy is good for is raising crickets." If the family name were ever to be redeemed, Hong decided long ago, it would be through Two Brother's scholarly attainments. What Hong wanted for himself was revenge. He dreamed of humbling the spiteful villagers who had forgotten the greatness of his mother in their zeal to belittle his father.

Will I ever see Father again, he wondered. Last night Lao Lu had hunched over the rickety table with a full cup and an old pack of elongated playing cards. They were almost too worn from shuffling for the courtiers and ladies in brocaded gowns to be visible, though the cards had been printed by woodcut blocks and colored by hand. Father was drunk on "frozen-out" wine—alcohol that remained liquid while the rest of the wine froze solid. Last winter Father had made a whole vat of it. Drink and cards were the only things that held his interest anymore.

Appraising his father's bleary eyes and sallow face, Hong had felt sorry for him last night—sorry along with angry at him for having ruined the Lao reputation. While cooking a farewell dinner for her two brothers, Big Sister had sobbed piteously, fearful they would never come home again. The responsibility of taking care of Father was now solely hers.

Stricken by remorse, Hong had thrust nine or ten coins into his father's hand. Lao Lu stared dumbly at the money. He got down then on his knees and kowtowed, then lay full length on the floor in obeisance as if his son were an emperor. Profoundly embarrassed by his father's groveling, Hong had chewed his lip to keep from crying out.

Now, as the trek began, Hong glanced sideways at Two Brother, who wore the blue gown and winged cap that identified him as a Flowering Talent. Could gege endure the rigors of a long journey, not only to Chengdu, but all the way to Beijing? Though tall and broad-shouldered, he was quite thin, pale, slow-moving. While other boys his age had flown kites and raced one another across the fields, Chen had sat in a candle-lit room and pored over his books. Were his legs strong enough for days of walking through wind and rain? Could his stomach accept the poor fare he'd surely eat on the road? And what sort of devious people would try to take his money or otherwise cheat him? Did Two Brother have an inkling of the difficulties ahead?

If Hong had known at that moment what was on his brother's mind, he'd have grimly declared, "How right I am to worry about such a silly fellow!"

Because instead of facing up to the rigors of travel, Chen was thinking of great poets of the Tang dynasty. Leaning forward to shift the pack's weight on his shoulders, Chen was recalling Li Po's poem about the province of Sichuan, which in Tang times had been called Shu. Li Po wrote:

> *The road to Shu is hard,*
> *harder than climbing to the heavens.*

On either side of the road were mountains rising out of the valley, their peaks shrouded today in mists. Eight hundred years ago Li Po had written:

> *Peak upon peak*
> *less than a foot from the sky.*

There was in his poetry a sense of rivers gushing and tumbling, just like the mountain streams of Sichuan.
And this wonderful line:

> *Dismal birds howling in ancient woods.*

The great Tu Fu lived for three years in a hut by a stream near Chengdu. He composed more than two hundred poems there.

> *If you draw a bow, draw the strongest,*
> *If you use an arrow, use the longest;*
> *To shoot a man, first shoot his horse,*
> *To capture rebels, first capture their chief.*

But how like Tu Fu it was to end this martial poem with a line that turned the meaning around:

> *What's the good of so much killing?*

Unable to gain a government post through the examination system, at the age of forty-three Tu Fu had obtained a modest position through the intercession of a friend. He was a failure in the world's eyes. He wrote more than fifteen hundred poems.
The great Han Yu, however, entered government service by passing the imperial examination with honors. He held many

posts with distinction. Although great, he was not as great a
poet as Tu Fu, or even Li Po.

"The river flows east and the gibbons cry at night."

"What did you say?" Hong asked.

"Did I say that aloud? I was thinking of a poem by Li Po."

The road was coming out of the valley into the foothills of
a mountain range that they'd cross before reaching Tianquan,
where the district examination had been held. Two Brother
had been there, and later, for the county exam, had gone
farther, to Mingshan. So already in his life Two Brother had
traveled a distance three days from the village.

After only two hours of walking, Hong was farther from the
village than he'd ever been before. Just as a rain shower
reached them, pattering down on his broad-brimmed field hat,
for the first time Hong felt the exhilaration that comes from
traveling. He thought of Wujiang, doomed to remain in the
village for a lifetime, and with the rain poking little holes into
the dusty surface of the road, Hong felt sorry for his old friend
as he and his brother bent forward into a downpour that
obscured their way eastward.

For two days they labored through the mountain passes,
following the tortuous paths between spruce and lindens with
heart-shaped leaves, through groves of birches and ancient
larches. The rain kept up a steady tattoo on conifers and flocks
of sheep that huddled on sumac-covered hills. As the travelers
dipped up and down the trails, passing tea plantations and
mulberry orchards, they noticed isolated farm huts perched
high above narrow valleys virtually lost in fog that heaved and
churned like a tidal sea. Then they came down into foothills,
the rains ever present, walked through Tianquan, and turned
slightly southward through the larger town of Yaan, then northeast to the county seat of Mingshan, where Chen had earned
the title of Flowering Talent. Now it was Chen's turn to be
farther from the village than he'd ever been before. The two
brothers entered a new world.

It was a world of chili-pepper farms, weedy cabbage patches,

stands of many varieties of bamboo: speckled, dragon, scaly,
phoenix-tailed. And the rain never ceased. Carts were mired
to their axles or overturned in mud. What had once been dry
gullies were now the mealy channels of rapid little streams.
Paths gave way, sending travelers down into water-filled hol-
lows, against rocks and tree trunks. Chen would have halted
on many occasions to slip and slide down a hill to help someone back up, but Hong resolutely urged him on. Their progress
had been so slowed by the downpour that they were in danger
of getting to Chengdu after the examination had begun.

Nor did things get better when they emerged from the hills
altogether and reached the edge of an alluvial plain. Here the
Qingyi River, a tributary of the mighty Min, snaked northward
and crossed the main east–west route through Sichuan. The
Qingyi, clogged by silt, was gorged with backwash pouring off
the mountainsides and soon overran its banks, flooding wheat
fields and the road, so that the brothers slogged knee-deep
through muddy water for a half-dozen miles before coming to
a small hill where a farmhouse stood. They paid the farmer to
let them stay in his stable.

Exhausted, they threw themselves down in the hay. After a
few minutes, Hong got up, shuffled over to the farmhouse, and
bought two bowls of cooked rice from the farmer's wife. No
sooner had he settled in the dry hay beside his brother, their
chopsticks hovering above the steaming bowls, than they had
an argument. It was the first of their trip.

It began with Chen worrying about his mulberry-bark paper
getting wet, though they had meticulously wrapped it in yak
skin before leaving the village. Too tired for patience, Hong
waved his chopsticks indifferently. "There's nothing we can do
about it. Either the paper gets to Chengdu dry or it doesn't.
Don't worry yourself about it."

"I do worry myself about it. If my paper were your crickets
and you were me, you'd be throwing your arms around, shouting."

"Do I do that?"

"You do when you're angry."

"Thank you, Two Brother."

"Forgive me, I'm just worried. If they let personal paper into the examination, I'll need mine."

"You don't know whether they will or not. You're worrying before you need to worry."

"I need this paper," Chen fretted. He rarely complained, and Hong knew that when he did, it always had something to do with his books or writing materials.

Annoyed, Hong said testily, "People need a lot of things, but things don't always need them."

Chen guffawed. "That sounds like a quotation of some sort."

"Well, it isn't."

"Why do you fear being wise? You *are* wise sometimes, didi," he acknowledged, using the affectionate term for "younger brother." "There's no disgrace in being wise or clever."

Hong nodded cursorily, working his chopsticks over the steaming mound of rice.

"Mencius said," continued Chen, "that the great end of learning is nothing less than to seek for the lost mind."

Hong paused at his eating. "What's the lost mind?"

"Mencius doesn't explain, but I assume all of us have a lost mind, in a way of speaking."

"What's the good of talking about the lost mind if you don't know what it is? Let me tell you, gege, what a lost mind is. Our father's mind is a lost mind. It wanders around the village without him. When it gets lost, so does he. That's when he gets drunk. He drinks in order to find his mind, but it's always gone somewhere else. That's when he cries in his cup. He can't find his lost mind. And I don't think reading the Classics will help him find it."

They heard a cackling sound from the darkness of a horse stall behind them. "I don't understand what you're saying, but you're young gentlemen! I saw the winged cap when you came in! Are you going to eat all that rice by yourselves?" While speaking these words in a tremulous but rasping voice, a bony-looking man opened the stall gate and came into the final light

of day that fell through the open doorway and enabled the
brothers to see a long narrow face, a crooked mouth.

"This is our meal," Hong told him sharply and plunged his chopsticks down into his bowl. "We'll be eating all of it."

In response, the man squatted against the opposite wall, maintaining a respectful distance. "May you enjoy it, young gentlemen. I was only asking."

"What are you doing here, sir?" Chen asked politely.

The fellow hooted and struck his knee as if he'd been told a joke. "The young gentleman calls me *sir*! Does this mean a change in my luck? Well, I work for the farmer. When I can't work in the fields, like today, his wife won't give me anything to eat. Not half a bowl."

Chen thrust his out. "Here, take some." He glared at Hong until the boy reluctantly thrust his bowl out, too.

Not having chopsticks, the man scooped up some fingerfuls of rice from each bowl and quickly swallowed it. "Ah, may ten thousand good things come your way, young gentlemen. I saw the winged cap: I knew you were not like other travelers. Are you going east?"

"Yes," Chen said.

"Is it flooding eastward?" Hong asked.

"Well, it's flooding here. It started just like this a few years ago. Daily rain. Then the Qingyi swelled up and overflowed for miles either side of its banks. Ten miles in every direction. I don't know how many died, how many villages washed away. That was when my own luck turned bad. I had a millet crop, but it went under the water."

"What's that sound?" Hong asked, startled. It was a loud chomping from still farther back in the stable.

"He's got a couple of pigs back there," explained the farmhand. "They're swilling rice slop. This farmer's very satisfied with his fields and livestock. Thinks he'll be rich." The man winked. "So did I think I'd be rich. But first the river flooded and I lost the crop and then I borrowed money from the Buddhist temple to start over. So I planted millet, but the temple fathers came to me even before the shoots came up, and they said until I paid the debt, they wouldn't let me work the land anymore. Not even hoe it. Shoots came up, but even when the baby died, the temple society warned me not to work the land or me and my family would be punished for it. They meant killed for it. I told the head of the temple society, I said how can I pay the debt if I don't work the land and bring in a crop and get money to pay the debt off? But the temple society wouldn't listen. They wanted to build a new temple and needed the money, and if they didn't get it from me, then they'd take over the land if I starved to death. I sat at the edge of my field and watched the weeds strangle my grain. We were eating tree bark, insects, anything. My other son got sick. Worms crawled out of his bottom, a whole army of them," the farmhand continued in a low, awed voice. "I won't forget the way he whimpered, as he touched his bottom and brought up worms on his fingers. 'Look at them,' he whined, poor sick little fellow, 'look at them!' Finally I smothered him. Yes, with a blanket. I couldn't stand it anymore—his terror when the worms began wriggling out of his nose and mouth. They still poured out after he was dead. You wouldn't believe it," he said with a sigh. "Then my wife, her belly swollen from the weeds we lived on, went out to beg in the village and came back to me beaten horribly. Next day she was gone. I don't know where. I didn't have strength to go searching for her. Finally someone took pity on me and gave me some millet gruel. I worked for that man a year for nothing. I didn't care if he hit me now and then. I was grateful he let me live."

After a long silence, Chen said quietly, slowly, "I remember hearing of the flood and famine. I had no idea it had happened so near our village. Within a few days' walk."

"No one knows on this side of a hill what's happening on the other side," the farmhand said. "This province is a hard place. It's hard to travel in, with the mountains and the plains and the rivers everywhere."

"That's what Li Po thought," mused Chen.

"What?"

Hong broke in here. "Do you think the way is safe eastward?"

"Yesterday I heard a man say it wasn't raining in the Red Basin. Flooding here, maybe a drought there." He chuckled grimly. "Maybe the gods never meant for people to live in the province of Sichuan."

They traveled the next morning under a metallically bright sun and a sky swept clean of rain clouds, which left the earth exposed to a raw, merciless heat. Not long after sunup the flood had receded from the fields and much of the road, and by midmorning the brothers were slogging through ankle-deep water and by noon were walking in mud. "He'll eat today," observed Hong.

Chen, who'd been reciting passages from the *Analects* in his mind, started as if coming out of sleep. "What did you say?"

"He'll work in the fields today, so the farmer's wife will give him a bowl of rice," Hong said.

"Ah yes," said Chen with a smile.

They were coming to more hills whose sides were terraced like huge staircases with tea plantations and castor oil bushes. By midafternoon the grass was dry enough to crackle underfoot. By late afternoon the brothers had descended to another plain dotted with millet and bean fields. Women were hauling wicker baskets filled with peaches down the road. Porters carried sacks of produce between shoulder poles that sagged from so much weight into the shape of curved bows. Hard-muscled boys about the size and age of Hong were running foot-pedaled irrigation wheels next to rice paddies. It was a crisply busy, highly ordered landscape, with no sign of flooding.

That night a balmy summer-like air enabled the brothers to sleep out in their bedrolls. They found a small wood at the edge of a field near a cotton gin; the gin had two wooden rollers moved by a treadle, and a light but steady breeze kept the balance wheel knocking rhythmically against its sides. But the brothers didn't mind; they slept soundly, their noses filled with the fragrance of tree peonies, of laurel, ginkgo, and ailanthus.

In the morning, when Chen awakened, he stretched and looked around at the trees, and quoted happily to his brother from Han Yu:

> *Nothing compares with poring through texts*
> *red brush in hand making notes in the margin*
> *What use is there in craving an excess?*
> *A few handfuls of grain are all I need.*

Lao Hong was capable of looking at Two Brother as if he were a complete stranger. At such times Hong felt two conflicting emotions: one, grudging admiration; and the other, disdain for someone out of tune with the world as it was—the kind of disdain he also felt for their father. These two emotions now filled Hong as he watched his brother stretch and recite ancient poetry as if this long, hard journey were nothing but a lark. The torment of his feelings about Two Brother left Hong surly and uncommunicative, though Chen didn't seem to notice, but drank from a nearby stream and smiled as if a sip of water were enough nourishment for the entire day.

That day they traveled through the Red Basin, so called because the soil of this broad plain was suffused with reddish sandstone. Enriched for centuries by the silt of flooding rivers, the fields here stretched as far as the eye could see. The horizon was obstructed only by the mounds of village cemeteries, which lay among bean patches and wheat fields.

Chen was in a garrulous mood. He told his brother that Confucius had been born in this month according to some authorities, and in the autumn or winter according to others. Master Kung once observed that by nature men are nearly alike; by practice, they become far apart. Why is that so? Chen asked without expecting a reply. He leaned forward in that characteristic way of his, taking weight off his back and letting his mind plunge into a tortuous web of ideas.

The road here was clogged with herds of goats and cattle, so only livestock could get by. Leading the way, Hong took them down paths alongside wheat fields so they could bypass the traffic jam. Chen scarcely noticed that they'd left the road; he was too absorbed by the question of human differences and similarities. What caused them? And was diversity better than unity? He began quoting Confucian philosophers on the significance of opposition in government and society. So-and-so believed this; so-and-so believed that.

Hong wasn't listening. Not only was he bored by such disquisitions, he was fully intent upon what his eyes were telling him, what in fact they had been telling him for miles without his paying attention.

This is what his eyes told him: You are looking at the beginning of disaster.

In the field he saw a great number of short-horned locusts crawling on wheat stalks or along the ground. They were young—nymphs without fully developed wings—but already they were on the inexorable march of primal instinct, advancing even before they could fly. From great reedbeds along the shorelines of the Aral and Caspian Seas, from countless Asian riverbanks, their parents had recently migrated and bred. An internal necessity propelled the young locusts forward, across rivers, over cliffs, through chasms A few adult locusts were flitting through the air, harbingering an immense swarm of winged monsters soon to evolve from the maturing nymphs. In a month, perhaps less, perhaps in a week or even a few days, thousands would be riding the wind, drifting in black, angry clouds over the fields, coming down in the evening when the temperature dropped. They'd settle over everything in a massive brown layer of clicking, clacking life. With their powerful jaws, in a single day they'd strip bare anything that grew, even trees of their bark. Wherever the locusts went, animals would starve. The fields would be reduced to a few withered stalks, leaving famine to sweep the land.

This is what Hong told his brother.

Chen gave him an appraising frown, then stooped and stud-

ied a few locusts for a moment. "How do you know this is going
to happen? Does this idea come from your cricket friends?"

Hong nodded. "The old carpenter Peng told me about a
locust plague."

"I don't know your cricket friends," Chen said with a touch
of superiority.

"Peng lived through a locust plague. His family lost a whole
millet crop in less than a day. In that amount of time these
things can eat fifteen times their own weight, Peng says. No
one knows why they swarm and fly. For many years they're just
locusts and do little harm. Then suddenly they start moving
like this . . ." He pointed at the ground. "Notice how they're all
heading in one direction? And they multiply and multiply and
multiply so awfully fast and swarm and cover the sky, and when
they come down, Peng says, nothing's left where they light.
I've heard him tell stories about the plague many times."

"You really believe a few locusts crawling around can mean
a plague's on the way?" Chen asked incredulously.

"I don't know. Have you ever seen so many locusts before?
Look at them. And all heading east?" He realized that his
brother had never bothered to look at insects in his life. "Anyway, if they do swarm, who knows where they'll go? They're
heading east now, but they might change direction. Once they
swarm, Peng says, they let the wind carry them. North, south,
east, west—"

"West? Toward our village?"

Hong enjoyed moments when his brother asked questions
that he could answer. Judiciously, he replied, "They could turn
around and go westward as far as the village. It's up to the fates
and the wind."

"And then?"

"As Peng says: famine follows the locust."

"That won't happen to our village," Chen declared.

"Why not?" Hong snapped.

When the scholar, overwhelmed by the idea, could find
no answer, Hong said more gently, "Well, the chance of its

happening is small. The land's big. The swarm would probably
come down at another place."

"Yes, that's what I think, too," Chen said with a smile, and his smile remained while they journeyed farther eastward, passing one village after another: ponds, vegetable patches, white houses with black timbers. "Chengdu shouldn't be far now," Chen exclaimed as they entered yet one more village.

He had scarcely uttered these optimistic words before some men rushed from a lane and shouted at them, "Stop there! You're under arrest!"

The magistrate, a lean angular man half-smothered in a brocaded robe, sat on a heavy mahogany chair in the "legal room" of his large villa. Now and then he ate a sweetmeat from a gold plate on a table beside him. The two brothers stood, arms bound behind them by tethers, with guards at their back.

"Remove the ropes," commanded the magistrate. When this was done, he said to the brothers, "Open those bedrolls of yours."

They did, and when Chen uncovered his writing materials, the magistrate leaned forward curiously. "Let me see that ink stone. Is that jade?"

"Yes, Your Honor," Chen said, taking the stone up to the magistrate and bowing. "It was my mother's ink stone."

The magistrate raised his eyebrows. "Your mother could write?"

"Yes, Your Honor."

After inspecting the stone, the magistrate handed it back. "So you say that's your mother's ink stone. Do you really expect me to believe it?" He smiled so broadly that the guards smiled, too. "Why do you think you've been brought here?"

"I don't know, Your Honor."

"You wear the gown and cap of a Flowering Talent. Do you

really expect me to believe *you* are a Flowering Talent? Let me tell you why you're here. People like you have been coming through my neighborhood for days now. They pretend to be scholars going for the provincial, but in fact they're charlatans. They write terrible poems at a high price for gullible merchants who want to put such drivel in frames and look good in front of neighbors. These wandering impostors claim to sell influence in Chengdu. They ask huge fees for small legal services, pocket the money, and run. They beg commissions as go-betweens in business deals for farmers, and end up with all the business. They lay waste our countryside like a swarm of locusts, deceiving poor ignorant souls who work hard for a modest living, and I won't have it any longer. I'll see to it that *scholars* like you learn to stay away from my territory. Granted, most of them are a lot older than you, and should know better. I'm surprised someone so young would try such a stupid thing. Anyway, young man, you are detained. And can expect twenty lashes with a whip in the morning in my courtyard." He raised his hand to signal the guards to take Lao Chen away.

"But, Your Honor," spoke up Hong, "my brother has his diploma from the county examination and his badge of rank."

The magistrate hesitated. "Let me see."

Chen dropped to his knees and proceeded to paw through the bedroll, searching for his Flowering Talent's diploma and his badge of rank, civil service Grade Nine. An embroidered cloth to be worn on the chest during official functions, the badge of rank was called a Mandarin Square. Grade Nine was represented in the embroidery by a couple of earthbound quail pecking at the grass. The top Mandarin Square, worn solely by the Grand Secretary to the Emperor, showed two stately cranes soaring above the clouds. What Chen found in the frantic rummaging was his Mandarin Square. What he also turned up accidentally was the sealed and dangerous letter from his schoolmaster to someone in Chengdu.

Fearful of the magistrate noticing the letter, Hong leaped forward and dramatically seized the Mandarin Square. "Here, Your Honor!" he cried, holding it high.

"I see it, I see it," the magistrate mumbled irritably. "Crooks get hold of badges easily. I've seen half a dozen Mandarin Squares in the last week. Where's the diploma with his name on it?"

On his knees, Chen looked up from the objects scattered around his bedroll, one hand nearly touching the letter. "I know the diploma's here, Your Honor. I just can't find it."

"You just can't find it," repeated the magistrate sarcastically. When he raised his hand again, the guards stepped forward.

"Wait!" Hong shouted, adding respectfully, "Your Honor!"

"Well?" The magistrate glared.

"I can prove my brother is what he says he is."

"Without a diploma that's hardly possible."

Hong hesitated, the effort of quick improvisation evident on his taut face. Then abruptly he smiled. "With all respect, Your Honor, it *is* possible. My brother will recite any passage from the Classics you ask for."

Popping a sweetmeat into his mouth, the lean, hawk-faced magistrate grinned. "Careful, boy. Don't play with me or you'll get a whipping, too. I know my Classics. I was once a Flowering Talent myself."

"Ask for any passage," Hong urged.

Thoughtfully, the magistrate studied the calm pale face of the so-called Flowering Talent. "If I ask him," the magistrate said, turning with a frown to Hong, "and he answers incorrectly, I promise you, you'll also be beaten."

"Please, Your Honor," said Hong, "ask him."

"Very well, then. From the Lu version of the *Analects*, quote paragraph twenty-seven of chapter fifteen."

With scarcely a pause for breath, Chen recited: " 'The Master said, "When the multitude detests a man, inquiry is necessary. When the multitude likes a man, inquiry is equally necessary." ' "

"From the Hsun Tzu, Yang Ching edition, part three, chapter nineteen, give me the opening argument."

Instantly Chen recited: " 'Man by birth has desires. When these desires are not satisfied, he cannot but pursue their satisfaction. When the pursuit is carried on without restraint or limit, there cannot but be contention. When there is contention, there is chaos. When there is chaos, there is dissolution. The ancient kings—"

"All right, all right," said the magistrate impatiently. After asking for two more quotations and receiving two more perfect replies, the magistrate wagged his head from side to side. "Well, all right. That's proof enough, indeed. No one quotes like that who isn't a Flowering Talent." He smiled approvingly at Chen. "Thanks to your brother's resourcefulness, you're free to go."

"Here! The diploma!" cried Hong, who had been rummaging through the bedroll (and concealing the sealed letter).

Taking another sweetmeat and a sip of tea, the magistrate declared, "After such a recitation, the diploma's no longer necessary."

That day they crossed the mighty Min River by flatboat and came upon a vast system of canals, dams, waterworks, and high embankments. The irrigation system provided for prosperous crops of rapeseed and sugarcane and allowed little farms to surround themselves with groves of bamboo. In this rich land the pigs and poultry lived on a variety of grains under the shade of orange and apple trees. The road, very wide now, was crowded with herdsmen switching their goats and with farmhands hauling wheelbarrows and with porters, two abreast, balancing shoulder poles from which dangled bolts of cloth, hardwood furniture, iron tools. As the brothers tramped onward, they noticed farm women staring at Chen's winged cap and blue gown while grinding rice and grain on stone mortars with heavily scarred pestles.

The brothers had said little for hours. Finally Chen quoted the Master: " 'When you have faults, don't be afraid to abandon them.' By that I mean myself. I mean that I need to abandon my faults. I need to remember where I put things. I shouldn't have misplaced the diploma."

"Never mind," Hong said generously. He did not add, "And

you let that dangerous letter lie there like a sparkling jewel."
Ever since leaving the magistrate's village he'd taken charge of the Flowering Talent diploma, the schoolmaster's recommendation of the Lao family to the provincial officials, and the dangerous letter addressed to someone in Chengdu. These, along with Zhu Tong's letter to a former battalion commander—all secured in yak-skin wrappings—were now carried inside Hong's shirt and warmed his ribs.

Moreover, he had won on the issue of the banner.

The banner had earlier been a source of contention between the brothers. Although in his elegant calligraphy Chen had written CANDIDATE FOR THE IMPERIALLY DECREED PROVINCIAL EXAMINATION on a cotton banner before leaving home—bowing to the insistence of both Hong and Big Sister—he'd argued against carrying it into Chengdu. "I know it's done by some candidates," he said, "but it's not in the spirit of Master Kung to be so boastful. He'd never approve."

"Don't worry about his approval," Hong had told Two Brother. "He won't be there to scold you. Confucius hasn't scolded anyone for the last two thousand years."

Chen had cleared his throat. This was his usual expression of disapproval when Younger Brother said or did something outrageous.

Sheepish now after his failure to locate the diploma and hide the dangerous letter, Chen agreed that Hong could display the banner as candidates traditionally did—but only at the gate, not before.

After a few hours' walk the next morning, Chen squinted into the sunlight and called out, "I see something on the horizon! A low haze to the east. It must be the city."

Instead of confirming what his brother saw, Hong halted and took off his bedroll, removed the banner, and quickly attached it to a wooden frame with cord. Then he stared into the distance. "Yes, that's the city."

"I said don't show the banner before we reach the gate," Chen declared.

"Don't worry about it. Just look for those hibiscus shrubs."

Centuries ago, so the story went, a feudal lord had planted hibiscus along the top of the wall that stretched for twelve miles around the city.

Clearing his throat, Chen informed his brother stiffly that the flowers were surely no longer there and anyway they couldn't possibly be seen at this distance. But he said nothing when Hong gaily hoisted the banner and let CANDIDATE FOR THE IMPERI- ALLY DECREED PROVINCIAL EXAMINATION ripple in the wind.

There, just ahead of them, rose the huge arched West Gate of the city. Its thick, nail-studded doors were open to a stream of wagons and pedestrians, all eager to funnel through the first gate, through a walled courtyard, and then through the second gate with its high forbidding towers. Traffic was backed up, however, because of customs inspection by a team of officials, some of them armed with cudgels and swords.

"Kublai Khan and his Mongols nearly destroyed this city," Chen observed, appraising the immense stone walls. "That yangguizi, that foreign devil they called Marco Polo, he visited here, too." When his brother said nothing, Chen glanced at him. "Did you hear me?"

"Yes?" Hong was watching the customs officers inspecting packs and burlap bags. They stuck swords into straw-filled wagons, patted the shirts of peasants, rifled through bulky goods. "What are they looking for?" Hong asked a man waiting in line ahead of them.

"You can't bring jewels into Chengdu without paying. You can't bring in jade or ivory without paying. You can't bring in firearms at all."

"What else are they looking for?"

The man grimaced with amusement at Hong. "Anything they fancy that you have. Best give it up without an argument." The man stared hard at Hong. "What are you afraid of, boy? Are you a fierce rebel? Anyway, with that"—he pointed to the banner Hong carried—"you're quite safe."

And it was true. When the brothers reached the front of the

customs line, an official asked with a surly frown if there was
a diploma to go with that banner.

"Do you want to see it?" asked Hong, wondering if he could slip the diploma from his shirt without revealing the other items.

"No, go on, go on," the official told them, waving impatiently.

And so they were inside the provincial capital of Chengdu.

As they walked down the narrow streets, buffeted by a hurrying throng, Chen told his brother that they must visit Tu Fu's cottage and also the country house near Cinnamon Tree Lake that had been built by the great scholar Yang Shen.

"You better register first," Hong said. "Then we can find a place to stay." He asked people several times where the reception station was, but no one slowed down long enough to give directions, so Hong waited until a little old woman came along. Grabbing her arm, he held it until she told him where to go.

After fighting their way through the crowd—the banner ripped, so Hong threw it away—they finally arrived in the north section of the city, at a large courtyard, where a long line of men stood in front of a Buddhist temple; next to it a sheet of paper was stuck on a pole: RECEPTION STATION: PROVINCIAL EXAMINATION.

"We waited forever to get into this town," grumbled Hong, "and now we wait again."

This time Chen wasn't listening. His lips moved soundlessly and serenely in the recitation of poetry only he could hear.

Hours later the brothers emerged from the temple, where Chen had registered and delivered the letter of recommendation brought from his village. It was stamped with the incised stone seal of the schoolmaster, his name and official position in thick red ink. Then an assistant examiner told Chen that he couldn't take his own paper into the examination but must buy paper here at the temple. So Hong opened the money pouch and paid for three answering-sheet folders of thick white paper, sixteen pages to the folder, and twenty-two vertical columns to the page—space enough, the man explained, for no more than twenty-five characters in each column. On the cover of each folder Chen wrote his name, age, and physical characteristics ("tall, thin, a mole on left wrist"). Then he gave these folders to a collector, who handed him a receipt to redeem them at examination time, two days hence. Hong also paid for special paper so that Two Brother could write rough drafts of the answers.

When finally they left, Hong sighed wearily. "Nothing's worse than waiting. Did you notice how many old men are candidates?"

"Are they? I suppose I was too interested in the answering sheets to notice. The paper's better than mine. Thicker. It'll take a good ink-brush impression."

"Much older. Forty, fifty years old. At least half of them. I thought the candidates would be more your age."

"Maybe they wait for many years before applying."

"Why would they do that?" Hong wondered.

"To make sure of their preparation."

It sounded like something that Chen, not anyone else, would do. "Let's find a place to stay," Hong suggested.

And so they wandered into a poor district, where papers were pinned on nearly every door, advertising rentals for the examination period. Although many of the dwellings were no more than shacks, they were terribly expensive. Without his having won the cricket fight, Hong realized, they wouldn't have money enough to stay anywhere in this city. Good old Fire Star, he thought. But there wasn't time for a nostalgic memory of his mighty black warrior. "Let's try here," he said, pointing to a ramshackle little house no better or worse than the others.

Soon they were unloading their bedrolls in a small windowless room, partitioned by a dirty old sheet. In their half there was a rickety table, a washbowl sitting on it, and one chair, nothing else. With the money the old landlady charged for this half room, Hong might have bought an ivory-lidded cricket cage. That's what he was grimly contemplating when someone called out from beyond the sheet, "Fellow scholars, welcome to Chengdu. I am Shen Ding."

That said, a skinny man in his mid-thirties pulled the sheet aside and stepped into the brothers' half of the little room. He had a fleshless sallow face, his large eyes made larger by high cheekbones and sunken cheeks. Hong had never seen anyone so thin. Shen Ding's Adam's apple stood out prominently like a round stone. Long bony hands protruded from the sleeves of a threadbare shirt that hung on his skeletal frame like a gunnysack.

He stared at Chen's blue gown and cap lying on the table. "We'll be taking the exam together," Shen Ding said with a friendly smile. "Come now, let's go have some tea." He added when Chen looked uncertain and Hong frowned, "Be my guests, please."

As they left the house (the wizened old lady glaring at them from her open doorway), Shen Ding told the brothers about his life. He did it with the ease of someone who hides nothing from others. As a boy he'd shown intellectual promise, so his father had sacrificed comforts to have him tutored in the Classics for more than a decade. This effort had been rewarded; Shen Ding became a Flowering Talent at the age of twenty-five. "Older than you," he told Chen with a wink, "but younger than most." His luck had changed, however, as he then failed the provincial exam every three years for the last dozen. To make a living during this time for his wife and three children, he tutored the sons of local officials and landlords. "Some of these boys should be turned over to Japanese pirates." Pursing his lips, as if considering the importance of his next remark, the skinny man said, "So this is my fifth attempt. I must succeed, I must!" He made this declaration with a finality that had both brothers staring at him. It seemed so ominous that on a generous impulse Chen patted his arm and declared, "You will succeed! You will!"

They came to a teahouse and sat in bamboo chairs beneath an awning, where they could regard the busy thoroughfare. "I know some of these candidates," Shen Ding claimed with a grimace, pointing at men who strolled arm in arm down the street. "We've all failed together."

"Why are so many of them older?" Hong asked, studying the strollers. "And all without beards?"

"They shave them off, trying to look younger. Candidates under twenty-five have a different set of questions—easier. So when they register, the old fellows falsify their ages, claiming they're boys no older than you are, Lao Chen. When they hand in their applications, they give a bribe to the collector and erase twenty or thirty years from their age. These men have little or no interest in scholarship. That I can swear. They've tried countless times to pass."

"Why do they try so hard," Chen asked, "if they don't care about scholarship?"

Ding threw a surprised glance at the young scholar. "Out there in the west where you come from, they don't tell you much about the politics of the exam, do they. They tell you only of the glory if you pass."

Chen acknowledged his ignorance with a smile.

Their tea came, and Ding paid. Carefully, proving himself a man habitually short of funds, Ding put each square-holed copper coin on the table as if it were a precious stone. "There'll be five or six thousand people taking the exam."

"How can that be?" Chen asked in alarm. "Fewer than a hundred succeeded in our county exam. That should mean only five or six hundred for the whole province."

Ding blew hard on the surface of his tea to cool it. "Anyone who took the exam before is eligible. Candidates who first tried thirty years ago will be at the gate on exam day."

"I still don't understand," Chen said, "why they try so hard if they don't really like the life of a scholar."

"Why do they try? Because if they pass and become a Recommended Man, they can't be dismissed from office for incompetence or charged with petty crimes, and they pay no taxes, and people give them money for literary services. Ah, it's worth trying for!" By the anxious look on his face, Shen Ding was including himself among those hoping finally to pass. "Look at that young man across the street," he whispered abruptly. Ding was staring at a blue-gowned Flowering Talent not much older than Chen. He was swaggering along in the company of two young women.

Chen noted that.

"There," said Ding, "is a young man who will pass."

"How do you know?" Chen asked curiously.

"He's the son of a great landlord north of here. He's been tutored in Suzhou and Beijing for years. You can be sure the Chief Examiner from Beijing and his deputy and the Examination Supervisor and his assistants and proctors have all banqueted at the family mansion. That young man will pass no matter what he writes in the answer book."

"I thought position and money are no guarantee of success," Chen said. "I thought all candidates are treated equally."

Ding sighed and finished off his tea. "So they are, officially. And common men do succeed now and then. But it helps to have influence and money."

"I believe that," Hong put in, giving his brother a dark look for sounding like an innocent. Without knowing the actual facts, Hong had surmised the truth of Ding's explanation long ago. Back in the village Chen had refused to believe him; now Two Brother stared disconsolately at his untouched cup of tea.

"If you aren't drinking that," Hong said, "give it to me." When Chen didn't respond, Hong reached out, took the cup, and quaffed the liquid in a couple of swallows.

"One out of a hundred succeeds at the provincial," Ding declared, staring at his own cup.

Both young men were so depressed that Hong wished to be somewhere else, flying a kite or playing chess or watching one of his crickets eat a specially prepared mixture of mosquitoes and rice gruel. It was no fun being a scholar. And at least that was something to be thankful for, Hong thought: he had no desire to be one.

Shortly after midnight on the eve of the provincial examination, a cannon went off; half an hour later, three more cannon shots boomed across Chengdu. By that time Chen and Shen Ding had mumbled goodbye to the sleepy Hong and were hurrying on their way. Chen carried in his bedroll, at Shen Ding's suggestion, a large earthenware pot for drawing water and enough cooked rice and fruit to last three days and two nights of incarceration, because nothing except water was supplied to the candidates once they entered their cells.

Chen and the older Shen Ding had become fast friends in the last two days. During long conversations Chen had assessed Ding's chances of passing the provincial. In his opinion, they were extremely good. He told Three Brother that their new friend was absolutely sure in his grasp of Confucian principles; he had a fine memory for quotations; and a sample of his calligraphy displayed a thorough mastery of the Running Style. "Wrinkles on a demon's face" was his method of choice for modeling brushstrokes (Chen preferred "eddies of a whirlpool"). Perhaps Ding's poetry was somewhat weak—technically accomplished, but lacking in rhythm and imagery. "Yet he'll succeed!" Chen declared, smacking his hands together.

The Western Capital Examination Compound lay next to the largest of Chengdu's lakes. A forest of torches set on stone ramparts lit up the early morning darkness. Bursts of golden light fell on the breeze-stirred water. Already a huge crowd was assembling at the Great Gate for roll call, tossing a multitude of shadows against the stone walls.

"Here's where we separate," Shen Ding said. "Look there." He pointed to lanterns and banners held above the gathering candidates. "We're grouped by home district. Where did you take your district exam?"

"Tianquan."

"So find the banner for Tianquan." For a moment Shen Ding
hesitated. "When we first met," he began slowly, "I thought
you were a country boy without any chance. But after our talks
these last two days, I think you might make it. Yes, you just
might."

Chen thanked him profusely and reiterated his own enthusiasm for Ding's chances. "You too! You'll pass! I know it!"

Then Chen went looking for the district of Tianquan.

He expected to see the nine others who had passed the
district examination with him—and sure enough, he recognized some of them standing together: men in their twenties
and thirties. Not one of them acknowledged Chen when he
approached, but gave him suspicious, morose glances, for he
had beaten them all at the district level. At least four times
that many other candidates were waiting around the Tianquan
banner. They were all much older. Some were reciting aloud,
others were moving prayer beads through their fingers, still
others were chattering loudly about this and that, spreading
rumors and complaining about the long wait. All of them
looked anxious.

One of the assistant examiners periodically conducted a roll
call. Like the other assistants, he wore a green robe and black
shoes trimmed at the sides in white lacquer; they were extremely thick-soled, which added a half foot to his height and
made him as tall as Chen. After nearly two hours, the district
group was led to the banner of Mingshan, where, among the
milling scholars, Chen spotted the candidate who had taken
first place at the county examination. The eyes of First Place
and Third Place briefly met, wavered, looked away. Here, too,
the size of the group was augmented by scores of older candidates, so that by dawn, when the final roll call was held, there
were hundreds collected around the Mingshan banner, maybe
a thousand.

Assistant examiners went through the multitude, calling for
silence, warning them of "being stamped" if they kept up such
a babble.

"What's 'being stamped'?" Chen asked a man nearby.

"If you don't know that," the man sneered, "how can you take the exam?"

"Pay no attention to him. He's already failed a half-dozen times," another man told Chen. "Being stamped means being kicked out. Any infraction of rules can get you stamped. Do what you're told and keep your mouth shut."

Just as the sun came up, the huge metal-bound doors of the Great Gate finally swung open, and by orderly procession, banners flying, each group proceeded into the Western Capital Examination Compound.

As he entered the main courtyard, Chen noticed tall watch-towers on the surrounding walls. Each tower was packed with guards looking down on the teeming crowd. Though he had never been in a prison or even seen one, Chen imagined it must be something like this. He stood in line, awaiting his turn at the inspection table, but didn't reach it until almost noon. By then it was blazing hot, and some of the candidates removed their robes, stripping down to loincloths. Many shuffled over to the water platform and got a drink from the large jars standing there. For the most part the waiting scholars kept silent, fearful of being stamped, but a few whispered among themselves and Chen overheard them say that there was only one entrance to the compound; once the examiners and candidates were all inside, the latch bar on the Great Gate would be sealed; no one, not even the Chief Examiner, could leave until the first session of the examination was declared over. He heard them say that if someone died during that time, the body would have to be wrapped in straw matting and flung over the wall. It had happened in the past.

What interested Chen more was what they said about the inspection. If you got caught hiding the tiniest crib note, even a blank piece of paper, you were stamped and the inspector earned a reward for vigilance.

Finally Chen came to the head of the line and faced a quintet

of inspectors, who roughly went through everything in his
bedroll. "No paper?" one asked him.

"No, sir."

"Don't call me sir. I'm nothing but a soldier. Any books?"

Chen shook his head. The man slowly and methodically frisked him from the top of his head—running fingers through his unruly hair—to the soles of his feet.

"What's this?" A soldier held up a bean-jam dumpling that had been wrapped among the foodstuffs in Chen's bedroll.

"Food for my stay."

"Yes?" With a knife the inspector sliced open the dumpling and mashed the contents with his thumb, grinning all the time at Chen. "I guess you're right. It's not old Confucian gibberish. It's real food."

Chen was passed through and given an entry certificate, after which he followed the line to the second gate, where there was yet another inspection. He heard someone say that if any irregularity was found here, the inspectors at the first gate would be punished.

By the time he got through the second inspection, it was midafternoon. Hungry, Chen ate the mashed dumpling, along with two others, as he waited in another line beyond the second gate. A burly young soldier approached, waving his arms, herding Chen and a score of other candidates into a group. In a harsh voice he ordered them to wait.

"What else would we do," an older man murmured under his breath.

After a while the stocky young soldier returned and told them to follow him. He led the way through an inner third gate, called the Dragon Gate, which opened upon a grand avenue extending as far as the eye could see. It was lined on either side by entrances to narrow lanes; each lane was flanked by small brick cubicles, the Hao She—examination cells.

"Find your own lane," the soldier yelled out angrily. He pointed to identification numbers written on banners at the entranceway of each lane. "You're supposed to be so clever. Don't ask me for help. I can't read."

"Don't let him bother you," the man next to Chen said. "The guards all hate us. They know if we pass, we can bully people like them for the rest of our lives."

On Chen's entry certificate was written "Lane 52, Cell 15A." Of the twenty men in his group, he was almost the last to find his lane—far down the long avenue—and for the first time since awaking this morning, he felt anxious. This sense of apprehension increased when he located Hao She 15A near the closed end of Lane 52. The tiny cell was twice as tall as it was wide, without door or window. As it was used only once every three years for the specific purpose of the provincial examination, the Hao She was badly in need of repair. Pulling aside a torn old curtain, Chen walked inside and looked in dismay at his examination room. A section of roof had collapsed in the far corner; weedy vines snaked along the rain-streaked bricks; with each step he had to brush away cobwebs. Assistant examiners had announced that candles in the rooms were illegal; anyone using one would be stamped. So the candidates could write only while the sun was shining through the doorways. There were three sets of wooden brackets projecting at different heights from wall to wall. Three boards were stacked at the entrance. Awkward though he was, Chen managed to fit each of them into brackets so that the top board served as a shelf, the middle as a desk, and the third as a chair. Done with that task, Chen stared at the packed-earth floor, wondering how he'd spend the night here. His body was much longer than the cell—surely no more than five feet square. He'd have to curl into the curved shape of a shrimp or bend his legs and sleep half sitting up.

While thousands of candidates were still being processed, Chen had nothing to do but sit in Hao She 15A and wait until morning. Now he knew what people meant by feeling jittery. So far in his scholarly life, Chen had been fortunate. During the other examinations he'd been calm. When people asked

him how he felt, Chen always claimed to be at ease. Only Third
Brother really believed him. The pressure of these examinations was legendary for the sickness and even insanity it caused among candidates. Chen had merely followed instructions, read the questions, written the answers. His mind had been at ease like a bird sitting on a branch.

Hao She 15A, however, filled him with newfound dread, a fluttery sensation in his fingers and behind his eyelids. Had the long wait intimidated him, Chen wondered. Or perhaps he was confounded by so many people, such a complicated procedure, and the endless avenue, and the network of numbered lanes, and the interminable cells without doors or windows, tall enough, but not wide enough for a full-grown man to sleep in comfortably. Could he endure the hardships awaiting him? He didn't fear the examination questions; he did fear the dingy little room and the heavy tread of patrolling guards eager to catch rule breakers. He was frightened by an awareness of countless other men nearby, breathing in the darkness, waiting and hoping. Tomorrow their ink brushes would race across paper—thousands of ink strokes every moment of the day. No wonder a candidate needed the virtues of a dragon, a donkey, a wood louse, and a camel to get himself successfully through such a test!

At sunset he left 15A to visit the latrine at the lane's end and then walked back to the grand avenue and filled his earthenware pot at a water platform. Groups of candidates were still being led in by sullen guards. Returning to 15A, Chen arranged his writing materials on the shelf and stretched the bedroll out on the earthen floor. He lay down, knees up, back of his head against the wall, eyes following the slow passage of constellations across the gaping hole in the cell's roof. Perhaps he dozed briefly, but for most of the night Lao Chen was awake, struggling with this new sense of apprehension. Often, when he felt himself drifting at last into sleep, something behind his eyes awakened him. It was like a small animal inside his head, scurrying around noisily in the dry straw of a stable.

———

So he was fully awake the next morning before sunrise when the guards began yelling in the lanes and minor officials came to each cubicle with answering sheets. Chen waited at his doorway. A man took three folders from a large pile carried by an attendant, read off Chen's name, age, and district, then the physical characteristics: tall, thin, a mole on left wrist. The official nodded solemnly when Chen held out his wrist. "Give me your receipt," the official demanded briskly.

Chen had it ready; he'd put the receipt on the shelf where he could see it, fearful of misplacing it. With receipt in hand, the official gave Chen the answering-sheet folders.

"Do I begin now?" Chen asked.

The official grinned at him. "If you wish. Except it might be better to wait till you have the questions."

The attendant snickered.

It was not until an hour later that another official came down Lane 52 with the question sheets.

Chen took his and, without looking at it, placed it on his desk and smoothed out some wrinkles in the paper. Next he took his writing materials from the shelf board and placed them at his right hand.

He picked up the oblong of white jade, his mother's ink stone. Lovingly, he turned it around in the early morning light now drifting through the open doorway and the gaping roof. The craftsman who had shaped this ink stone of jade must have used something hard, much harder than steel, something like crushed garnet, to polish such a hard surface. White was a strange color for an ink stone, and when Mother had initially ground the lampblack stick against the sloping wall of white jade, the trough had been stained forever, giving the ink stone both dark and light hues. It was the opposition so loved by scholars—the yang and the yin, the light and the dark, hard and soft, man and woman, heaven and earth. Because the stone's grain was so fine, it wasn't easy to grind an ink stick against its surface. But the ink produced was smooth; it had the wished-for thickness of oil.

Chen took up an ink stick and began grinding, and as he

ground it against the stained jade, his mind became calmer. And when he added some water to the mixture of pine soot and glue, creating an ink of viscous consistency, his mind grew still, as motionless as the jade itself. He twirled the hairs of his brush in the mixture, testing its density. This ink was correct; it would not dry out too quickly or flow too easily.

Now for the first time he looked at the question sheet. The mind behind his eyes was like a huge red sun: imperturbable, silent, encompassing. Calmly, steadily, he began to read. After reading the first question, he picked up the fox-hair brush, holding it so the hollow space in the palm of his hand could have held an egg. Liking a rather dry brushstroke, Chen used a smaller brush than was customary. He knew what the answer should be. All that remained was to render it precisely by the use of sure, accurate brushstrokes. After a pause, Chen lowered his brush and with a deft flick of his wrist caused a black slash to appear on the white paper. He had made the first stroke of the first character.

While Two Brother waited in line for hours to reach his examination cell, Three Brother tramped the bustling streets of Chengdu, awestruck by the energy and color of what he saw: markets with straw ware and bamboo ware and silks and pottery (and crickets for sale, most of them guoguo, the big fat singing kind); Buddhist monasteries, Taoist shrines, parks, tombs, governmental palaces.

But mainly he ate.

Never had he seen so much food of such variety. He stopped at one food stall after another, sampling strange dishes. He especially liked translucent noodles in a bean sauce topped with finely minced pork; the burly vendor, a jolly and garrulous man, explained that the dish was called Ants Climbing a Tree because bean sauce stained the noodles a reddish-brown color like tree bark and the tiny pieces of pork looked like ants. Hong ate steamed bread filled with sweet beans; he ate carp with charred red peppers; he ate braised river eel and Lion's Head meatballs; he ate crispy-skin chicken, glazed in honey and vinegar; he ate soft-fried lotus flowers, orchid-petal chicken strips, duck smoked in camphor and tea leaves.

Hong ate until the sweat broke out on his forehead. He felt bloated and queasy. Staggering back to his room, he fell into a long, troubled sleep. Next morning, when Two Brother was hunching over the board in his tiny cell, ink brush poised over the answering sheet, Hong got up as slowly and sluggishly as a very old man. Head in his hands, he decided to assuage his guilt for such gluttony by doing something constructive.

He'd deliver the schoolmaster's letter to its destination here in Chengdu. On the outside of the sealed scroll, in calligraphy less distinguished than Two Brother's but still impressive (Hong prided himself on being a good judge of handwriting), the schoolmaster had written:

YE PAN

SOUTHWEST CHENGDU

That was all. Sticking the letter inside his shirt, Hong set out, lowering his eyes at the sight of each food stall he passed. Along with eating himself sick, he'd wasted precious funds yesterday. So he hoped this fellow Ye Pan would give him a reward for bringing the letter; that was the chief reason for delivering it.

Locating Ye Pan was not easy, because the southwest section of Chengdu was a hodgepodge of buildings shoved close together within a maze of narrow lanes. And people were not inclined to help him. How different this was from home! Villagers accompanied a stranger to his destination, even if it meant an hour's walk. Hong began to despair of finding Ye Pan in this scurrying multitude, but he kept asking for Ye Pan! Ye Pan! Ye Pan! His effort was sometimes rewarded by a rough push or a muttered curse. Finally a porter hauling a wheelbarrow

filled with soybean bags gave him a glance and a quick answer.
"Ye Pan, the barber. Down that way. On the left."

"How far?" called Hong.

But the porter trudged on.

After a long walk that brought him to the extremity of the southwest part of the city, Hong despaired once more. But suddenly, on the left, there it was: a barbershop facing the street. A richly gowned woman sat on an overturned cask, while a man arranged her heavily oiled hair into a configuration that reminded Hong of the wings of a butterfly. To add body to the design, the barber was weaving some false strands of hair into the real ones. He fidgeted, inspected his work, and stepped nimbly around, inserting a number of pins and small ivory combs into the rich black mass, while the well-dressed woman held up a mirror and watched him working at the back of her head.

Hong stayed across the street, hidden behind baskets stacked high, peeking around them to make his own appraisal of Ye Pan. Was there anything dangerous about the fellow? He wore an ankle-length gown, its top gathered and cinched under a broad leather belt. Above the waist he was bare and muscular, his face deeply seamed by weather and years of living. He didn't look dangerous, but the more Hong studied this barber, the more he seemed unlike other men. He looked, in fact, mysterious, surely powerful. He might have been a general in one of the ancient stories or a fearless voyager who traveled across the seas—it was in his high-cheeked face, his fiercely staring eyes. Yet he chatted playfully with the elegant woman and seemed to amuse her while his graceful fingers put finishing touches to her decorated hair. After the woman paid and the barber bowed grandiosely at her departure, he turned completely around and crooked his finger in Hong's direction.

Confident of being well hidden, Hong didn't think the barber was crooking his finger at him.

"Yes! You!" the man called out in a ringing voice that had passersby turning to stare. "You, boy! Come here!"

Hong didn't hesitate longer but at this call of undeniable

command scooted across the street and stopped obediently in front of the barber Ye Pan.

"What do you want from me? A haircut?" The robust barber grinned. "I lived in the north years ago, where a tribe called the Manchu cut the hair of their slaves in a special way. They shave the front of the head and let a long braid hang down in back. The Manchu make their slaves wear this queue because it reminds them of horses—slaves and horses looking alike. If the Manchu ever conquer our land, we'll all be wearing queues. Want me to fix you with one?"

When Hong backed away in alarm, the barber laughed. Then instantly his face turned dark and threatening. "Why were you spying on me, boy?"

Hong answered truthfully. "I was watching you, sir, because I need to know something."

"Know what?"

"Sir, if I can trust you. If you are . . . dangerous."

A fat man came along and started to lower his bulk onto the overturned cask.

"Shop closed, sir. Shop closed," Ye Pan told him with a dismissive wave. When the disappointed customer had waddled off, the barber turned back to Hong. "Am I dangerous and can you trust me? Go in there and wait." He pointed to a curtained room behind the shop. Hong obeyed. Then Ye Pan went outside and put up the large wooden panels that closed his shop to the street.

Sitting down on a stool, Ye Pan pointed to another one in the cramped room, which was lit only by a small circle of sunshine coming through an overhead window. Under the man's steady gaze, Hong gingerly sat down. He noticed posters of gods on the wall: Paki Tai with his sword, Kuan Yin sitting cross-legged on a lotus, Na Cha skating along on his fire wheels, and a large painting of the red-faced Kuan Ti, God of War. "Now tell me who you are," Ye Pan demanded. "And tell me how I might be dangerous. Tell me everything."

In the barber's voice there was a chilling note that warned Hong to be truthful or he might find himself in more trouble than he could dream of. Even so, he would hold back the letter for a while. To hold it back, of course, he would have to lie.

8
7

When Hong had finished his story about the journey to Chengdu for his brother's examination, the barber remained silent awhile. Finally he said, "So your brother is taking the provincial. I have a feeling you aren't impressed by such glory."

"Our mother would have wanted him to succeed."

"But don't you care?"

"For his sake, I do. As for me . . ." Hong shrugged. "There are other things in life besides examinations."

"More important things," agreed the barber. "The examination system is corrupt. The government is corrupt. Rich landlords bury bags of money around the house. They love heavy doors with metal knockers and tall vases and black furniture and aren't like other men." He was on his feet, pacing as he talked. Hong suspected that the strange barber had quite forgotten him. Ye Pan ranted on about landlords: how they levied outrageous rents on their tenants, embezzled funds, bribed officials so as to seize land illegally. And the temple associations were no better, though officially organized to protect the common man's property. Ye Pan stopped pacing and turned with a scowl to Hong.

"Are you a draft of wind?"

"Sir?"

"A spy!"

"No, sir."

"You haven't told me your reason for coming here."

"Yes, sir, I have. Our schoolmaster told us to see you while we were in Chengdu and pay our respects."

The barber guffawed as if responding to a joke. "Fei Qun told you to come and pay your respects? I think you're a clever boy, which is why I'm curious about you—why I'm treating you like a grown man. But I also think you're not sure what to do—whether to trust me or run. I think whatever it is you've come to do, you should do it *now*."

"Yes, sir." Hong was fearful of confiding in this fierce man, who was clearly more than a barber. "But I told you the truth. I've done what I came to do. I've paid my respects in the name of my schoolmaster."

"You're a brave boy, but a foolish one. Don't you realize you may never leave this room?"

Hong wasn't shocked by this threat. It was something he could expect from this man. But should he risk his life for a letter? And one written by someone he didn't even respect, much less like? And how could he expect a reward unless he delivered the letter?

Even so, Hong heard himself lying in a brightly confident voice. "I've done what I came to do, sir: paid respects in honor of my schoolmaster, Fei Qun."

The barber stared thoughtfully at the boy, who met the unflinching appraisal with one of his own.

After a while Ye Pan sighed. "I don't believe you," he said bluntly, "but I suspect you'll let me know your reason for coming here." Then he smiled broadly. "But that will be when you're ready."

Hong said nothing.

"Boys like you are rare," Ye Pan continued. "There's a need for boys like you—who have both wits and courage."

"Thank you, sir."

"Do you think I'm flattering you? I think you think so. Well, I *am* flattering you, but I'm also speaking the truth. There's a need for boys who keep their mouths shut, do what they're told, and serve a great cause."

"A great cause, sir?"

"Yes, a great cause. Does that interest you? Wait here." He went out back and shouted at someone. When he returned, Ye Pan sat down and looked at his clasped hands. He spoke calmly, in careful detail, as if explaining something to an equal, not to a boy.

So Hong listened.

Ye Pan spoke of oppression and the need for people to overcome it. Even the Master understood that idea. Confucius believed a ruler derived power from the people and the people expressed the will of heaven. So if a prince failed to give the people justice, he must lose the mandate of heaven. Then it was the people's duty—their *duty*, not their choice—to replace him. "Did your scholarly brother ever teach you that?"

"No, sir."

"I believe you're listening."

"I am, sir."

Throughout history, continued the barber, brotherhoods had been secretly formed to overthrow tyranny and establish justice. He ticked off their names on his fingers: the Bright Moon Society, the Yellow Sand, the Big Swords, the Red Spears, the Righteous Fists, the Heaven and Earth Association, the League of Hard Bellies, the Way of Pervading Unity, the Heavenly Gate Society, the Fans, the White Robes, the White Lotus Society.

He explained the White Lotus in more detail. It was a Buddhist sect that had gone underground a few hundred years ago. The White Lotus was created by five monks who survived a Mongol attack on their monastery. Growing strong on a creed of universal justice, the secret society had managed to liberate patriots from jail, burn official buildings, eliminate greedy landlords and scheming magistrates. The White Lotus had undermined the authority of a corrupt government until it collapsed and made way for a new era of harmony. That new era had been established by the first Ming Emperor. But his successors had grown weak, until now the whole country was again facing disaster.

"Do you know who that is?" asked the barber, his gaze fixed on the wall painting of the War God.

"Yes, it's Kuan Ti."

"Kuan Ti is patron of the White Lotus. Before becoming a god, he was a great warrior. He wielded a sword called the Black Dragon and rode a horse called the Red Rabbit."

Hong stared at the painting. Red-faced Kuan Ti was seated on a tiger skin, with the face of a tiger emblazoned on his green robe. "My name means 'red'; my sign is the tiger," Hong said with pride.

"Then you should be a disciple of Kuan Ti. He protects us from corrupt rulers."

A bent old man came through the back door, carrying a tray. On it were two teacups, a pot, and a variety of dim sum tidbits. Hong was astonished—the barber was treating him like an adult guest!

After tea and dim sum (yesterday's gluttony forgotten, Hong ate heartily), the barber asked with a sly glance at the boy, "Tell me what I told you about the secret societies and the White Lotus."

Hong promptly answered, "People should fight against injustice. Even Confucius says so. But they must do it secretly."

"Why do you think, boy, I've told you so much?"

Hong thought a moment, munching on a soft bun. "So I'll trust you."

"Exactly."

Hong thrust his hand inside his shirt and came out with the letter. "This is for you."

When Hong started for home, his belt pouch was filled with copper coins and his mind with images of ancient warriors, horses galloping through darkness, the clang of swords on the ramparts of a city wall.

"Come here tomorrow," Ye Pan had told him.

Nothing would keep Hong away. After giving Ye Pan the letter, he had trembled in both fear and anticipation. Would the man punish him for lying? Or realize he had lied only to protect himself?

Having read the letter, Ye Pan turned to the boy with a deep frown.

Is the frown for me or for what the letter says, Hong wondered.

When Ye Pan spoke, his voice was gentle. "Have you any idea what Fei Qun's letter says?"

"No, sir, it was sealed, so I didn't read it."

"Meaning you'd have read it if it hadn't been sealed?"

Hong said, "Yes, sir."

"Why?"

"The schoolmaster told my brother the letter could be dangerous. If I knew what was in it, maybe I'd know how dangerous and why—and protect us from it."

"That's true. What made you carry the letter if it put you in danger?"

"Two Brother is Confucian. He had to respect the wishes of his teacher."

"That's not why *you* carried it."

"Oh no, sir. If Two Brother carried it, he might get caught. And also"—Hong paused, studying the barber's cold face—"I carried this letter in the hope of getting a reward for its delivery."

"Then why didn't you deliver it, get paid, and run off? That way you'd avoid danger."

"Because I think . . ." Hong was not sure of his own mind. "I think I was . . . curious. What made the letter dangerous? I was curious."

"Curious enough to put yourself in danger?"

"I think so. Yes—I was. If the letter meant danger, then I wanted to know why."

"Boys like you are rare." Ye Pan reached into his own money pouch and brought out a handful of coins. "So here's your reward. Go if you want."

After Hong counted the coins, thumping them on the floor to judge if they were counterfeit, he placed them in his money pouch and sat there motionless.

"I said, go if you want."

"Yes, sir. But—I'd like to know more."

"Know more about what?"

"The White Lotus. How people fight injustice."

Ye Pan said harshly, "What do you know, boy, about injustice?"

"I've seen it in the village. On the way here we met a farmer who'd lost everything because of it. I know there's injustice."

The barber sneered. "Don't tell me you care about stopping it."

"I don't know. But I know what it is. I know it exists."

The barber nodded approvingly. "Well said. Come here tomorrow."

And so the next day, while Two Brother tackled a new set of questions in his tiny cell, Three Brother returned to the barbershop. This time he didn't hide across the street. Instead, he walked up boldly and at the barber's signal went behind the curtain. He was content to wait. He had to know more about things that had caused him a sleepless night. All those men bound in secret brotherhood—was Ye Pan one of them? And the blustery old schoolmaster, Fei Qun? What could two such different men have in common? What did the letter say? What did they intend to do? Overturn a corrupt government? What government? Local officials in a few villages? Or did they have great plans? Did they dream of toppling the Ming Emperor? How could they do such a thing? With huge armies? Where would they get them? Or by assassination? How? By slipping into the Forbidden City with knives? In a dozing reverie he recalled words from the day: Mongols, Righteous Fists, bribery, justice, mandate of heaven, and the fearsome Kuan Ti whose red face and tiger symbol linked the God of War to Lao Hong of a small village in the west of Sichuan. He felt that fate was standing just behind his shoulder, breathing hot breath against his cheek.

At noon of the third day, shortly after a cannon shot went off, Lao Chen organized his folders, packed away his writing materials, earthenware pot, and bedroll, and took his answers to the main compound, where receiving stations were located. He found the banner for his district of Tianquan. An assistant examiner sat behind the table. When Chen started to hand over his folders, the examiner gave him a surprised look. "Done already? You're the first in."

"Yes, I heard the cannon sound."

"Just because the cannon sounds doesn't mean you have to
stop work." The man smiled tolerantly. "Nobody pays attention
to it. Ignoring the end of a session is an old tradition. Take
more time. Everyone has until evening."

"No, thank you." Chen shoved his folders toward the examiner. "I have nothing more to say."

The examiner shrugged. "I'm sorry to hear that. Well, then, relax until the cannon sounds tomorrow morning."

"Thank you," Chen said cheerfully and left the compound.

On his way back to the boardinghouse, he stopped to buy a new batch of cooked rice and more fruit for tomorrow. Noting his scholarly dress, the grocer asked Chen how the examination had gone.

"The worst part was waiting."

"And you have two more sessions to go," said the knowledgeable grocer, who appraised the gaunt young man skeptically. "They say it gets worse and worse. You need a strong body more than a strong mind."

Chen smiled. "I know I'm thin. I count on you to give me good fruit so I'll have the strength."

This forthright and friendly remark caused the grocer to set three more peaches in the pile. "Free!" he declared.

When Chen returned to the boardinghouse, the old woman who had rented the room stood in the doorway, barring his entrance. "You owe," she told him.

"I thought my brother paid."

"Price of room has gone up. You owe."

Chen had only ten copper coins left after paying for the fruit. He took them out and handed them over.

"You owe more."

"Is my brother here? He has money."

Reluctantly the old woman stepped aside and let the young scholar go into his room. It was empty. That meant Shen Ding was still in the compound, finishing his work. Where was Hong? Abruptly Chen felt exhausted; it was all he could do to stretch his bedroll out before falling asleep.

When finally he awoke, a candle was burning on the little

table and Three Brother was squatting nearby, staring at him.

"It was all right," Chen assured his younger brother, who looked anxious. "I had to write on three themes from the Four Books. I chose the *Great Learning*, the *Discourses of Mencius*, and the *Doctrine of the Mean*." He pursed his lips thoughtfully. "I didn't choose the *Analects* because I wrote on it for the district and county. Then we had to compose a poem in the ku-shih style." He stared into the distance as if recalling his effort. "They wanted the second, fourth, sixth, and eighth lines of each stanza to rhyme. They wanted seven syllables to the line instead of five. That made it interesting. In honor of Tu Fu, I wrote about the mountain streams of Sichuan." He turned to his brother. "The old woman stopped me when I came in—"

Relieved by Two Brother's buoyant mood after the first session, Hong waved off the problem of the landlady. "I told the old demon we had Lao family members in Chengdu. They'd be glad to slit her throat for much less than she asked for the room." Hong chuckled.

"You threatened her life?"

"Well, she's a cheat. We paid in advance, and that's that." He reached into his pouch and counted out ten copper coins. "Is this how many you gave her? She swears it was ten."

"I think so."

Hong walked over and placed the coins in his brother's pouch. "Don't worry about the old demon. She won't bother you again. I'm pleased, Illustrious Brother, that the test went well. It did go well. Isn't that so?"

"In my opinion it did. There was no difference from the other exams." Chen didn't tell his brother about the initial panic he'd felt this time. Hong was a tough boy except when it came to these examinations. To keep Three Brother from worrying, Chen was determined to show good cheer however he felt.

"We're going out to eat now." Hong jumped to his feet and clapped his hands. "There's a specialty they have here

called Ants Climbing a Tree. And don't tell me you aren't
hungry."

"I'm not."

"Come, come, come." Hong gestured with both hands as if herding sheep. "Get up, Lao Chen, and eat! You'll need your strength tomorrow."

Rising with a sigh, Chen said, "I can't argue with you."

"No, you can't. Remember that," Hong declared, sounding ten years older than he was. "Don't argue with me."

When they returned from their noodles and minced pork, Chen was shocked to find that Shen Ding hadn't returned from the compound. In fact, the brothers had almost fallen asleep in their bedrolls when the door creaked open and the older scholar shuffled into the room. He was tiptoeing past them, trying to be quiet, when Chen sat up. "What happened? Shen Ding, are you all right?"

"Oh yes, don't bother yourself," he muttered. "I just took my time." He lifted the dividing sheet and went into his own part of the room, but almost immediately returned to squat down beside Chen. "What did you think of it?" he asked.

"I liked the poem, the seven syllables to the line. It was a challenge, even though the rhyme scheme was conventional. I thought—"

"But the essay," Shen Ding interrupted. "They wanted only three themes for discussion. Why not one theme for each of the Four Books? Instead you had to leave one book out. Wasn't that a trick question? I believe everything depends on the choice of books. Which three did you choose?" When Chen told him, Shen Ding said bitterly, "I picked wrong. I shouldn't have picked the *Analects*. Don't you think it was an error? I suppose almost everyone picked the *Analects*. You were right to pick the *Mencius*. It's the hardest to understand, so most people probably avoided it. You won't bore the examiners who read your essay, and there won't be as many to compare it with. I made a mistake. I chose the *Analects* because I knew it best. I made a stupid error." He put his head in his hands.

Chen leaned from his bedroll and patted the older scholar's

arm. "The *Analects* is the deepest core of Confucian thought. You did right to select it."

"You think so? Then why didn't you select it, too?"

"I wrote on it before. I needed a change."

"Ah, you're very confident," Shen Ding observed wistfully. Getting to his feet, he went back to his half of the room. Hong listened in the darkness. Soon he heard his brother breathing rhythmically and calmly, but heard fitful coughing from the other side of the sheet. Shen Ding was not sleeping. Hong could imagine him lying there, fists doubled, tense, with eyes wide open, fixed on the black ceiling. He recalled something Two Brother often quoted: A discontented mind is like a serpent wishing to swallow an elephant. Hong was imagining a snake crawling up the leg of an elephant, then ants crawling up the trunk of a tree, when suddenly he, too, fell asleep.

Shortly after midnight a cannon shot boomed across the rooftops of Chengdu. Thoroughly awake, Chen got up and dressed. He called out to Shen Ding, but got no reply. Lifting the sheet, he saw to his dismay that the exhausted man was still asleep. "Shen Ding!" he called out.

Hong went around his brother, knelt beside Shen Ding, and shook him roughly; at last the older scholar burbled, opened his eyes, and stretched. "I should have finished earlier yesterday," he murmured. "I'm so tired."

Hong said coldly, "Get up. My brother has to leave soon."

Shen Ding got up.

When the second cannon sounded, Chen and Shen Ding were halfway to the examination compound. "Will it be exactly as before?" Chen asked. "I mean roll calls and searches and long waits in the sun?"

"Exactly as before." Shen Ding sighed wearily. "They say if two or three people don't go mad during an examination, it's been a failure. Yesterday's question about themes—was choosing the *Analects* a serious error? Did I ruin my chances?"

"Not at all. I'm sorry I didn't choose it," lied Chen.

When they parted at the Great Gate to join their respective

groups, Shen Ding's mood had changed for the better. He called out, "Don't worry! Just stay calm! That's the important thing," waved gaily, and hurried away.

The second session was not altogether the same as the first. Each candidate was assigned a new cell. This was done to discourage anyone from hiding notes for use during a subsequent session. That afternoon it began to rain. When Chen located Hao She 22B, he felt himself lucky, because the roof of this cell was intact. He'd have a dry night before the examination continued the next day. That wouldn't be true of the poor fellow who drew Hao She 15A!

While Two Brother was going through the laborious ritual of gaining entry to the second session, Hong rushed off to spend the day at Ye Pan's barbershop. Sitting in the back room, he waited patiently for Ye Pan to have some free time between customers. Then he leaned forward eagerly and listened to the man talk of many things, of brotherhood and justice and secret signs, blood oaths, passwords, sacred numbers. Ye Pan explained that numbers had special meanings: one meant unity; three was the number of creation because everything proceeded from it; five was the greatest of numbers because it represented life and God; six was the least important number; seven stood for death. He took Hong into another room, farther back in what seemed to be a maze of rooms. Here he showed the boy certain objects on a table and explained their meaning. The short sword lying there meant the oppressors must be killed; a red lamp distinguished truth from falsehood; an ink brush wrote upright laws; a white fan revived the spirits of dead heroes; a yellow umbrella recalled the first great Ming Emperor; a mirror allowed the brothers to see in themselves their inner strengths and weaknesses. There were also teacups whose positions on a table had deep significance.

"All this and more is learned by brothers of the White Lotus," Ye Pan said.

"It must be difficult to join."

"Of course. If secrets aren't kept, people die. The Lotus stands against oppression; therefore, it represents danger for those in power. Only men of honesty and courage can join the Lotus."

"Someday I wish ..." Hong let his wish trail off.

Ye Pan finished it for him. "You wish to join."

"Yes, sir, I do."

"Tell me why."

Hong said nothing.

"Are you light-headed and frivolous?" Ye Pan asked harshly.

"I don't know why. When I lived in the village, that was enough for me. But seeing the world beyond it, I want to live differently from the way I lived there. And I think of the farmer who lost everything. It would feel good to help him. That's all I can say."

"Those are your only reasons?"

"That's all I can think of," Hong admitted, crestfallen.

"You've given an honest answer." Ye Pan put his hand on the boy's shoulder. "The Lotus is always looking for the rare boy. The Lotus needs him."

"What can a boy do for the Lotus?"

"More than you imagine."

"Tell me, sir."

"Well, he can carry messages, observe things. A boy looks as innocent as a rabbit, but at heart he can be a tiger. He can go in and out"—the barber made wavy lines with his outstretched hand—"where a grown man would be stopped. A boy can see what's happening. He can be the eyes and ears and quick feet of the secret brotherhood." Ye Pan smiled grimly. "If he's that rare boy I spoke of."

"Do such boys join the Lotus?"

"Of course. They're always welcome."

Without more thought, Hong asked, "Would I be welcome?"

Ye Pan stared so long and thoughtfully that Hong wasn't sure the barber had heard the question. Finally Ye Pan said, "This is a password." He spread wide the five fingers of his left hand. "It stands for the founding monks who fought the Mongols at Shaolin Monastery. The answer is this." He made a circle with

his thumb and first finger. "It stands for the circle of heaven
and earth. It's where the yin and yang are united. It represents
the will of the Lotus. There are other passwords, of course."

"Please tell me, sir."

"No, they're only for brothers. But remember this. If you're
ever in trouble and sense that a brother of the Lotus is nearby,
call out the number *fifteen*."

"Fifteen."

"Three is birth, five is life, seven is death. Added together,
they make fifteen. Fifteen is the number of souls uniting in the
body to form man. When a brother of the Lotus hears 'Fifteen!'
he comes running. He'll give his life to help whoever shouts
that number." Ye Pan was staring at Hong from those fierce
dark eyes. "When a candidate is questioned by the brotherhood, he's asked, 'Which is harder, my sword or your neck?'
What do you think he should answer?"

"My neck."

"Come here tomorrow."

Once again Chen finished early. The assistant examiner took
his answering folders without surprise, but said to the young
man with a sarcastic smile, "You have nothing more to say? If
everyone was like you, the readers would have an easy time
of it."

"Oh, didn't I write enough?" Chen asked with a frown. "I
filled all the pages."

"You did?" The examiner leafed through them and gave
Chen an astonished look. "How did you write so much and
copy it out already?"

"I didn't write drafts. My first copy is the final copy."

The examiner gawked at Chen, then thumbed rapidly
through the papers, looking for smudges, cross-outs, sloppily
formed characters. The handwriting was flawless. Looking up
with an apologetic smile, the examiner said, "Well, then, relax
until the cannon sounds tomorrow."

Chen got his third ration of cooked rice and more fruit from the grocer, who added nothing free this time but advice. "I hope you haven't made friends of the others. They say it's a bad practice."

"Why?"

"You make a friend and trust him. He tells you the wrong things to do. He points you in the wrong direction."

"Why would he do that?" Chen wondered.

"You're rivals, aren't you? Only a few Recommended Men come out of the exam, am I right? You remove one rival, you have one less to worry about. Don't take advice from anyone."

"Thank you, I'll remember," Chen told the grocer, but only to be polite. He would never suspect Shen Ding of deception. At his back he heard the grocer shout, "Man's mouth is only two flaps of skin, so don't pay attention to what comes out of it!"

Arriving at the boardinghouse, Chen saw the old woman at her doorway; she took one look at him and scuttled into her room. His room was empty again. Where did Hong go during the day? That question only just occurred to Chen. He knew, of course, where Shen Ding was. So Chen spread out his bedroll and almost instantly fell into a dreamless sleep. This time he awakened before Hong came in.

"It was all right, didi," he began. "We had five questions on the Five Classics, none too difficult. They made us reproduce the first paragraph of our answer to the first question for the first session. I suppose that's to prevent substitutes from coming in and taking the second part of the exam for you. What do you think? Didi?"

"What?" Hong was sitting cross-legged on the floor, chin in hand, staring at the wall.

"I asked, didi, don't you think they made us reproduce the first paragraph in order to prevent cheating?"

"Oh yes. I think so."

Chen began pacing, hands at the small of his back. "I wrote on the *Mencius* about the mandate of heaven, where Master Meng is asked if the Emperor can give the world to another. I paraphrased Master Meng's answer as follows: 'When the

Emperor presides over the sacrifices and treats the people well, he is accepted both by the people and by heaven. The world is his. But if the Emperor tries to give it to someone else because he is the Emperor, he can't succeed. Only heaven can give the world to anyone, and only with the consent of the people. The Emperor cannot do it.' That was my first paragraph; I remember it well. He stopped pacing and turned to his brother. "Didi?"

"Yes. He rules only if the people are satisfied with him. Otherwise they'll throw him out."

Hong's interpretation added a note of rebellion that Chen hadn't included in his paragraph. But there was no need to point that out. "So that was the test today," Chen said. "What did you do?"

"I delivered the schoolmaster's letter."

"Ah, I'm glad you did."

"Ye Pan gave me money."

That didn't seem to interest Chen, who stared at the room-dividing sheet. "I'm worried about Shen Ding. I'm worried because he worries too much. He didn't commit a serious error by choosing the *Analects*, but I don't think he was convinced. Worrying too much could hurt his chances, although I'm confident he'll get through."

"And will you get through?" Hong asked sternly.

"There's one more session to go."

"But if it's like the two others, will you get through?" Hong persisted.

"If I don't, there's something wrong with the readers." It was less a boast than a statement.

"Are you really that confident?" Hong was now smiling.

"I read the questions, I understood them, I wrote my answers. I wrote the poem in the form they asked. And I left early."

"But isn't leaving early dangerous?" Hong was now frowning. "Shouldn't you take all the time they give you?"

"If I used all the time, that would be dangerous."

"I don't understand."

"I don't know how to explain it. If I used all the time, my mind would swim around like a fish."

Usually their conversations about study and examinations ended this way: with the brothers turning away from each other, as if taking different paths across a field. At last Hong broke the silence by insisting that they go out to eat.

When they returned, Shen Ding was still gone. "I'll wait for him," Chen said when Hong pulled out their bedrolls and placed them side by side.

"Don't do that," Hong warned. "You need all the sleep you can get."

"I slept this afternoon, so I feel fine. I'll wait for him."

Hong shrugged, got into his bedroll, and closed his eyes, but behind the dark lids he was seeing visions of heroes protecting the land from evil lords. He was still awake when the older scholar finally returned. He heard Shen Ding eagerly question his brother about the test. His brother's voice was patient, soothing; Shen Ding's voice was high-pitched, rapid, and shaky. That night Hong fell asleep only after hearing his brother's calm breathing. He knew that Shen Ding would get little sleep.

The next day began with a cannon sounding. The two scholars left together. As they trudged through the darkness, Shen Ding said, "Do you have any money with you?"

"Yes," Chen said, "a little."

"Whatever you have, give it to the examiner when you hand in your final answers."

"Isn't that bribery?"

Shen Ding guffawed. "My friend, you're very innocent. That's why I'm trying to help you get through. Everyone bribes on the final day."

"But I thought—"

Giggling, Shen Ding gripped Chen's arm. "That's just the point—you don't think. Put your money between the leaves of your folder. It's the only way to get through."

That day followed the previous pattern. Chen found himself in a dilapidated cell worse than the others. But for a sense of well-being he could draw on yesterday's nap and last night's abbreviated sleep. Next morning he was given the final question, which had been written by the Chief Examiner, who had come all the way from Beijing under an edict from the Emperor. It was an excessively long and rhetorical question, the answer to which was simple enough, Chen thought, because by displaying his scholarship, the Chief Examiner had explained the answer in writing the question. Chen wrote out a straightforward critique of Tang polities in the latter half of the ninth century—beneath all the fancy language, this was what the question asked him to do. He took it to the receiving station shortly after noon.

The assistant examiner smiled at him. "First again. Did you find the question easy?" He wagged his finger in mock warning. "Remember, the Chief Examiner wrote it."

"Yes, it was easy." Chen handed over his folder.

"Well, then, when the next cannon sounds, you'll know if you passed." The man regarded Chen solemnly. "Somehow I believe you will."

"Thank you," Chen said politely and left. He had not put money between the leaves of the folder. Had he committed a serious mistake? After all, Shen Ding had explained the consequences for not giving a bribe: you didn't get through. On the other hand, the grocer had warned him to be careful of such advice.

Ultimately, Chen had not put money in his folder because Confucius would have despised him for it.

Chen could do nothing but wait for the results to be posted. Thousands of exams had to be read behind the locked and sealed Great Gate, where examiners and clerks must remain— even their corpses, if any—until every paper was graded.

Shen Ding explained the procedure to his friend. All the papers were first studied for poor handwriting. If a paper had too many cross-outs, smudges, or miswritten characters, it immediately failed. Next, several thousand clerks took the remaining original papers—the "black versions," since they had been written in black ink—and recopied them in red ink. Copying the original was to prevent examiners, many of them tutors, from recognizing the handwriting of a candidate who had studied with them. Then proofreaders compared the "red" and "black" versions for copying errors. Proofreading corrections were made in yellow ink. Both versions were then sent to the custodian, who retained the black originals and sent the red copies through a single narrow door into a section of the compound where associate examiners read and graded the papers. These readers wrote their remarks in blue ink. "Without merit" or "mediocre" meant fail; "excellent in style and content" and "recommended" meant a paper had passed. Assistant examiners, with the help of clerks, next gathered together the work of each candidate for the three sessions and determined who had passed the entire examination—failing one session resulted in failure overall. The passed papers were then seen by the Chief and the deputy examiners, who made the final ranking. They used black ink. The deputy wrote the character "chu" on the red-ink copy; then the Chief Examiner wrote "chung" beneath it, forming the compound chuchung— "passed," along with the numerical ranking. This was repeated on the black version. Both versions were preserved, and the black originals would be forwarded later to the Board of Rites in Beijing. Because only numbers identified the winning papers, those numbers had to be matched with names on the applications. Finally, the custodian supervised the placement of actual names on each chuchung folder. At the end of such a long, involved process, the administrators were just as exhausted as the candidates.

Chen still liked Shen Ding, but ever since handing in his final work without including a bribe, he'd been suspicious of the older scholar, if against his will. After two nights of waiting for results to be posted, Shen Ding went out and got drunk. He staggered back to the room and ranted for hours about the

unfairness of the examination system, which favored the rich,
he claimed, and discriminated against people like himself who
had wives and children to care for. Abruptly Chen asked him
if he had offered a bribe with his final paper.

Caught off guard, the drunken scholar said, "No, of course
not." His sallow face wrinkled into a grimace.

"But you told me to put a bribe in with my paper."

"Ah, well, I didn't have money, that's why. I have mouths to
feed. But you have no one to care for. Did you do what I told
you? Did you put your money in?"

"No, I didn't. Confucius would not approve."

The drunken scholar laughed merrily. "*Confucius*? Do you
honestly care what a man thinks who's been dead two thousand
years? You should have included a bribe. I thought you would.
I was certain you did! Country boys need help in these exams.
You're a fool for not doing it."

The next day, when they went together to the examination
compound to see what was happening, they found an official
paper nailed on the huge door. It listed the names of candidates
who were now barred for life from examinations. They had
been guilty of trying to bribe guards and examiners.

Chen turned to the older scholar. "Did you know this would
happen?"

Shen Ding swallowed so hard that his prominent Adam's
apple bobbed like a cork. "No, of course not."

"You've been here before. Have you ever seen them bar
people for life for doing what you told me to do?"

The older man shrugged his thin shoulders. He didn't answer the question directly, but muttered, "Sometimes they're
strict and sometimes not."

Chen said nothing. From that moment on, however, he kept
to his side of the room-dividing sheet. He read his books and
wrote some poems. He wrote a poem about the betrayal of
friendship, and he waited.

Meanwhile, Hong was living his own new life. Had Chen
known of it, the two brothers would have been further apart

in their understanding of each other than ever before. Though puzzled by Two Brother, often Hong went away from their conversations with a saying that applied to his own life. One of Chen's sayings stayed with him these days: "I dreamed of a thousand new paths, but woke and walked down the old one." Hong vowed not to walk down the old one unless all other paths were cut off—only Chen's failure in the exam could do that. Otherwise, Hong would take one of the thousand new paths open to him.

He was going to join the White Lotus.

He was, of course, sworn to secrecy even before the ceremony took place. "Sworn Brother"—Ye Pan was already using the term for an initiate—"when shall the ceremony be? A newcomer chooses his own date to take the oath."

"So my brother won't know, Righteous Uncle, I think it should be when he's at the banquet."

"What banquet?"

"For those who pass the exam."

"Oh? What if he doesn't pass?"

"If he doesn't pass, Righteous Uncle, then I won't join the Lotus and we'll both go home. He'll need me with him then."

"Is this how you make important decisions?" Ye Pan smacked his right fist against his left palm. "With one blow?"

"Yes, sir, I do. But he *will* pass and I *will* join. We'll take the path leading far away, not the old one home."

Smiling in approval, Ye Pan said, "A rare boy."

Chen languished four days, reading and writing. Shen Ding went out drinking every night, which especially annoyed Hong because it reminded him of Father. Very late one night Shen Ding came in laughing and woke the brothers up. He'd been carousing with other candidates who told a story called "The Seven Phases of the Examination."

"When you enter the compound carrying your baggage, you're a beggar," Ding said. "Getting searched, you're a prisoner. Entering your cell, you're the larva of an insect. When you finish the exam, you're a sick bird released from its cage.

Waiting for results, you're a restless monkey on a chain. When you fail, you're a poisoned fly. When you calm down and find out you've broken all your things in anger, you're a pigeon who's smashed its own eggs." Ding laughed uproariously. "Come on, country boys! Don't you see how funny that is?" In the bony face his eyes were shining fiercely.

The next morning, hearing a cannon go off, they hurried to the examination compound. A crowd was gathering around the Great Gate.

"List's posted!" Ding cried. He rushed forward, separating himself from Chen, who patiently joined the candidates at the rear and awaited his turn to reach the front, where a large placard had been nailed on the gate. Of nearly six thousand candidates, only about sixty had passed: one out of a hundred. The first five places in the sequences of names had been left blank, so the list began with the sixth-ranked Chujen, or Recommended Man.

Jostled and elbowed by anxious candidates looking for their own names, Chen stood there a long time before realizing his name wasn't there.

He had failed.

Backing away from the placard, he moved through the crowd and beyond it and stood looking at the lake, which sparkled in the sunlight. Shen Ding came alongside him.

"So you failed," said the older scholar.

"Yes. I looked for your name but didn't find it either."

"I won't try again," Ding said firmly. "But of course, that's what I said last time. It was the *Analects* that ruined me. I knew it."

"The readers didn't read my answers right."

Ding laughed scornfully. "That's what we all say. Be a man and admit you weren't good enough."

"I was good enough."

"Oh? Were you? Then stick around for the Chief Examiner when he comes out and posts up the leaders. The list isn't complete till he posts the top five." Ding laughed again. "I really believe you'll wait around to see. Well, why not? The first time people take the exam and fail, they usually do that—hope against hope they're in the top five. I admit I did. But that was four exams ago, when I was a Flowering Talent almost as young as you." Ding turned and started to walk away. "So wait, then. Enjoy yourself."

Chen did wait. For nearly two hours he stood in the broiling sun along with a couple of hundred other candidates, most of whom, he had to admit, were young, like himself. Perhaps Shen Ding was right—the older candidates knew better.

At last, in a bright ceremonial gown and accompanied by a dozen associate examiners, the man sent from Beijing by the Board of Rites on the Emperor's authority, the Meritorious Chief Examiner, strode from the compound. On spaces left empty at the head of the list, he pinned the names of the top five candidates. Then in red ink he put his personal seal on the placard. The provincial examination was over.

When Chen reached the front, he saw LAO CHEN, TIANQUAN DISTRICT, in the fifth place.

The next few days were a blur of activity. Chen spent a good deal of time in the examination compound. Along with other Chujen, he met and drank tea with officials who days ago would not have glanced his way. He was also taken into the presence of an elderly examiner who had made the final evaluation of his work.

Gao Shi had a small but elegant office in one of the main buildings of the compound. He offered Chen tea and looked the young man over. From years of too much study and too little exercise, Gao Shi had become a huge, rumpled man with heavy jowls only partially hidden by a long gray beard.

Chen noticed that Gao Shi had kindly eyes.

"I don't know the west where you come from," confessed the fat old scholar. "Do you have any men of letters in your village?"

"No, Honorable Gao Shi."

The old man cleared his throat in embarrassment. "Please,

Lao Chen," he said, "don't address me as 'Honorable.' I'm not
accorded that title. Just call me Examiner or Gao Shi."

"Yes, sir, Examiner."

"I hear you handed in your first draft."

The old examiner must have learned this from the official
who took Chen's answers at the district table. "If I know what
to write, I write it only once," explained Chen. "So I had no
reason for making another copy."

"I also hear you left very early."

"I had nothing more to say."

"Well, you said enough. You were interesting on the *Mencius*. And that was a charming poem about the mountain
streams. I, too, enjoy Tu Fu. There's a tendency these days to
rank him third or fourth among the Tang poets. I still put him
first."

So they talked awhile, and when Chen left, he not only liked
Gao Shi but had laid the ground for revering him as he revered
Tu Fu.

Two days after the test results were made public, Hong told
Ye Pan, "My brother's been invited to the Banquet of Auspicious Omen. Two nights from tonight."

"Then that's the night of your initiation."

At the Banquet of Auspicious Omen, all guests first turned
in the direction of Beijing to thank Emperor Chia Ching by
whose imperial grace the provincial examination had been
held. There was music and toasts with hot wine. Lao Chen had
the honor of sitting next to Gao Shi, his acknowledged mentor.
A member of the Chengdu Opera sang a song with words
from a poem called "Yu, yu, cry the deer!" which described a
memorable feast given by an emperor for his officials long
ago. This song introduced a special moment during the banquet, when each Chujen bowed to the examiner who had
recommended him for passing. Toasting with a thimbleful of
wine, the Recommended Man acknowledged his eternal debt
and discipleship. Lao Chen called Gao Shi "my Master
Teacher."

The old man lifted his own wine cup. "I pledge to be your mentor for the rest of my life. We have a bond now that can never be broken."

While such oaths were being sworn in the great examination compound, another ceremony was taking place in the rambling house of a barber. Lao Hong took off his blouse and put on a white robe, which symbolized death to the old ways. He was barefoot and had scrubbed his face hard to wash it clean of the dust of injustice. Smoky incense filled the candle-lit room where he waited.

At last the door opened, and a man also in a white robe signaled him to enter the next room, where at least a dozen other men waited. Ye Pan stood in front of an altar on which statues of the gods stood crowded together. A large portrait of Kuan Ti hung above the altar.

Ye Pan held a struggling rooster in one hand, a long sword in the other. When Hong stood before him, Ye Pan raised the sword and deftly cut the rooster's head off. Blood squirted everywhere, splattering the white robes of both Hong and Ye Pan. Then, as he'd been told to do, Hong put out his right hand so that Ye Pan could grip the middle finger.

"Do you wish to join this family?" Ye Pan asked.

"I do."

Ye Pan drew the sword blade slowly and deeply across Hong's finger. When the blood was flowing freely, Ye Pan held the boy's hand over a bowl that contained blood from the rooster.

"Your blood," said Ye Pan, "is mixed with the blood of generations of the White Lotus. The blood of the rooster represents every drop of blood spilled by the brotherhood in the name of justice. Is this bond what you wish?"

Hong knelt at his feet. "It is." He recited the correct line. "Where brothers lead I will follow."

"Will you abide by the Thirty-six Oaths?"

"I will."

"Do you understand if you betray the Lotus, you will die?"

"I do."

A red lamp was glowing in the room, illuminating the taut faces of the witnesses. Hong was prepared to answer their questions.

One called out, "Where did you come from?"

"From the Red Flower Pavilion," Hong replied, "where I was instructed in the bonds of loyalty and the five virtues."

"How many roads could you have taken?" another called out.

"Three."

"Which road did you take?" still another asked.

"The middle road."

"Why?"

"Because it was the broadest. Every man can walk on it if he wishes. It is the road of justice."

"Rise up," Ye Pan commanded, and when the boy did, his mentor embraced him.

The other men came forward, too, and embraced him. In his ear he heard the same word again and again and again, "Brother . . ."

Two Brother and Three Brother got home at nearly the same time. Shen Ding was already there, drunk as usual. "What did you do?" he asked Hong, whose finger was wrapped in bloody cloth.

"Someone tried to rob me on the street," Hong said. "He cut me with a knife."

"You don't lead a charmed life like your brother here," Ding said with a bitter smile. "He just came in before you. He was telling me about the great banquet."

Chen, embarrassed, had told him very little.

"Not everyone leads a charmed life," Ding continued. "I don't. I have a wife and three children to feed. I tutor the brats of rich landlords for a living. I dream of selling them to Japanese pirates. I have taken that exam five times and failed it for any number of reasons. This time I chose the wrong book. But your brother here, who lives a charmed life, selected the *Mencius* instead of the *Analects*, and so he goes on to

Beijing as a Recommended Man and I go home to my half-starved kids and overworked wife and no future. You see, it's true. Not every one lives a charmed life. For example, from the place you came from—beyond Mingshan, isn't it?—a plague of locusts has overrun whole villages. People will be starving soon. The strongest will eat. The thieves and bandits will eat. Stories came into Chengdu today that they'll be eating dead bodies where you come from. Isn't that what happens after a locust plague? Murder, starvation, looting? I believe the people where you come from don't live charmed lives either." He turned his sodden face and weary eyes toward Chen. "I knew early that you could make it. I wanted very much to like you because you were a nice fellow. As you would have it, a Confucian man," he said with a wry smile. "But I hated the thought of your becoming a Chujen and my going home with nothing, with hard work and no reward to look forward to. So I told you to bribe the examiner out of spite. Out of spite!" Surprised that neither brother reacted to him, Shen Ding waited a few moments, then, in anger and frustration, swept the dividing sheet back and staggered into his own half of the room.

"Don't pay any attention to him," Hong said contemptuously. He sat down on the floor and waved his bandaged hand toward the dividing sheet. "He's nothing but a rice bucket."

"Did you hear what he said? What if it's true?" Chen felt weak, stunned. "What if the locusts did get to our village?" He pictured Daiyun shuffling forward on her lily feet. Such a small, inexperienced girl could never fight for a handful of rice. In the aftermath of a locust plague she would be among the first to die. Chen closed his eyes and saw vividly her heart-shaped face.

"You worry too much," Hong declared irritably. "If the plague turned back to the west, the wind would have to shift completely around. Most of the plagues head east, don't you see, so it would be a very rare thing to happen." He waited for a reaction from Two Brother, who said nothing but looked at the floor. "Well, there's nothing we can do about it," Hong proclaimed briskly. "We leave for Beijing soon." Again he waited for a response, and when none came, he added, "The rice bucket over there is lying. No one can know what's happening back home. If the plague did hit there, it would take many weeks for word to come out. A plague sets a wall around a whole area. So how could the rice bucket know what was happening?"

Chen said nothing.

"And if people tried to get in or out, they'll be murdered by starving people or bandits. The rice bucket is right about that."

Chen said nothing.

"For my part," said Hong, "I worry about only a few. Big Sister, Wujiang, a few others maybe. And Father," he added. After a long silence, during which he stared at the floor, Hong glanced over at his brother, whose eyes were filled with tears. "You mustn't think about it," he told Chen.

"Tu Fu said, 'A lonely boat is moored to the heart that yearns for home.'"

"That's true enough. But there's nothing we can do. And you're a Recommended Man and our goal is Beijing before the next exam begins. What's the good of yearning? I remember one of your famous sayings: 'On the eastern mountain, tigers eat men. On the western mountain, tigers eat men, too.'"

"Why are you saying that?"

"I may be wrong, but I think it means one place is as good as another. And it's against yearning. Yearning for home is no better than yearning for somewhere else. Yearning for things to go right helps nothing. Yearning for a nice pleasant world is foolish. Yearning for winds to carry the locusts eastward instead of westward is even more foolish. The thing is, you haven't time for yearning. You have to finish something. And I'm to go with you."

Next morning they awoke to find Shen Ding gone. He had left a note.

FORGIVE ME. NOW THAT I WILL NEVER SEE YOU AGAIN, I CAN WISH YOU SUCCESS AND MEAN IT. I DO, CHEN. YOU ARE TRULY A FLOWERING

TALENT AND DESERVE TO BE A RECOMMENDED MAN. AND I WILL TRY AGAIN AT THE PROVINCIALS THREE YEARS FROM NOW. NEXT TIME, HOWEVER, I WILL AVOID THE *ANALECTS*.

SHEN DING

Because Two Brother was brooding about the chance of a plague overwhelming their village, Hong got him out of Chengdu as quickly as possible and on the road to Chongqing and the great Yangtze River. He convinced Chen they must hurry. In truth, they had more than enough time to reach Beijing before the municipal examination began. By asking around, Hong had learned it should take a few months of steady if leisurely travel to reach the capital from Chengdu. But the farther from the village he dragged Chen, the less chance of his brother heading back home. That would indeed be a fruitless and perhaps fatal journey, in Hong's opinion. At home they used to say, "If you plant melons, you reap melons." The saying meant you got what you paid for. And if you went where you shouldn't, you suffered for it. Two Brother never looked where he was going. He could be in the dead center of a locust swarm before knowing it. He'd wonder why his arms and legs were covered with crawling, clacking, six-legged, hard-winged horrors and why there was nothing to eat and why those haggard riders bearing down on him with swords drawn wanted anything he might have, even his life.

Hong believed he must point his brother's nose toward the rising sun and keep it there. Fortunately, Chen had no idea how long a trip to Beijing might take. When Hong told him at least half a year, Chen accepted this dubious estimate as pure fact. The province gave each Chujen a generous travel allowance, so Hong figured they could add his cricket winnings to it and have money enough to keep them on the way to Beijing for a long time.

So in unnecessary haste they left Chengdu and took the

southeast road for Chongqing. Each, unknown to the other, carried a letter for delivery—Chen in his bedroll, Hong inside his shirt.

From Gao Shi, Deputy Supervisor of the Chengdu Provincial Examination, Lao Chen held a letter for someone in Wuhan, a city on the way to the coast. The old man stroked his long beard and sighed. "If only I could go myself. It's beautiful on the Yangtze, especially the Three Gorges. But it's also dangerous. As you can see, my young friend, I'm no longer equipped for the rigors of travel." With a smile he made a gesture as if to heft the bulk of his stomach. "Meng Dafu is an old friend of mine, soon to be a new friend of yours. You'll find him interesting."

Lao Chen looked at the sealed letter. Nothing more than Meng Dafu's name was on it. "Will I have trouble finding him?"

Gao Shi chuckled. "I think not."

After waiting for more explanation and receiving none, Chen dutifully put the letter away. He'd not tell his brother about it. Hong might feel obligated to deliver it as he had done the schoolmaster's letter in Chengdu. As a Recommended Man, Chen must personally see the Gao Shi letter through to its destination. A saying of Confucius convinced him of his duty: "The gentleman makes demands on himself; the inferior man makes demands on others." In other words, if you agree to deliver a letter, you must do it yourself.

Though indifferent to Confucian principle, Hong felt the same way about the delivery of letters. His need to keep a letter secret from Chen didn't come, however, from the desire to relieve his brother of responsibility. It had nothing to do with Two Brother. Hong had sworn to keep his link to the Lotus concealed from everyone. So when Ye Pan gave him a letter, it was a foregone conclusion that he'd keep it secret. Ye Pan told him one thing only: the letter was a coded message for someone of great importance in Beijing. Hong didn't ask what the message was. He appreciated the sense of his remaining ignorant of it. If he were to be stopped by authorities, they might torture him to find out what the letter meant. If he knew nothing, he could tell nothing. Ye Pan warned him, however, that they'd learn from him who sent the letter.

"Let's assume they capture you," Ye Pan said coolly. "They'll ask politely who gave you such a strange letter. Then they'll demand to know. Then they'll start hurting you."

"I'll never tell them," Hong claimed.

Ye Pan shook his head. "If they torture you long enough and skillfully enough, you'll tell them that and anything else you know. You'll tell them where I live. You'll tell them I'm a barber and describe my house and everything in it. You'll tell them about your initiation and the secrets you swore never to reveal. You won't be able to help yourself. You'll even make up things to tell them. Luckily for you, they'll kill you when they think they have enough. Then you won't suffer anymore or feel the guilt of betraying your vow."

"Is it really possible? Could I betray you?" Hong cried in dismay.

"Of course it's possible. After all, you're flesh and blood like anyone else."

"If I ever betray you, Righteous Uncle, what happens then?"

"They'll come for me and I'll suffer the same fate, unless I have a few moments' warning. Then I'll keep them from torturing me, too, and learning what they want to know."

"You mean, kill yourself?"

It was not necessary for Ye Pan to reply.

As the brothers walked into the countryside beyond Chengdu, people stepped aside and respectfully let Chen pass. On his winged cap he wore a new duck-shaped emblem of woven silver and gold—the mark of a Recommended Man. He also wore one of his gowns that identified him as a scholar (he had two new ones now—both paid for by the province). On the left breast was sewn a Mandarin Square for Grade Eight of the civil service, represented by two swans drifting on a pond. In Chen's bedroll was his diploma, stamped with the governor's seal. To further establish Two Brother's fame as they traveled through unknown countryside, Hong had paid to have

a large banner made of silk, which could be unfolded and
hoisted on a pole. In large red characters the banner said:

VICTORY NOTICE

THE HONORABLE LAO CHEN HAS PASSED THE SICHUAN

PROVINCIAL EXAMINATION IN FIFTH PLACE

CHUJEN LAO CHEN PROCEEDS TO THE MUNICIPAL

EXAMINATION IN BEIJING

PLEASE MAKE WAY

When Lao protested that such a notice was shamefully arrogant, Hong scoffed with a wave of his hand. "I saw banners just like it all over Chengdu. Most of the Chujen have them made for traveling. They get you lodgings and food when there are none. We'll use this banner before we're through. You'll see. Everyone bows to the rich man; every dog bites the man in shabby clothes. I think that's an old saying, isn't it? And I remember something you once said about humility being false."

Chen quoted it correctly for him. " '*False* humility is genuine arrogance.' "

"See what I mean?" Hong grinned in triumph. "We're not being arrogant if we carry the banner when things look bad. We'll be humbly seeking help from those who respect scholarship, so it's true humility if we raise the banner high."

Chen didn't point out how specious this argument was. He let it go, however, because the banner gave Three Brother so much pleasure. He seemed to be happier about the high ranking in the provincial than Chen was himself. With a little prodding, Chen decided ruefully, his brother could turn out vain and boastful. The modest young scholar was glad, therefore, that Hong didn't know about the Messengers of Congratulations.

Actually, Hong did know. He had learned in Chengdu that a messenger was sent to the home of every new Chujen. Standing in front of a successful candidate's house, the messenger cried out, "Congratulations, Most Honorable Scholar!" until the whole town or village knew about it. Of course, the man would expect a reward for his effort, but it was a small price for a family to pay, as the achievement and the praise attending it trickled down to the furthest-removed cousin and nephew. This did not apply, Hong noted, to the Lao family. For one thing, Lao Lu would be lying drunk and penniless inside the house when the messenger came. For another, no messenger would venture into country plagued by locusts.

We can count on nothing but ourselves, Hong decided. So he argued further for the expediency of taking the banner along. "If we find ourselves in a bad place, we lift the banner and walk forward with the raised chin and unseeing eyes of an emperor. It could get us through."

Chen grumbled, but conceded the common sense of Hong's insistence on such a display, if safety was at issue.

What Chen didn't know about was Three Brother's possession of something secret and dangerous that could identify him as someone just as special, in his own way, as a scholar. Hong kept an oval ivory charm in his money pouch. Given to him by Righteous Uncle, it was engraved with the fierce-looking image of a bewhiskered god with the muscular body of a monster without feet. The characters for BUDDHA, TIGER, and DRAGON were written across its large belly. On the left shoulder were the words INVOKE THE GUARDIAN OF HEAVEN, and on the right shoulder, INVOKE THE BLACK GODS OF PESTILENCE. When rubbed between thumb and first finger, so claimed Ye Pan, this talisman invoked the Yin and the Yang, the Shadow and the Sun, the Passive and the Active, the Good and the Bad, the Valleys and the Mountains, the Cold and the Heat—in fact, all the oppositions in life that a man must endure. A charm of such universal application might help a sworn brother through the worst of times.

And so the Lao brothers trudged in an easterly direction until reaching the Jialing River. There they turned south and followed the river toward its meeting with the great Yangtze. One day after another, beneath cloudless skies, they journeyed past a long string of red sandstone hills covered with pine forests and terraced fields. Harboring their secrets, they talked little until Hong began asking his brother questions about history.

Chen's eyebrows went up. "You're interested in history? This is the first I knew of it."

Affecting nonchalance, Hong said, "I've always been interested in history. I mean, in the way governments rise and fall. In rebellions. That's the sort of thing that interests me."

"An interest in violence seems understandable from a handler of fighting crickets," Chen observed testily. Even so, he entertained his brother with the story of China in perpetual upheaval, beginning with the Chou, a nomadic people from the northwest, who swept into the country twenty-five centuries before, using three-man chariots to overthrow the Shang rulers.

Palace intrigues and assassinations brought the Chou dynasty to a close. Although the next government lasted only fifteen years before rebellion toppled it, during this period the Chin Emperor built the Great Wall.

The Han followed. It was characterized by constant turmoil, ending finally with the army's defeat by a Taoist religious group, the Yellow Turbans.

"Wait," Hong said. "These Yellow Turbans, were they a secret society?"

"They began that way, before they recruited large armies. Why?"

"I don't know much about secret societies."

"For my part," Chen said, pursing his lips in judgment, "I don't approve of them. They claim superiority in their doctrine of universal salvation. But by making such a claim, they undermine the established way of things. Master Kung wouldn't approve either."

"But isn't their aim to bring about order?"

"Well, I suppose that's a stated aim: the establishment of social order."

"I thought Confucius believed in order."

"He did. That's his main principle."

"Didn't he mean a just order? What you said about the Chin

Emperor, that he brought about order but at the cost of everyone's happiness, would Confucius like that?"

"No."

"So your Master wanted order with justice. If a government was bad, didn't he believe in overthrowing it?"

"So he did, so he did," Chen said impatiently. "Do you want me to continue?"

Hong nodded, kept his mouth shut, and listened to his brother describe a history of further chaos after the fall of the Han dynasty. Four hundred years passed before China was stable again. The first Tang Emperor defeated a number of rivals for the throne. His victory brought relative peace for three hundred years. Then new rebellion broke out, ending with the creation of many small kingdoms, all of them warring against one another. At last a strong military leader unified the country under the Sung dynasty. But it, in turn, didn't last long. The empire split, with the northern part dominated by people who came from beyond the Great Wall. Secret societies rose up to overthrow those foreigners. That was two hundred years ago, when a great general defeated them and began the dynasty now ruling, the Ming.

"There," Chen said with a smile, "you have it."

"Rebellion. Secret societies. Uprisings and downfalls," mused Hong. So his brother had told him what he needed to know: China had always been a country devoted to the idea of righting wrongs and replacing poor rulers with good ones. Two Brother confirmed what Ye Pan maintained: the will of the Chinese people must prevail as it had always done through the centuries. To fight for justice was their heritage.

Hong thought of sacred scissors to cut the bonds that held China to foreign aggressors; an ink brush with which to write just laws; an old red lamp to distinguish truth from falsehood; a mirror in which to look and find his true nature. He had entered the Circle of the Lotus, and this made him new.

As they walked, he glanced from side to side, fearful of a "draft of wind"—a spy who might smell him out as a brother of the Lotus and run to the authorities. What if they took him up and tortured him? He'd never talk, never reveal secrets, no matter what Ye Pan said. There was something stronger in the mind than in the body. His mind would never let his body betray him.

Engrossed by such musing, Hong scarcely realized they were on the outskirts of a village. A crowd was standing in a circle in a nearby field. When a farmer came along, Hong asked him what was happening. The man explained that it was a festival in honor of Lei Tsu, Thundering Ancestor, the god of ripening fields. Leaving the road, the brothers walked toward the gathered spectators, who were watching twenty or thirty girls, most of them about Hong's age or slightly older, dancing with sticks. Actually, the sticks were bamboo rods about three feet long, decorated at the end with bells and tassels. To a rhythmic beat each girl was striking her arms, legs, back, and stomach with her stick. So many sticks, hitting the young bodies in unison, caused the bells to jingle merrily and the tassels to sway. In a half circle, a chorus of older women was singing a song in praise of Thundering Ancestor. Farmhands and villagers were clapping encouragement and drinking from goatskins.

Hong glanced warily at his brother. He was not surprised to see that Chen was transfixed by the dancers, especially by one girl who smiled at the tall young man as she whacked herself while jumping from one foot to the other.

Hong said, "Let's go," but Two Brother never moved or shifted his gaze.

Hong nudged him. "Let's go. We have a long march today." The girls had formed a single file, which dipped and swayed like the long sinuous body of a dragon. When the middle of this multiple-jointed dancing creature passed by, the girl smiled brightly at Chen.

"Gege, I said let's go! We have a long march ahead."

A middle-aged man sidled up just then and touched Chen on the sleeve. "Honored sir, I see on your gown a mark of very special distinction. I noticed it immediately." He chuckled at his own cleverness, thrusting both of his hands into the long sleeves of his own gown.

A landowner, Hong thought. A rich landowner.

"We're only a small village, but I like to think we have a certain knowledge of the world," the man continued. "I myself make it a point to read one book a year. What do the sages say? It escapes me now, but the idea is the mind must be as active as the body."

Chen was shifting his gaze from the garrulous man to the dancers—to the one dancer. "Yes," he said vaguely.

"I note from the emblem on your cap," the man continued, beaming, "that you're a Grade Eight, a Chujen. From your youth I gather you're a new Chujen. Congratulations."

"Thank you, sir," Chen said politely, his eyes on the dancing girl.

"What rank?" the man asked crisply.

Chen turned to him. "Sir?"

"I asked your rank in the examination."

"Oh, fifth, sir."

The man's mouth dropped open in wonder. "I am honored, we are all honored, Recommended Man! Fifth! As the gods are my witness, we have never had someone so high as a Fifth passing through our village."

When Chen failed to answer, his attention now wholly on the girl, the man realized what Chen was looking at, smiled, and plucked the young scholar's sleeve again. "Do you like our Thundering Ancestor dance?"

"Ah, I do, sir."

"That girl"—he pointed to the one who was commanding Chen's interest—"is my humble and worthless daughter."

Now Chen looked at him and never heard Three Brother, who was muttering under his breath, "Let's go—we have a long march ahead."

"Permit me to offer you and your companion," the man said with a triumphant smile, "something to eat and a night's stay in our humble and worthless little home, which, though poor enough, will be vigilant in affording you all that can be had in this region, I can assure you."

Hong winced and stopped saying, "Let's go." Grudgingly he

fell behind his brother and the talkative man, who gripped Chen's elbow familiarly. His monologue unending, the fellow led them to a large farmhouse nearby, stocked with a pond for fish and a barnyard for pigs and endless fields of wheat, sesame, and onions.

At least we'll eat well, Hong thought. But he feared the girl.

On their third day at the Ma farmhouse, Hong watched distastefully as Two Brother strolled with the girl, Weijun, in the garden or sat with her in the courtyard. Landowner Ma was also watching—spying would be a better word—from around corners, his eyes twinkling, his mouth set in such a fatuous smile that Hong began to hate him.

"Let's go," he told Two Brother when finally they were alone for a few moments. "The food is very good . . ." Actually, he felt that the household cooks were wonderful. Hong had eaten the best meals of his life here, but was willing to sacrifice them to get away safely. "And the Ma family is nice, but, gege, it's time we left. What's wrong?" He noticed that his brother suddenly looked sad.

"I'm thinking of Daiyun. If the locusts did come, the village wouldn't be starving yet. Isn't that true?"

"Not for weeks. Not until normal supplies gave out."

"But then I see her in my mind, wasting away, hungry, trying to find a scrap to eat."

At least he wasn't thinking of the girl here, Hong thought. "Remember, Daiyun's family is rich," he pointed out reassuringly. "If anyone survives in the village, they will. They have servants to protect their granaries."

Chen brightened.

"But I can see why you're thinking of Daiyun," Hong said. "You're comparing her to this girl here."

"Well, yes."

"There's no comparison," Hong said briskly. "This girl has rough hands. She dances with a stick but can't play a lute. Her face is red from too much sun—and it's fat, not narrow, like Daiyun's. And her voice is scratchy and much too high. And she giggles all the time and says nothing of interest. She's nothing at all like Daiyun. Not in any way."

"You seem to have studied her closely," Chen said with a laugh.

"There's not much else to do here. Except eat. I must admit the food's good, but we have to move on."

"Landlord Ma wishes me to stay," Chen admitted with a little sigh. "This morning he asked me to marry Weijun and help him with his estate. He has properties all over this region. He'd put me in charge of some of them right away."

"He wants to boast of a Chujen for his son-in-law. But you told him no."

"I told him I'd think about it."

Hong was shocked, horrified. He sat down on the bed in their room and stared at the floor. Would all his brother's work come to this? Marriage to a dull girl and a lifetime of coping with that windbag of her father?

"Very well." Hong slapped both knees decisively. "You stay here and think about it. I'm going on."

"Why would you go on without me?" Chen asked, alarmed.

"You'll be settling down here. You don't need me anymore. So I'll have the freedom to see what we started out to see together. I'll go down the Yangtze and travel all the way to the coast and reach the ocean and then head up the Grand Canal and visit the great capital of the world. I'll make my way, so you stay here and think about it and then marry the girl with rough hands and spend your evenings listening to her father talk about a book he read last year. Goodbye."

When Hong got up, Chen rushed to him and placed both hands on his shoulders. Looking down at his muscular brother, the tall young scholar frowned deeply and said, "All right, then. I've thought about it. I won't stay here. I'm going on with you."

Part Two

They were on the road early the next morning. Weijun stood at the courtyard gate, eyes shining with tears that she wiped away with a silk kerchief. Her father, less restrained, rode a donkey alongside the departing brothers, begging Chen to stay. Not only would he let his new son-in-law manage the properties, he would give the Honorable Recommended Man two of them for himself.

When Chen politely declined the offer and kept his eyes on the road, Landlord Ma upped the number to three.

Then four.

Kicking the donkey, Landlord Ma rode a few paces ahead of the travelers, turned, and blocked their way. "I'll give you five of my seven properties. Five! I'll put it in writing, so the title is yours alone, without encumbrance. Do you hear me?" The man's face was crimson, his chest heaved, and in his urgency he kept digging his heels into the donkey, which reacted by kicking up its rear feet, nearly unseating the rider.

When the brothers continued silently on their way, Landlord Ma rode behind them for a while, then had to move off the road because of porters bearing huge bales on shoulder poles. From the ditch he began yelling at the brothers' backs. "Not good enough for you, is that it, Recommended Man? Do you think you can triumph in a place like Beijing? The true scholars there will eat you alive and spit you out and howl with laughter! So go on and make a fool of yourself! I wouldn't want a son-in-law so stupid! I've been courteous to you, as a gentleman should, but since you behave so rudely, I'll confess you never did impress me! Never! If I hadn't seen the diploma with my own eyes, I wouldn't have believed such a simpleminded country boy could rank at all in a district, much less rank fifth in the provincial. A miracle not likely to be repeated! Hear me! You won't make it in the capital, that's certain! Not a backward boy from the Western Mountains! They'll laugh you out of Beijing! So don't come running back here and expect a generous welcome! The only welcome you and that brat of a brother will get is a cudgel across the back! Hear what I'm saying? Hear me?" Rising up from the saddled donkey, the landlord's rather portly body swayed this way and that as he kept yelling at the pair long after they had reached a pine-covered hill and disappeared over it.

They walked in silence for a long time before Hong, who had been glancing at his brother's glum face, finally spoke up. "Are you thinking of her?" he asked.

"Yes, I am," Chen admitted.

"Well, she's not so bad, but think of the father!"

"What are you talking about?"

"Weijun."

"What does she have to do with it?" Chen asked in surprise. "There's no plague here."

"Ah, that's true," Hong said with a smile of relief. "Rich people like the Kuo family keep huge stores of food for emergency. Daiyun will always have something to eat. And the next planting will come soon enough, and then the harvest. She'll become a big, strapping girl." In his desire to paint a rosy picture, Hong nearly made the mistake of adding, "Ripe for marriage!"

Again they walked in silence, letting the countryside hold their attention. They passed whole houses built from rocks the size of a man's head. They passed lakes and sulfurous springs and flourishing stands of trees that filled their nostrils with the fresh scent of conifers. Clouds roiled overhead, sending down a foggy drizzle, and then the sun burst through skeins of gray to light up the dark surface of the Jialing River. Fog was sucked into valleys among wooded hills that had been rising from the landscape for the last few hours.

"That hill there," Hong called out suddenly. "Far off there, ahead!" Little orange dots gleamed on its distant sides just emerging now from the rainy mist. "Aren't those tiled roofs? And so many of them!" Without waiting for Two Brother's confirmation, he cried, "We've come to Repeated Good Luck!"

The city of Chongqing meant Repeated Good Luck, a name given to it in commemoration of its prince becoming Emperor during the Sung dynasty. Commanding a rocky peninsula above the mighty river, Chongqing was also called the Furnace of the Yangtze, being hot and humid even during autumn. The Yangtze had its own name, the River of Golden Sand—a misleading epithet, since the jagged curves of the Yangtze's channel were filled with grimy silt for much of its 3,500-mile journey from the western interior to the sea.

The brothers had never seen anything like Chongqing. Wooden houses rose from stilts that clung to the steep promontory. Everything seemed at a tilt, unstable, ready in one good gust of wind to blow over and topple into the confluence of the Jialing and Yangtze. It was a crumbling, gritty, unkempt place. Everything was connected to everything else by countless steps like an intricate spiderweb of stone. Most people got up and down the stairways in sedan chairs of bamboo carried by lean, muscular men who stared only at the next step, yet trudged successfully through the maze to arrive where they were supposed to be. They deposited their passengers without a murmur until haggling began over the price of the ride. The brothers gawked at surefooted ponies that also navigated the raked stones. They expected at any moment that one of the shaggy, swaybacked animals would lose its footing and be catapulted down the terraces into the water far below.

But Hong was not so overwhelmed that he couldn't think of the main thing. "Someone in Chengdu told me they have good pickled vegetables here, and the local dumplings should be tried, and they do fine things with bean curd, gege. Let's eat."

They stayed in Repeated Good Luck only long enough to arrange for passage down the Yangtze to the city of Wuhan. At the waterfront office, a young clerk looked Chen up and down, appraising the winged cap and the skinny fellow who wore it. "So you're a Chujen," he said with a sneer.

"Yes, and for that reason he gets a better price on the passage," Hong declared.

"Oh? And who are you? Grand Secretary to the Emperor?" the clerk said haughtily. "I've studied the Classics myself, and you know what I think?" He turned his narrowed eyes Chen's way. "Talking with someone of true wisdom for one night is better than studying books for ten years."

"That may be true," countered Hong, "but where do you find someone of any wisdom these days, much less *true* wisdom? Certainly not in Chongqing."

The young clerk glared at the boy a moment, then turned again to Chen. "Does your Grand Secretary always speak for you?"

"I have a letter of introduction from the Provincial Governor," Chen said, patting his travel pouch.

"It isn't there," Hong muttered, opening his own pouch. "It's here." He took the officially stamped letter from his pouch and handed it over.

Sullenly the young clerk undid the red ribbon, unrolled the letter, and read a polite request—actually a veiled demand— for the Chujen bearing the document to be shown the respect bestowed on scholars of his station. He should also be given low rates and special privileges whenever available to others of similar status.

"Since you know so much about wisdom," Hong said to the frowning clerk, "you can understand the wisdom of doing what the governor says."

Silently the clerk complied, but only after Hong studied the rate chart and made sure that Chen's passage was half the regular price. For himself, Hong expected to pay full fare. That was just.

"My ancestors and I thank you," he said to the clerk with a little bow, then smiled at the young man's effort to control his anger. So he added, "My brother, who knows such things, once told me there are Five Blessings. I hope that all five descend upon your house: longevity, health, riches, love of virtue, and a natural death, which in your case may not be possible. Good-bye, sir."

When they were outside on the wharf, where cargo boats were being unloaded by stevedores, Hong burst out laughing. "We made a fool of him."

Chen wasn't smiling. "One of these days your impudence will get you into grave trouble."

"And of more importance, Master Kung would not approve. Yes, I know." But Hong had nearly forgotten the incident, so absorbed was he by the hectic activity on the dock. Long lines of porters were hauling bales straight up the paved slopes toward Pipa Shan hill. Meanwhile, awaiting their turn to be unloaded, numerous junks lay at anchor, their canvas sails circled by cawing white birds and their long oars sticking over the gunwales at angles like the spindly legs of a locust.

"Think of it!" Hong exclaimed. "Tomorrow we go down the Yangtze!" He was dismayed to see his brother staring blankly into the distance. "What are you thinking about now?" Hong asked in exasperation, for he wished to share his excitement.

"What he said."

"What who said?"

"Tu Fu. 'Survivors can manage to live on, but the dead are gone forever.' "

"That's right," Hong agreed. He hoped his voice sounded cold, because he mustn't be sentimental about the people back home. Not with a brooding Two Brother. "We're alive. And tomorrow we go down the Yangtze. And surviving it might be difficult, especially if we go at it half-asleep instead of wide awake."

Shortly after dawn, they went down to the harbor, getting clumsily in the way of cargo, rope slings, hawsers, and shouting stevedores. At last they found their vessel—an old shallow-drafted junk. She carried quadrangular lug sails. Bamboo battens enabled them to be folded up and let out like an accordion, and though they were so patched that they had the threadbare look of a poor man's laundry, such ribbing kept them strong enough to hold the wind. Her five masts were staggered off the midline and tilted fore and aft; this kept each sail from getting becalmed by the one in front of it. The elevated poop deck was square-shaped; the huge rudder centered below it was perforated to make handling in swift currents easier. On each side of the flared bow a round red eye was painted so that evil water spirits could be watched for. Hong explained each of these features to his brother, having heard a cricket handler often boast in meticulous detail of his years as a freshwater and seagoing sailor. Belowdecks at the stern was the passengers' cabin, nothing more than a cramped space with some planks attached to the bulkhead for beds. It reeked of fish.

So complained an old merchant who arrived shortly after the brothers. "But it's better than the last I was on. On that one the crew cooked their lousy meals in our cabin. They drank and fought, too. It was worth your life to sleep there. What's the wings for?" An old gnarled hand pointed at Chen's winged cap. "What have we got here—a grand official?"

Hong explained in rather lofty tones who his brother was.

The old merchant stared at Hong. "Can your hand cover the sky, boy?"

It was a saying familiar to Hong, who had heard it applied to himself many times. People meant by it, Do you expect me to believe your lies?

"We have a diploma to prove what we say." Hong motioned to his brother, who, grimacing, shook his head and fiddled with his bedroll to avoid more of this boastful talk. "Not only is he a Chujen, but he ranked fifth in the provincial," continued Hong.

The old man sighed. A porter had hauled four large sacks and a bedroll into the cabin for him. "I don't care what your brother does or is. All I care about is getting these bamboo wares to Wuhan. What is there in this dismal life to care about except business? Hey, boy?"

Hong glared at him for an answer.

Under the old man's watery eyes were bags of flesh the color of earth. After a long, thorough appraisal of Hong, the old eyes began to twinkle. "The Tiger! I'd bet my life you were born under the sign of the Tiger."

Astonished, Hong admitted that he was.

The old man grinned. "I rarely miss, boy."

Chen had wandered out on deck, but Hong remained behind, curious about this old fellow who had guessed his birth sign.

"What are you two really doing?" the merchant asked.

"I already told you."

The old man waved off Hong's blunt assertion. "My honored father used to say, 'Misfortune goes out where disease enters in—at the mouth.' "

"I'll have my brother recite. He'll amaze you," Hong promised.

"What do I care about recitations? Three times a year I take my best merchandise to Wuhan, where people appreciate good quality. Aside from these trips, I sell all the year around, every year, every week, every day, and I have done so ever since I was your age or younger. I like this journey on the great river. It's never failed to fascinate me, though I stopped taking it for a year. That's when my wife died." He paused, studying the boy. "Is this your first trip downriver?" When Hong nodded, the old man said, "It was hers, too. We hit a shoal and broke up and she drowned. That was fifteen, maybe sixteen years ago. Are you boys selling anything?"

"No, I told you."

"I know you told me. Are you joining the army? I hear a soldier's pay is better in the east. That's because they're fighting Japanese pirates these days."

"The boat broke up and your wife drowned? Do such things happen on the river?"

The old man began chuckling. "Do such things happen? Oh, indeed! Why, the Yangtze is a *devil* of a river. Otherwise, who would think her fascinating?"

Hong began to look at the wrinkled old merchant in a new light. Though claiming only business mattered, this ancient seller of bamboo ware was at heart an adventurer—and sprightly enough to travel with men a fourth his age. Hong liked him.

"Where do you come from, boy?"

"I told you."

"Yes, you told me the west. North is peace, east is happiness, south is strength. West is danger."

That's right, Hong thought. West is danger. West is crawling with untold numbers of whirling horrors that have ceaseless jaws and six long legs.

Their conversation was interrupted by a long, rhythmic banging from the deck.

"Don't be alarmed, young soldier-to-be," the merchant said dryly. "That means we're getting under way."

Hong rushed out on deck, where Chen was holding on to the rail and looking toward midships, where a sailor stood with a hammer and beat it against a huge sheet of iron attached to the mainmast. He was warning the harbor that the ship had left its berth for the broad sweep of the Yangtze.

After leaving Chongqing, the junk sailed on a leisurely current into the broader reaches of the great river, with pagodas and Taoist temples along both banks. The brothers stood at the midships gunwale and watched the river towns go by with their cobblestone streets and tiny shops and beyond them the terraced rice paddies and thatched cottages of villages.

"Nothing dangerous here," Hong muttered.

His brother, laughing, gripped his arm. "Is danger what you want, didi?"

"The old merchant says there's danger, so I look for it, that's all."

"A beautiful tranquil river," observed Chen with a contented smile. "Honorable Gao Shi also said it's dangerous, but then he's quite fat."

Hong glanced at his brother; the expression on Chen's face was more relaxed and happy than he had seen in months. Perhaps the soft landscape sliding by and the river breezes appealed to older brother. He was better off without women around him, Hong decided. All Chen needed was books. But would it always be so? Brooding on their future, Hong feared the examinations in Beijing. If Lao Chen did succeed, would he continue to need a younger brother? Would he want a town mansion and beautiful women and rich clothes and private audiences with the Emperor to satisfy his vanity? Hong had no idea what might happen, and he told himself on the *Floating Lily* (the grandiose name of the dilapidated old junk) what he had told himself even before Chen took the district examination: Mother would have us see it through to the end. What happens then is up to the gods.

There was hardly time, however, to wonder about the future now, when the present was so demanding. They huddled with the old merchant and a few other passengers under the flapping shade of the mainmast. The sun's glare turned the Yangtze's otherwise unruffled blue surface into the bright chaotic look of shattered glass. The deck got so hot that their straw sandals felt close to burning, but it was better to be abovedecks than in the cramped and stinking cabin.

The merchant, Lin Shi, told them the legend of the Three Gorges. Long ago, before anything was written down, Emperor Yu the Great hacked apart a mountain range with his magical ax in order to drain a lake that had submerged the entire province of Sichuan. That was why the gorges were so sheer: they had been cut through with a gigantic blade.

And suddenly, as if a giant had blown out a candle with one breath, the sun vanished in clouds and the sky darkened until the river looked like a broad sheet of slate. The old merchant chuckled at the awestruck expression on Hong's face. "Maybe you're beginning to see the great river for the strange creature she is," Lin Shi said. "Look." He pointed toward the north bank, where the *Floating Lily* glided by a walled town. "They sell oranges and peaches in Wanxian. But their bamboo ware is not as good as mine. It's not as tightly plaited."

Three hours later they passed the town of Yunyang, where great battles had been fought nearly two thousand years before. "The head of General Chang Tsei is buried in a temple there. They say it talks whenever a rebellion's about to begin."

"Has it talked recently?" Hong asked with such eagerness that the merchant laughed.

"You sound, boy, as if you wanted it to talk long enough and loud enough to bring down the Emperor!"

Because of a new change in the river, Hong was spared further scrutiny. Waves were building on the Yangtze, its slate-gray surface broken as if chips of stone were cascading down a mountain.

"We're coming to the first gorge, the Qutang," explained Lin Shi. He squinted at three men who stood on a cleated plank at the stern, gripping a huge oaken tiller. "Nobody pays any attention to them until the rapids begin. Then you know your life is in their hands."

The captain, a short wiry man, appeared on the poop deck. "I'm told," the old merchant whispered, "he's a Hakka from the south and a former pirate, but a good man on the water."

Suddenly the brothers felt the hull of the old junk start to quake, while the tumultuous roaring of the river filled their ears, and a thin, violent spray swept over their faces. Shallow here, the Yangtze was dotted with huge boulders around which numerous whirlpools surged. A lashing, foaming rapid spilled around bends that the tillermen, on the captain's shouted instructions, had to navigate. Stripped to the waist, they worked in unison to turn the great rudder in conformance with a narrow channel that twisted like a snake among treacherous rocks. Above the old junk rose the towering Qutang Gorge, its shiny black sides as cleanly hewn as if a magical ax had indeed cleaved straight through the granite.

"Is this dangerous enough for you?" Chen asked his brother with a grimace.

"What did you say?"

Neither heard a word the other spoke, not even when they repeated themselves by cupping their hands and yelling.

Then, abruptly, it was over. They were out of the gorge, sailing along, if not tranquilly, at least without a wild buffeting from the river.

"That wasn't so bad," Hong grumbled.

The old merchant grinned at the boy. "Qutang is the first and smallest gorge. We have only begun."

It was getting late, so the captain moored alongside the riverbank at a bend calm enough for the anchor to hold. In the morning, when the junk returned to mid-channel, the brothers stood at the gunwale and watched sampans heading upstream. The small brown boats were hardly moving forward against the current, although boatmen on them were poling frantically.

Joining the brothers, Lin Shi said, "It usually takes a week to go downstream from Chongqing to Yichang. That same four hundred miles going upstream, against the current, can take two months. Wushan's not far ahead now. It was named for a mountain where witches lived."

The brothers scarcely heard him. They were listening to a heavy rhythmic sound coming from around the next bend in the river. Then they saw three long lines of men struggling across sharp-edged boulders on the north bank. Hawsers as thick as a man's arm were draped across their shoulders, as they leaned forward, the ropes becoming taut or slack as the current ripped and shifted in the river below.

"A Yangtze tracker worked for me," said Lin Shi. "Hardest worker I ever saw. Hauled bamboo in a wheelbarrow from a village twenty miles away. Would do anything rather than come back here and do *that*." He gestured toward the line of two or three hundred trackers who were hauling one of the twelve-hundred-foot hawsers forward across the rocks, inch by torturous inch. As they wobbled along like overburdened ants, the trackers chanted intermittently and the tracking bosses shouted at them to keep going. "If you inspected the bank over there," Lin Shi said, "you'd find rope marks etched into the stone.

That's how many centuries they've hauled boats upstream on this stretch of river. That tracker who worked for me died only last year," he told Hong. "Not much older than your brother. Lungs gave out from a youth spent here."

At that moment a large junk hove into sight around the bend. On its bow a group of men were banging gongs and beating drums in rhythm so the trackers ashore could time their slow, measured steps. The characters QIN CHAI—By Imperial Commission—fluttered on a white banner at the top of the main mast.

"A deputy officer from Beijing is on that junk," Lin Shi declared solemnly. "Everything on the river must yield to it." And indeed, the *Floating Lily* moved dangerously close to the south bank, clearly establishing right-of-way for the official and his party aboard the junk.

"Someday," Hong said to his brother, "you'll command the same power."

"Yes, why not?" the old merchant exclaimed merrily. "And bring me along, will you? I'd like to know what it feels like on such a boat, making the world clear out of your path!"

They approached Wushan soon and docked there to unload cargo, take on passengers, and stay for the night. "If you were sailing right now through the next gorge," Lin Shi told the brothers when they bedded down in their cabin, "you could see the moon only when it was directly above the gorge."

"Why?" Hong asked curiously.

"Because the cliffs are so high and close together. There's only a tiny ribbon of sky right above you." He held his weathered thumb and first finger an inch apart. "I can see by your faces you don't believe it."

"Well, I've yet to see anything really dangerous," Hong said pointedly.

"Those boulders in the Qutang weren't big enough and mean enough for you?" asked the old merchant with a broad grin. "All right. Just wait. We have more coming."

———

So early the next day, plowing through a mist as thick as soup, the *Floating Lily* entered Wu Gorge, where again the travelers experienced the Yangtze's torrential fury. Above the howl of rolling and churning water, Lin Shi shouted in Hong's ear, intent upon teaching something to the boy he'd befriended. He pointed out smaller gorges leading off from the Wu. In some of them lived golden-haired monkeys and mandarin ducks. He waved in the direction of Goddess Peak, a stone pillar that stood on the tallest of mountains hereabouts. From a distance it was said to resemble the youngest of twelve fairies who guided ships along the Yangtze. Nearly always she was shrouded in mist, but to anyone who happened to see her, the Wu Fairy brought good luck.

Hong called to Chen, but Two Brother was solitary this morning and stood by himself, his long figure hunched over the gunwale. So Hong squinted alone through the swirling fog.

"See anything?" asked the old merchant.

"No."

A few minutes later, old Lin Shi asked again. "See anything?"

"No."

"Then you won't," the merchant declared briskly and folded his arms. "We are past the place of seeing her."

But Hong persisted. Five minutes later, he cried out, "I see her! I see the pillar on top of a mountain peak! There!"

"No you don't!" But the old man scrambled to his feet. "Where?"

"There!"

Following the boy's outstretched finger, the old man squinted into the drifting veils of mist and then let out a whoop of his own. "I see her, too! After so many trips, I see her! This is the first time!" Draping his arm around Hong's shoulder, the old fellow beamed with pleasure. "Thanks to you, boy! Good luck's coming our way. There's no doubt about it."

Hong also felt a thrill of pleasure, and not because of any possible good luck. It was caused by the old man's arm thrown familiarly across his shoulders. And it struck Hong that his own father had never done anything like it.

"The danger is a hoax," Hong grumbled to his brother when they had sailed through the thirty miles of Wu Gorge. "Those men at the tiller know every rock and shoal. For them it's like riding a donkey down a road. And look at the Hakka captain. Was a man ever more sure of himself?"

Chen shook his head doubtfully. "I've been looking at this water. I don't trust it."

"*You* don't trust it?" hooted Three Brother. "You don't have to trust it. Only the captain and those three at the stern with the rudder, they have to trust where to go on it. A river in itself isn't dangerous."

"Does your old merchant tell you that?"

"No, he's like you. He says the third gorge, the Xiling, is the dangerous one. And I suppose after that he'll say the next stretch of river is the most dangerous and then the stretch after that and after that." Hong chuckled with confidence, as if he had sailed the Yangtze all his life.

Studying his brother, Chen frowned. The boy was exuberant and boastful and took up with anyone who came along, for example, this grubby seller of bamboo ware. Even so, when Hong wasn't beside him, Chen looked around anxiously; and when Hong wasn't there to be seen, Chen saw Three Brother in his mind and the imagined sight made him smile.

Hong was spending much of his time on the *Floating Lily* with the old merchant, who continued to lecture him on the great river. The largest of the three gorges, the Xiling, actually consisted of four smaller ones: the Gorge of the Sword, the Horse Lung and Ox Liver Gorge, the Soundless Bell Gorge, and the Gorge of Shadow Play.

"Where did all those names come from?" Hong asked.

"No one knows. Centuries ago they got these names. Think of how much water has passed through this channel," Lin Shi mused. The old merchant loved the Yangtze.

Before reaching the first part of Xiling Gorge, they sailed calmly past countless orange and peach orchards. It was a serene moment, and the dozen passengers lined the gunwale,

enjoying a placid river breeze and intermittent sunshine. From
belowdecks came the chirping of caged birds, the grunt of
pigs, the yapping of dogs whose flesh was considered a delicacy
at feast time on the tables of the wealthy.

And then once again the mood of the Yangtze turned around.
The first gorge loomed ahead, the clouds lowered, the rapids
crashed against shoal and half-submerged rock. The channel
narrowed ominously to nothing more than fifty yards across,
so that the port strakes of the *Floating Lily* nearly touched the
side of a junk passing upstream.

"Come over to starboard," Lin Shi urged. "You can look
straight up at the gorge, and it seems to be toppling over."

Hong went with him, and sure enough, when the boy looked
up at the precipitous shiny wall of rock, it seemed to be lurch-
ing over into the river.

They were so occupied with this phenomenon that they
didn't notice the junk heeling over as it spun around a sharp
bend from which a half-dozen rocks projected, like immense
spikes driven into the wall of the gorge. The old merchant had
turned to the boy with a grin. "What do you think of it? Huh?
Isn't the river an old devil? Aren't these gorges like nothing
else?"

Scarcely had he spoken these words when the junk veered
again, slipping so close to the south wall that one of the projecting rocks, perhaps six feet long, nearly grazed the starboard
gunwale.

It happened so fast that Hong, remembering, would never
know if he got out a final cry of warning. Turned away from
the projecting granite, old Lin Shi had opened his mouth to
say something when the rock, like a sweeping arm, caught him
in the back and hurled him over the side. Hong had only an
instant to see the old man rolling and tumbling, eyes staring
and mouth opening into an astonished O, before foam covered
the tossing body and rippling water sucked him into its depths.

It happened that fast, before Hong could even scream, let
alone seek help. Then he was rushing along the tilting deck
toward the captain, who stood high above him on the poop.

His yelling didn't break the captain's concentration until minutes later, when the *Floating Lily* had passed through this highly dangerous part of the Gorge of the Sword. "What is it, boy?" the captain shouted down testily.

Hong told him and was horrified to get no more response than a cold shrug. Much later, after the *Floating Lily* had successfully picked her way through a maze of shoals and rapids, the captain came down into the cabin, where Hong was curled up, facing the bulkhead.

The short powerful man sat on the bed plank and studied the boy. In a voice so quiet and tender that Hong turned to stare at him, the captain said, "I've sailed these gorges a hundred times, and each time my heart is in my mouth. I knew Lin Shi well. He traveled this river often on business. I saw him talking to you. He liked you, boy, and I can see you liked him. But in his eagerness to tell you things, he didn't stay vigilant. You can't do that on the Yangtze. He forgot where he was for just a moment, and . . ." The captain opened his hands, palms upward. "If you travel in this world, you must be prepared for the consequences. I'm sorry. I liked Lin Shi, too."

Neither Hong nor the captain realized that Chen was standing in the shadows. After the captain left, Two Brother came over to the bed plank and knelt beside Hong.

"It was very strange," Chen murmured.

"It was my fault. He was talking to me and didn't see the rock coming. Alone, he wouldn't have been so foolish. I did it." Hong was looking up at the plank above his head; Lin Shi had slept there.

"Tu Fu said—" Chen began.

"I don't care what Tu Fu said!"

After a long silence, Hong muttered, "Well, what did he say?"

" 'In these troubled times I have drifted here and there. Returning home alive is but an accident.' "

"Yes, I believe that. But we . . ." He turned to stare at Two Brother. "We're going on."

Next day, when the *Floating Lily* had passed the gorges, the captain sent someone for the sacks of bamboo ware and the

bedroll. Nothing was left in the cabin to prove that the old
merchant had been there. The brothers went topside.

Looking down at the choppy waves, Hong said, "Perhaps the
locust swarm was blown away from the village."

"Do you think so?" Chen asked hopefully.

"I'm almost sure of it."

"Why?"

"I don't know." But Hong knew. Having seen the old man
swept away, he couldn't bear the idea of death.

Day followed day on the treacherous Yangtze, with bends
and eddies enlivening its rapid passage downstream. Trackers
were everywhere, hauling the upstream boats between rocks
and shoals, hunching nearly parallel to the earthen banks and
crawling with slow insectile determination among boulders.
There were other gorges of less tumult and danger, though
their rocky sides often leaned close enough together to blot
out all but a tiny shaft of sunlight.

The brothers talked very little. Standing at the rail, they
stared at the surging tons of river while days lengthened into
a week and the *Floating Lily* sailed through the central province of Huguang, known as the Granary of the Empire. Hillsides
terraced in tea and lac-tree orchards alternated with plains
sectioned into wheat fields and rice paddies. Nowhere else,
claimed a grain merchant who had cozied up to the wearer of
a scholarly winged cap, were there so many varieties of rice:
white-hemp rice and wild-goose rice and pig-fat rice and tiger-
skin rice and sword-point rice.

Chen listened politely, answered questions, bowed respectfully to the merchant when they met on deck. Hong was not
even courteous, but turned away. His rudeness was lost on the
grain merchant, who simply wanted to brag at home of having
met a Chujen, Fifth Rank, on a junk bound for Wuhan.

Chen understood that his brother's behavior resulted from

the death of old Lin Shi. Hong might behave impudently at times, but at heart he was good-natured and loyal. When the hillsides leveled out and vanished into a broad plain, Chen even said to him, "I think you miss your old merchant."

"Maybe so." Hong shrugged, as if trying to appear indifferent.

"Do you fear talking to other people?"

"Why should I fear that?"

"Because you might talk to someone and like him and call him friend and then by accident something might happen to him. Having friends can mean losing them, so why have any?"

"You didn't get that from books."

"Lin Shi's death wasn't your fault."

"How can you tell what is or isn't my fault? Do you think your Master could tell?"

"I think he could."

"For myself, I think something is my fault only if I can control it. Did your Master believe we control our lives?"

"Yes, he did."

"But we can't control everything. Some things we can't control. What did he say about that?"

"Wisdom is learning to distinguish between what can and can't be controlled. Then you know what you're responsible for." Chen added, "It's the work of a lifetime."

Unraveling such thought was wearisome, so Hong changed the subject. "Lin Shi was more of a father to me than our own ever was."

"I wonder if Father is still alive ... if Daiyun is, and the others. Will it ever be possible to know what's happening on the other side of the mountain or beyond the sea?"

"That's not an interesting question."

Chen guffawed. "Master Kung would say the same thing! We must deal with what's here and now."

Hong regarded Two Brother for a long time. "Sometimes I think you're only a lot of memorized words. But here and now you looked into me and saw what was there. It's hard to believe, but you knew what I was feeling. I'll never really know you, gege," he said with a touch of wonder.

The old junk glided past one lake after another, all shimmering beyond the fields and rimmed by willow trees. Because the willow's gracefulness made it traditionally a symbol for woman, Hong was reminded of his brother's weakness. And that reminded him of Daiyun, perhaps starving to death. And that reminded him of Chen's unrelenting speculation about the fate of the entire village. Lin Shi's death encouraged in Hong the surfacing of emotions that had been carried deep within. He couldn't deny certain things now. For example, he, too, worried about the village—about everyone there, not only a few. Staring at the unfamiliar riverbanks and the blue lakes beyond, Hong saw in his mind's eye the twisting lanes and muddy ponds of home. Lin Shi was only the second person he'd seen die; the first had been his mother. He had seen many crickets die, but that wasn't the same. He didn't want the people of his village to die. He didn't want a plague of locusts to bring on starvation. He hated to think of streets becoming as silent as a fallow field, of the last survivors fighting weakly over a few grains of rice, of vultures sailing over the rooftops and their circles of flight growing smaller. The thought of that happening weighed on him until with great effort he managed to rid himself of it altogether, like a burdensome sack carried too long. He was helped by recalling something Two Brother had once quoted from one of those philosophers or poets: "The most stupid thing you can do is try to change what can't be changed." Lao Hong vowed never to be so stupid again.

Wuhan, the junk's last stop, was actually three towns that huddled together at the confluence of the Yangtze and Han Rivers. Hankou was a small fishing port on the plain to the northwest; Hanyang occupied several hills to the southwest; and Wuchang, oldest of the three, stood on the right bank of the Yangtze, its high walls overlooking the river traffic that headed upstream and down. When the brothers debarked in

Hanyang, Chen insisted on taking a ferry across the river to Wuchang and finding a place to stay there.

"What does it matter if we stay in Hankou, Hanyang, or Wuchang?" Three Brother wondered. "We're here only to book passage on another boat downstream."

"I have business in Wuchang," Chen announced. "I have a letter for someone there."

"You never told me." Hong was both surprised and hurt. "Why didn't you tell me?"

"Well, it is my business."

After studying his brother, Hong said, "All right, then. Do what you must." After all, he had letters of his own to deliver. Two Brother knew about the Suzhou letter for an army commander, but not about the Beijing letter for someone important in the White Lotus. So they both had their secret commitments of honor. If Chen wished to go his own way, let him. Smug in his own independence, Hong added, "After finding a place to stay, we'll get some sleep and tomorrow you go about your business."

Though upset by Hong's easy acceptance of his secrecy, Chen decided to maintain it, at least for a while. They traveled across the river in silence and found lodgings in the south, a flat, ugly part of town. They ate a frugal meal of rice and mushrooms—Hong grumbling—then strolled for a time through a market selling hog bristles, tallow, and goatskins. That night, after Hong fell asleep, Chen went to the landlord and asked where he might find someone by the name of Meng Dafu. To his surprise, the man answered without hesitation. "Near the Yellow Crane Tower." He gave directions. "Ask from there."

Next morning, without waking his brother, Chen left for the hilly northern part of town. He located She Shan, the tallest hill in all of Wuhan, climbed it, and strolled past a Buddhist temple made of white stone. Someone showed him the Yellow Crane Tower, a pavilion given that name because a god flew past there long before, seated on a yellow crane. A few steps beyond the Yellow Crane Tower, he asked a passing man where Meng Dafu lived. Instantly the man pointed to a high wall facing the street on the corner. "If he's in this town, you'll find him there. If he's in hell, look for him *there* . . ." Cackling, the man pointed to the ground.

Chen was tempted, as he'd been last night with the landlord, to ask who Meng Dafu actually was. But surely Gao Shi would prefer him to find that out for himself, so with the letter in hand, Chen walked up to the heavy wooden door and banged on it three times with its large dragon-shaped iron knocker.

The door opened a suspicious crack; an eye looked out. After Chen announced the purpose of his visit—to deliver a letter from Gao Shi—an old man who wore the black uniform of a servant opened the door wider and inspected the tall young man, his gaze lingering on the winged cap. "You'll have a way to go, Chujen, before delivering that letter. Meng Dafu no longer lives here. He's gone to Suzhou."

"Where in Suzhou?"

The old man threw up his hands. "How should I know? They say Suzhou. It's for you to find out more. Or do they give those winged caps for nothing?" And he slammed the door shut.

Back at the lodgings, Chen told Three Brother of his failure to deliver the letter. "Don't you have a letter from someone for someone in Suzhou?"

Hong was offended by such casual indifference to his own commitment of honor. He never understood Chen's ability to recall huge chunks of poetry while forgetting the simple but important details of actual life. "I have a letter from Zhu Tong to his former commander. From the moment we set out, I swore I'd deliver it," he claimed loftily.

"Good. Then we must both go to Suzhou. It's my duty to see that Meng Dafu gets this letter."

Next day the Lao brothers took passage on a three-masted junk. As the canvas sails unfolded, batten by batten, the staggered masts filled out with cloth that billowed, then held firm. The Yangtze meandered through minor gorges in a southeasterly direction. The eight crew members and ten passengers settled into a monotonous daily routine. Chen stayed much of the time in the cramped cabin, bent over his texts by candle-light. He could have read on deck, but the passing river traffic and changing landscape were distracting. Hong liked to sit near the sailors, who talked of their lives while mending sails or splicing cordage. From them he learned something about seamanship and the great river. One old sailor had spent most of his life on seagoing vessels. His description of foreign lands fascinated Hong, who vowed then and there to visit them all someday. The old man spoke of piracy with the zest of some-one who missed the excitement of attack on the high seas. He had contempt for the infamous Japanese pirates called Wokuo—the dwarfs—who sailed out from their small islands to harass the shipping lanes marked for the China coast.

"But the Wo were much weaker than supposed. Savage, yes, very brutal. They killed anyone in their way. But they weren't real sailors, true men of the sea. Trouble with the Wo," he said, while jamming a wooden fid through strands of a hawser to separate them, "was their ships. These ships they called hagai-bune were small, no match for ours. Flat-bottomed, narrow in the beam, and low in the water, they were almost powerless against our ships. Ours had high strakes like a city wall. Their builders held the planking together with little iron plates in-stead of nails, so when a hagaibune was rammed in battle it fell apart. They used dry straw to plug up holes instead of hemp and tung oil, so no wonder they often sank. Put masts along the center line, never staggered them like ours. That's why they could sail only in favorable winds." Pursing his lips judiciously, the old sailor concluded, "The Wo were nothing. They never deserved a reputation for sailing, much less plun-dering anything more than a fishing boat. We Chinese gave them their reputation."

"I've heard that," a young sailor claimed. "They say seven of every ten pirates are Chinese. Yet everyone fears the Wo."

The old man winked. "That's what the real pirates want. The real ones are mostly Chinese from the south. By blaming the Wo, they shift the blame from themselves and keep robbing the rich Chinese from the north." He sighed. "But the time of prowling the high seas is past. Pirates today spend as much time on land as they do on water. They might as well call themselves soldiers for the little time they're on ships." He spit contemptuously. "The days of truly sailing a pirate ship are gone."

The young sailor laughed and with his own fid poked the old man playfully in the arm. "Is that why you work on a river junk? Can't find a good pirate ship to sail on?"

The junk came finally to Juijiang, a port for handling tea and Jingdezhen porcelain. Behind Juijiang lay the Lushan, mountains where rich merchants traveled by sedan chair into the cool shade of conifers during the sizzling heat of Yangtze summers.

After taking on some bales of tea, the junk left Juijiang and set sail for the northeast, conforming to a looping change in the channel. The ship passed Pengze and the thriving city of Anqing, with its high stone walls facing the shoreline like a fortress. The junk had just left Chikou behind when, at a bend in the river, it was set upon by a pair of small two-masted junks, not much bigger than fishing boats.

A crew member yelled, "Pirates!"

Crouching behind some deck-stored bales amidships, Hong heard the first cannon shot whiz through the rigging and splash into the water beyond. The old sailor, an ex-pirate himself, had been wrong: his former shipmates still plied the waters of the Yangtze. The astonished boy saw a brass cannon with its long barrel mounted on the deck of one attacking ship. He saw the fuse lit, its length sputter and snake a moment before setting off a flashing charge of gunpowder. The boom resonated across the river, sending a flotilla of fishing boats out of mid-channel toward the shore, like a covey of frightened birds.

Rotating at great speed, two cannonballs joined by an iron chain whirled into the junk's foremast, smashed two spars, and fell to the deck, where the tangle of metal spun around fiercely before slamming into two crew members, decapitating one. The other, the old sailor, lay gasping with his right arm torn off. Another volley swept the helmsman off the stern. The fourth shot from the cannon spewed bits of broken pottery, stone, and iron chips across the deck. Hidden behind the bales, Hong heard them hit the wood, clatter like furious hail. He saw two more crewmen go down.

By the time the fifth volley arced into the rigging, the junk, without a helmsman, was adrift, settling broadside into the current while the remaining crew, including the captain, leaped off the stern and let themselves be carried away.

Joined on deck by his incredulous brother and other passengers, Hong remained helplessly motionless as if waiting to greet the boarding party that was soon to come. Both two-masted junks were already alongside, as if shepherding the larger ship as dogs do a wayward sheep.

"Give me your letter," Hong whispered and gripped his brother's arm.

"But—"

"Give me your letter!" Hong demanded again, while taking the White Lotus charm and his own two letters from his money pouch.

When Chen reluctantly handed over the Meng Dafu letter, Hong gripped them together with the charm. He rushed over to a dead crewman and removed his broad-brimmed conical sun hat of straw. After putting the letters and charm inside its crown, Hong jammed the hat on and pulled the brim securely down around his head.

"But—they'll find the things if they search—" Chen began.

"And they'll be angry that you tried to hide anything."

"Never mind. Be quiet. Say nothing—and hope."

He had no sooner admonished his brother than a dozen men in ragged black trousers and shirts, each carrying a sword or a knife, appeared over the port and starboard gunwales.

They didn't bother with the passengers but proceeded immediately to throw the dead and wounded overboard and get the junk under way, so that minutes later, when a couple of cargo ships appeared around the bend on their way upstream, there was nothing to see but a few torn sails and cracked spars and men working at the helm. Rounding the bend, the pirates maneuvered the captured junk close to shore and anchored. Then they gathered the passengers on deck and looked them over.

A bearded pirate ordered them to throw their money pouches on the deck. They all complied without a word. Then he stepped up to inspect them individually. To Hong, who stood at the end of the line, he said gruffly, "What's under the hat?"

Raising his chin to reveal a smiling face, Hong called out, "Brother to a great man!"

"What great man?"

Hong nudged his brother. "This great man."

Squinting at Chen, the pirate stared briefly at the winged cap with its gold and silver emblem. Another pirate, curious, fingered the Mandarin Square for Grade-Eight civil service on the left breast of Chen's gown. Then the two pirates moved to the other passengers, stopping to ask for occupations and reasons for traveling: three cotton farmers, all going to market towns; two hardware merchants headed for coastal cities to make purchases; a tea plantation supervisor bound for Wuhu to arrange for sales; a Buddhist monk assigned to a new monastery; and a prefectural magistrate from Anqing on the way to visit his married daughter in Wuxi.

While the questioning took place, Hong noticed a half-dozen raiders prodding bales and prying open chests. They all spoke Chinese, not Japanese, during this inspection.

The two merchants were questioned, then shoved and kicked when they both swore that they had no money aside from what they had dropped in pouches on the deck.

A tall raider, who seemed to be in charge, raised his eyebrows. "You're going to the coast to buy goods, am I right?"

The merchants nodded.

"You're going to buy goods without gold? Bring me gold right away or you're dead men!"

Both rushed to their quarters and returned within minutes, carrying leather-wrapped ingots of gold. The pirates laughed.

Next the chief raider approached the magistrate. "So you're visiting your daughter in Wuxi. That is benevolent of you. How long have you been a magistrate?"

"Eleven years."

"Eleven years. Commendable." He turned to smile at his companions. "Think how many of us he must have sentenced to death in eleven years."

"I had no men such as . . . you . . . come before me," muttered the trembling judge.

"No? Good. And none will ever come before you in the future." The pirate waved to his companions, three of whom rushed forward and grabbed the magistrate, leading him away toward the raised poop deck and behind the mast there. They couldn't be seen from amidships, so when the air was filled by a terrified cry, followed by a scream of anguish, the other captured passengers never saw what happened. There was the heavy sound of a splash. Then the pirates returned without him.

The chief raider sauntered over and studied Chen a long time. "What are you?"

"A scholar."

"Rich?"

"No."

"But important?"

"No."

"Why, then, the cap and the emblem? Young but important?"

"No."

"You lie." He motioned for two raiders to take Chen aside. "This one goes to the King Who Purges the Seas."

Heart in his mouth, Hong watched them lower Chen into the boat to starboard.

"Nine Dragons," the chief pirate said to a short but very muscular man, "take the others ashore. We'll unload this cargo downstream and sail down a way and meet back there."

Nine Dragons nodded. Rounding up the remaining passen-

gers, including Hong, he ordered them to jump into the small
junk on the port side.

Meet back there, Hong wondered. Where was back there?
Someone shoved him roughly against the others and muttered
to them, "Do as you're told or you're dead men." And when
Hong looked frantically over his shoulder to find Chen, all he
could see was the other small junk vanishing downriver, its
stern obscured by bellying river mist.

He had no money, but the true valuables were under his
broad-brimmed conical hat.

Hong was thinking that as the junk's rowboat reached shore
and a load of prisoners and raiders climbed out. The hefty
Nine Dragons led the way up the embankment and onto a path.
They moved in single file with pirates ahead and behind and
prisoners in the middle. No weapons were visible. The prisoners were unbound. They might have been a work party sent
out from a tea orchard or a rice paddy. But their captors had
made very clear that one false step would mean death. The
most threatening raider went by the name of Mountain-Splitting Ax. He was young, not many years older than Hong, so
perhaps that encouraged him to pick on the youngest of the
prisoners. Mountain-Splitting Ax, narrow-shouldered and no
taller than Hong, came up to the boy when they rested by the
roadside. Smirking, he said, "Your brother was singled out for
special torture because he wears a strange cap on his head and
two swans on his chest."

"There's nothing strange in what he wears," Hong insisted
boldly. "The cap means he's a Recommended Man. The two
swans mean he's an Eighth-Grade civil servant."

Mountain-Splitting Ax leaned forward and yelled, "Shut up!
You're nothing but a fool. You don't make sense. Who's to tell
me I can't finish you off right here? Then I won't have to listen
to your lies anymore. The thing is, not one of you will bring a

fen's worth of ransom. If it was my choice, I'd slit all of your throats here and now and go on lighthearted. You're worthless baggage, a sack of stones!"

During the day, while the party marched alongside fields of wheat and rice paddies and tea orchards, Mountain-Splitting Ax would seek out Hong in the line and prod him brutally in the back with a stave. "Get going, little boy." Hong was built far more powerfully than he was. "If you can't keep up with men, you deserve the same as that weakling brother of yours."

The party circled around the small city of Qingyang and waited in a nearby forest, while two raiders bought food at the market. Next morning, they passed a small detachment of soldiers on the road. One of the merchants, perhaps obeying a sudden impulse, yelled out at them, "Good morning!" When a couple of the soldiers turned and stared at him, the merchant giggled nervously, waved, and said nothing more.

Stopping in another woods at noon, Nine Dragons sat on a tree stump brooding. Then he conferred with two other raiders, who motioned for the offending merchant to follow them. The four went off for a long time, and when they returned, there were only three.

Nine Dragons said to the waiting prisoners, "We told you. Didn't you believe us? Next time one of you makes a mistake, we'll leave two of you behind. Get up and let's go."

Jingxian was a military post on a tributary leading to the Yangtze. Outside the walled garrison was a village where peasants from the surrounding neighborhood brought their produce and lumber for sale.

This was before the raiders had come along two weeks ago, overrun the outpost in a surprise night attack, executed the troops that surrendered, and taken over the barracks for their own. The surviving merchant had overheard a pirate mention the garrison town of Jingxian as their destination. That night, as the prisoners sat in a group beyond the raiders' campfire, he turned to Hong, for want of someone better, and whispered, "We're going to Jingxian. It's an army post they've taken over. It's what they do these days. They wipe out garrisons and live at the posts for a while. They use garrisons or sacked towns or river markets for their base, then move on. What's our country coming to when cutthroats take control of whole areas?"

Mountain-Splitting Ax, noticing the merchant talking to Hong, got up from the fire where he'd been finishing a bowl of rice and rushed to the prisoners, all of whom cringed at his approach.

"What were you saying?" He asked Hong, not the merchant. "Nothing."

Bending over, the raider took a swipe at the boy, who ducked and made him miss. Angered by his own ineptness, Mountain-Splitting Ax pulled out his knife and slashed it through the air. "Boy!" he bellowed. "Get up!"

Nine Dragons was on his feet, too. Yelling at the enraged knife wielder, he came up and stood between Mountain-Splitting Ax and the young prisoner. "If you have your way," he said angrily to Mountain-Splitting Ax, "there'll be no one left to ransom. I want no more of them killed, understand?"

Reluctantly, Mountain-Splitting Ax backed off and returned to his rice bowl.

Glowering at Hong, the leader said, "You! For someone so young, you have a good opinion of yourself. I've seen it, I've been watching. You have a brother of some kind of importance, so you think you're better than anyone else."

"No, sir," Hong declared. "I do not."

"Never mind. Just remember," the leader said, patting his own sheathed knife, "one wrong step . . ."

They reached the garrison town of Jingxian. Nine Dragons was soon conferring with the pirate leader there, who was called Heaven-Ascending Monkey. They brought the prisoners, one at a time, into a tiny smoke-filled room that smelled of fish. It was explained to each prisoner that his life depended on how much other people thought of him. If they were willing to pay ransom, then his life would be spared under certain conditions. To this effect, he must supply the names and addresses of family and loyal friends who had money. An attempt to play false would bring death. Once the requests were delivered, the ransomers would have no more than two weeks to deliver the money to an agent in Wuhu.

Two of the three farmers protested. They had only poor families and no rich friends. Even if their fields were sold, such a large amount of money could not be collected.

Heaven-Ascending Monkey was a long-faced, morose-looking man, who never showed the hint of a smile. "If I were in your shoes," he said, "I'd send the request and see what happened. Maybe some of your relatives have money hidden in the ground."

One of the farmers shook his head. "If they do, they won't dig it up."

"Are you saying, then, you refuse to give names of ransomers?"

The farmer threw up his hands in frustration. "If I had names I'd give them. But I have none. I can't raise the money."

"Then you will be executed," Heaven-Ascending Monkey told him calmly.

Again the farmer threw up his hands.

"Take him out and execute him."

When that farmer had been dragged out, the other one suddenly recalled a source of money. He surrendered the name and address of his second cousin who lived near Anqing.

They never called Hong. He waited in a windowless little room next to the armory.

So far he had been lucky, but in a situation like this he couldn't expect his luck to last. One thing he must do was hide his charm and the White Lotus letter somewhere else than under his hat. Now that he was held inside, it would be suspicious if he wore a broad-brimmed hat all the time. As it was, he had been terrified of the hat's being knocked off his head. So he flattened the White Lotus scroll and folded it into the smallest square possible and placed it, along with the little charm, under his left foot at the arch. Then he tightened the thongs of his sandal until there was no space visible between it and his foot. He still had the other two letters—Zhu Tong's to a former commander and Examiner Gao Shi's to a friend, Meng Dafu—but if they were found under his hat, he could justify carrying them as a favor. He left them nestled in the crown with a rag thrown over them.

Hong had dealt with this problem shortly before Mountain-Splitting Ax dropped by to warn him that his time on this earth was short.

"If there was money, it would be raised for your brother in the gown. But by now he's dead. So who would put up money for you?" He laughed harshly and walked away. Then the door opened and a boy younger than Hong came into the room.

He squatted in the far corner and stared at Hong until the prisoner snapped, "Well, what do you want? Have you come to gloat and watch me die like a coward? That I won't do."

"Be calm, friend," said the boy. He couldn't have been more than twelve—bony and small at that. "I just came by to tell you not to worry. You're young enough to run messages. That's what I do. They like to keep boys for work like that."

Hong remembered what Ye Pan had said about boys, at least the rare ones, who could scuttle unnoticed through a town like a stray dog and pick up all sorts of information.

"My name is Lao Hong."

The boy shrugged. "Call me Yao."

"Nothing more?"

"Aren't you tired of names?" He made a face. "Nine Dragons, Heaven-Ascending Monkey. They think a name can make them brave and smart."

"And don't forget Mountain-Splitting Ax."

They laughed together a moment. Then the small boy grew serious. "Whatever happens, always agree with them. Say yes even when you're thinking no." He got up and went to the door. "Remember that and everything will go fine."

Later that day a tall, husky pirate came for Hong and took him for interrogation to the smoke-filled room that smelled of fish. The two leaders sat regarding him closely. They asked him to explain once again who his brother was. Then the garrison leader, Heaven-Ascending Monkey, asked him if he wanted to live.

"Yes," said Hong, feeling his lips trembling.

"What are you prepared to do in exchange for your life?"

"What I must do."

"No. You mean, what we tell you you must do."

"Yes, Honorable Sir."

" 'Honorable Sir.' I like that." But Heaven-Ascending Monkey wasn't smiling. "Will you join us, work for us, do what we ask?"

"Yes, Honorable Sir," Hong said without hesitation.

"That means disavowing everyone else."

"Yes, Honorable Sir. I do."

"Good. You mean that?"

"Yes, Honorable Sir."

"Good. Are you ready to wash yourself clean and dedicate yourself to us? Run errands, spy, kill if we ask it?"

"Yes, Honorable Sir."

"Good." The raider pointed to a tub in the corner with a ladle. "Go over there and wash yourself clean. That means sins, commitments, loyalties to anyone else. Do you understand what I'm saying?"

"Yes, Honorable Sir. I pour water over myself and wash away the past."

"Good. Smart boy. You'll be useful. So go wash."

Hong went to the tub and picked up the ladle. Filling it with water, he poured it over his head and clothes.

"No, no, no," said Heaven-Ascending Monkey. "You must take off your shirt, trousers, and sandals. Everything. You must be truly clean."

Trembling, Hong took off his shirt and trousers. Dutifully he poured another ladleful of water over his body.

"You have forgotten something," Heaven-Ascending Monkey pointed out in a cold voice. "Your sandals. I said everything."

Hong stood there motionless, holding the ladle.

"Your sandals," said the leader. "Take them off."

After more hesitation, Hong finally reached down and took

off the right sandal, then ... the left, flipping it over on the ground.

Nine Dragons leaped up. "What's that? Under the sandal?"

Hong could find no words for a reply. He was putting on his clothes, breathing so loudly that it must have been heard outside the room. He reached under the left sandal at the same time Nine Dragons did, and the next instant received a blow on his head, then another and another until he lost consciousness.

When he came to, Nine Dragons was shaking a crinkled piece of paper in front of him. "What's this? Can you read?"

Hong nodded.

Flinging the paper at him, Nine Dragons commanded him to read it aloud.

" 'A thousand rabbits,' " he mumbled, " 'become fierce after cock crows ten times. Or sleeps after tiger growls or blinks thirty times at sun.' "

Looking up, he handed it back to the raider.

Heaven-Ascending Monkey now took over the questioning. Weren't these nonsensical words some kind of code? And this charm—a monster without feet—did it have a secret meaning? And what about this prayer to the Guardian of Heaven and the Black Gods of Pestilence?

To all these questions Hong remained silent. He was thinking of the charm's power. When rubbed between thumb and first finger it invoked the yin and yang, the ultimate power of the world. Never had his mind traveled deeper into the circle of the White Lotus!

"Speak, boy!" Nine Dragons yelled. "What does it all mean?"

"I don't know. I carried the letter for someone."

"What's his name?"

"Someone from my village. Maybe it was Wang. I think it was. Yes, it was Wang Fulei."

"You're lying, boy." Heaven-Ascending Monkey got up from the table, walked around, and knelt by Hong, who was sitting propped against the wall. "Let me tell you something. We know how to make you talk."

Hong knew that. Ye Pan had told him that people could torture him until he invented things to confess. But he didn't believe it. He would never talk. The Lotus would be proud of him, and for a few astounding moments of revelation, he felt this was his destiny: to suffer and die in silence.

"Do you have any idea what I'm telling you?" Heaven-Ascending Monkey asked in a voice that sounded almost sympathetic.

"Yes, Honorable Sir. I bought the charm somewhere, I forgot. Someone named Wang gave me the letter in the village."

Heaven-Ascending Monkey sighed and rose to his feet. "Do you know what I think? I think you're a messenger for someone bent on causing trouble in this country. Not that I mind. I like the idea of this country having trouble, because that means more money for those who know how to get it. So it'd be nice to know if we can profit by what you're doing. Do you understand what I'm saying?"

"I understand, Honorable Sir."

"Stop calling me that," the raider demanded irritably. "So I'm giving you one last chance. Who gave you this message and why and what does it mean and who is it meant for?"

Hong stared straight ahead. He was a sworn brother under the protection of Kuan Ti, once a great warrior who wielded a sword called the Black Dragon and rode a horse called the Red Rabbit and now a god. Which is harder, my sword or your neck? he thought just before the first blow came.

They beat him for an hour.

When they threw him back into the dark room near the armory, Hong crawled around, hoping to find the pitcher of water that had been there earlier. It had been removed.

Then the door opened and in came the boy Yao, who was carrying something. It was a pitcher of water.

"They said to let you have one drink. But have two," said Yao, extending the pitcher, which Hong took eagerly and drank from, swallowing rapidly. He kept his lips hard against the clay vessel, though they were puffed and bleeding.

"I'm sorry," Yao said. "But you must have forgotten what I told you. Otherwise they wouldn't have done this."

"It wasn't like that. I agreed with everything. Then I had some bad luck."

"Yes, I heard about it. You have some kind of letter they think is coded. You forgot what I said. You should have told them what they wanted."

Hong looked at the thin, narrow-chested boy. "Have they sent you to break me down?"

Extending the pitcher again, Yao laughed merrily. "Of course they have. But that doesn't mean I'm really their spy. Save yourself, Hong. Tell them what they want to know. You're too young and unimportant and poor to kill."

"I have nothing more to tell than I've already told."

Staring hard at him for a moment, Yao sighed, took the pitcher away, and got to his feet. "Goodbye, Hong. This may be the last time we meet."

The beatings began the next morning. Hong felt a tooth go. He couldn't see out of one swollen eye. His left ear throbbed but otherwise seemed no longer to be there. His whole body ached, but aside from screaming, he had let no other sound pass his lips. Again and again he saw in his mind the characters for BUDDHA, TIGER, and DRAGON written across the large belly of the monster without feet. Sometimes he plunged into the circle of the Lotus, spiraling downward through a long dark tunnel until at the end of it he heard someone yelling and knew that that someone was himself.

He had passed out numerous times. Then he was looking up into the scowling face of Nine Dragons, who was bending over him where he lay in bloody straw.

"We're done being nice to you," said the raider. "Now you're going to be hurt."

Another face, narrow and cold, appeared next to Nine Dragons'. "Have you heard of the Thousand Cuts?" asked Heaven-Ascending Monkey. His voice was as level and still as the surface of a pond. "They begin easily enough. With a little knife a few incisions are cut on the chest or maybe the arms. It depends.

Then the cuts become deeper, longer, more . . . complicated. That is, they curve and crisscross and come back again like spiderwebs thrown one upon another. One upon another. You see? They're no longer limited to a simple surface like the chest and arms. They go all over the body. They miss nothing. Do you understand the meaning? The whole body, the entire body, every inch of it, every tiny part of it, receives attention from the knife. In special quite terrible ways. Believe me, boy, you'll come to a point of such agony that you'll be screaming more for us to end your life than to stop the pain. You have nothing to say? Very well."

The face of a third raider appeared in the one-eyed circle of Hong's vision. He was an older, bearded man whose mouth twitched every now and then. He held a small thin-bladed knife. It seemed appropriate for peeling a peach.

Four other raiders then came along and held Hong down on the straw. The man with the knife knelt beside him and put the blade at the boy's navel. Hong had one last awful glimpse of it flashing in the candlelight, before he felt just the tip of the blade pricking against his stomach.

"We begin easy," the bearded man told Hong. "Just like he said."

Hong felt the first sharp sliver of pain as the blade slid through the outer layer of skin. Then the pain traveled on a long, unending path upward in a diagonal sweep across his ribs and lung on the right side. The pain ceased. Then once again he felt the first prick, the increasing power of the pain as steel sliced through the skin on his other side, and he screamed. On the third path upward from his navel, Hong heard himself pleading for them to stop.

They stopped.

"You have anything to say?" It was the calm, measured voice of Heaven-Ascending Monkey.

Hong had his eyes closed, kept them closed, while he listened to the frantic sound of his own breathing. Then he heard himself say in a surprisingly loud voice, "No!"

And once again the first impact, the uniqueness of the sensation of pain, and then its spreading course through his body, like a heavy stone tossed in water, sending out circles of waves. There came a time when he felt there was no standing it anymore. That was when his mind became suddenly calm, as if detached somehow from his body. It floated over him for a few moments. From it came words once spoken by Ye Pan. "Remember this. If you're ever in trouble, call out the number *fifteen*. Three is birth, five is life, seven is death. Added together, they make fifteen. Fifteen is the number of souls uniting to form man. When a brother of the Lotus hears 'Fifteen!' he comes running."

Before passing out, Hong heard himself shouting again and again, "Fifteen! Fifteen! Fifteen! Fifteen! Fifteen! Fifteen!"

When he awakened, he looked into the anxious face of the boy Yao. Then, glancing down, he saw that his whole torso was wrapped in bandages.

"Yes," said Yao. "They'll take good care of you until the end. Tomorrow will be much worse than today. The next day will be unspeakable. The day after that you will, mercifully, die. By then, of course, you'll have said everything and more."

Hong said nothing. He was feeling pain.

"Can you listen to me?" said Yao.

Hong nodded.

"And look at me?"

Hong realized he had closed his eyes. Opening them, he looked at Yao, who was holding up his left hand, all five fingers spread out. Then the boy made a circle of his thumb and first finger.

"What do you see?" Yao asked.

"The five monks who fought the Mongols at Shaolin Monastery."

"And then?"

"Yin and yang united. It's the will of the Lotus."

"Yes," said the boy with a smile and gripped Hong's arm. "You see, I was outside the room when they started the Thousand Cuts. I heard you yell 'Fifteen.' "

"So," breathed Hong.

"We are sworn brothers," said the boy. "And before the sun comes up, we must be out of here, or you're a dead man—and so, probably, am I."

In spite of pain and fear, Hong refused to leave unless somehow they got back his letter and charm. Reluctantly, his young sworn brother agreed, but warned, "If we're caught, they'll make the Thousand Cuts last a day, maybe even two days, longer."

Yao reasoned that he could remain here in the room without arousing suspicion. He had already been used to interrogate the prisoner, so his presence here was fitting. And they posted no guard. "After all, they needn't check on someone as badly hurt as you are," he told Hong while studying the wounded boy anxiously. "Can you walk?"

"I will walk."

To pass the time they told their personal histories, relieved of secrecy by the passwords. Yao had survived a terrible tragedy when only ten years old. Wo pirates from the main Japanese island of Honshu had sacked his town and taken many hostages. Then they rounded up all the children and threatened to kill them if they didn't murder any captured citizens who weren't ransomed. They even showed the children how to hack someone with a sword. Before this awful event took place, however, Yao had escaped.

"Would you have killed people from your own town?" Hong asked.

"Yes. If it meant my own life if I didn't."

Then he had wandered from place to place, living as a beggar and a thief. Luckily, he met a member of the Lotus, who initiated him and taught him the art of spying. He had been assigned by the Lotus to spy on the river pirates.

"Why?" Hong asked.

The boy shrugged. "I don't know why. The Lotus wants to know everything the pirates do and how they think. Do you understand the coded letter?"

"No."

"You see? It's not our job to understand why we do things, we just do them. My orders were to watch the river pirates, so I joined up with Heaven-Ascending Monkey a year ago. I don't mind saying I didn't know until the last minute whether he'd take me on or kill me. I'm a smart boy, and he needed one to spy in market towns and around docks."

"So you spy for the Lotus and pirates both?"

Yao grinned. "Sometimes I forget who gets what information." He shook his head in amused acknowledgment of his complex life. "Through a sailor on a Yangtze junk we meet every month or so, I get information out about the pirates. He tells the Lotus what I tell him. I don't know how."

"Who is the King Who Purges the Seas?"

"Oh, that's the famous Wang Chih." The clever young spy described the King Who Purges the Seas. Originally a smuggler of silks and of sulfur used for making explosives, Wang Chih allied himself with Wo pirates from the Japanese islands. He improved Wo ships, taught their crews to use crossbows skillfully, and expanded his dealings in contraband: brocades, silver, gold, swords, fans, dyes, paintings. His accomplices in China were shipowners, government officials, landowning gentry. Wang Chih was the greatest of pirates.

"They took my brother to him," Hong declared.

Yao pursed his lips thoughtfully. "They must think he's worth a big ransom. Wang Chih wouldn't deal with anyone unimportant."

"Mountain-Splitting Ax says they took my brother away only to torture him."

Yao snorted contemptuously. "They could have brought him here for torture. Pay no attention to Mountain-Splitting Ax. All he can split is a twig."

Hong lay back and absorbed the pain of his bandaged wounds. Once he got up unsteadily to test his legs, which so far hadn't been cut. "I will walk," he declared.

As the night wore on, Yao devised a plan. The headquarters, where Hong had been tortured, was also where Heaven-Ascending Monkey kept everything valuable, aside from captured loot. Headquarters was guarded by one man, usually a Japanese, since the chief raider trusted the Wo more than his own people. Yao knew who was on guard this evening—a man from Tanegashima Island who liked strong drink, especially a fiery white spirit made from sorghum grain. "I keep a bottle of maotai hidden," Yao confessed with a giggle.

"Do you drink it?" asked Hong, surprised.

"No, I just keep it. I don't know why, but I've always known the day would come when I'd find a use for it. And the day has come." His plan was to get the Japanese guard drunk, then enter the headquarters and find Hong's things.

Hong regarded his sworn brother a long time before saying, "You'll risk your life for me?"

"It's the will of the Lotus. All my life I've had nothing, no family and no money, but when I joined the Lotus I became someone. I have my own honor now."

Hong nodded. "Yes, we both do. I told them nothing."

"I know. It's known all over camp. You said nothing."

"And I'd say nothing, no matter what they did."

"You really believe that?"

"Nothing could make me tell. I don't care if they cut me ten thousand times."

"Well, then believe it," Yao said with a wry smile. "And perhaps it might be so. But you won't have to find out. We'll get out of here, you'll see!"

He reached into his shirt and came out with a wide piece of leather long enough to reach around Hong's waist. "You can wrap your valuables against your belly. If someone gets them there, you won't worry because by that time you'll be dead."

Hong glanced around. "Where's my hat? I've got something inside it."

"Do you mean these?" Again Yao reached into his shirt, and brought out the two letters.

Hong placed them against his belly, wrapped the leather around, and started to tie the ends. But the pain made it difficult, so Yao took over the task.

"I sold your hat," Yao confessed with a smile. For the third time he reached into his shirt. "For these!" He displayed two links of sausage. Taking one for himself and handing the other to Hong, he said, "Let's have a feast before we go. It may be our last."

It was close to midnight when Yao sauntered down the path between the barracks where the garrisoned soldiers were sleeping. Staggering but determined, Hong had earlier made his way to the south wall, crouching there in the darkness alongside a section of planking that Yao had long ago noticed was weak. With a couple of good shoves, he declared, it would give way.

Yao dug up his bottle of maotai and went to headquarters. He had no trouble persuading the Wo guard to have a drink and another and another, until finally the inebriated guard fell into a stupor. A few minutes later the boy had joined Hong at the wall. He gave Hong the letter and charm, wrapped in yak skin for protection by Heaven-Ascending Monkey—it had been a measure of the pirate's belief in their value. Yao said wistfully, "When the Lotus took me in, I wasn't given a charm. Maybe someday." For a few moments he studied the garrison wall. Tentatively he put his hand on one of the boards, a thick piece of pine, and shoved. The board wobbled in its place like a loose tooth.

Yao grinned. "It'll come out easily."

While Yao leaned his shoulder against it and pushed, Hong undid the leather strip and slipped the White Lotus message and the charm next to the two letters against his stomach. In spite of the pain, he tied the ends of the leather securely. Yao was right. The valuables would be removed from there by someone else only if Hong was dead.

Yao was having difficulty. He was too small to exert much pressure against the plank. Yet after a number of tries, he managed to move it backward a little and create a gap. A few more pushes and there was almost room for them to squeeze through; they needed only a few inches more. Yao shoved the neighboring board.

It didn't move.

He shoved the board on the other side. It didn't move either.

"Ah, we have trouble," Yao muttered in dismay. He pushed Hong aside when he moved up to help. "Save your strength. They post guards at the gate, and there could be others beyond the village. We might have to run, so save yourself."

Again the thin boy shoved at the board. Nothing. Telling Hong to wait, he went away and returned shortly, in his hands an iron-headed ax with a long, thick haft. Hong wondered how the boy had managed to lift it, much less haul it all the way to the wall.

"If you hit the board with it," Hong warned, "they'll hear the noise."

"I know, so be ready to run."

"What if you hit it and it doesn't move?"

"Then they'll catch us."

"You'll get the Thousand Cuts, too."

Yao nodded as if it were a probability too obvious to talk about. "If we don't get out now, they'll be at you tomorrow, and then tomorrow night you won't be able to escape, and the next day you'll be dead. And that's no good," he said. "No, it isn't, because you're on a mission. You've a coded letter to deliver. That's important." He lifted the ax over his head with difficulty, its iron head swaying like a cobra. "Now or never, Hong!"

The ax came down against the board, cracking and loosening it. But in the dark silence the ax blow sounded like the sharp report of a fired gun. Yao used the ax then for a battering ram, and pounded it rhythmically against the board, which finally edged forward, creating another few inches of gap. "One more," he gasped and slammed the heavy ax into the board

again. It gave way entirely. The loosened board offered sufficient room for the boys to climb through and out of the compound.

"Go, go," Yao urged, shoving Hong forward. "You first!"

Hong hesitated, aware of men shouting and footsteps approaching.

"Go go go!" pleaded the small boy, pushing him hard, so
hard that Hong fell through the gap in the wall. "Don't worry
about me! I'm in *the circle of the Lotus!*"

Hong struggled to his feet and, with a final backward glance,
staggered away. Every inch of his torso came alive in the new
pain caused by so much motion. He shuffled into the darkness,
heading for a distant flickering light in the village. Should he
circle it or wait there for Yao? Voices behind him were raised
harshly. Among the deep male voices he heard Yao's high
young trill, but words didn't separate out from the general
sounds of surprise and anger. What was Yao telling the soldiers? They must have found him at the wall with the ax. Maybe
he told them the ax was to protect himself from intruders. Yao
was a clever boy. He might tell them, look, someone has pried
the boards loose and entered the compound. They might believe it for a while. Hong paused to listen for more sound,
but nothing broke the ensuing silence. The soldiers must be
prowling through the grounds, searching for intruders. What
would they think when they discovered a guard drunk and a
prisoner missing? Yao was not following him, so Hong realized
they had taken the boy along to check his story. With a stifled
cry of dismay, Hong lunged forward. He couldn't wait longer.
He must circle the village and make for the distant fields.

In the first light of day he saw a farmhouse rise out of the
irrigated rice paddy that he'd been trudging through for what
seemed an endlessly dark time. His wet legs felt numb from
slogging through cold sucking mud, and by moonlight, when
he opened his shirt, Hong could see dark spots where blood
had seeped through the bandages around his chest.

The farm consisted of a low-slung stone house, a yard and

pigpen, a storage shed, and a barn. Hong opened the barn door and crept inside, smelling the warm pungent odor of hay and manure. In the dawn light filtering through cracks he could make out the barn's occupants: an old swaybacked mule, a few tethered sheep, some chickens. He threw himself down in a hay mound piled high in a corner. Curling up, Hong fell asleep, but not before the small narrow face of Yao loomed out of his shadowy thoughts. Hong blinked and the image vanished.

Yao. They had him, they were holding him down, they were letting him have a look at the knife before using it.

Hong sobbed violently. He knew what was in store for Yao; the crisscrossed red lines festering across his own chest and back reminded him only too well. Furious at the loss of the coded letter, Heaven-Ascending Monkey would take out his frustration on the boy. They'd keep Yao alive at least one or two days longer than other victims who received the Thousand Cuts.

Hong cried himself to sleep.

He awakened with a start and sat up straight despite the pain it caused him to move so quickly. He was looking into the startled eyes of a girl about ten years old. She held a feed bucket in each hand and wore a farm hat, a torn black tunic and trousers, and wooden clogs.

"Don't scream," Hong urged. "Please don't scream."

The girl stood motionless as if transfixed by the sight of this boy sitting in the hay, bloody bandages swathing his chest.

"I got away from pirates," he said.

She stood there.

"They cut me before I got away. That's the reason for this." Hong touched his bandaged chest. "I'm sick." And he realized he was. His head burned with fever, his wounds throbbed hotly. Licking his dry lips, he felt dizzy. "If you tell anyone," he muttered, "they might give me back to the pirates. Do you understand?"

She stood there.

Hong felt himself losing consciousness. He slumped over on his left side and with his right eye watched for the girl to do something.

But all she did was stand there.

The next time Hong awoke, he was staring into two faces, both hovering anxiously over him. The second face belonged to another girl, who was older, perhaps his own age. He slowly repeated his story.

Thoughtfully the girl studied him. "Behind here's a stall where Father kept the other mule before it died. Father never goes in there anymore. We'll put you in there."

The girls helped him rise and led him through a back door into a stall that smelled musty from disuse. They arranged some hay for a bed and laid him down. Then the older girl removed the dirty, blood-caked bandages and washed the suppurating wounds. Meanwhile, she sent her younger sister to see what Father and the farmhand were doing and then to get some cloth for bandages.

"Father mustn't see you," she told Hong. "If there's money in turning you in, he'll turn you in."

Little sister returned with a pair of old trousers, which big sister tore into strips. Finished with the bandaging, she let Hong drink from a bucket. "I'll be back later with food. Rest. You're burning up."

And so for a while—how long? Three days? Four?—he stayed hidden in the mule stall, eating soup when the girls brought it, sleeping otherwise, allowing his strong young body to fight the infection. At last the fever broke. He was able to rise. Many cuts were scabbing over, though others were still inflamed, the flesh around them proud and painful. He paced up and down the stall, hearing beyond the barn walls men calling to each other at work. Once he heard someone enter the barn, and through a crack he saw a woman kneeling beside the chickens to collect eggs.

If he were caught, what would happen to the girls? Surely their parents would beat them for hiding someone worth money. Hong sat dejectedly in the stall, wondering what had happened to his brother and to Yao and what might happen to the brave girls and to himself. It seemed that his destiny was to bring trouble. He thought of giving himself up and protecting the girls by denying that they'd helped him. He thought of surrendering to a terrible fate, of getting it over with it by returning to the garrison post of Jingxian. He felt old, perhaps older than his own father. There was good reason to give up. After all, the pirates dominated this countryside. Once the word got around that there was a reward for turning in a wounded captive, he'd have no place to hide when he left this stall. He might scuttle here and there like a crab, but inevitably he would die. All the effort of escape would end in the Thousand Cuts anyway.

But within the yak-skin wrapper, strapped by cord now around his waist, was a letter entrusted to him by the White Lotus Society. He would deliver it because now he had a double commitment. He must preserve his own honor and that of Yao as well. The boy, who must be dead by now, deserved no less.

And so Hong held on, ready if need be to assume the guilt of ruining two girls who were risking everything to help a stranger. A week or longer passed. When he walked around the stall, many of the incisions still caused him nicks of sharp pain, but not enough to impair his movement. He was ready to go on.

It was at sunset when both girls came with soup. As usual, they sat with him while he ate. Hong glanced up frequently. "What's wrong?" he asked the older girl.

"Nothing."

"Something's wrong. Is it because of me?"

The girl hesitated, then nodded, looking down at the stall floor.

"What's happened?"

"Nothing yet. But Mother asked today where I go when I'm not working. And she accused the farmhand of eating too much and he swore he didn't and they argued and then she asked me where I thought all the food was going. She gave me a strange look."

"She won't wait any longer," Hong declared. "Tomorrow she'll follow you here. Tomorrow they'll know about me."

The girl looked at the floor.

"So I'm glad I decided to leave," Hong said.

"You decided that? You're leaving? When?"

"Tonight."

Little sister shook her head. "No," she muttered, "no, no, no."

"So soon?" the older girl asked in alarm. "We can hide you in the woods."

"We can," little sister agreed eagerly.

"You've helped long enough," Hong told them. He felt the frustration of not knowing how to thank them, so he merely added, "I won't ever forget." But then something occurred to him, and he smiled. "My brother once told me a great thinker said, 'Kindness is more binding than a loan.' Do you see what that means? I'll always owe you."

"You owe us nothing," the older girl said with a frown.

"I owe you my life. And I'm glad to owe you so much. That way I'll never forget. We're bound together. I will owe you until I die."

After midnight he left the barn for the first time in two weeks. There was a full moon, which drenched the barnyard in milky light as he crept past the pigpen and the shed. The girls had brought him a hefty little sack of cooked rice to take along. Had they put themselves in danger by giving him so much rice? What if their mother, now suspicious, kept track of how much was left in the rice tub?

But there was nothing he could do. Thankful for his strength, Hong strode beyond the farmhouse into the fields, led by the moon in an easterly direction. Something else his brother used to recite: "No end in sight to the days of my wandering." Chen used to say it was the saddest line in poetry. Ah, Two Brother. Are you still alive? Was Yao right, that they'd hold you for ransom? Or was Mountain-Splitting Ax right, that they'd single you out for special torture? Which was it, Two Brother? Ah, tall, foolish, impossibly smart Lao Chen!

By daybreak Hong had traveled a long way. After a nap beneath some alder trees, he discovered a stream and drank from it in long, deep swallows. After satisfying his thirst, he gobbled down a small handful of rice, then went on.

The countryside was changing. The land was flat here, the air warm and drowsy. As he plodded forward, Hong saw isolated farmsteads that had pens filled with sheep and black pigs. The piglets had long, hairless ears that touched the ground when they waddled along. Often the little farms were surrounded by privet bushes and evergreen loquat trees laden with yellow fruit and bamboo groves. Going through one such grove, he noticed the early sunlight falling with a greenish tint to the ground. There were many rice paddies. He saw three men holding a horizontal rod while they walked slowly on a tread-mill that turned a feathery-spoked wheel whose little trays lifted water into the paddy. His progress was made cross-country, through fields and myriad woods dense with birch, poplar, and different kinds of fir. He scattered a flock of sheep in one field; in another he passed by successive orchards of persimmons and pears. He gobbled down half a dozen pears before forcing himself to stop. They could make him sick if he ate too many.

Now and then he opened his tunic and inspected the bandages. No blood was seeping through, but many of the cuts were painful to the touch. Often he wanted to lie down somewhere and wait for something, anything to happen without his making it happen. But he had two letters to deliver, along with Chen's, which he would try to deliver also. He stopped only to catch his breath and rest his legs; then he was up again, traveling eastward, which should take him toward Suzhou and the coast.

Sometimes he crossed roads where porters were carrying bales on shoulder poles and merchants led ponies loaded with hemp. There were carts, too, transporting wine in baskets of willow twigs waterproofed with oilpaper. It was a bustling country, so he had to be wary. Anyone might turn him in.

He was coming through a dark stand of scrub oaks when he glimpsed ahead, between tree trunks, a road and a column of soldiers walking along it. They were dusty, tattered, carrying multipronged spears, crossbows, rattan shields, bows and quivers, and a few muskets. A forest of weapons, held at all angles, sprouted from the long, serpentine line. Pairs of artillerymen carried on their shoulders the brass barrels of small cannon. For a moment Hong wasn't sure what to do. Then on an impulse, with a determined sigh of decision, he ran out alongside the shuffling column, fell into step, and shouted at the soldiers, "Where is your honorable leader? I must see him so I can find Commander Ma! Wherever Commander Ma is, I must go!"

The soldiers who noticed him at all merely snickered or laughed outright or called him obscene names or angrily told him to go away. The company of a hundred men plodded on, leaving a wake of billowing dust behind in which Hong stood blindly as if buffeted by waves of the sea.

Minutes later, recovering himself, he was walking in the ditch alongside the column of soldiers, yelling once again: he must see their captain, who must help him find Commander Ma. A few grumbling men picked up pebbles from the road and threw them at him. But he kept coming back, kept shouting, kept ignoring their warnings and jeers. When finally they halted for a rest, he squatted at the perimeter of one squad and waited like a faithful dog.

Hong had seen the captain at the head of the column. If he rushed up there and yelled for attention, the officer's aides would surely turn him away. His only chance of getting to the officer was through men in the company. So Hong waited, hoping his dogged patience would convince them to help him. He sat cross-legged and watched them give him uneasy glances. He could hear a couple of soldiers talking about him.

"It's not natural," one said as he held a pouch and scooped rice from it into his mouth. "Look how he sits there!"

"Oh, he's just a crazy boy."

"Don't be so sure. He could be a vengeful ghost. They say ghosts like to haunt soldiers."

The other soldier grunted skeptically. Smaller and older than his companion, he had the weathered face of a veteran.

"Has the boy got a shadow? I've seen none."

"That's because the sun's overhead," noted the veteran. "Nobody is casting a shadow. Does that make us all kuei?" He laughed contemptuously.

The younger infantryman was broad-shouldered and bewhiskered, without a thumb on his free hand. "Look at him look at us," he muttered with a scowl.

And indeed, Hong kept his eyes fixed steadily on the ten-man squad lounging beside the dusty road.

"What do you want, demon?" The bewhiskered soldier yelled at him suddenly. "We don't like kuei following us! Go away!" He made the shooing gesture of scattering chickens.

Hong shouted boldly, "Take me to your honorable leader!"

"Hear that?" the soldier asked his companion incredulously. "That's an angry demon. He'll do harm."

"He's a crazy boy," declared the veteran with a sigh. "Save your strength. We've got a long march today."

The suspicious infantryman got to his feet and walked over to Hong. "Get up."

Hong got up.

"Leave him alone," urged the veteran.

"Let's see if you're human or a ghost," said the bewhiskered soldier as he placed one big hand on Hong's shoulder.

The boy muttered in a low furious voice, "Get your four-clawed dragon off me."

The soldier gawked, while his squad mates tittered behind his back.

Hong flung the man's hand off his shoulder. "You're a fool if you believe in demons. You're like a blind man carrying a looking glass."

Getting up, sensing trouble, the veteran wagged his head in disapproval. "Boy, you've just put meat in the path of a tiger."

"Yes," said the soldier without a thumb. "Mountains don't turn, but roads do. You'll see," he added with a kind of cheerfulness that was ominous. The squad, getting slowly to their feet, made a circle around the two.

Even so, glaring, Hong stood his ground. "Take me to your honorable leader. That's all I want."

"That's all you want," the soldier repeated. "You tell us what you want and we obey. Is that the way it is?" he asked in that cheery, deadly voice. "You'll change soon enough, boy. You won't be making demands. You'll be calling *me* 'Honorable Sir' before you know it. You'll turn, boy, you're going to turn fast." And with that he struck Hong across the mouth. The blow was so hard that it whirled Hong around and flung him to the ground. But slowly he got up.

The soldier took a step forward—it was a leisurely enough movement. Gripping Hong's tunic, he ripped it open. Then he struck again. Hong went down again. Wiping blood from his lips, he began struggling to rise.

"Wait," said the veteran, motioning the bewhiskered soldier away. "Just look at him."

The gathered squad stared at the boy, who couldn't yet rise. The torn shirt revealed a chest wrapped in blood-caked bandages.

"What happened to you, boy?" the veteran asked, squatting down beside Hong, who had managed to get himself only to a sitting position.

"I was taken by river pirates," he said. Responding to this blunt, chilling statement, the whole squad stepped back and gave him time to recover.

Then he described the boarding, the executions, the forced march to the garrison of Jingxian. Without mentioning the coded letter, he told them of the Thousand Cuts.

There was a short intake of breath among the listening soldiers.

He described his escape with another boy who got caught, then his trek across country, his fear of being retaken.

When he stopped talking, there was silence. The veteran leaned forward to give him a comforting pat on the shoulder. "We'll take you to the captain, boy."

A week later, Hong was still with the company as it proceeded in a northeasterly direction, bound for a rendezvous with other elements of the Third Army Group. There were rumors. Certain regiments would be shipped northward to join a brigade from the Second Army Group and defend the Great Wall from attack by Mongol cavalry under Altan Khan. Young soldiers grumbled about the transfer, their reluctance confirmed by veterans who had once served at the Mongolian border. They claimed that the Mongols drank blood mixed with yak milk to give them strength. Riding from sunup to sunset, they nourished themselves on meat cooked by the heat of friction between their pony's skin and their saddle. They took no prisoners. They used three kinds of arrows, depending upon their distance from the target. If one man ran in battle, his entire squad was executed. Their complicated flag signals allowed them to change tactics almost instantly. They often pretended to flee, then attacked their pursuers with withering fire from ambush. They counted the losses of their foe by taking ears, which were hauled before the Khan in big sacks like harvested grain. No one wanted to fight the Mongols.

Hong listened, too. Hearing his story, the sympathetic captain had allowed him to come along with the troops. Without mentioning the letter he carried, Hong claimed that he must find Commander Ma in order to pay respects from a village friend of his, Zhu Tong, a former comrade-in-arms of the commander. The captain, a man committed to debts of honor himself, believed the story, especially after learning that the boy had stood up to a beating from one of his own soldiers (punished for it by ten strokes of a whip that left the bully almost as bandaged as the boy he had struck).

Hong was hoping to leave this company when it joined the Third Army Group. He might then accompany a battalion being transferred to the Fifth Army Group, to which Zhu Tong believed his old commander would still be assigned. The army was reshuffling a few of its chiliads—units of a thousand men—from one group to another, so it might or might not be true. By this tortuous military route Hong hoped to reach Commander Ma. He couldn't take a shortcut by setting out on his own. Every soldier he met discouraged him from traveling alone through this embattled countryside. Led by the infamous Wang Chih, raiders were causing more trouble south of the Yangtze than ever before. And there was another thing to consider—something Hong hadn't known until now. When his captors began the Thousand Cuts, they had carved the character for "Wo" on his chest. If ever he were caught by pirates again, the scars would prove he had once been their prisoner. Think of their fury when they learned he had humiliated them by escaping! As one soldier warned, "With you they'd go a step beyond the Thousand Cuts. I don't know what it is, but I've heard they do something more terrible. Never get caught, boy. Slit your own throat first."

So he stayed with the company, always close to the veteran who had protected him. Ping Zhai, for that was his name, explained many things to Hong about army life. Like Zhu Tong, he lamented corruption in the military. Officers stole from their own troops. Men nowadays could bribe their way out of hard duty. There was low pay and too much time spent in digging ditches rather than in fighting. And like Zhu Tong, he bragged about discipline in the past. "So many of the new troops are mercenaries. They lack pride and training. In the old days we'd have brought Wang Chih to his knees without trouble. But these young troops, they hear the sound of battle and shake like leaves. They're in it for pay, not honor. That's the reason they're cowards."

One night they bivouacked outside of Yixing, west of the huge lake of Taihu. Next day they were joined by two regiments, then a third the following day, a couple of more battalions and half a dozen unattached companies, until the force had swollen to nearly four chiliads. The entire force moved a few miles farther south to Dingshuzhen, a village known for its pottery kilns. The force put up tents made of so many layers of cloth that arrows couldn't penetrate them. Hundreds of horses and mules came in from the countryside, hauling supplies and produce. Hong watched messengers gallop into camp, banners flying on their lances.

He felt the deep swift pulse of excitement that spreads among men preparing to fight. Is this where I really belong, he wondered, fascinated by archers at practice in nearby fields. He stared awestruck at the rich brocaded robe of a visiting zongpingguan, a brigade general, who had come to see the du zhihui shih, the wei commander.

One afternoon he was squatting near the headquarters tent, hoping to see more great men, when Ping Zhai came along with news. Their captain had arranged for Hong to accompany a battalion that was joining the Fifth Army Group a few days' march away. Politely Hong thanked him, though he didn't wish to leave here where such a large, exciting army was encamped.

But then Ping Zhai added, "I learned something about the officer you're looking for. When your friend served under him, Ma was a chiliarch—he commanded a thousand men. He's now regional general of two wei. That means he has twenty thousand men under his command. He's a Zhen Shou, a Grand Defender!"

"When do I leave?"

"Tomorrow, boy."

In retrospect, it would seem like no time at all before Lao Hong stood before the paunchy, long-bearded, gray-haired man who sat lounging in a chair outside his headquarters tent. The bivouac was within sight of the outcropping of rock on which most of the town of Zhenjiang was built.

General Ma scrutinized the boy severely before speaking.
"They say you were tortured. Show me."

Hong dutifully opened his shirt, where some of the bandages had already been removed, revealing long, welted lines somewhat resembling spiderwebbing.

"Why did they do it?" the general asked, frowning. "I've never heard of them wasting the Thousand Cuts on a boy."

"Because I was carrying a letter for you," Hong lied, having already devised the story. "They wanted to teach people a lesson."

"What lesson?"

"If people carry messages for the army, they'll pay for it."

At last the general smiled faintly and pulled on his long beard. It was a reasonable explanation. "They had completed the first day?"

"Yes, Honored Grand Defender."

"I thought so. They usually move to the legs and face on the second day." The general added rather coldly, "You were lucky."

"Yes, Honored Grand Defender."

"Well, do you know what was in the letter?"

"No, Honored Grand Defender. I never read it."

The general gave him a glance of surprise. "Why not?"

"Zhu Tong never told me to read it, so I didn't."

"I see." The general sighed. "And you came all the way from Sichuan? All that effort for nothing."

"But, Honored Grand Defender, I have the letter." While taking it from the yak-skin wrapper tied around his waist, Hong described his escape with another boy who had stolen the letter from the pirate stronghold.

General Ma's eyes widened.

"I wouldn't have left the garrison without it," Hong declared.

"Where is the other boy?"

"Caught." Hong swallowed hard. "Dead by now."

"Yes, I suppose he is." Curiously the general studied Hong. "If you agree to carry a letter such a long distance, you must be prepared for consequences. Why else did you leave Sichuan?"

Hong told the general about his brother, a fifth-ranked Chujen. They had been traveling to Beijing for the palace examination.

"So you have a Recommended Man for a brother? Where is he now?"

"Captured, too. They took him in another boat downstream."

"A Chujen? They must be looking for ransom."

"They were taking him to the King Who Purges the Seas."

This revelation brought a sudden smile to the general's face. "Destiny is strange," he said. "I, too, am going to see the King Who Purges the Seas. I mean to see him at the end of my sword." He reached out for the letter, soiled and crumpled, but still legible.

After reading it, he looked solemnly at the boy. "This is a good thing you have done, bringing me the letter. A soldier lives for the respect of those he leads. This"—he tapped the paper—"is the highest measure of respect. A man who once served with me accords me praise that I'll never forget. It's what a soldier lives for: a good reputation with those he leads."

For a few moments he seemed to forget Hong. Stroking his beard, he seemed to plunge backward through the years to another time. Tears filled his eyes. He began musing in a low soft voice. "Zhu Tong had a black mustache that curved down like the claws of a crab."

"Yes, but it's gray now," Hong said with a smile.

"And swayed when he walked. More like a sailor than an infantryman. Yes, I remember clearly. He saved my life twice."

"Honored Grand Defender, he said three times."

General Ma nodded with a laugh. "That's possible. Offhand, I remember twice. Yes, Zhu Tong. One of the best men I ever led into battle. We were in Burma with the Third Army Group of the Southwest. Saw action against the Maw Shan. Took the city of Ava after a long siege."

"You tore down a river dike and flooded the region. Then they couldn't get food smuggled in and you starved them out."

"Ah, he told you that. Did he tell you we went next against

the Kalmucks in Mongolia? We used the Square Formation and battle wagons. Good tactics against cavalry."

"He told me that, too, Honored Grand Defender."

"Best lancer I ever had. Good, as I remember, with the crossbow, too. Zhu Tong. Always reliable."

"You liked to use the Mandarin Duck Formation, even though it was old-fashioned."

"Yes, and I still do. These young officers like innovation for its own sake. Did he tell you how many years we served together?"

"Sixteen, Honored Grand Defender."

"Ah, I thought it was less. Sixteen." The general stroked his beard thoughtfully. "How times flies." Once again he grew pensive, one hand on his ample lap, the other motionless on his beard. "Well, boy, you have done both me and Zhu Tong an admirable service. You've proved brave and true. Is there something I can do in return?"

Without hesitation Hong said, "Yes, Honored Grand Defender. You're going to fight the King Who Purges the Seas. I want to go along."

The general smacked his knee and chuckled. "And so you shall. We'll find out what has happened to your brother. I promise you."

Next day a messenger brought news.

Troops of the Third Army Group had retaken the garrison at Jingxian.

Nine Dragons had been killed, but Heaven-Ascending Monkey had escaped.

What about the prisoners held there for ransom? None had survived the attack. Hong had been brought in to hear this.

"Is there something you want to ask?" General Ma said to him.

"A boy named Yao—was he there?" Hong asked the messenger, who smiled faintly at this naïve question and looked for the general to answer it.

"We don't keep track of boys," Ma said bluntly. Then he added, "You'll probably see many die in war—both men and women, young and old. Accept it as life."

Hong looked at him steadily. "I will, Honored Grand Defender."

Thereafter the general kept Hong by his side, as if grooming the boy for a military career.

That same afternoon a messenger came from the opposite direction and reported that Wang Chih was embarking on a full-scale operation in the south. The raider had taken the town of Yuyao, upstream from the port city of Ningbo. He had with him a strong land force of five hundred men, half of whom were swordsmen from the island of Kyushu. Japanese, observed the messenger, might be inept sailors, but on land they could be formidable warriors, and these swordsmen had been hand-picked by the King Who Purges the Seas. From this little town Wang Chih meant to control the shipping activities of Ningbo; eventually, after his army grew strong enough, he planned to sack the great city of Hangzhou.

In consultation with his staff, General Ma decided not to send the two wei of twenty thousand after the outlaw. The movements of a large army would be too unwieldy, too noticeable, too powerful. Such a force would frighten the raiders away, only to have them turn up somewhere else. Ma meant to send an expeditionary force, consisting of one chiliad of a thousand men, southward by different routes in four regiments. They'd regroup at Shangyu, fifteen miles west of Yuyao, then force-march at night and take Wang Chih by surprise at dawn.

But even then there was a good chance of Wang Chih's escaping. Often cornered, he had always squirmed out of every trap. Ma meant to prevent his escape, which would probably be by river to Ningbo, then down the broad estuary to the sea. There Wang Chih could reach one of the islands beyond the river mouth, which provided a haven for smugglers. Ma brought in a naval officer attached to the Fifth Army Group. They planned a joint operation. Half a dozen war junks would leave the Yangtze, sail down the coast, and lie off the delta entrance, ready to intercept any boats heading from the roadstead for the open water of the East China Sea.

General Ma would lead the expeditionary force personally, leaving the remaining troops with a deputy to defend Wuxi and Suzhou in case other raiders attacked those cities.

Sitting quietly in a far corner of the headquarters tent, Hong heard everything. Initially, he'd been in awe of the imposing general, but without liking the heavyset officer's coldness and severity. As time went on, however, Hong had chances to watch him consult his staff, listen patiently, evaluate their opinions in order to arrive at his own decisions. The general let down his guard sometimes, allowing glimpses of a leader deeply concerned with his troops' welfare, steadfastly loyal to those who served him. When the expeditionary force left its quarters near Zhenjiang and moved southward, Hong not only admired but liked the old man. He understood why Zhu Tong had regarded his ex-commander with such affection.

On this warm autumn morning the general rode on horseback behind the leading file of infantrymen. Hong walked next to the horse, watching its tail flick rhythmically at a cloud of flies hovering around its flanks.

Intent upon their march, the soldiers rarely spoke. The column moved swiftly, silently except for clinking metal, snorting horses, the grinding squeak of wagon wheels, the accumulated breathing of more than two hundred men, who scarcely glanced at the passing landscape: fields of flax, flocks of sheep, fishponds.

Hong took in everything. He squinted at distant hills where tea orchards and rows of mulberry trees clung to the terraced sides. Sometimes he thought he could smell salt air even though the ocean was miles eastward. He stared at a forest of ancient pines, struggling to survive. He saw white pigs with swaybacks and black ducks and shaggy ponies browsing in a field. Although the fate of Two Brother was never far from his mind—darkening it like a cloud over the sun—Hong could not help smiling now and then from the excitement of being here, along with marching men. They were embarked on a great adventure, as the road unraveled hour after hour. Perhaps General Ma had divined in him what he really was: a wandering spirit infused with the desire to meet challenges beyond his imagining.

It took a week to reach the outskirts of Hangzhou, a thriving city famous for its immense lake. The regiment hastened past tea factories where the green leaves of Dragon Well tea were drying in trays over twig fires. Despite fatigue, the troops quick-timed alongside the Qiantang River until they came to West Lake, its shore lined with weeping willows and peach trees.

Here the general called a halt. The men were grateful for this respite from a demanding march, but General Ma hadn't stopped only for their sake. He had a debt of honor to pay.

Taking members of his staff and the boy with him, General Ma located on the northern shore of West Lake a Buddhist temple and a tall brick stupa, then climbed a nearby hill dense with laurel, poplar, and birch.

Hong wondered where they were going, but knew the general well enough not to bother him with such a question. Slowly but surely, Hong was learning the disciplined ways of an army man. When it was time to know, he'd be told.

And so he was. The general turned and motioned over his shoulder for Hong to join him.

"We're going to the tomb of Yueh Fei," he said, explaining further that Yueh Fei had been a Sung dynasty general who defeated the wild Jürchen tribes streaming down from Mongolia. Four jealous traitors had plotted his downfall. Arrested and unfairly accused of crimes, this great warrior and patriot had been beheaded.

Near the end of General Ma's explanation, they reached the summit, where a temple stood. On a stone arch above it four characters were incised. BI XUE DAN XIN: BLOOD OF JADE, HEART

OF CINNABAR. Past the arch was a huge courtyard, then the main hall, which featured a wooden statue of Yueh Fei and a ceiling decorated with cranes, the symbol of immortality.

"Have you read *The Romance of the Three Kingdoms*, boy?"

"No, Honored Grand Defender. But I know of it through my brother."

"Then you've heard of General Tsao Tsao. After committing terrible crimes in pursuit of power, he said, 'I'd rather betray the whole world than let the world betray me.' These are famous words. What do you think of them, boy?"

When Hong hesitated, not sure of how to reply, the general continued. "Tsao Tsao was wrong. Better to be betrayed than betray. Without honor a soldier is nothing."

Leaving the temple, they headed for Yueh Fei's tomb, the path lined with dark cypress trees and stone lions, rams, horses. The tomb was actually a round tumulus with a surrounding fence painted blue and a tall granite stele placed in front of the mound. To the right stood two cast-iron statues, with two more to the left. They represented the four traitors—a minister and his wife, a prison official, and a jealous general—who knelt with hands tied behind their backs.

General Ma did a full kowtow in front of the tumulus. He knelt twice and knocked his forehead twice against the ground. Hong knew enough about ritual from his brother to understand that the officer couldn't kneel three times, for that honor was accorded only the Emperor. Then General Ma lit a joss stick and thrust it into a sand-filled bowl on a pedestal beside the tumulus. After long minutes of meditation with closed eyes, during which time his lips moved in a soundless prayer, the general turned suddenly and faced two of the cast-iron statues. To Hong's surprise the army man kicked one of them viciously and spit on the other. Turning, he displayed similar contempt and hatred for the remaining traitors.

General Ma wasn't through. With his entourage following, he headed down another path until he arrived at a wooden pavilion. Sheltered inside it was a pine stump. "Here," he said to Hong, "they beheaded Yueh Fei." Motioning for his adjutant, who came forward with a bunch of chrysanthemums, General Ma took the bouquet and laid it on top of the stump. Again he stood a long time in silence. Then, with a sigh, he turned and said to his followers, "Such a man will never die. He represents the best in us. And the suffering he endured only encourages us to be like him: generous, brave, determined."

Sitting around a campfire that night, revived by the day of rest, troopers of the Fifth Army Group smelled the lake air and listened to monkeys chattering in dense woods beyond a nearby pagoda. One of the soldiers said, "I know Hangzhou." He described the food of this region: West Lake vinegar fish, snow-white shrimps cooked in Dragon Well tea, stewed duck tongues, steamed rice with lotus leaves.

Hong's mouth watered. He was suddenly racked by home-sickness, hungering for the food of his own region.

The soldier laughed at Hong's look of intense longing. "It's clear this boy likes to eat. They say around here that in heaven there's paradise, and on earth there's Hangzhou."

The following night Hong dreamed of things he had seen in Hangzhou during their passage through it that day: parasols that resembled stalks of bamboo when closed, but revealed painted landscapes when unfurled; fans with slats made of sandalwood and an overlay of silk; chopsticks of tortoiseshell and scissors of ivory.

The scented breezes off West Lake, the temples and pavilions and luxury of stores that he gawked at while the column shuffled along the streets of Hangzhou—all of this prepared Lao Hong for withdrawal from harsh reality, so he was taken by surprise when the regiments regrouped at Shangyu. They were getting ready for combat! But combat was still an idea to him. Next evening he moved closer to reality when the troops set out by moonlight to cross the fifteen miles that separated them from Yuyao.

When the light of dawn began spreading across the eastern sky, the regiments were drawn up on the swampy ground before the unwalled town. They were going to attack, fight, kill.

They were going to kill, he thought. Kill. How many men were entering the last day of their lives? Standing beside the mounted general on the summit of a small hill, Hong stared down at the enemy—Wang Chih had not been surprised at all. The bandit's troops were already waiting in front of the tree-shrouded little town. General Ma was commenting to an aide, "I've heard that Wang Chih had good spies. Now I believe it."

A burst of sunlight over the town's foliage twinkled on the unsheathed blades held by Japanese swordsmen. Their Chinese comrades stood beside them with long spears, bows and arrows, a few muskets. Hong suspected that the Fifth Army Group was better armed, but he dared not ask anyone. General Ma's voice, crisp and authoritative, called out as subordinates rode up, received orders, and rode away. They filed down the slope to join squads in formation across the swampy ground.

Hong recognized the formation: it was the venerable Mandarin Duck, described lovingly by Zhu Tong. Two shieldmen walked in front, one carrying an elongated five-pointed shield and the other a small round rattan shield. Their objective was to screen the men following them, but those with the rounded shields were also expected to throw short javelins. Next came two men carrying bamboo trees fixed with antler-shaped ends to obstruct the opponents' aim. Behind them were four lancers, whose twelve-foot-long weapons were the heart of the offense, since they could be wielded effectively at considerable distance from the foe. At last came two rear-guard men with three-pronged spears, from which arrows propelled by firecrackers could be fired; they were the second line of striking power.

This was the basic ten-man unit, led by a corporal. For any success the ten men must act as a single unit. No individual heroism was expected or wanted. They were rewarded and punished as one. Hong studied the tree carriers and recalled Zhu Tong's admiration of men strong enough to carry something so big and unwieldy into combat. Also assigned to each of these infantry squads was a musketeer. Zhu Tong would have contempt for them. He believed in close-contact weapons, not these newfangled guns, some of which had fancy names like "thunderbolt guns" and "wine-cup-muzzle cannons" and "cartwheel exploders." Attached to this force were half a dozen heavy cannon called Big Storms, because when fired they scattered shot like hail. A Big Storm's jug-like cartridge contained tiny iron balls stacked in layers, then plugged with wood and sealed with mud. It was used at point-blank range; its wooden ties had to be driven into the ground before firing to prevent it from hurtling into the air. He watched the gunners tapping the ties with large mallets.

Hong had been with the army long enough to understand what he saw: how battle formations were drawn up, how each sort of weapon was used. He possessed a knowledge of warfare denied to the casual observer. Yet when the first wild outcry turned both opposing lines into little clots of running men, Hong knew instantly he was ignorant of battle. He watched the two wavering lines break apart as they started to close. Squads that had seemed so neatly delineated were becoming chaotic packs of men rushing forward with dangerously pointed objects in their hands. He saw fire lances shoot iron chips and broken pottery out of bamboo barrels. Their targets, living men, burst apart some thirty or forty yards away. Then those same fire lances were used as pikes in the close combat that ensued.

When the swampy ground became a writhing mass of screaming men, Hong began walking downhill. Without realizing it, he was going toward the battle.

"You! Where are you going?"

Hong turned to see the glowering commander.

"Come back here!" General Ma yelled.

Hong hesitated. He had no idea what he was doing.

"Come back here, fool! You're not ready!"

Chastened and bewildered, Hong returned to the summit of the hill, where, for the next hour, he watched the terrible scene below. For a while he merely felt a sensation of horror, as he watched arms being severed (especially by Japanese swords-men) and lances slide through stomachs and arrows pierce eyes. But then he began to observe in a different way. He was thinking about what he saw. He began to separate the general mayhem into significant events, until the fortunes of each side shifted, changed, took the early shape of probable outcome.

The Mandarin Duck formation, though untidy in action, did in fact hold together. Shieldmen and bamboo-tree bearers did manage to screen off the lancers, who skewered many of the foe unable to get close enough to use swords. Half a dozen Big Storms, mounted on a knoll, sent a hail of iron balls into the raiders, mowing them down like stalks in a wheat field.

He noticed officers on horseback shouting new orders to their men. The right flank, urged on by these commands, curved around Wang Chih's main force until it reached the rear. Soon the men were lunging at the enemy's backs. This encircling movement confused Wang Chih's force and broke the spirit even of the formidable Japanese, who joined their Chinese companions in a thwarted attempt at escape. They scattered like geese into the woodland, flung themselves into the small river, dropped their weapons in the haste of a wild, panicky retreat.

Hong cheered.

Aware of what he'd done, he turned sheepishly toward the general, who guffawed.

"Yes, boy! We've won! Cheer all you want. It's the time for cheering."

But minutes later, Hong was facing what neither Zhu Tong nor General Ma had told him about.

All across the battlefield, where wounded men lay in groan-ing anguish, Ma's soldiers armed with broadswords were pick-ing among the dead for the enemy. These corpses they decapitated, dumping the bloody heads into large gunnysacks brought along for that purpose.

While Hong was staring at this gruesome scene, a young corporal whom the boy knew trudged up to him. The corporal was nursing a slashed forearm. "What's wrong, boy? You look sick."

Hong said nothing.

"The heads bother you? You'll get used to it."

Hong said nothing.

"The War Board suspects false reports of victory. We need proof. And that's what heads are—proof."

Hong said nothing.

"To gain First-Class Merit," the corporal went on, "we need no less than one hundred and sixty-five heads. That's the fixed number. The heads are sent to Beijing." Gripping his bloody arm, the corporal gazed dully across the battleground. "I'm sure there's enough. One thing about Ma, he won't cheat. Some commanders do. I served with one who didn't have enough heads for First-Class Merit. He had us go out and kill some neighboring farmers and bring in their heads. As I remember, we needed something like thirty to reach the limit of one hundred and sixty-five." He smiled but wagged his head ruefully. "Sometimes war is very foolish," he muttered and walked on, trailing his wounded arm like a banner on a windless day.

Revulsion at the taking of heads didn't deter Hong from crossing the battlefield. Cross it he must to enter the liberated town. That was where Chen might be.

But to Hong's dismay and despair, his brother wasn't there. Nor were any hostages, nor was Wang Chih, who, predictably, had boarded a fishing boat and headed downriver when the battle appeared lost.

Leaving most of his force to round up the defeated raiders, General Ma commandeered some fishing boats in the neighborhood. Next morning he set out with a small contingent for Ningbo, which was where the outlaw and perhaps fifty men were headed, eyewitnesses in Yuyao claimed.

So Hong found himself on the crowded deck of a fishing boat that wriggled like a tadpole along countless narrow streams toward the port of Ningbo. Rivulets flowing down from mountains to the west were channeled here by a network of canals into tiny lakes and inlets and finally into three rivers. At the confluence of these rivers, Ningbo had been built.

When the general's pursuing boats arrived at Ningbo, his agents soon learned that Wang Chih had left for the sea in a coastal junk. It was then that Hong fully understood and admired General Ma's two-pronged attack from land and sea. If his war junks had arrived at the river mouth as planned, they should be waiting for Wang Chih when he got there.

The general's boats headed down the estuary among nameless little islands, densely covered by mangrove. It was hot. Mosquitoes annoyed everyone, even the impassive general, who also swatted and cursed at them. The pursuing party couldn't reach the entrance to the delta by nightfall, so the boats pulled up into the weeds and waited for morning. All night the sleepless men heard one another slapping at horseflies and mosquitoes. When dawn allowed them to see their faces, they grimaced at the hollow eyes and bite-covered cheeks.

But they were rewarded for persistence, because as they poled into view of the river mouth, they saw a small, anchored junk surrounded by a half-dozen warships—those sent from the Yangtze to intercept Wang Chih if he escaped to this point.

When General Ma reached the flagship and went aboard, he learned that Wang Chih wished to negotiate. He'd exchange a dozen hostages for free passage across the strait to an island sanctuary.

One of the hostages was a vice governor of Zhejiang Province. Others were merchants of various standings. There was also a young scholar.

General Ma asked the naval officers what they thought.

They'd dealt with Wang Chih before. He'd not hesitate to execute the hostages.

The general nodded in agreement. "It would be a grave breach of honor if we sacrificed a high official like a vice governor to our own appetite for glory." Glancing at Hong, who stood in a dark corner of the cabin, he added, "There's also the young scholar. I want him out, too. And the merchants are men of standing. I believe we should accept the scoundrel's offer."

The naval officers were relieved, because that was what they thought, too.

"After all," continued the general, "we'll have isolated Wang Chih. He'll be as good as caged on that island. It's only a matter of time before he'll venture out. Then we'll take him."

Nothing that Lao Hong could remember in his life had ever given him as much joy as watching his tall lean brother in the winged cap—now torn and battered—step out of the dinghy next morning and climb the rope ladder to the deck of the warship. Nothing could compare with that moment, unless it was when he embraced Chen before the assembled crew.

Once they were alone, Chen described to his brother the worst thing about his captivity. The pirates had given him nothing to read, nothing in all that time, but had laughed in his face whenever he pleaded for something to look at, even an old astrology pamphlet or a list of items on a bill of lading. He spent days with his wrists tied behind his back, the bonds so tight sometimes that the flesh swelled and throbbed. When he moved too slowly for their satisfaction, the pirates cuffed him. One knocked out a tooth—he displayed the gaping hole halfway back on the lower right side—and another pirate in a willful fit of anger kicked him so hard in the ribs that he still carried a bruise and felt pain when he took a deep breath. But none of this compared to days without books, without a thing to read, without a single written character to contemplate. All he'd seen had been rolling decks, grimy sailors sullenly at work, unshaven pirates honing their knives. He craved a return to the life of the mind.

So he was happy when Hong suggested that they set out for Suzhou, deliver Examiner Gao Shi's letter to Meng Dafu, and then head for Beijing to prepare for the examination.

The brothers had accompanied General Ma to Ningbo, where he was going to remain a few weeks, freeing the region from remnants of Wang Chih's outlaw force. When Hong spoke to him of leaving, General Ma was not happy.

With unconcealed contempt the general first regarded the tall, thin Chujen. Turning to Hong, "I expected better of you," he said. "I thought your life was with us."

"I thought it might be, too, Illustrious Grand Defender. But when I saw my brother again, I knew I must go with him."

"Does your brother live your life for you?" General Ma asked sarcastically. Not expecting an answer, he added, "During the battle you started down the hill toward the fighting. Do you know why?"

"No, Grand Defender."

"Because you wanted to be part of it. Excitement took you by the throat and shook you till you didn't know what you were doing."

"Ah, that's true, that's what happened."

"I, too, felt that way the first time I saw combat. Some people do, some don't. Those who don't should stay clear of the military. But you belong with us."

"Thank you, Illustrious Grand Defender, but I'm only a village boy from Sichuan."

"The lotus flower rises from the mud but doesn't smell of it. Where a man comes from doesn't matter. What a man is, is what he makes of himself."

"You honor me, Peerless Grand Defender. But where my brother goes, I go. At least," Hong added, "until he takes the examination."

"If you decide then to join the army, come to me. I'll help you," said General Ma. "You have the makings of a true warrior."

Before leaving Ningbo, they had the good fortune of receiving hostage compensation from the army. In theory, a failure of government to protect the citizenry must be atoned for by financial reparation, but in practice it was rarely done. The brothers learned, however, that General Ma had insisted on it. They were given funds to continue their journey—funds augmented by Chen's status as a Grade-Eight civil servant, with the monetary privileges of that rank.

They booked passage on a small cargo boat headed for Hangzhou.

Sailing northward on one of the myriad rivers of the region, Chen said to his brother, "I'm glad you didn't stay with the army. There's an old saying: 'Bandit one day, soldier the next.'"

Hong turned and squinted critically at his brother. "General Ma was never a bandit."

Chen nodded sheepishly. He didn't upset his brother further with another old saying: "The fame of a general is built on ten thousand rotting bones."

They spoke little after that. Hong was staring beyond the riverbank at countryside through which the Fifth Army Group's expeditionary force had marched. He had thrilled to the sounds of horses and men on the way to battle. He had never felt so alive. Yet his brother had always been with him, even then, a sorrow in his mind like a great black cloud across the sun. Now he stood beside the tall young man, whose absence had darkened everything. Chen looked woebegone in the torn winged cap and dirty gown, yet they identified him as a scholar of distinction. It was an honor to be such a man's brother.

"I missed you," Hong told him.

Chen turned and smiled down at him. "While I was a prisoner, I always thought of you. I thought of you through the words of the great poet Li Yu: 'The grief of separation is like springtime grass. However far I go, I find it growing still.'"

Reaching Hangzhou, Hong insisted on trying out the regional food. He had not forgotten the soldier at the campfire, joyously describing it. Hong had once heard someone say, "A good chef knows at least thirty ways to prepare the simplest thing, such as bean curd." After eating steamed duck liver and meatballs shaped like lion heads, Hong declared grandly, "In Hangzhou the chefs must know a thousand ways to prepare bean curd!"

The brothers purchased bedrolls and sandals, had Chen's winged cap repaired, and had his scholar's gown mended and cleaned. From a street vendor they bought two broad-brimmed hats like the one Hong had used to conceal the letters and his White Lotus charm from the pirates. The purchase of a new pouch allowed Hong to keep their treasures more comfortably in there. He wore the new conical hat anyway as protection from the sun. Although autumn had arrived, heat and glare persisted in this delta country. He and his brother were tired of water travel. Instead of using the Grand Canal, which started in Hangzhou, passed through Suzhou, and meandered north-ward almost all the way to Beijing, they decided to walk the nearly one hundred miles to Suzhou.

Next morning, exchanging the smiles of travelers who have gone through much together and savor the idea of going through more, the two brothers began their trek. It was a cloudless morning, already warm before the sun had gone midway up the eastern sky. The land was both heavily farmed and densely wooded. There were many lakes and small rivers, some of them festooned with fishing nets. Catalpa trees lined the dusty road for their shade and beauty.

Chen recited poetry under his breath. Hong looked from side to side, glad to be alive in this serene and fertile country.

In five days they entered the city of Suzhou, founded twenty-five centuries ago and renowned for its maze of canals, its textiles of silk, and especially its gardens, rockeries, and pavil-ions. Even Chen gave up his interior recitations and stared at the famous city.

They found a room in a small house built on the bank of a canal. Vines crawled up the wall, lending their bright green to the mossy, discolored stone. It was a lovely place, though the fetid canal water lent the air a pervasive stench that had Chen grimacing and holding his nose.

"It's only midday," Hong said from the window, where he could see sampans gliding along, sculled by men naked to the waist, their sweaty muscles gleaming in sunlight. "Go deliver your letter to Meng Dafu."

When Chen hesitated to leave, Three Brother urged him on. "Yes, go do it. Do your duty. Be a dutiful Confucian."

"Thank you, then," Chen said with a frown. "I will." He asked for the letter from Hong, who had been carrying it tied to his waist.

Leaving the house, Chen stood flat-footed in the street. He had no idea where to go. Everyone seemed in a hurry. A man was setting up his cookshop on the corner. It consisted of a charcoal burner, two paper lanterns, a stack of drawers, some bowls. He had carried the entire contraption on his back. That night, in a sweet plum sauce he'd cook dumplings stuffed with sweetmeats that were carried in the drawers. Chen saw that the vendor was too busy to answer questions.

But then a lantern seller came along, carrying his wares lashed to a shoulder pole.

"I need to find a certain Meng Dafu!" Chen called out.

Without looking at him, too intent upon his burden, the lantern seller muttered, "I know, I know. He lives near Wang Shih Yuan."

So even here, in a city unfamiliar with him, Meng Dafu was so well known that a street vendor knew where he lived.

Garden of the Master of Fishing Nets.

All his life, Lao Chen had heard of it, so he was shocked to hear that living near this famous garden was the man he sought. He had no trouble obtaining directions to Wang Shih Yuan. He found himself on a narrow road canopied by sycamore trees; they laid a green skein of leaves overhead, so that the light filtering down cast an eerie hue on pedestrians below. Guided by his instructions he walked into a cobbled alley and came at the end of it to a plain-looking doorway. Did this inconspicuous entrance lead to the most wonderful of gardens? An old man was sitting on a stoop next door, drinking tea.

"Sir, is this Wang Shih Yuan?"

The man nodded.

"I'm looking for someone who lives nearby. His name is Meng Dafu."

The man smiled. "Down there." He pointed to an even narrower lane. "Third house on the right. Are you a brave man?"

"Why?" Chen asked fearfully.

"From what I hear, it takes a brave man to enter that house of demons."

Gao Shi's letter seemed to burn in the hand that held it. The tea drinker's warning frightened him, yet with a sigh of decision, Chen walked to the third house—a large stone one, two stories high—and pounded on the door. A servant opened it a crack, reminding Chen that the same thing had happened in Wuhan. Once again he repeated his story about delivering a letter. This time when a servant looked him over, there was disbelief in the watery old eyes, for what should have been a splendidly dressed Chujen was a rumpled young man in a mended gown. But when Chen raised the soiled, half-torn letter to eye level, the servant let him in.

"I was held by pirates," Chen said in explanation for his appearance.

"Well, I could see something had happened," the old man said with a sniff. Dragging one foot, his entire body tilted to the right, he led Chen through a succession of cobblestoned courtyards in what was obviously a large compound. One courtyard, entered by a moon gate, contained a rock garden, potted flowers, and mulberry trees. Another courtyard was filled with jars in which, from the pungent smell, a mixture of something was fermenting, protected from sun and rain by woven hoods of split bamboo. The old man, noticing Chen's curiosity, mumbled, "Soybeans, wheat, salt, bitter herbs. Master loves the terrible stuff. No one else in the world can eat it." They passed through yet another courtyard, this one smaller than the others. On a stone bench a girl was sitting.

Chen nearly halted. She was beautiful, though upon noticing him staring at her, she whisked open a silk fan and held it up to hide her face.

"Come along," ordered the servant gruffly. "Did you have trouble finding this place?"

"People seem to know Meng Dafu."

The servant grinned. "They think he's a devil because he makes things. Did they tell you the house is filled with demons?" The old man laughed. "Don't be embarrassed. It happens to everyone who visits here."

They arrived finally at a plain wooden building, windowless, but tall and broad.

"Wait," the servant told Chen and went inside. After a long time he appeared and crooked his finger. "Go in."

Chen found himself squinting through murky light furnished by candles set on tables everywhere. The room contained numerous objects, so many of them of such variable and unfamiliar shapes that he couldn't focus on one. And then at the far end of the room, he noticed a skinny little man in a peasant smock sitting cross-legged on the floor among piles of paper.

"I don't eat meat. Meat contains unhealthy things, so I eat my own meatless concoction I call Meng food. I'm sure my man told you it's terrible stuff. He tells that to everyone, so I give my own explanation before anything else is said. Well, come here, come here, Chujen. Give it to me."

Hurrying forward, Chen bowed low and extended his hand, which held the rolled letter from Gao Shi.

That was the beginning. And what Gao Shi had prophesied was true: Chen almost immediately had a new friend. But Gao Shi was only mildly correct about the young scholar finding Meng Dafu interesting—Meng Dafu was the *most* interesting person he had ever met.

As Chen told Three Brother after the first day, "Meng Dafu makes things."

"What things?" Hong asked with only mild interest.

"Umbrellas of strange shapes, wheelbarrows equipped with sails, a three-sided plowshare of iron, a spinning wheel. He's working on a new kind of match. He has made a magic lantern."

"What's that?" Hong asked with genuine interest.

Chen explained that prancing horses painted on a revolving tube were thrown by lamplight against a wall in such a way that they seemed to be moving. "He's made a pulley to lift a barge from canal to canal. He knows how a mechanical clock works. Did I tell you of the spinning wheel?"

"Yes."

"It's driven at great speed by a belt between a big wheel and a little wheel. He wants to develop a chain drive, too."

"I don't understand a thing you're saying," Hong grumbled.

"I don't understand myself. But you can spin more silk because of this wheel."

"Is this what he does all day?"

"All day, every day," Chen conceded with a smile. "He makes things." Chen took something from his pouch. About a half foot long, it consisted of four bamboo struts attached to a cork seated on the end of a pole; when a string unwound rapidly from the pole, the feather blades of the struts rotated and lifted into the air.

"Is that what he makes?" scoffed Hong. "That's a bamboo dragonfly. Wujiang had one his uncle brought from Canton."

"Meng Dafu says someday they'll make one large enough for a man to sit in, where the cork is. And when the blades turn fast enough, he'll fly into the air like a bird."

"Do you believe that?"

"If Meng Dafu says so, I believe it."

"Like you believe anything Confucius said. You believe things too easily."

Accustomed to his younger brother's skepticism, Chen did not respond to it.

Hong was unaccustomed, however, to the assertive manner his older brother was now displaying.

"We'll stay here awhile," Chen said.

"But why? Aren't we finished here?" Hong opened his hands out.

"I'm going to watch Meng Dafu make things. He's asked me to come every day to watch."

"Every day? For how long?"

Chen was accustomed to his younger brother's persistence. So he merely said, "Please don't ask me that again, because I don't know. When I'm ready to leave, I'll tell you."

He neglected to tell Hong about the girl. The following day, when he appeared at the house, Meng Dafu's servant gave him a low, respectful bow of welcome. But as they walked through

the labyrinth of courtyards and small gardens, the servant
turned suddenly and said, "About that girl."

"What girl?" Chen asked disingenuously.

"She's the Master's only child. Wife Number Two, her mother, died last year. Wives Number One and Three, both childless, pay no attention to her. Never mind them anyway. You won't see them. Number One stays in the west wing, Number Three in the south. What was I saying? Ah yes. Remember one thing: the Master dotes on Yuying. He is jealous of anyone who speaks to her aside from me and Cook and her own servant. If you wish to keep coming here, stay away from Yuying."

So every day Chen went to Meng Dafu and watched the little man make things. Meng Dafu was at present consumed by an interest in printing books. Five centuries before, a man named Pi Sheng had invented movable type, but, made of clay, the characters broke easily, so they proved impractical for use in printing.

Meng Dafu sat on a high stool opposite Chen in the candle-lit laboratory. "If type could be used again and again and in every sort of combination, think of how the world would change."

To Chen's surprise, Meng Dafu decided to reproduce for his guest the original experiment conducted by Pi Sheng. First he cut some characters out of sticky clay, baked them, and placed them in an iron frame; the bottom was coated with a pasty mixture of resin, wax, and ashes. When the frame was filled, so that the whole thing made a solid block, he warmed the bottom of the frame. The paste melted enough for him to press the frame with a board and smooth out its surface. The block of type became as even as a whetstone. He inked the surface and pressed a sheet of paper against it. "There's your page." Heating the bottom again and for a longer time, he loosened the individual characters until they fell out of the frame. "You see? Saved for the next time and the next."

Meng Dafu held up one of the characters, its top edge cracked. "But here's the problem that Pi Sheng never solved.

The clay he used lasted only a few times. There must be another way to make type strong and yet clear."

Meng Dafu described his own experiments. He had tried various hardwoods, such as the honey locust, the pear, the jujube date, all of which woodblock printers used. He tried to harden them further by treatment with polishing substances and minerals. "Nothing succeeded. Wood lasted only a little longer than clay. So look what I'm working with now." His face lit up in a smile, like that of a boy at play, as he led Chen to another part of the room, where a table was filled with crucibles, retorts, and mortars.

"I'm mixing tin and lead with this silver rock." He picked up a crystalline piece of antimony. "It hardens tin and lead, so the type made from them should be sharp and clear." Meng Dafu sighed in blunt acknowledgment of defeat. "But I haven't got the right proportions yet. When I do, the rest will be easy. I'll make hundreds of impressions without any loss of sharpness in the characters. Do you know what that means?"

"More books printed," Chen declared. "More and better and printed faster."

"But for one problem. Can you guess what it is?"

Rubbing his jaw, Chen thought awhile before replying. "There are so many characters," he said.

"Thousands."

"Yes, thousands. And to set this type you would have to find them all quickly. But how? If you made all these thousands of characters you'd have a jumbled pile of them."

"That's the problem."

Chen stroked his jaw thoughtfully. "You must store them in a special way."

"What special way?"

"Put them together so they can be easily found," Chen continued. "Classify them . . ."

Meng Dafu gestured impatiently. "Yes, don't stop. Go on."

"In foreign countries, so I've heard, words are written by how they sound. If we wrote them in that way, too, we'd need fewer characters, isn't that right?"

Meng Dafu nodded. "Characters are combined by sound, so we'd need only thirty or forty. But we write our language by how things look, not how they sound." He sighed. "To make type for each unique character is a great problem. In this the barbarian foreigners are lucky."

Chen said nothing.

"Think about this problem of handling so many pieces of type," Meng Dafu said. "Tomorrow, tell me what you think." He demanded it in a voice of such authority that the young scholar lay awake half the night.

The next day Meng Dafu asked immediately for an answer.

Chen had it ready. "Store the type in a large revolving table."

"Why revolving?"

"To get at the type quickly. Build compartments in the table. Store the type in them according to classification."

"What classification?"

"Any kind will do, just so long as characters go into different compartments. I thought of using strokes."

"What do you mean?"

"Strokes used in making a character—the dot, sweep, curve, hook, and angle used in writing them out. You could have a one-dot, two-horizontal-sweep, one-hook compartment. And a one-dot, two-horizontal-sweep, two-hook compartment. And so on. If strokes of a character are too complicated, so you can't use that method of classification, there's another way."

"Tell me."

"By sound."

"But we can't use sound like they do in foreign languages."

"No, but we can use sound in another way—according to *rhyme*. Our language has many rhymes, so why not put characters together according to them? I thought of using the *Official Book of Rhymes* as the method of classification."

Meng Dafu shrugged. "A friend of mine has already thought of that."

"Forgive me, Honorable Meng, for saying what's obvious."

"Oh, it isn't obvious. Using strokes is an obvious way to classify, but not using sound. Only after working months on the problem did he think of using strokes and rhyming sounds together. And he never did think of the revolving table. That idea was mine—after an equally long period of thought. You seemed to have come up with our solutions overnight."

Embarrassed, Chen began to apologize.

"Stop that," Meng Dafu demanded. "As long as solutions are found, it matters little who finds them. To seek and find the truth wherever it leads—that's the soul of what we do."

Chen felt that the inventor was regarding him curiously. It was an intense look, now familiar to Chen—Meng Dafu reserved it for something he was working on.

"In his letter," said the inventor, "Gao Shi called you the best scholar to come from Sichuan in years. But this can't be true." Meng Dafu was nervously hefting a big crystal of antimony, as if this repetitive action might help him arrive at a difficult decision. "If it were true, why would you waste yourself on the imperial exams? Especially if you could stay with me instead and do work of real importance? Do you think some old scholars parading around the Forbidden City could hold your interest for long? Do you realize I'm asking you to become my apprentice? Do you have an answer?"

When Chen merely gawked at him, Meng Dafu shook his head. "Go on, go away. Come back tomorrow and we'll say nothing more about it. But one of these days, give me an answer."

Lost in speculation about this offer, Chen didn't watch where he was going when he left the laboratory. Shuffling through a moon gate into a courtyard, he nearly collided with the inventor's daughter. Carrying a flower vase, Yuying dropped it in surprise, shattering porcelain across the cobblestone.

There were profuse apologies on both sides. Chen bowed; she bowed. They both claimed the blunder. But before going their separate ways, they said other things, mostly nonsense about the weather. Somehow they also managed to say something about Wang Shih Yuan.

How had that happened and why, Chen wondered while leaving the compound. He'd told her that he loved the Garden

of the Master of Fishing Nets (never having been there). She
loved it, too. She went there early almost every morning. She had smiled; he had smiled.

Garden of the Master of Fishing Nets.

Almost every morning.

Early.

Chen's step became airy and brisk as he walked down the sycamore-lined streets of Suzhou.

The tall willowy girl was there before him. She rose from a stone bench when he entered the second courtyard. She wore a loose high-collared gown of a purple color with sleeves far longer than her arms, so her hands were hidden from view. Her eyebrows were plucked and penciled, her cheeks powdered a thick white.

Chen had heard even back in his Sichuan village that the most beautiful girls came from Suzhou. Yuying's skin—her forehead being free of powder—was as pale as alabaster. Her mouth was shaped by lip rouge into a tight little bud of crimson.

"This garden," Yuying said in a high tremulous voice, "is the only place my father lets me go alone. I know it better than my own room. Let me show you."

For an hour she escorted him through courtyards, around a small lake, down corridors of the two-storied house, no longer occupied. She was an effective guide, pointing out the design of plum blossoms in the paving, the rugged grandeur of Tai Hu rocks that stood in clusters like stone flowers, a tiled roof so curved that when demons landed on it, they were cannonaded back into the air. Chen strolled by her side past shrubs and magnolia trees and little groves of delicate bamboo and ancient cypresses gnarled by time, mutilated by lightning. They walked inside pavilions placed for rock viewing and halted in front of white plaster walls lined with dwarf trees and rows of earthenware pots holding herbaceous plants. When they went inside the house, Yuying explained the subtle illusion of hua chuang—living windows—so called because their frames held compositions of rocks and flowers that were actually outside the house: still-life paintings created by architecture. By her thorough explanations, Yuying made the little one-acre garden seem like an illusionary trick in itself—many times bigger than it really was.

But Chen heard little and retained even less of what the girl said. All he could think of was the guide. Her feet had never been bound and were therefore of normal size, unlike the lily feet of Daiyun. Because of the heat, there was a touch of moisture on her upper lip. To uncover her hands, the girl flipped her sleeves gracefully. Chen had a look then at long white fingers—but none of them with a two-inch nail, sheathed in gold, such as Daiyun wore. With her ten fingertips Yuying caressed the convoluted shape of a Tai Hu rock, pitted by centuries of swift water rushing across its surface. Her touch was like a butterfly lighting on stone.

All of a sudden Yuying turned and started to rush from the courtyard. She told him it was getting late. When Chen followed, she warned him they must not be seen entering her father's house together. He must stay here awhile. "Tomorrow?" she asked over her shoulder while continuing to hurry. "You won't disappoint me?" Not waiting for his answer, Yuying hastened on.

So he remained a while longer in the garden, his eyes filled with the sight of galleries and courtyards and a profusion of flowers. But his eyes saw nothing. In his mind's eye he was watching the tall slim figure of the retreating girl, her purple gown billowing in a gust of wind, her unbound hair flowing like dark water.

Tomorrow, he was thinking.

Tomorrow.

What was happening to older brother?

That question haunted Lao Hong's waking hours. He was

perplexed and frightened by Chen's newfound independence of spirit that allowed him to make decisions on his own. Each morning, very early, Chen left the room and each evening returned to it simply to eat and sleep. His outburst of enthusiasm about "watching Meng Dafu make things" had been replaced by a determined silence, as if he guarded against an impulse to share his feelings with anyone, much less with a younger brother.

With little else to do but wait and brood, Lao Hong walked the streets of Suzhou, asking himself questions. Was this strange fellow Meng Dafu casting a spell over Two Brother? Who besides an adept at magic would build a magic lantern and imagine a bamboo dragonfly large enough for a man to fly in? Did the man cast a shadow? Was it possible that Meng Dafu was a gui—an evil spirit disguised as human? Ghosts came back from the land of the dead seeking revenge against those who looked happy. That was Chen's mistake. He looked happy these days. It might anger a gui enough to bring down sickness, insanity, death. Was the maker of things a gui?

These terrible questions drew Hong far from the center of Suzhou. He trudged into the outlying fields, laid out tidily along meandering rivers and canals. He watched the farmers work. The women wore white kerchiefs, blue cotton tunics, black pajamas, and short aprons as they squatted beside the furrows. They culled out ripe lettuce and tied it in bunches with twists of straw. They huddled and probed and cared for the fields with the intensity of caring for infants.

A tall man with two large wooden bowls on a shoulder pole went among them, watering the plants. At a riverside he filled his emptied bowls and returned to the field. No motion was lost as he detached the buckets from the pole and scattered water across a vegetable patch.

All of this reminded Hong of home. He felt a tightening in his throat, a sudden rush of tears. If the locust plague hadn't killed them, villagers were working in their fields today, right now, just as these farmers were doing. And kites were flying and crickets were being tended to.

Until this moment he'd never felt the full power of home, the sharp ache of homesickness.

But by the time he returned to the city, Hong felt another emotion as strong: the need to protect his brother from harm. He asked people in the street where he might find a wizard.

Within a short time, Hong was brushing aside a dirty cloth curtain and entering a tiny shop where an old woman sat behind a table chewing garlic.

"I need a charm," Hong explained. "I have money."

"What kind of charm?" she asked cautiously.

"To protect my brother from a demon."

"Oh? Is a demon threatening him?"

"I think so."

"Will he be wearing the charm?"

"No. He doesn't see the danger."

"Best, then, to make a charm of paper. You need only to have the right things said, then burn it." A racking cough seized her and for some moments she wasn't able to speak. Then, clearing her throat, the old woman told him hoarsely to return in the morning and the charm would be ready.

When Hong turned to leave, she called out, "Wait! The money!"

Next morning she had the charm ready. It was a piece of red paper inscribed with magical words: "The Heavenly Master, the Thirty-six Spirits of the Great Bear, the Spirits Dwelling in Sun and Moon, the Spirit of the Sea Monster who rescues fairies from the watery depths, hear this plea and banish all fear." The old woman clapped her hands sharply and uttered a long string of incomprehensible sounds. She then told Hong that by his burning the charm, the evil surrounding his brother would disappear.

"Does that mean Meng Dafu will die?"

"No. Only the evil part of him will die. People don't understand the gui. It inhabits a human but doesn't take full possession of him. So it's possible to remove a gui without also killing the human who carried it."

That relieved Hong, who had spent a sleepless night wonder-

ing if to protect his brother he might have to kill someone.
The paper was duly burned, and Hong sat back with a smile
of contentment. At least he no longer faced a demon. His rival
for control of Two Brother was only a man now.

"You mentioned Meng Dafu," the old woman said, glancing
sideways at him from baggy eyes. "He's a strange man but well
known. Did Meng Dafu carry the gui we burned?"

In answering yes, Hong also supplied the circumstances: his
brother, a Chujen, was being instructed by Meng Dafu in magic.
It was an honor, after all, to have a Chujen under your spell.

"Your brother is a Chujen? A great scholar? There's money
in that," the old woman observed. "I have strong powers, boy,
though I rarely use them. I must be convinced they're serving
a good purpose. In you I see a troubled boy who at heart is
honorable and loyal. It would be my privilege to intercede on
your behalf."

"Intercede?"

"If there's anyone I can call up from the dead who might
offer you advice, I'll do it. I sense you need help in a special
way."

"I'm afraid of my brother's deciding to stay here and failing
to take his exams. But I can't talk to him anymore."

"So you need to consult a wise and benevolent ghost?"

"Yes." And with growing conviction, Hong added, "That's
what I want, that's what I really want."

"Do you have a ghost in mind? Otherwise, I'll choose for
you."

"My mother."

The old medium sighed. "I am a Wu, diviner and wizard, so
what I tell you is true. To do this thing is difficult because the
closer the ghost is to you, the harder the task of conjuring it.
That's a law of the universe. It costs a good deal of money."

"I'll pay," Hong said eagerly.

"Come tomorrow at this time. You'll speak to her ghost."

The next morning Chen entered the house of Meng Dafu
and accepted the offer to become the inventor's apprentice.

"Be fearless, young man," said Meng Dafu. "Never compromise in seeking the truth. That's why, long ago, I refused a public career. This is my world. In it I'm able to create something new from wood and metal and air." He swept out his arms to include the whole laboratory. "Now that you're joining the truth seekers, a small band of special men, you have the right to know the Great Secret." He waited for the young man to absorb that remark. "What you see here is only a little part of what I do. What I'll tell you now is the Great Secret. We are close to finding immortal life!"

Having made that strange declaration, Meng Dafu led the young scholar out of the laboratory, through a corridor, and across a courtyard to a smaller building. It was also windowless, but with at least half a dozen smokestacks rising from its roof.

With his hand on the door, Meng Dafu turned to appraise Chen for a few moments. "Do you know what cinnabar is?"

"No, Honorable Meng."

"Quicksilver comes from it. You roast cinnabar and get quicksilver. But cinnabar is much, much more. Ah, much more!" Again he studied Chen intensely. "There's a principle in the universe: all metals are debased forms of gold and cinnabar, the only pure substances on earth. This is another principle: nature strives to regain its purity. Therefore, all metals would become gold and cinnabar if they could. Do you understand?"

"I think I do."

"Prepare," said Meng Dafu, opening the door, "to enter the world of the Red Bird and the White Tiger."

Lao Chen found himself in a room far more cluttered than the other laboratory. What dominated here was a number of bellows, stoves, ovens, and furnaces, surrounded by bins filled with minerals of different shapes and sizes. On dusty tables stood rows of crucibles and forests of retorts, some of which were connected by bamboo tubing. The air reeked from a pungency of burnt sulfur and charcoal, along with other smells borne on acrid gases that brought tears to Chen's eyes. There were metal balances for weighing substances, along with ham-

mers, tongs, and chisels. There were three-legged cauldrons
built with an upper and a lower compartment for distilling
liquids.

Through this bewildering chaos of chemical and mineral,
apparatus and equipment, Meng Dafu walked serenely like an
old poet enjoying the solitude of his garden. He was talking
all the time, lecturing, explaining. "The Red Bird is fire; the
White Tiger is the spirit of metal. Fire and metal hold the
secrets of life. I am a member of the Wai Tan Society. Our goal
is to find the elixir of immortality. In the First Man the yin and
yang were perfectly balanced, so in him the distinction between life and death vanished. Such balance was then lost, and
so we are born, live, and die. What we must do"—he turned
to stare at Chen—"is restore that balance. Then death will end.
How is this done?" Meng Dafu picked up some bright red
crystals from a table. "By purifying cinnabar. I have friends
who seek the elixir through gold. But I'm sure the right path is
through cinnabar." He rolled a few of the red crystals between
thumb and forefinger. "It's capable of supplying a vital force
to the body. But first it must be heated and cooled, heated and
cooled a great number of times, in complex mixture with other
things. When finally purified, it will surely be the sought-for
elixir. And so through it we will ascend to heaven in broad
daylight." Meng Dafu shook his head sadly. "No one has yet
transformed cinnabar in this way. But it will be done, it will!"
Face flushed with emotion, Meng Dafu added, "That is my
dream."

Meanwhile, Hong arrived at the Wu's house, where he
waited in a tiny anteroom until called by the old woman. Her
back parlor was lit by one candle. A cloud of incense drifted
lazily through the hot, close, smoky air. The old Wu ordered
him to sit opposite her at a small table.

"Have you been good to your mother's spirit?" the Wu
asked briskly. Her old hands were folded in front of her, each
finger wearing a large ivory ring with a fierce human face
carved on it.

"When she died," Hong said, "my father climbed up on the roof and made a hole so her spirit could escape from the house."

"Your father did right."

Hong didn't say what he was tempted to say: it was the only thing my father ever did right. Instead he told the Wu that before leaving the village he'd gone to her grave and offered incense, cooked rice, and flowers to her spirit.

"You did right," declared the Wu. "This makes my task easier. There's nothing harder to conjure than a ghost made angry from neglect. Put your hands on the table and touch mine." Her mottled hands opened wide, each thick-knuckled finger outstretched. Hong put his hands out in imitation of her. The Wu touched each of his fingertips with her own.

"Close your eyes," she commanded. "Think of your mother. Help me bring her out of the nine levels of the air."

Closing his eyes, Hong worked mightily to see his mother in his mind. Her image appeared, faded, came again and wavered and went away and came again: a heavyset woman with hair swept back into a large black knot and with plucked eyebrows painted into wide blue arcs. She wore a quilted jacket with full sleeves and heavy clogs with thick wooden soles. She carried a fan and a book.

"She's coming down now," the Wu announced in a voice so low that Hong strained to hear it. "Floating down through the levels. She's not smiling, but not frowning either. She looks expectant. That is good. She's coming down down down, floating out of the sixth level, now the fifth. She's coming down quickly. That is good."

Hong felt a tremor pass from each of her fingers to his.

"Now, remember, you must ask questions. Don't be frightened of her voice. Ghosts sound different from us. Be brave. You're lucky because she wants this. She's ready to talk, and many ghosts aren't. She's coming toward me, she'll be with me, and in me soon. Wait. Keep your eyes closed."

He held them tightly shut, hearing from across the table odd little sounds: clucks, groans, sharp cries, as if something violent were happening.

"Open your eyes."

When he did, Hong was astonished by the change in her expression. The Wu's gaze was fixed straight ahead; spittle bubbled on her withered lips; her whole body seemed rigid, as if cut from wood. "My son," she called out in a voice so hollow and booming that Hong nearly leaped to his feet. "Don't be afraid," said the ghostly voice. "Speak to me."

Trying to speak, Hong found to his dismay that words wouldn't come out. He kept swallowing until finally he spoke. "Mother," he said, "are you happy where you are?"

"I am, son. I'm happy in the ninth level. But I'm worried because of you. Tell me why I'm summoned."

He explained his fear of Two Brother's remaining here under the spell of a maker of things.

"When I died, what did I ask of you?"

"To see that he took the examinations. He's a Chujen now, but he shouldn't be satisfied with it."

"You're right, son. Keep your promise and get him to Beijing."

"But if he says no? Two Brother has changed, Mother. He doesn't listen to me."

"Tell him he must do as I ask. Or a ghost's fury will haunt him forever. Tell him!" Her deep voice reverberated in the small room; the candle wavered from the Wu's powerful expulsion of breath.

"And if he won't listen?"

"Tell him!" The fingertips touching his were trembling violently.

Breaking contact, Hong jumped to his feet. "But what else can I do besides tell him?"

"Tell him." The voice seemed to get softer, as if moving rapidly away. "Tell him ... tell him ... tell him ..."

"Mother! Stay! I miss you!"

But the Wu's face had changed again. Her eyes opened; her

lips stopped trembling. She wiped the sleeve of her robe across her drooling mouth. Her body relaxed, slumped as if in the aftermath of great effort. The Wu looked around curiously. "Did she come? Was she here? I felt her nearby, approaching me, but then . . . nothing."

"She was here," Hong muttered, hunching over the table.

"Did she advise you?"

"My brother must go to Beijing."

The Wu smiled wanly and drew a kerchief across her sweaty forehead. "Good."

"But that was all. She didn't say what to do if he refuses."

"You should be ashamed," the Wu snapped. "A ghost, even a wise one, can't do it all. We humans must act on our own. Don't send her back with a sense of failure. Don't be ungrateful."

"Oh, I'm not! To think I talked to her! Mother was happy. That's what she said. Happy! Oh, I miss her!" Hong folded his arms on the table, laid his head against them, and sobbed for a long time.

When finally he looked up, the Wu was smiling. "You got your money's worth."

When Hong returned to the lodging house, Two Brother was waiting for him. "I've decided to become Meng Dafu's apprentice," Chen announced.

"All right. After you go to Beijing."

"I thought of taking the exams and then returning. But I'm afraid Meng Dafu won't take me back."

"Go to Beijing. Mother wanted it. I was there when she died and it was her last wish. I promised her."

"It was your promise, not mine," Chen observed coolly.

"But it was her wish, not mine."

Neither said anything for a while. Finally Hong told him about the Wu and speaking to their mother. "She said you must finish what you started. You must go to Beijing."

"I don't believe in your Wu. I have no faith in magic."

"Because Master Kung had none?"

"Because he was right to believe in this world, in the here and now. The Wu never spoke to Mother."

"Mother told me you must go to Beijing."

For a moment Chen seemed to hesitate. Then he maintained in a sharp, clear, determined voice, "The Wu never spoke to Mother, and neither did you. I'm staying here. This is where I want to be."

Every morning they met at the Garden of the Master of Fishing Nets. Sometimes they sat together on a stone bench, close enough for Chen to feel the warmth of her thigh next to his. A couple of times he touched one of her hands when it appeared from under the sleeve. This contact brought from Yuying a startled gasp of alarm.

He had to make clear his love. "I'm staying because of you," he finally told her. "I don't care for elixirs of immortality. I don't believe they can be made."

The girl's mouth rounded into a circle of fear. "If my father heard you say that!"

"But you won't tell him?" he asked hopefully. "You want me to stay? You want me to, don't you?"

"Of course I do," Yuying answered uncomfortably as she turned her gaze toward a white plaster wall.

As days passed, he got to know more about Yuying. Her father had seen to her education, which was remarkably good for a girl of Ming times. She read the Classics, could recite from them. She played chess. She played the lute. Her calligraphy was as fine as Chen's own. She liked to write in the Slender Gold Style because, in her words, "it's as hard as crystal and as clear. I'm mastering the shaping line 'Wrinkles on a Demon's Face.' Do you know it? Of course you do, but people don't, I hear, and yet they call themselves calligraphers."

He'd been surprised to learn she was eighteen, only a year younger than he. Yuying looked no older than Daiyun. Why had her father waited so long to see her married? But he dared not ask. He listened.

Indeed, he listened every morning, for no sooner did they meet in the courtyard than Yuying let go with an unending stream of words, as if dammed up for years in the isolation of her father's house.

"I like dry-brush painting. Do you agree that Hsu Tao-ming was the greatest of scroll painters? Or do you like the misty poetics of Mu Chi? But my favorite work comes from the Northern Sung period—the flower-and-bird paintings. Do you agree? There's such movement, such freedom. But I never have liked Hsieh Ho's Six Principles of Painting. Too much stress on copying. Don't you think? What do you think? Do you consider Ni Tsan one of the immortals? I don't. His painting is too sparse and solemn."

Chen followed, a step behind, as Yuying led the way through courtyards and galleries. He was thinking of the warm sensation against his leg when they sat side by side on a bench. Often he suggested that they sit together, hoping to recapture the experience, but usually she preferred to stroll—and to talk.

"Wen Zheng-ming lives nearby, you know, and he's a friend of my father, though I've never met him. He sat for examinations just like you, only he never succeeded in twenty-eight years of trying. Just think. Even so, he's the finest calligrapher alive and his paintings of trees are exceedingly memorable. Don't you agree? What do you think? But of course many great artists failed their examinations. Tang Yin was an exception. Son of a grocer—did you know that? Son of a grocer, he passed his districts at fifteen and his provincials at twenty. He failed the palace exams, though, because a friend of his, also a candidate, bribed an official and implicated Tang Yin. But you already know that, don't you? Everyone should. His portraits of women are wonderful, don't you think? Do you agree? And Tun Chi-chang was a scholar, too. He became tutor of the Crown Prince and President of the Board of Rites. In his districts he placed

second instead of first because of poor calligraphy. Can you
believe it of him? Did you know it already? He overcame this
weakness by sheer willpower. And look at him now. I consider
him the third or fourth greatest calligrapher of our time. Do
you agree? Where do you rank him? On second thought, I rank
him a bit lower. Perhaps fifth. What do you think? His chief
model was Mi Fei. Now, Mi Fei . . ."

And so it went. Chen found himself thinking of Daiyun while
listening to Yuying. Had the plague come to the village? Was
Daiyun strong enough to survive? She had lily feet and a fingernail two inches long on the small finger of her left hand.
She was only fourteen, but capable of arguing like a shrewd
old woman. Her bold, saucy spirit made him smile. He had
always discussed the Tao with her. "We can do without rules
if we're devoted to the Tao," he used to say. "The Tao is beyond
is and is not." Usually she'd upbraid him for being pompous.

He never spoke of the Tao with Yuying. Even if he tried,
most likely she wouldn't hear him.

Why did she talk so much? Was she simply nervous or was
she frightened of something?

Those questions were answered one morning when he per-
suaded her to go inside the lake-viewing pavilion and sit
awhile. Their thighs touched, warmed. Did she notice? Chen
couldn't tell, because she stared resolutely ahead while describing the romantic but terrible life of Yang Kuei-fei, an
emperor's mistress, who was strangled with a silken cord for
her extravagances and infidelities.

On an ungovernable impulse, Chen broke suddenly into her
discourse. "We always meet here. Can we meet somewhere
else?"

Yuying turned and looked at him with startled eyes. "Somewhere else? I thought you liked the garden. You told me so,
you told me you did, you said, 'I like this garden.' Didn't you?
I love this garden. I've been coming here every morning for
years, I don't remember how many, but—"

"Yuying. Please listen."

She took a deep breath and said nothing.

"We're never alone here. People come and go. I want to be alone with you."

"Alone?"

"Yes. The two of us."

"The two of us," she said, as if repeating a phrase in a foreign language.

"I thought, maybe, if I came early enough some morning, I might come to your quarters. I know where those are. In the south wing, past the little pond with flowerpots beside it. Yours is the second little building on the right."

She was staring wide-eyed at him. "You want to come to my quarters?"

"I thought some morning . . ." He cleared his throat, aware from her expression that Yuying hadn't thought of such a thing until this moment. "We'd be alone. Talk. It would be different from this."

"Yes," Yuying said in a thin shaky voice. "So different. Do you know my father wishes me to marry someday?"

"I'm sure he does. Perhaps someday," Chen began, but stopped short of making a sudden bold proposal of marriage. He said vaguely, "We should talk more about it."

"To a man of means and standing," Yuying continued as if unaware of his saying anything. "A man of means and standing, you must surely realize, would never want a woman who had let another man into her quarters. Never under any circumstances. Any whatsoever. For it's said—"

"Yuying." Chen reached out to touch her sleeve; thinking better of it, he pulled his hand back. "You don't understand." It was a lame beginning, for he didn't understand either. Or rather he understood only now. He had been trying to seduce Yuying without being fully aware of his intention. "Coming to your quarters was an innocent suggestion," he stammered, knowing it had not been innocent at all.

The girl was on her feet, her heart-shaped mouth trembling. "You have insulted me. You have taken me for a flower girl of the streets!" With that, her face half-hidden in flowing sleeves, Yuying turned and rushed away. She trailed behind her a little frenzy of sobs and cries.

Leaping up and gripping the pavilion's rail, Chen watched in dismay as the girl vanished around a courtyard wall. Two old men in black were staring awestruck at him, unable to comprehend such turmoil in the serene garden they were visiting. They halted halfway across a tiny bridge that was only three strides long. Chen smiled cheerfully at them. That was his reaction to the girl's wild departure—a cheerful smile. He realized, to his amazement, that he felt relieved. He did not want Yuying. He surely did not want to marry her. He had wanted nothing more than her beauty for a while.

And he did not want to be Meng Dafu's apprentice. In fact, he had never wanted it. Many of the things that Meng Dafu had made were wondrous. He was brilliant. He understood the working of mechanical clocks and could envision the day when bridges would be suspended over gorges. His desire to produce more and better books would have been admired by Confucius. But at the same time Master Kung would have strongly disapproved of someone who wanted to make elixirs of immortality and machines that could fly.

It was all clear to Chen now, clear enough for him to realize how lucky he was for things to end here. Fortunately, Yuying had never thought of him as a real suitor. He had been little more than available—someone who would listen to a girl hungry for companionship. His mild touch had alarmed her; his suggestion that they have a love affair had offended her. Yuying had managed to save him through her own pride and fear.

Chen glanced down at goldfish in the lake; they moved slowly as if suspended in a soft, warm, gelatinous substance. How peaceful they were.

He smoothed his robe in preparation for leaving the garden. It was time to set things straight. He'd go to Meng Dafu and confess to a lack of true interest in science. He'd beg forgiveness. He'd blame himself for a failure to understand the high principles of alchemy. Humbly he'd thank the inventor and say goodbye. They'd part as friends.

While walking to the Meng house, Chen rehearsed what he would say. Then his mind raced beyond the imagined scene to a resumption of his journey with Three Brother. He saw them walking down a long road together, happily singing a peasant song of Sichuan.

Approaching the house, he noticed some workmen next door placing thick cottony paper in the window frames so they'd retain heat during the coming winter. Life went on for some people just as it did for goldfish: calmly, almost without incident. If he saw Yuying before leaving the Meng household, he'd apologize. Perhaps they'd nearly bump into each other. He had reached the house, so there wasn't time to prepare a speech of repentance.

When he knocked, the door opened a crack, then widened. The old servant was standing there, his face pinched from the tension of frowning.

"It's you," he hissed at Chen. "What have you done? She came in here screaming. You insulted her at Wang Shih Yuan, is that right? You came on her suddenly from behind and tried to grab her? Ah!" The old man threw up his hands in disgust. Getting control of himself, he leaned forward, one hand extended, nearly touching Chen's sleeve. "Get away from here at once! He'll have bullies after you. Master's beside himself with anger. He dotes on the girl. A Grand Secretary or a prince of the realm wouldn't be good enough for her. No one ever will be. But *you*! How could you do such a thing! Go, go quickly. I'll not recover from such a blow! You seemed like such a fine young man, and I've heard Master say smart, too. Why did you do it? Why did you ruin everything? When the elixir was ready, you'd have been one of the first to become immortal. And then the flying machine—you'd have flown through the air. So why did you spoil everything?" He stopped talking, cocked his head as if listening. "Go, go quickly! Get away before he has you murdered! Go! Go!"

Little was said between the brothers. Chen simply announced his decision to leave for Beijing immediately. Hong didn't question this change of heart. It was enough to be on the road once more, to have a mutual goal sending them forward again.

They left that afternoon for the Grand Canal. This thousand-year-old waterway was the chief means by which food and other supplies got from the south to the capital of Beijing. The brothers paid for space on the deck of a riverboat that was canopied amidships with heavy thatch. Soon they were moving northward under the power of three boatmen. Two of them in tandem worked a thick wooden oar at the stern. They took a step backward, a step forward, with one of them working the oar itself and the other pulling a rope attached to oar and deck, a motion that accelerated the rowing stroke. The third oarsman, at the bow, pushed off the bottom with a long bamboo pole, walked forward to midships, then hustled back to gain purchase for another push. In this fashion the boat, loaded with gunnysacks of barley and wicker mats, made headway on the crowded canal.

As they felt the excitement of renewed adventuring, the brothers smiled at each other and watched the vertiginous world of the Grand Canal flow around them. Naked to the waist, their skin the color of polished walnut, scullers maneuvered their craft through the choppy main channel. Small river junks with high sterns and patched sails were overtaking and passing one another port to starboard, their weathered strakes nearly grazing. Wicker baskets hung over the gunwales. Women bailed water from their sampans with earthenware bowls and blackened pots. Dumpy scows were lashed together along the canal bank, laundry flapping from stem to stern. These ancient riverboats served as the permanent home for people who rarely stepped ashore. Tables on the forecastles held sauce bottles and rice bowls. Kettles that burned charcoal on poop decks were filling the air with swirls of pungent smoke. Wild shouting also filled the air as sailors argued over right-of-way or yelled greetings to ex-shipmates on tugs, barges, sampans, cargo rafts. Along the shoreline footpaths there were armies of porters carrying shoulder poles or pushing two-wheeled carts. Well-kept farmhouses stood nearby in fields lined with bushes and willows. There were cherry trees and vegetable gardens.

The brothers experienced an illusion special to the canal: they saw the sails of ships rise out of wheat fields. Because the canal snaked through the countryside in wide loops, its traffic often seemed to be traveling on land—sailing through rice paddies, sculling through farmyards.

"Are you glad to be here?" Hong asked shyly.

"Glad to be here?" Chen leaned forward and touched his brother's arm. "At this moment I'd rather be here than anywhere else in the world."

At the town of Gaoyou, the canal boat moored. A forest of sampans and junks lay alongside the banks. Nothing was moving beyond this point, a surly boatman told the brothers. When they asked why, he pointed northward as if that were an explanation. Leaving the boat, they went into Gaoyou, which was crowded with distraught passengers and boat crews. They noticed a sallow-faced little man sitting against the wall of a grain shed. His smile encouraged Hong to question him.

"Why isn't anything moving north?"

"Because the Yellow River is still flooding."

"How far is that from here?"

"About seventy miles. But the land south of the river has flooded for more than thirty. The stretch of canal between Huaiyin and here is closed. I've come from Huaiyin myself. In my younger days I'd still be there, working on embankments. But it's not for someone my age. It's hard work carrying baskets of mud, and it's frustrating when the banks don't hold and they slide away like mush. Anyway, I've seen enough of flood and famine." He sighed. "I've seen people howling from hunger and tearing their hair out when they had the strength. After a flood eight years ago, I saw human flesh sold in a market. I've gone into villages where whole families committed suicide. They lay together neatly in rows. I've been in other places where they banged on iron gongs all day, trying to drive off evil spirits causing the famine. What they did was make noise enough to waken the poor souls that just died." He grunted in acknowledgment of his own morbid witticism. Then he studied the brothers.

"Are you going to Beijing?"

Chen nodded.

"Picked a nice time, didn't you. Usually the floods come earlier in the season, not this far into fall, but then no one ever accused this river of being reliable. So you're headed for Beijing. Would you take some advice?"

When Chen nodded again, the little man explained that the waters had probably receded by now from much of the countryside, so they could take the road due north to Huaiyin. There they might get transport across the river. There were no bridges and little ferry service except at Huaiyin, so it was the only way they could get beyond the Yellow and continue to Beijing. The trip to Huaiyin should take at least three days, so they'd need a dozen fistfuls of pickled rice wrapped in oiled goatskin to keep it waterproof. There wouldn't be a single bite of food to buy on the way. Looking the brothers up and down, he added, "Get yourselves walking sticks and sharpen the ends."

"For spears?" Hong asked.

The little man smiled grimly. "You'll be going through flooded country. Remember that. Water's been in everything. Every storage bin, every grain cellar, every pot and jar has either been buried in mud or washed away or ruined by water. That means nothing to eat. That means when two young fellows like you come along, looking well fed and healthy, people will just naturally want what's in the bundles you're carrying."

"Thank you," Hong said. They had brought along some buns filled with bean sauce. He took them from a bundle, peeled back the soggy paper they were wrapped in, and held them out. "Share with us," he said. "Then we'll get rice and sharpen our walking sticks and go north."

And so they did as the little man suggested. They trudged up the northern road that led to Huaiyin. A mist descended like the slow smoke of a waning forest fire. Gray silt, left by the receding river, oozed thickly across the leachy soil, making the eroded meadows as smooth as butter. Nature was transforming the land into featureless bogs and swamps. The brothers slogged through a silent world of endless fog. They came to a river that lay south of the Yellow, but at such an angle that the brothers didn't need to cross it. They stared in horror at the eddying water that carried the flotsam of human life along its channel: bits of clothing, pots, a weeding pole, entire sections of wood-framed buildings, bloated corpses.

Carts stood empty, sunk to their axles in mud. A crow clutched the tiles of an overturned roof and cawed defiantly at crumbling walls and sagging doors.

Entering a village, they smelled damp clay but saw no one, not until they reached the last huts there. Out of a doorway staggered two men holding pitchforks, yelling weakly for food food food!

The brothers pointed their walking sticks at them, warily turning as the circling men wobbled and lurched, hardly able to hold the pitchforks.

Hong thrust with his makeshift spear and bellowed, "Out of here!"

Backing off, mumbling, the attackers shuffled away like sleepwalkers and reentered the dark hut they had come from.

"Food," the brothers heard at their back. Across the road, two women, one middle-aged, the other young, were sitting against the earthen wall of another hut.

"Food," the older woman muttered, one hand half-uncurled.

Without hesitation Chen went to her and bent down. He
ladled some rice into her palm.

She didn't eat, but turned and offered the handful to the
younger woman, who stared straight ahead, ignoring her. The
eyes of both women were sunken, their pale lips covered with
slime. Their skin looked hard, leathery, and the older woman's
belly hung down like a deflated pouch.

When the young woman refused to eat, refused even to
acknowledge the offer, the older woman lifted her rice-filled
hand and munched slowly. To swallow seemed painful. After
she had chewed awhile, eating a small portion of the rice, she
poured the rest carefully into the pocket of her blouse. "May
the gods bless you," she muttered at Chen. "We got here I
don't know how." She seemed confused by what she was saying. "Our whole village went down. My granddaughter
drowned, I think. My daughter"—she glanced at the younger
woman—"this one—was swept away. No, not this one. I have
three daughters, good girls, and two sons, and four grandchil-
dren, one girl, three boys. It filled up everything until everything washed away. Two horses, goat, some dogs, I think. They
were taken straight across the field, swept away like twigs,
swept away by so much water I wonder where it came from.
We lived on tree bark. Ah yes, that's when granddaughter died.
She didn't drown. She was one that starved. Another one did,
probably all the others did. And Two Daughter here has
stopped eating. Look at her. She won't eat again." The woman
shook her head sadly. "No, my Number Two girl won't ever
eat again."

"Give them more rice," Hong said. Chen poured more rice
into the older woman's lap. She touched it with her fingertips,
idly, as if it were worthless.

"Will they"—Hong looked in the direction of the two men
with pitchforks—"hurt you?"

The woman smiled wanly. "They will if they can walk. They'll
take the food."

"What can we do?" Chen asked.

Hong shook his head. "Nothing. Except this." He walked over to the hut where the men had gone inside and poured about two handfuls of rice on the ground at the doorway. "Maybe they'll let the women alone. Or . . ." Hong didn't finish the thought, because he knew Chen would not consent to murdering the men in order to save the women.

The brothers looked at each other. "There's nothing more we can do," Hong said, hoping that Chen didn't see his lips trembling.

After three days, as the man in the shed had predicted, they arrived at Huaiyin. Refugees from the west had already reached there. They lay in the streets, groaning. The air was infected with the stench of the unburied dead. Hands waved at the brothers, reached out to pluck at their sleeves, their trouser legs, until they had to kick out and pull away and hurry on.

Getting to the docks, they saw the river.

Rising in the plateaus of Central Asia and called for centuries "China's Sorrow," the Yellow River had meandered three thousand miles through the central plain. For most of each year a sluggish river, the Yellow's bed had gradually choked up with silt until its channel was narrow and shallow. Monsoon rains had done the rest. Floodwater sloshed over riverbanks, smashed dikes, and flowed across immense areas of coastal plain toward the sea.

What the brothers saw, when they looked down at the Yellow's shifting channel, was a great rampaging surface that reminded them of a huge beast flexing its muscles. Under the hammering of water, the banks had become an evil-smelling treacle, sliding away from the river's swell. Peasants, joined by local soldiers, were shoring up the levees with bales of kaoliang roots pounded into place against the tamped soil. Hundreds—men, women, and children—were toiling with baskets, hauling mud, building up retaining walls. Doggedly they struggled in the deep mud to contain the beast. Boats were rowing back and forth across the river. They came alongside the dock, their large sweep oars at rapid work trying to keep them upright in the current. The boats swung in and out, fighting the beast beneath them, as passengers boarded. Horses, tethered to stern railings, were forced to swim across. One was lost. Its reins, poorly tied to a rail, slipped free, and currents drew it into mid-channel, where it turned and rolled, unable with its earthbound hooves to get a purchase on empty air or raging water. The great round rump glistened. The mouth opened in a rictus of terror, and the bulky shape was pulled into distant mists farther downstream.

"Don't stand here if you can't pay to cross," a boatman growled at the crowd massed around the dock. "It's dangerous out there. We don't run back and forth for nothing."

Pushing forward with others, the brothers finally reached a boat at the wharf. A boatman collected passage and allowed them to board. One impatient man rushed by and climbed into the boat. A hulking boatman threw him over the side, and he had to cling to a piling for dear life, until a few people dockside reluctantly helped him back up. The sun was setting like a rust-colored ember. When the brothers' sampan was packed, the boatmen shoved off with poles and entered a thick, lowering fog. The brothers watched themselves become entangled in webs of cloudy dusk. Though side by side, they could hardly see more of each other than nose, mouth, eye sockets, yet they saw something else approaching the gunwale—something big in the water like a huge fish. It was not a fish but the entire earthen wall of a village hut, crumbling yet still intact enough to ram straight through the sampan if they collided. By skillful maneuvering, the oarsman managed to veer away from its path. That massive rectangle of earth, plaster, and wooden beams continued its antic tumbling seaward. Then the Yellow became as dark as death, and before they gained the opposite shore, their own faces turned in the final light into murky featureless objects, much like the land they had walked through for the past few days.

"What are you thinking?" Hong asked when they left the boat and struggled up the muddy bank.

Chen said nothing.

Later, when they had found a farmhouse along the road and paid for the privilege of lying in the hay mound, Hong asked again, "What are you thinking?"

"Do I seem as if I'm thinking?"

"You're always thinking. Tell me. What are you thinking now?"

"Of a poem by Ho Sun."

"Tell me."

> *"The traveler's heart has a hundred thoughts already,*
> *his lonely journey piling mile on endless mile."*

Hong said quietly, "You're thinking of Daiyun."

Chen said nothing.

"She's alive. I'm sure of it. They all are."

Chen said nothing.

"Well, there's a chance. And since we don't know, we shouldn't despair."

Chen said nothing.

"We must just go on."

For a long time Chen said nothing. Then, turning to his brother, he said, "We just go on."

Fearful of delays on the Grand Canal and weary of water, they headed north by foot on a road that led through the towns of Shuyang and Xinyi into the hilly and fertile province of Shandong. During this week of steady traveling, they spoke little except to discuss food and lodging. But one morning Hong questioned his brother's silence if only for something to do besides walk.

"Did you hate to leave your friend the great inventor?" Hong asked suddenly.

Chen glanced at him, surprised by the question. "No, I didn't hate to leave him. Why do you ask?"

"You were thinking hard just now. So I ran through my mind
what you could be thinking of."

"I was thinking of something Meng Dafu once described." So Chen in turn described it to his brother: a famous clock built by Su Sung five centuries before. More than thirty feet high, it was driven by water power, but its entire movement depended on machinery created by man: wheels and shafts, hooks and pins, interlocking rods and stopping devices. Ninety-two bronze manikins struck bells and beat drums to mark the passage of time. It contained a celestial globe to show the motions of sun, moon, and planets. Because of jealousy and political intrigue, Su Sung's clock was pulled down and destroyed only a few years after it was built.

"Did this Meng Dafu make gunpowder?" Hong asked, impatient with the story of a clock.

"He's not interested in gunpowder or fireworks. But he can make both."

"How?"

"By mixing sulfur and carbon and something called saltpeter. More saltpeter, bigger explosion."

"If you had stayed," Hong mused thoughtfully, "you'd have learned all he knows and more. You'd have become a maker of things."

"And flown through the sky and become immortal?" Chen laughed. "I'm content to walk on the earth and die when my time comes."

"So you didn't want to stay?"

"No," Chen declared. And that was true. "I'd rather write a poem than build a bridge."

"I'd rather fight crickets than do either," admitted Hong with a laugh of his own.

The truth was, Chen's brooding had been caused by something other than a clock destroyed a half millennium ago.

Actually, he had been thinking about Qufu, the birthplace of Confucius. They were heading in that direction. Today they would stay in Linyi, from which one fork in the road northward went on to Jinan and the other to Pingyi and Qufu. If they took the left-hand road, they'd reach Qufu in four or five days. Perhaps he'd never have the chance to see it again, Chen thought. The problem was Hong. The closer they got to Beijing, the more anxious he became—fearful, perhaps, of another delay. Of course, the Qufu route would add little to the distance they traveled on their way to Beijing. But that would not bother Hong anyway. Three Brother would worry about going to the hometown of the Master. After all, Chen understood in himself the pull of the name Qufu; it meant history, it meant the graveled paths walked by the Master, the temples worshipped in, the landscape beloved by that venerable man. Hong deserved better than waiting on an older brother's whim, as he had in Suzhou. Chen resolved to say nothing about Qufu.

So it was with delighted surprise that Chen heard his brother bring up the subject himself as they entered the town of Linyi. "When we stayed at that farmhouse the other night, I talked to the farmer," said Hong. "He told me that at Linyi the road branches off in two directions. One leads to Jinan and the other leads to Qufu. Isn't that where your Master lived?"

"Yes, in Qufu."

"Both roads lead north. We'd get to Beijing either way."

"We could go the Qufu way," Chen said, trying to hide his eagerness, "if we wanted to." After a long pause, he asked timidly, "Do you want to?"

"I'd like to see where the man lived who has such an influence on my brother. Yes," Hong said, "I want to."

Chen wasn't fooled. "In payment for letting me have my way," he said with a smile, "I promise the next time you ask something of me, I'll do it."

Next morning they took the left fork for Qufu.

"I hear the finest plums grow in Shandong," Hong observed.

"It's said that Lao Tzu was born under a plum tree. That's why some of his teachings have a sharp edge, a tartness to them. Do you know why the plum tree's a symbol of longevity?"

Hong looked down at his sandals as if more intent on where they were going than on his brother's explanation.

"Because plums grow on withered-looking branches—the

tree looks very old but still bears fruit." Chen waited a moment before adding, "You follow Confucius, though you don't know it."

Hong snorted.

"You're honest, kind, loyal, and loving. Those are the four essential virtues, according to Master Kung."

"Come on, gege. Your Master Kung wouldn't have liked me. I'm nothing but a village boy from Sichuan."

"The Master believed a man's nature was more important than his birth. Many of Confucius' disciples came from the poor. He would have hoped for more respect from you, more attention to courtesy, more restraint in opinions—yes, I'm sure of that. But he'd have seen in you the four essential virtues. You're wrong, didi: he would have liked you."

"You have those long legs," Hong grumbled, "but they go twice as slow as mine. That farmer also told me there's a famous inn on this road. It serves hot sausage, sour vegetables, and strips of pickled bean curd. If we walk fast enough, we'll be there before sunset."

As they entered the town of Qufu four days later, they saw an old man coming along the road with a bamboo cage. There was a lark inside, and he was causing the cage to sway back and forth, so the bird got its exercise. The sight reminded Chen of Old Shen, who used to take daily walks with his own songbirds. And Old Shen reminded the young scholar of Big Sister and Father, of the embittered schoolmaster and the whole village. But the swaying cage ultimately brought him to the most precious memory of all. In his mind's eye he saw Daiyun doing embroidery. She glanced suddenly up at him to say something disapproving, but with her eyes shining.

Hong also turned to watch the swaying bird and the old man on their outing together, so he scarcely saw the granite lions seated imposingly at the south-facing entrance to the temple. Like most temples, this one, dedicated to Confucius, had its buildings and courtyards arranged along a north–south axis. The brothers walked in, following a long, shaded avenue lined with ancient pines and flanked by commemorative stelae, whose tall granite shapes had the stately look of trees in a timeless forest.

Not wishing to bore his brother, Chen resisted the temptation to dawdle in front of each stele and read its poetic praise of Master Kung. They went straight for the Great Hall. In its portico stood ten imposing pillars, each carved from a single block of marble, with dragons coiled in relief around the column, slithering among puffs of stylized cloud.

Inside the hall were statues of the Master and his disciples. Set under a silk canopy, Confucius was depicted as a bulky long-faced man who wore a hat shaped like a mortarboard. As the brothers stood quietly there, music from another building carried through the temple: bronze bells, stone chimes, lutes, and deep-voiced drums.

Hong was watching his brother, who seemed transformed by the experience of being so close to his Master, dead now for two thousand years. Chen was mumbling a prayer or a poem or maybe a passage from one of the works attributed to Confucius. Discreetly, Hong backed off a few steps to give his brother more privacy.

"What now?" he asked, when finally Chen turned away and left the temple.

"The tomb."

Hong shrugged indulgently. "Very well, then. The tomb."

What was called the "Kung Forest" lay north of town. Planted within the cemetery walls were countless pine trees. Their smell discouraged Wang Xiang from going inside. He was a demon that devoured the brains of the dead. In this pine-scented enclosure many generations of the Kung family were buried. It was actually an immense park entered through a stone gateway with a chiseled inscription: ETERNAL SPRING. Evergreens and cypresses, rising from thick undergrowth, stood in towering grandeur above chunky sculptures of stone dogs, goats, lions, dragons, and horses. There were other figures, discolored by centuries of rain. These were disciples of the Master, their hands clasping granite scrolls, their bearded faces and hunched shoulders expressive of immense energy focused on a beadlike zone of contemplation. Their flared caps were similar to the winged one worn by Lao Chen.

Neither brother spoke as they crossed a stone bridge and walked down the avenue of honor called the Spirit Road. It was shaded by ancient evergreens and flanked by panthers, griffins, and rain-streaked scholars of stone.

The tomb of Confucius was nothing more than a plain earthen mound. Nearby stood two granite sages and a stele engraved so skillfully that the stone had the wet, yielding look of brush and ink against rice paper. Chen kowtowed three times, granting Confucius the same respect as an emperor. Hong kowtowed also, but only twice.

Then the young Chujen began to mumble, his expression as fixed as those of the granite scholars who formed the Master's timeless entourage.

Hong felt no comparable reverence, yet his brother's worshipful contemplation of this tomb reminded him of General Ma at the tomb of Yueh Fei. And then, as time passed and a breeze stirred in the pines, Hong recalled his own grief in the backyard where he had buried Dragon Legs and Fire Star—not in gold coffins but in the gourds they had occupied during their honorable lives.

Finally Chen turned away, tears in his eyes. When they started out of the cemetery, he said, as much to himself as to Hong, "In front of his tomb, standing there, I imagined the Master traveling from prince to prince. They wanted to learn from him, not about virtues but about understanding the ways of men, so they might overthrow their enemies. I saw them growing impatient with his message of right action, loyalty, and kindness. His words grew tiresome to them, and they turned away. Confucius died without office, without political favor, without a personal estate, almost without honor. What do you think of that, brother?"

After a long silence, Hong said, "I think it's what any man must face when he's uncommonly wise and loyal and kind."

Next day they returned to the temple and the Kung Forest

so that Chen could pay homage once more. In a vast courtyard they discovered a small pavilion that surrounded a juniper tree. According to a nearby stele, the Teacher of Ten Thousand Generations had planted this tree with his own hands. That meant the old juniper had been growing in this weather-hammered soil more than three hundred years before the Great Wall was built. They were contemplating its scraggly limbs when a man hurried up, bowed, and asked them please to follow him. The Illustrious Vice Secretary of the Ministry of Rites at Qufu respectfully requested a few gracious moments of a Recommended Man's valuable time at his humble little office whenever possible.

Having delivered this flowery speech, the man, who wore a long velvet robe, added, "He wants to see you now. At your convenience, of course."

"But why?" Chen asked.

"You've been seen here, Chujen. Someone of your standing is always welcomed by the secretary."

Chen nodded with a smile. He was thinking of Yuying, who hadn't felt he was of sufficient standing to be her suitor.

Hong didn't have to be told that his own gracious presence was not required. He sat on a bench outside the Kung residence. This mansion was ordinarily closed to everyone except family and staff. Idly he watched some soldiers having lunch under a shade tree nearby. They drank water—too poor to buy tea—and bolted down wheat cakes, slurping and grunting and hunched over as intent as wolves. Blunt-faced peasants, they had glowing cheeks. Hong thought of home.

Meanwhile, Chen accompanied the messenger through the expansive mansion and through courtyards with matched pairs of porcelain stools and moss-covered rocks and pools. Finally he was introduced into the private office of Wei Xi, Vice Secretary of Rites.

An austere-looking man with a wispy beard, Wei Xi was seated at a rosewood desk; behind him hung a scroll of mountains in a mist. With a flourish of one long sleeve, the secretary offered his young visitor a seat. Chen sat down on a divan of carved ebony with a marble back.

They exchanged ornate pleasantries, which seemed to gratify the official, who might not have been sure that the young man understood the niceties of polite society.

"You're on your way to Beijing for the examination?" Wei Xi finally asked.

"Yes, I'm traveling there with my brother."

"Your province?"

"Sichuan."

"Your ranking?"

"Fifth."

The official nodded approvingly. "And I gather you've stopped here to pay respects to the Master?"

"I have, Honorable Secretary."

"Had you come last month, you might have joined us for Master Kung's birthday celebration. This year we sacrificed thirteen oxen, forty sheep, and sixty-three pigs. The music was wonderful, the dancing as good as I have ever seen here. We debated the question: How can man adjust the social order to the cosmic order? Does that question interest you?"

"It does, Honorable Secretary. It's central to the Master's thought."

The secretary frowned, as if annoyed by having so young a man tell him what was central to Confucian thought.

But fired by a chance to express his own ideas, Chen went on. "I think I would start by stating the difference between Confucian and Taoist attitudes toward the concept of the Tao. For the Taoist the Tao is a mystery revealed by an abandonment of rational thought. For the Confucian the Tao is a way of seeking virtue. I find a clue to this problem in Master Kung's words, 'I never blame heaven.' He is telling us to forget the cosmos. We must look within ourselves for answers. We must make perfect the social order, then wonder if it conforms to the cosmic order. But we needn't wonder then. It surely does conform. Like the horse coming before the cart, the social order comes first and heaven takes care of itself. In a sense the question has only one part: How do we order society?" Chen stopped there, realizing that he'd gone on much too long. He was acting like Yuying—starved for someone to discuss things with. Though he loved and admired his brother, Chen hadn't talked philosophy with him during their long trip together. Opportunity now at hand, he had said too much. Indeed, his insensitive garrulousness had provoked the secretary: the official's lips were twitching.

Even so, the official tried to smile. "Your ideas are most interesting," he said in a voice thin from the effort of hiding his annoyance. "However, duties prevent me from carrying our discussion further." He picked up a sealed scroll that lay on his desk. "Given your standing as a scholar and your obvious devotion to our Master, you are, in my estimation, the appropriate person to carry this letter to Beijing." Before handing it over, he studied Chen a long time. "You'll make sure it gets to Censor Tang Wangai? In the name of our Master?"

"I'd be honored to carry it. I'd guard it with my life and give it only to him."

After a few thoughtful moments, the secretary said, "You were seen kowtowing three times in front of the tomb. Three times. Is that correct?"

"I know three is reserved for the Emperor," Chen admitted without hesitation. "But I believe the same respect is due the Master."

"Even though such behavior is treasonable?"

Chen said nothing, but his unwavering eyes met the cold gaze of the official.

Finally Wei Xi looked away. "Yes, I believe you," he said, his lips pursed as he gave Chen the scroll. "If you have breath in your body, you'll deliver this letter." He added with a tight little smile, as if the act in itself were difficult, "Because you'll be delivering it in the name of the Teacher of Ten Thousand Generations."

Next morning Hong shook his sleeping brother. When Chen rubbed his eyes, Hong said firmly, "Now keep your promise.

You said you'd do what I ask. I ask you to get up and go to Beijing. Without more delays, without second thoughts about what you're doing. Just go to Beijing and prepare for the exam."

Chen nodded compliantly. "That's what I'm going to do. Because I promised—and for another reason."

"What other reason?"

"My belief in the Master. You gave me a chance to renew it. Traveling took me far away from him."

"So did your great friend Meng Dafu."

"That's true. More than you know," Chen added without explanation. "And I lost sight of the meaning of my study. All those years of reading and learning were for a reason—for something else besides passing examinations. Qufu taught me what I already knew. I want to know the mind of Master Kung and follow wherever it leads."

Hong smiled thinly. "Right now it leads to Beijing."

So they left that morning. Hong turned, as they began walking, and said, "We must just go on. You promised, remember?"

Chen said, "Of course I remember."

Chen kept his promise by traveling thereafter with the intensity of a monk on the way to a newly assigned monastery.

They went forward single-mindedly day after day. They walked through a landscape that had become flat, yellow, with dark blue hills in the distance. They passed cabbage patches, vegetable gardens of turnips and cucumbers. Wheat stalks, shorn ankle-high, looked cold and brittle in the crisp morning light. Ducks drifted idly in quiet little ponds. Once a squadron of geese waddled across the brothers' path on the way toward a place wet and hidden. Whirling leaves, brittle as shells, crackled in the wind. In a village they bought padded jackets against the cold. They bought apples and persimmons from smiling peasants, and in almost every town now they saw deer hanging from rafters and hares dangling by their long ears in butcher shops.

The world had become quiet and peaceful again. Hong remarked on it in wonder as they stared at brick cottages and men leading mules into fields. The horizon seemed to stretch forever under a light enlivened by unseen particles of dust that gave it a golden tinge. The north wind began to howl, but the brothers leaned into it in silent determination.

They had been traveling in this austere manner for more than three weeks when Hong said abruptly, "Why is it so? People were swept away. Others starved. Everywhere you looked, the world was in the grip of demons. And now this! No one has a care except bringing in the harvest or shooting game for feasts. Why is it part of the world suffers and part of it prospers? Why can't something be done when things go wrong? Why couldn't we do anything back in that village where the two women were? Why? Tell me what your Great Master would say."

"He would say you do good by helping others. But knowing what is good and doing what is good are not the same. Circumstance may prevent you from acting on what you know."

"So your Master would have said leave the women there."

"I believe so. We had no chance of saving them."

"At least not the younger woman. But the older one?"

"She wouldn't have left her daughter."

"But we could have made them safer. We could have killed those two with the pitchforks. All they were good for was killing someone."

"I thought of killing them."

"You did?" Hong was surprised. "Why didn't you say something?"

"Had I told you I thought of killing them, you'd have agreed, and we'd have killed them."

Hong considered the possibility for a moment. "Yes," he said, "we would have."

"Of those four people who, if any, might survive? We can only guess. Perhaps the two men had the best chance of surviving. And what if they did survive? They weren't murderers at heart. Circumstance drove them to despair, and despair to desperation, and desperation to violence. But say they survived

and we met them years later. As merchants they sold us something, invited us to tea, proudly introduced us to their families."

Hong said nothing, but fixed his gaze on cedars and cork
trees and nut-bearing hickories that stood off the flat, straight
road. At last he snorted contemptuously. "If your Great Master
had gone through that same village, who knows what he'd have
done?"

"That," Chen said, "is true. He'd have tried to see what was
good to do and then tried to do it. But circumstance could
have entered in, twisting everything beyond reason. Then, like
us, he'd never fully rid his mind of what he could have done
but didn't do. Master Kung was very human. That's why his
thought has lasted so long."

"Ha," scoffed Three Brother, but without conviction.

Later in the day he cried out, "Look there!" Tight curls of
black smoke were rising above the fields ahead. They made a
dense cloud clear across the horizon. Many tiny things were
glittering through the smoke in the distance. "Tile roofs," Hong
suggested. "We're coming into a city, a big city. We've gone
through Guan and Yufa. This must be Beijing at last!"

Beijing was a huge city, swept at intervals by dust-laden
winds coming out of Central Asia, and frequently threatened
by nomadic hordes from beyond the Great Wall. Only recently
the sole capital of China, having shared that honor before
with Nanjing, the city possessed stout walls forty feet high and
fourteen miles long, with formidable watchtowers rising at
intervals above the tiled roofs. There were four cities, actually.
The Tatar City lay northward, a hilly expanse dotted with small
lakes. The Imperial City came next, with armories, spacious
parks, government buildings, and the mansions of high officials. It contained within its precincts the Forbidden City, home
of the Ming Emperor, with public audience halls toward the

front and private quarters toward the back. The Emperor's needs and those of the palace women were serviced by twenty thousand eunuchs who had been organized into a dozen bureaus that ran everything from the kitchen to the palace guard. South of this royal sanctuary was a sprawling residential area called the Chinese City; most of the people lived there.

Passing through the Chinese City, the Lao brothers went straight to the Beijing Examination Compound. It was located in the Imperial City (Gao Shi had so instructed Chen). There the young scholar checked in as Chujen, Fifth Rank, Sichuan Province. He was given not only expense money but an address for housing, because every candidate at this academic level was a guest of the state.

This time the brothers didn't lodge in a grim little boardinghouse but in a private home owned by the widow of a former vice director of parks under the Ministry of Public Works. The widow was not there but at another estate in Tianjin, so a staff of a dozen servants greeted the scholar and his brother at the villa, not far from the Imperial City. Two other Chujen were already guests, with two more scheduled to arrive before the examination began.

The villa—actually a compound of a dozen buildings—had a large courtyard and a duck pond. Hong stared in awe at the richly decorated rooms: six-foot mirrors set in heavy wooden frames; benches with footrests and fluffed cushions; glass cases containing flower arrangements of jade; ostrich plumes set in tall ebony stands; tasseled chandeliers; vases five feet high; paintings and panels of calligraphy on every wall. Everywhere he looked, there was a clutter of splendor unlike anything he had seen before. It made him nervous. His insecurity in the face of such opulence must have showed, because during a stroll through such rooms, he heard a tinkle of laughter behind him.

Turning, he saw peeking around a tall flaring vase a skinny girl of about eleven or twelve. "Who are you?" he asked sharply.

The girl stepped out and boldly returned his look. She had

two long braids that reached the small of her back. "Who are
you?"

"Why were you laughing at me?"

"Because you looked so . . ." She couldn't find words, but laughed merrily.

"Who are you?" he repeated severely.

"Daughter of Number One cook. Are you a eunuch?"

"No," Hong said, shocked. "Why do you ask such a thing?"

The girl shrugged her thin shoulders. "There's so many in Beijing. Poor families castrate their boys and try to sell them to the imperial staff. The lucky are bought, the unlucky join the street gangs. The way you're looking around here, you seemed poor enough to be one of the Volunteers for Imperial Duty."

"I am Lao Hong," he announced measuredly, "Three Brother of Lao Chen, Chujen, Fifth Rank, Sichuan Province."

"Oh, as grand as that?" the girl said sarcastically. "You certainly do come from the provinces. Here in Beijing there are more Chujens than donkeys in the street—almost as many Chujens as eunuchs."

"You seem more like the grand lady of the house," Hong countered, "than just a cook's daughter."

"Number One daughter to Number One cook," the girl corrected. She had both hands on her hips. "Remember, if you try to steal anything, I'll be watching. You won't get away with it."

The brothers took a few days to acquaint themselves with the great city. They strolled through one market after another, staring at crimson marriage candles as tall as a man and toy cranes dangling from sticks. They noticed letter writers crouched under awnings with their writing materials spread on overturned boxes. They heard the noise of barbers clacking their metal clippers (Hong thought of Righteous Uncle, Ye Pan) and the blare of a trumpet blown by a knife sharpener announcing his presence in the neighborhood. And they watched a rickshaw puller tie mittens on the handles of his vehicle in anticipation of a sharp drop in temperature. A single file of heavily laden camels from Mongolia shuffled past them, snorting and coughing. They stood flat against a wall while a courtier passed in a sedan chair so big that it was divided into a bedchamber and a reception room, staffed with two attendants, and hauled by forty bearers. They stopped at an open market where a caravan from Central Asia was displaying its wares. The brothers gawked at saddles of red leather, figured carpets, stirrups of chiseled iron, peaked hats of fur with floppy brims. Sun-darkened women stood beside the horses wearing silver earrings, red jackets, green turbans. When the brothers bought nothing, the women jeered in a foreign language.

The Laos strolled along streets called White Tower, Iron Lion, Dry Fish, Perpetual Repose. They were startled when they first heard a sound common in the city: a raucous whirring overhead, made by temple pigeons with whistles fastened to their wings.

After this first overwhelming experience of Beijing, the brothers settled back into their lives. They had their clothes cleaned and their hair cut and went their separate ways.

Lao Hong headed straight for the Imperial City, where, he had learned from the house servants (but not from Fufang, the cook's daughter), he could find the Red Horsemen of the Western Esplanade. At the massive gate to the Imperial City he was halted at the checkpoint, and no amount of arguing with the guard there would get him in, even though he waved the torn letter from Ye Pan in the man's face.

Getting nowhere, Hong took a deep breath and tried something else. "Tell me this, Illustrious Sir," he said to the guard, "do the Red Horsemen ever come out?"

The guard responded to "Illustrious Sir." "Of course. Every evening, just before sunset, they ride out to give their horses some exercise."

So Hong waited the rest of the afternoon, until the sun dipped under the high wall of the Imperial City. And as the guard said, the huge gate swung open and a squadron of Red Horsemen of the Western Esplanade rode out into the broad avenue fronting the gate. They wore sleeveless leather jerkins over crimson shirts and peaked leather hats and crimson trousers with leather boots. Arrow quivers crossed their backs diagonally. Each carried a shiny steel pike.

Standing near the gate, Hong yelled at the formation of riders leaving two abreast, "Sun Qi! Sun Qi! I am fifteenth son of your sworn brother! *Fifteen!* I am fifteenth son of your sworn brother! Sun Qi! Sun Qi!"

The entire troop of a few hundred men passed without one reining up or giving him a glance.

Crestfallen, Hong was about to leave. Then he reconsidered and decided to try once again when the Red Horsemen returned. It was dark when they approached the entrance to the Imperial City, now lit by torches in sconces. Hong stood alongside the troop and shouted the same message until the last horseman disappeared through the gate. Even then Hong waited, unsure of what to do next, and as he stood there, a guard gestured to him from the gateway. Reaching the gate, Hong noticed a Red Horseman waiting inside.

"You, boy," the rider called.

Walking past the guard, Hong came to the horse's side and stared up in the torchlight at the frowning rider. "Who are you?" the man asked gruffly.

"Are you Sun Qi?"

"I am. *Fifteenth* son of your sworn brother."

Hong extended his hand to show the rolled letter, but without giving it up. "From Ye Pan."

"Follow me," the rider said, and so in this manner Hong entered the Imperial City of Beijing for the second time.

The renowned mounted guard called the Red Horsemen lived in barracks, but as an officer Sun Qi had his own private quarters. Hong waited in an anteroom while Sun Qi changed into a robe and sipped some hot tea provided by an adjutant. Then the Red Horseman took the boy into a small windowless room lit only by a single candle. Half of the room was a brick platform covered with mats, cushions, and carpet, with a low table and a cupboard. Hong had never seen a kang before—a feature of northern living. Sun Qi told him to climb up and sit down. When Hong did so, he felt sudden warmth from the heat delivered by internal piping below the whole platform.

Sitting opposite him, Sun Qi waited and, when Hong did or said nothing, asked for the letter.

For a moment Hong hesitated, as if unsure even now to give it over. Finally, with a sigh, he did.

Sun Qi read it carefully, then studied the boy a long time before speaking. "Tell me why you brought this letter."

Hong explained that he was accompanying his brother, a Chujen, from their home village to Chengdu, where he had met Ye Pan. Then they had come on to Beijing.

Sun Qi nodded silently. He had a long, brooding face with beetling black eyebrows and a skeptical curl to his mouth. "If you wished me five blessings, what would they be?"

Hong felt relieved that they were starting the ritual of identification. "Long life, health, riches, love of virtue, and a natural death."

"Where were you born?"

"Under a peach tree in the Red Pavilion."

"Where is the Red Pavilion?"

"In the land of suffering in the valley of truth."

"Why is your face so yellow?"

"I am troubled about my country."

"Why is your coat so old?"

"It was handed down by five ancestors."

"Who were they?"

"Five monks who survived betrayal and attack."

"Have you entered the circle?"

"I have. At the home of Ye Pan I entered the circle. He led me into it."

"I demand of you a last and final proof that you're a fully initiated brother."

Hong recited:

"Before parting, the five ancestors composed
A verse which heroes have never disclosed.
But if to brothers this was shown
They'd know they were not alone."

Sun Qi nodded brusquely. "Then tell me the verse."

"No."

"Recite the verse!"

"No."

"Why?"

"Because there is no verse. The secret of the White Lotus is so deep that there's nothing more to say."

The darkly somber face of the horse guard broke into a smile. "Good. Good, boy. You're truly a sworn brother." Picking up the letter, he said, "Do you know what's in this?"

"Yes."

"Were you told not to read it?"

"Yes."

"But you read it anyway?" Sun Qi asked angrily.

"Pirates caught us and made me read it. They asked me many times what it meant. They had me read it; they read it to me themselves. I know it by heart." Hong closed his eyes and said in a singsong voice, " 'A thousand rabbits become fierce after cock crows ten times. Or sleeps after tiger growls or blinks thirty times at sun.' "

"Yes, you certainly know it by heart," Sun Qi observed.

"While they were cutting me, I saw each word in my mind. I know the message better than my own name."

"Cutting you? What do you mean?"

Hong pulled off his shirt and exposed the crisscrossing, vinelike scars that covered his chest.

"The Thousand Cuts," murmured the shocked horseman.

"I would have felt all thousand had it not been for Yao." Hong described their attempt at escape and Yao's sacrifice.

"Truly a sworn brother," Sun Qi said. "When they cut you, what did you tell them?"

"Nothing."

"Well, did you tell them who gave you the letter?"

"No."

"You never mentioned Ye Pan?"

"Never. I'd never do that."

The Red Horseman smiled wryly. "Come, they cut you twenty, thirty times. After the first hundred you'd have said anything."

"No. Not after the full thousand. I'd never say anything."

Sun Qi studied the boy closely. "Never mind what you would have done. What you did do was good enough. So good, in fact, I'll tell you what the message says." He explained each code word:

a thousand = number of men
rabbits = Sichuan force
cock = New Year (Year of the Cock)
ten times = ten days
sleeps = disbands
tiger = general of the White Lotus
growls = decides not to attack
blinks = waits
thirty times at sun = one month before deciding

The code meant therefore that a thousand fighting men in Sichuan Province would wait for ten days after the New Year before attacking, or they would disband if the Lotus leader decided not to launch a full-scale attack, or they would wait one more month before making a final decision.

"Have I helped, then?" Hong blurted out.

Sun Qi smiled coolly. "Helped what? The message was false. There was no force, no decision to be made." He waited for the astonished boy to absorb those facts. "Ye Pan quite rightly wished to see if you can be trusted, so he wrote nonsense. But you did get the message here, so you *can* be trusted." In a softer voice, Sun Qi added, "I regret you suffered so much to deliver a message that meant nothing."

Hong looked down at his sandals a long time before responding. Then he stared directly at the Red Horseman. "But it did mean something. It meant I proved myself."

There was a teapot and cups on the table. Lifting the pot, Sun Qi said, "Have some tea, Sworn Brother. You are one of us now. The next message you deliver may well shake the empire."

Chen, too, went to the Imperial City, but entered by another gate without effort after explaining that he, a Recommended Man from Sichuan, carried a letter from the Minister of Rites at Qufu to the Honorable Censor Tang Wangai. A guard was even assigned to escort the young scholar past the villas and temples and supply depots and stables and residences of officials to the right place: a drab group of brown buildings in the north called the Censorate. This department supervised the morals of officials by inspecting their accounts, and recommended promotion of some, impeachment of others. The censors, responsible only to the Emperor, acted at times as judges and policemen, and therefore, so one of the servants had explained to Chen, were heartily despised.

The offices of the Censorate were appropriately austere, and that of Censor Tang Wangai especially so: huge dark desk, chairs, benches; and no paintings, no calligraphy. The only refinement was a joss stick burning in a sand-filled porcelain bowl. The censor wasn't there, so Chen stood with hands folded behind his back and looked out through a grillwork window at a cobbled yard and the weathered gray patina of an old wall. Chen waited a long time before a short portly man in a black, high-collared robe strode briskly into the room. Chen recognized the censorial breast badge—a fierce-looking monster called the xie zhi, which according to legend distinguishes good from evil by smell.

Amenities cared for, Censor Tang Wangai offered Chen a chair, then sat behind his desk as serene-looking as a Buddha. First he read the letter; then he smiled brightly at Chen.

"You must have made a splendid impression on Wei Xi for him to entrust such an important letter to you. Have you heard the old adage: 'Ruling a country is like cooking a fish; too much handling spoils it'?"

"Taoist thinking."

"Yes indeed. Yes, you know. And of course it's wrong, isn't it. Ruling a country takes a strong hand. Did you come through the flooded country?"

"Yes, Honorable Censor. It was very difficult."

Tang Wangai smiled even more brightly. "But difficulty doesn't stop you, does it. I, too, am impressed. So you ranked fifth at Chengdu. Will you make the first group of ten? There is nothing more impressive than the Calling of Names. All the Presented Scholars waiting in the presence of the Emperor— a sight to behold! I wish you well, young man. You have done me a great service by bringing this letter. I won't forget it."

That night, when Chen returned to their room in the widow's villa, Hong hadn't come back yet. Chen was surprised and went into the courtyard to see if Two Brother might be sitting on one of the porcelain tambours to "watch the moon washing its soul," as a poet once said.

But only the cook's girl was there, staring at the moon. "Looking for your brother?" she asked boldly. When he nodded, Fufang laughed and said, "A boy like that, new in the big city, there's no telling what trouble he might get into."

"I hope you're wrong," Chen said with a forced smile.

"Do you think you'll pass?"

It was a saucy question from a girl her age, but Chen calmly answered, "I think I will."

"Why?"

"Because I know the Classics. And I know poetry."

"You think well of yourself."

"Yes," Chen told her solemnly, "I do. I've worked hard and I'm ready."

The girl glared morosely at him a moment, then suddenly smiled. "I think you are ready. How I envy you!"

No sooner had the words left her mouth than Hong walked into the courtyard, now drenched in moonlight. "Did you have a good day?" he asked Chen quickly.

"Yes. And you?"

"Yes."

The girl started to giggle, so that the brothers turned to stare at her. "You don't sound like brothers," Fufang declared. "You sound like two officials meeting for the first time. Aren't you friendly?"

The brothers turned toward each other and for a moment seemed confused.

"Each of us has his own life to live," Hong declared, but with such pomposity that both brothers chuckled, then laughed outright until Fufang joined her laughter to theirs in the moon-washed courtyard.

The examination in Beijing was actually in two parts, the first called the municipal examination and the second, following shortly thereafter, called the palace examination. The first was the harder, since it culled out most of the thousand candidates assembled, leaving about two hundred to undergo the palace test, presumably designed by the Emperor himself, although the Minister of Rites aided him and sometimes wrote the main question. The final ranking of Presented Scholars came after the palace examination.

Lao Chen had access, through the Ministry of Rites, to the imperial library, and every day he went there to reacquaint himself with the world of scholarship. So much travel had shaped his consciousness into something more than a repository of ideas and words. He was far more aware of what went on around him. But the passing scene, however turbulent, must be rigorously pushed aside. He must replace it with his highly trained memory, which could conjure up a quotation in seconds and manipulate a rhyme effortlessly. Lao Chen had learned, however, one thing from travel that he would never forget: the world outside of literature and philosophy could be passionately interesting. He had always felt that most people

lived drab lives because they didn't know Confucius and Mencius and poetic styles—things that afforded him endless pleasure and excitement. This acquired knowledge of the world
beyond words allowed him a better understanding of Three
Brother and gave him the ability—sometimes—to share in
Hong's own raw, unmediated experience of life. Even so, they
kept apart during those autumnal weeks of Chen's preparation.

While Two Brother studied, Hong often met with members
of the White Lotus. They were a diverse group: artisans, military
men, local officials, a distiller, a singer from the Beijing Opera.
This score of men in the inner circle shared the desire to rid
China of corruption. They met at various places—at Sun Qi's
quarters (Hong was armed with a permit to enter the Imperial
City), at private houses, at teahouses, even at lakeside parks.
These meetings were usually short, the conversation elliptical
and difficult for Hong to understand, although the subject was
ever the same: to bring down the dynasty. At such meetings
they spoke of their adversaries. Mentioned most often was Ni
Fenglin, the most powerful eunuch at court. Unlike many of
the eunuchs, who were first-rate administrators and true servants of the state, Ni Fenglin used the Emperor's ear to further
his own ambitions. As Director of Palace Rites, Ni Fenglin had
total control of the palace staff. He wore a jacket with a python
design authorized by the Emperor. This made him equal in
public recognition to the Grand Secretary of the Inner Court,
who also wore the python badge, along with the Mandarin
Square of two cranes above the clouds. Aside from the Emperor himself, only Ni Fenglin could ride a horse within the
Forbidden City or be carried in a sedan chair within its con-
fines. This gave him a slight edge in prestige over the Grand
Secretary.

The leaders of the White Lotus feared that Ni Fenglin could
effectively become the ruler of China. Surely that was his goal.
He had created new policies to infiltrate all levels of government, to control the Emperor's access to information, to command the various investigatory organizations: the Eastern
Esplanade, the Ming Surveillance Office, the Office of Scrutiny,

and the feared Silk Robe Guard of the Red Depot. Standing
against such an array of spies and secret agents was the Western
Esplanade, an elite army unit that favored the Censorate and
the ministries.

Acting as liaison between the White Lotus and the Western
Esplanade was Sun Qi. Although the military believed in reform
and the Lotus in overthrow of the dynasty, both cooperated to
nullify Ni Fenglin's overweening ambition and influence. To
this end, the Lotus meetings were often devoted to an analysis
of officials who were for and against change. Hong recognized
the name of Tang Wangai; that was the censor to whom Two
Brother had delivered a letter. Perhaps an alliance was being
formed between Censor Tang Wangai and the Western Esplanade, with the Lotus as mediator. At least, that was how it
seemed to Hong.

During these complex and intense discussions, he tried hard
to sort out what was important. He had good reason for learning quickly. Another boy of Hong's age attended the meetings,
too. It was soon apparent to them both that they were competing for approval, that the membership was judging their com-
parative ability to carry out future assignments—one of which
could be of great significance. This assignment was often
hinted at, but never revealed. Both boys were given messages,
verbal and written, to deliver all over Beijing, so that within a
short time Lao Hong was familiar with all six ministries—Civil
Office, Revenue, Rites, War, Punishments, and Public Works—
each of which employed spies for the Lotus. He was sent with
messages to the Grand Court of Revision, the Imperial Academy
of Medicine, the Office of Music and Dance, the Court of Imperial Entertainments. He met vice directors, secretaries, clerks.
Slipping them pieces of paper or more likely whispering a
nonsense phrase, a name, or a date, he kept them informed of
meetings and plans and the shifting fortunes of people in high
places. Hong learned how to get in and out of buildings without
attracting notice. He brought food presumably ordered for
certain offices, used passwords and permits when appropriate,
posed as a distant relative or a servant sent from home. His

age helped. People seemed to feel that someone so young could be in an important government building only for good reason. When, rarely, he was questioned, Hong always had a ready answer that proved him to be as harmless as he looked.

Apparently his rival learned quickly, too. At the meetings they exchanged surreptitious glances, sizing each other up.

Meanwhile, Chen had been discovered by his own rivals. Three of them appeared at the library one afternoon and introduced themselves to Chen, who was startled to learn that they had discovered he was a Fifth Rank from Sichuan. Sounding him out on his history, they seemed relieved by his life in a village and his lack of Beijing connections. As Chen told his brother, "They think I'm a country boy."

"So you are," Hong said.

"Nothing but a country boy."

"You're a country boy and a lot more, gege."

Although confident of his powers, Chen wanted to prove himself to these new acquaintances. So when at the library one of them invited Chen to accompany them to dinner the next evening, he readily accepted.

Hong warned him, "Gege, they know little about you except your high ranking in Sichuan, so they fear you. You can't make friends of them. Remember Shen Ding."

Armed with that advice, Chen arrived in a cautious mood at the Fengzeyuan Restaurant. The first there, though on time, he waited in the vestibule, idly studying the wall hangings and red lanterns that lit the incense-filled room. He watched other diners arrive, many of them older men with young women in tow. The old saying "A stout cat is surely a thief" helped him meet the bulky men's stares. Adjusting his winged cap to let them know who he was, Chen grinned back.

Even so, the long wait made him nervous. To calm himself down, Chen played a game. In Chinese folktales there were godlike figures called the Eight Immortals, who were eccentric, flawed, but lovable. Chen named each of the three candidates after an immortal he resembled. One candidate was overweight, so he was called Zhongli Chuan after the potbellied god who carried a fan that made the dead come to life. Another candidate was capricious and boastful, so he became Lu Dongbin, who wore a sword across his back and carried a fly whisk, symbol of being able to fly and walk on clouds. The third candidate had an imperious manner and prided himself on his elegant taste, so he was Cao Guojiu, a nobleman who held a jade table that admitted him to the imperial court. And so here they came in: overweight Zhongli, whimsical Lu, and vain Cao.

When finally they arrived and greeted him like a long-lost friend, Chen felt himself smiling at three of the Eight Immortals.

Drawing aside the silk curtain and gesturing toward the red-lantern-lit interior of the restaurant, Cao said grandly, "This is the finest Shandong food in all of Beijing. We think Shandong is the finest cuisine in all of China. What do you think?"

"I'm no judge of food," Chen said bluntly.

They entered a private room, which held a long black table, elaborately set with fine porcelain and polished silver. On the walls were paintings, on the floor thick carpets. When Chen gawked at such opulence, Lu slapped him on the back and declared gaily, "Don't worry, my friend, about the expense. Dinner is our gift to a splendid colleague from the magnificent province of Sichuan."

Zhongli and Cao tittered.

And so they sat down. During the conversation that ensued, Chen sat quietly and learned a good deal about his generous companions. They were all sons of officials, it turned out. They could have entered government service without taking the examination, but they were taking it because advancement thereafter into the higher echelons of power came only to those who did well in the exams. This they freely admitted. They had attended the best schools in Beijing: the Correct Learning College, the Literary Enlightenment, the Fostering Rectitude Academy. They talked familiarly about past examinations, though this was the first for all of them. They gossiped about rampant cheating in the past, about candidates who paid substitutes to write their tests for them, about essays put near

the top of the list without even being read because their au-
thors had influence at court. Zhongli guffawed and pointed his
chopsticks at Chen. "Look at him! He looks sick. Do they think
out in the provinces that everything is truth and poetry in the
exams? What a rude awakening he's in for!"

All the while they ate and drank heartily. The trio competed
with one another in analyzing each dish, praising one and
disparaging the next.

"These snowflake prawns are saltier than you get in the
south, but tastier."

"This duck marrow soup rivals that of any found in Shandong
itself."

"The abalone in this dish is not quite fresh."

"The red sauce for this braised fish could be a bit sweeter,
but then, not even the finest restaurants are perfect."

Ultimately they all deferred to Zhongli's judgment, as the
stout young man declared this restaurant to rank within the
First Group of the city.

Chen ate little, but nervousness in the presence of so much
expertise prompted him to drink more rice wine than ever
before. It gave him a feeling of belonging with these roistering
scholars. It loosened his tongue, so that he confessed to having
given them the names of immortals. At first they smiled indulgently, for it seemed that the country boy viewed them as
legendary and lovable. Unfortunately, with a wink, he confessed to having reasons for calling them Zhongli, Lu, and Cao,
but refused to say more, though instantly they asked for an
explanation.

Reasons for calling them Zhongli, Lu, and Cao? The table fell
silent, as the trio considered those reasons. Did the country
boy's mischievous wink mean he had chosen them for the
immortals' most glaring faults? Could he possibly mean a glut-
ton, a buffoon, and a snob? The question was in each frowning
face: Could the country boy be that insolent? Chen glanced
blearily around and grinned.

Finally, to ease the tension, Cao raised his wine cup and

solemnly declared, "Yellow gold is plentiful compared to white-haired friends."

"A graceful toast," noted Zhongli.

"Indeed, an elegant toast," said Lu, "worthy of one of my dearest friends and a most promising scholar."

The three looked at Chen for a comment. Grinning ever more broadly, he said, "You fellows must be much older than I am. I haven't got any white-haired friends yet. Mine have black hair."

The three exchanged disapproving glances. "You don't seem to understand the meaning of my toast," Cao said coldly.

"Remember," slurred Chen, "I'm a country boy from Sichuan, O Immortal."

"Since you have immortality on your mind," said Lu, "tell us what you think of God."

"I don't think of God."

"Then what do you think of life and death?"

Chen laughed and tossed off his cup of wine. "Someone once asked such a question and got an answer he didn't like."

"Tell us about that," Cao asked pompously.

Chen turned to him. "A disciple asked Confucius what he thought of immortality. Confucius replied, 'Why must you ask such a question? You don't understand life—how can you understand death?' "

After a moment of silence, Zhongli said with a shrug, "Of course, we all know that. And we all know, my friend, you are quite rude."

"Rude and truthful are sometimes the same," Chen muttered with a scowl.

"Come, come," said Lu. "Since we're quoting the Master, here's one you might take to heart: 'When you have faults, don't be afraid to abandon them.' Like drinking to excess, like pretending to a superiority you don't have, like reaching beyond your station."

His companions smiled fiercely.

"As to that last point, my friend," Cao said, leaning forward to touch Chen's sleeve, "when you stand on tiptoe, you don't stand on firm ground."

"Let me interpret for you," said Lu. "When you let your ambition go too far, when you give up restraint in order to be what you are not, you risk losing everything."

"Yes," agreed Zhongli, popping abalone into his mouth. "What you must do first is know your limitations. Ask yourself, do I know who I am and where I come from?"

"Only fools know exactly who they are," Chen quoted the Master, "and where they are."

"Insolent," hissed Lu, who might have pulled out the immortal's sword had he worn it across his back.

Getting up unsteadily, woozy from so much drink, Chen upset a jar of wine, spilling it on Cao's silken robe. There was an outcry of dismay and disgust as Chen lurched forward and staggered out of the room.

At the widow's house, Hong sat outside on the courtyard bench, shivering while he waited up for his brother. Fufang came out, carrying a quilted blanket, which she put around his shoulders. Without a word she sat down beside him.

"He's dining with scholars," Hong explained after a long silence. "I wasn't sleepy, so I just thought I'd wait up for him."

The girl nodded. "Father told me about these scholars from Beijing. It's what they do with country boys they think are good. They get them drunk, make them lose confidence. There was a boy once who could have been in the First Group, but after they got through with him, he didn't even pass the municipal."

"That won't happen to my brother."

She studied Hong. "You're good to him. He's lucky to have you."

"And I to have him."

They said nothing more, but sat and waited until Chen staggered through the gateway. Fufang sat quietly in the shadows, watching Hong hold Two Brother's head while he vomited on the flagstones.

Two days later the brothers stood in the same courtyard and gripped each other, hands to forearms. "Good luck, brother,"

Hong said. "If the village survived, everyone in it must be wishing you good luck. Even Father. And Mother, wherever she is in the sky, must be sending you good luck, and we all do, and Daiyun. Good luck, good luck, brother."

Chen left for the examination compound. In a few hours the municipals would begin.

As in the provinces, the municipal examination took place over three sessions conducted in a vast sealed compound with hundreds of tiny cubicles. In charge was the Minister of Rites, who for this purpose bore the ancient title of Zhi Gongju, Metropolitan Examination Supervisor. To aid him, the Emperor had designated a Chief Examiner, three deputies, and eighteen associates, who were served by a virtual army of clerks, guards, and attendants.

Chen and the other thousand candidates were familiar with the procedure. It was identical to that of the provincials. They entered the compound by groups, underwent a thorough search of their belongings, followed an armed escort to their assigned cells, and awaited the fastidious distribution of questions.

When Chen got his test paper, he found one question each on the Four Books—the *Analects*, the *Mencius*, the *Great Learning*, and the *Mean*—and instructions to compose a poem in the ancient ku-shih style, using a seven-character line.

For a while he sat there, staring at the test sheet. Nothing came to mind for any of the questions. Unaccountably, his thoughts returned to the mother and daughter starving to death in a village where two desperate men lurked with pitchforks. Had so much experience on the road incapacitated him for the exacting work of scholarship and composition?

He sensed in himself a growing fear, a special kind which he had often heard other candidates describe but which he had never felt until now. It was the fear of not knowing how to begin. Then the fear became panic as he started to think of his own mind in a singular new way. It was either stranger or foe. Whichever, it was alien to him and would not do his bidding. It was a sulky, irritable thing, like a spoiled child refusing to listen. Getting up and pacing in his cubicle, he stood at the doorway and looked out at the cobbled avenue and the cell opposite his. Surely the candidate over there was breezing through the first question. Chen caught himself in the same predicament described by others. He must get out of it, he must, he must—but how? "The hunted tiger leaps the wall." Easier said than done. Did he have the strength and will to fight? He no longer trusted his mind to help him. His self-confidence was gone. And everyone must be far ahead of him by now.

A Taoist once said, "When you come to a fork in the road, take it." Remembering such a saying was good: it meant do something. The longer he hesitated, the worse his panic would become. He couldn't depend on his mind; well, then, he'd depend on his hands.

Sitting down, he stared at the ink stone, the half-dozen ink sticks, each of the four brushes, and the stack of blank paper. Everything was lined up neatly on his desk. His gaze returned to the ink stone, his mother's white jade ink stone. Picking it up, he turned the pale oblong in the morning light as he had turned it months ago in Chengdu. He rubbed its hard stained surface. He studied the light and dark hues that symbolized yang and yin, man and woman, heaven and earth. Everything he'd left the village with was now lost, except this ink stone, which he had kept by securing it to his waist with a band of leather after leaving Chengdu. Picking up an ink stick, Chen began grinding it against the hard white jade. It was difficult work. His hand moved back and forth with the same rhythmic motion as a farmer operating a treadmill to irrigate a rice paddy. Now, as in Chengdu, his mind grew calmer as he made a mixture of ink. By the time he created a black substance of smooth consistency, his mind had narrowed to a zone of clarity where each thought stood out as keenly as crystal. He had only to reach within this circle and take what he wanted. He had only to pick up a word or an idea with the fox-hair brush he held and place it on the answer paper.

Hong sometimes wondered if, had he not been sworn to secrecy, he would have told his brother about the White Lotus Society. Then he always arrived at the same answer: no, of course not. He knew the Lotus well enough now to appreciate its truly subversive nature. He heard stories from Sun Qi and others of corrupt judges being murdered, of prisoners being liberated from jail, of government buildings torched to protest unfair taxation. The activities of the Lotus stood squarely against the Confucian idea of social order. That was why Hong couldn't share his knowledge of rebellion with the only person he'd trust with such a confidence.

Aside from its political goals, the Lotus advocated something else deeply opposed to Chen's philosophy. The monks who had founded the Lotus were Buddhists. Most of today's brother-hood were, too. And one of the members had even given Hong the Pure Land Sutras to read. Never a skillful reader like Chen, he nevertheless could read these teachings, which emphasized faith in Buddha Amitabha. Founded by Hui-yuan, the Pure Land Sect asked only for the recitation of Amitabha's name in exchange for rebirth in Sukhavati, a haven for tormented souls and a paradise for the faithful. Skeptical by nature, the boy wasn't sure of any of this, yet in trying to imagine Buddha Amitabha, he envisioned a smooth round face, lips parted in a faint smile, kindly eyes, a serene expression unlike any he had ever seen. Such a vision comforted him. Back home, about half the villagers were Buddhists. Wujiang's family hosted many wandering bonzes, and so Hong was familiar with their austere garb and begging bowls and quiet manner. Hong's own parents had hung a paper likeness of the Kitchen God on the wall and perfunctorily lit a joss stick now and then to the Goddess of the West, but neither Mother nor Father had shown much interest in religion. Now Hong kept a dog-eared copy of the Pure Land Sutras within reach—and hidden from his brother.

After all, the reaction of a Confucian disciple to such doctrine was predictable. Chen would argue against having faith in paradise and a merciful god because they had nothing to do with this world. He would probably add that Buddhism was too gloomy in its emphasis upon suffering and detachment. Living a good life here and now was alone worthy of investigation. Confucius never worried about extraordinary things, such as light streaking across the night sky or monstrous births or snowfall in summer or owls hooting by day or thunder sounding from a cloudless sky. Hong could hear Two Brother's words droning in his ear: authorities cited, arguments repeated endlessly. To protect the Lotus from discovery and himself from boredom, Lao Hong nurtured a determined silence. In lonely solitude, he carried the burden and excitement of a secret life.

His own activities within the Lotus had expanded. He learned to follow people without detection, to observe salient features of their behavior and report precisely what he'd seen. He dressed and could act like a beggar. He wore the special black gown of a young eunuch attending the Inner Palace School and ostentatiously commanded shopkeepers to do his bidding. He carried a shoulder pole from which baskets of salt blocks dangled—physically, his most demanding role. He sold matches and wicks, picked rags, hawked herbal soup, and pushed wheelbarrows filled with lanterns. And all the while he was watching, studying, forcing his mind to remember every detail of what he saw. In the process the kaleidoscope of Beijing life was revealed to him. During his assignments within the city, Hong saw fierce bronze lions with gaping jaws, plum doors, moon gates, stone chips laid in a flying crane pattern to form a path. He visited the Pavilion for Worshipping Stones and the Pavilion of Drenched Blossoms and the Hall of Lapping Waves. He heard the soft tinkling of pagoda bells, then the next day stood outside old warehouses full of animal fur and straw, where for a copper coin the neighborhood homeless could burrow in like moles to keep warm.

Then one day he went to meet Sun Qi in a park north of

the Forbidden City. Most of the leaves had fallen, so the tree branches had a wild, angular look. When Hong saw the Red Horseman rise from a bench, someone else rose with him.

It was Hong's rival, who gave him a broad smile that looked ominously triumphant.

In the brusque way that the Lotus had of conducting business, Sun Qi got right to the point. One of them was being assigned to Harbin and one would remain here in Beijing.

Harbin. The very name gave Hong the shivers. Winter in Harbin lasted more than half the year. For something to do, people cut huge blocks of ice from the frozen rivers and constructed little villages out of them that melted only in late spring. From the look of his rival's face, Hong knew who was going to the city of ice.

"You," Sun Qi said, jabbing a finger at Hong's chest, "come back here at this same time the day after tomorrow. Goodbye."

When Hong hesitated, the officer growled, "Goodbye."

Glancing at his rival, Hong saw a grimly turned-down mouth. He went all the way home before feeling sure of the decision: that he would stay in Beijing and his rival freeze in Harbin.

Two days later, back at the park, he was not so sure that he had the better of it. But he soon learned that at least they were giving him an important if dangerous assignment. Leading the way along the icy bank of a small lake, Sun Qi explained it quickly.

Having received political support from officials both in and out of the capital, Censor-in-Chief-of-the-Left Tang Wangai had finally agreed to cooperate with the Lotus and the Western Esplanade in their scheme to assassinate the hated Director of Palace Rites, Ni Fenglin. One duty of a chief censor was to keep track of the daily whereabouts of high officials, and in turn they were obligated to supply him with itineraries and schedules. Tang Wangai was therefore the only man in Beijing who could foretell the movements of someone as wily as Ni Fenglin. The problem, of course, was Ni Fenglin's recent awareness of his own vulnerability. If anything happened to him, Ni Fenglin publicly maintained, it would be because the censor always knew where he was. In consequence, during the last few weeks Ni Fenglin had assigned operatives from the Silk Robe Guard of the Red Depot to a constant surveillance of Tang Wangai. Where the censor went, there went a silent band of spies in a variety of disguises. At the present time it was nearly impossible to contact him without their knowing, and from their brutal reputation they wouldn't hesitate to kidnap anyone who seemed in league with the censor. Kidnapping would be only the first step. Torture and death would inevitably follow.

"Compared to the Silk Robes," Sun Qi said grimly, "your pirates are surely schoolboys when it comes to torture."

"What is my assignment?"

"To approach the censor just long enough and close enough for him to say a few words. He'll give you a time and place."

"Where Ni Fenglin will be?"

The Red Horseman nodded.

"For your attack?"

The Red Horseman nodded again.

"How will you attack? A dozen men? Or a few? Or just one? With a sword? A knife? How?"

"That's none of your concern," Sun Qi said curtly. "You'll have only seconds with the censor. The meeting must seem accidental—perhaps two people bumping into each other. It must not arouse suspicion among the Silk Robes lurking around! But there's always the chance of it." He waited for Hong to respond.

"Yes," Hong said thoughtfully, "the Silk Robes could get suspicious."

"What then, Lao Hong? What could happen then?"

"They might catch me."

From his pocket Sun Qi took what looked like a large red berry. "If you're certain of being caught, put this in your mouth. Bite hard, chew, swallow as fast as you can. It's been filled with poison."

"Would I die quickly?"

"Yes, luckily for you."

They were both silent awhile. "Where will I meet the censor?" Hong asked.

"At the Ming tombs. There are details to work out. Perhaps you can help with them. Walk faster," commanded Sun Qi, who was increasing his pace around the ice-rimmed edge of the lake.

Because of his hesitant beginning, Lao Chen did not finish his first session ahead of time, but handed in his answering booklet late on the third day along with most of the other candidates. In line not far behind him was Zhongli, who grinned fiercely and called out, "Will you celebrate your brilliant scholarship by getting drunk tonight?"

Chen turned away and never looked back.

That evening, when he arrived at the widow's house, his brother was already there, sitting by a window, face turned to a flurry of snowflakes.

"What are you dreaming about?" Chen asked.

"Oh, crickets," Hong said with a wan little smile.

"Were you kite-flying again?"

"Yes." To account for his time, Hong had told Two Brother that he flew kites every day with some Beijing boys his age.

Chen shook his head. "I'll never understand how flying kites can keep you interested. Raising crickets, yes, and fighting them. But putting a few feet of silk up in the air and watching the wind blow it around? I'll never understand."

"No, I suppose you won't!" Hong said it so gruffly that Chen stared hard at him, wondering what had made him angry.

The next day Chen returned to the compound for the second session. There were five questions on the Five Classics, all of them requiring a formidable memory and keen scholarship. Having overcome his fear during the first session, Chen had no trouble in the second. He finished early on the third morning. His only surprise during all that time was to learn that two other candidates had finished ahead of him.

For the last session, he was given five essays to write on various topics: poetic forms of the Tang period; Confucius' relationship with his disciples; the chief philosophical flaw of Taoism; the meaning of "good" in the social order; and the place of filial piety in government.

Here he faced a new obstacle.

Never before had he worried about the quality of a question. Any question would do, as long as it gave his mind some kind of a challenge. It was the exercise of his powers that interested him; the question hardly mattered except for providing a path into his thoughts and memory. But, regarding these topics, Lao Chen was not happy. He disliked their detachment from his life, their lack of relevance to the long, tumultuous trek he had just made across the vast land of the Middle Kingdom.

Letting his mind wander freely through the experiences of the last months, Chen knew what he wanted to write about: the farmer and the temple society that had denied him a chance to work his land and save his family. The temple society should have put the farmer's need to save his family first and its need to build a new temple second. That's what Master Kung would have said. In this way Chen's own experience might enrich an essay. Or he could write about Shen Ding, who, after struggling so many years to succeed, finally placed first in the provincial. That was not true, of course, but think of the inspirational tale it would make! Again he recalled the flooded country and the women starving and the men lunging around with pitchforks. Could he make that, too, the subject of his essay?

Musing, he placed his elbows on the desk and for a time forgot about the examination. As if struggling from a demanding sleep, Chen blinked his eyes and stretched his long thin arms. He began mixing ink. It was time to work on the essays assigned.

On the third day of the final session he finished early again. This time he was not surprised to learn that five others had handed in their papers ahead of him. The competition was very great, he acknowledged. But when he walked away, the uneasy feeling that accompanied Chen from the compound was caused not by any sense of failure or apprehension but by the essays he had written. They said nothing of the world as he had come to know it.

After leaving the compound, he came to a broad avenue where a bridal procession was passing. Hidden behind gossamer curtains, the bride rode in a red sedan chair, carried by six stout men. Her feet would never touch the ground between her parents' home and her bridegroom's house, signifying the irrevocable change in her life. Chen watched until the bride and her family had vanished around a corner of the avenue. Back in the village they did exactly the same thing for a wedding, even though the distance between houses was sometimes no more than a hundred paces. Chen stopped and bought a steamed bun filled with sweet bean paste. Idly eating, scarcely aware of what he chewed, he stared down the street where the bridal chair had gone.

While Two Brother was meandering homeward from the final day of the municipals, Three Brother was bumping along in a broad-wheeled Beijing cart beyond the outskirts of the city. The driver, who held the reins of a shaggy pony, turned to look at his young passenger. "The tombs are there," he said, "over that hill."

Hong signaled him to stop. Getting down, he reached for the coins kept under his sandal.

"No," the driver said. "This is free, illustrious novice. I want to gain merit."

Hong nodded and twirled the wooden prayer wheel he carried. Stuffed inside each of a dozen slits in the wheel was a tiny paper with the name of Buddha Amitabha written on it. By spinning the wheel, the deity's name was invoked many times. "Bless you in the name of Buddha Amitabha," Hong said in a singsong voice to the driver and twirled the wheel again.

This morning he'd gone to a barber, who shaved his head

clean. Through the Lotus he had obtained this prayer wheel and beads and a saffron robe to go over his trousers and jacket. Sun Qi had inspected him carefully.

"You were right," he finally acknowledged. "This is the best possible disguise you could use. You seem like the perfect novice, Lao Hong. I can see you five years from now—a bonze with his begging bowl. And twenty years from now, the abbot of a monastery!" Sun Qi chuckled. "You're a clever boy. This may get you through."

As he walked over the crest of a dun-colored hill and looked down, Hong saw the Great Red Gate, which stood at the entrance to the necropolis of the Ming dynasty. The massive structure contained three arches and doors, the central one used only for bringing in dead emperors. No horses were allowed inside. Visitors coming to worship at the tombs went on foot. Many wore saffron robes, as did Hong. Others wore the mortarboard hats of officials or the leather jackets and swords of military officers. Descending the hill, the shaven-headed boy passed some leafless fruit trees and a grove of pines before coming to the Great Red Gate. He took a deep breath there, passed beneath the high arch to the left, and joined a thin but steady stream of pilgrims on their way along the Emperor's Road to the Ming tombs. Low-bellied clouds and a biting wind filled the afternoon. A thirty-foot stele stood on the back of a granite tortoise beside the avenue; it commemorated the reigns of emperors buried here. Flanking the snow-flecked avenue were huge stone guardians: lions, camels, elephants, rams, unicorns, and horses. Dry little gusts of snow swirled wildly around the massive stone figures. Farther on stood matching pairs of granite horses, generals, priests, and astrologers. They watched over the eternal sleep of a dozen Rulers of Men.

Hong was heading for the tomb of one such ruler—Yung Lo, third Emperor of the dynasty, who had died in 1424 after a reign of twenty years. The shaven-headed novice glanced from side to side, warily searching for pilgrims who seemed more interested in other pilgrims than in the Sacred Way. Fear made him see an agent of the Silk Robe almost everywhere he looked, so he gave up trying and concentrated on muttering "Buddha Amitabha" until pink and ocher roofs appeared over the forested valley ahead. The avenue of guardians ended at a portico that led into a copse of evergreens; beyond it and another three-arched gate lay a courtyard and a tile roof of imperial yellow. He had reached the Hall of Eminent Favors, where surely his own fate and perhaps that of his country would be determined.

Taking out a rosary with trembling fingers, Hong held it in one hand and the prayer wheel in the other. His heart beat faster as his lips chanted again and again the divine name of Buddha Amitabha. Passing a row of giant pine trees, he came to a triple terrace of white marble. At least a score of people were gathered at the third terrace around huge porcelain stoves used for burning animal offerings. The air smelled pungently of burnt fur and flesh. From behind the stoves a goat was bleating plaintively, awaiting its turn with the knife, as Hong climbed the steps and stood to one side of the stoves. Officials ranged around the great ovens, their hands steepled in worshipful gestures. Hong searched among their breast badges for a fierce-looking monster—the xie zhi design that would identify the wearer as Censor Tang Wangai.

And there he was: a short, heavyset man piously watching the smoke of sacrifice drift into the gray air.

The goat screamed, and its wriggling body was brought around the far stove, blood pouring from its slit throat. At this moment the censor looked quickly around. Hong caught his glance. It was enough to assure Hong that the censor knew exactly who he was.

Sacrifices made, the official party continued to perform its monthly observance at the tomb. Entering the immense hall (the novice following at a discreet distance), they walked to the wooden altar on which a funeral table lay. Here they all respectfully bowed their heads and observed a long silence, after which the tightly knit group broke apart. They walked off in twos and threes. Relieved at ending such a tense ritual, they discussed the weather, paintings they had recently bought, the rising price of good wine.

Now, wondered the boy—should it be now?

He followed Censor Tang Wangai and two companions from the hall into another courtyard. They stood in front of a Tang stele, regarding the quality of its carving and its message.

Now? Should it be now?

Glancing around, Hong saw at least a dozen other people in the courtyard. Were any of them Silk Robes?

It was now. He got the signal from Censor Tang, who turned slightly as if looking for something. The censor looked for me, Hong thought, even as his legs carried him toward the stele. The censor was standing to the left, a couple of feet separating him from his companions, as he appeared to be studying the right edge of the upright slab. Hong came forward, slowly, with great effort controlling the speed of his approach. Then he was there, nearly close enough to the stout little man to reach out and touch the censorial badge on his robe.

Without turning from the stone pillar, which he seemed to be studying assiduously, Censor Tang whispered, "Temple of Heaven second day next month at noon."

Hong moved instantly, if slowly, around the tall slab, still muttering "Buddha Ambitabha" under his breath. Then he turned and walked away, leaving the censor and companions to discuss the calligraphy carved on this stele eight hundred years ago.

Hong could scarcely breathe from excitement, fear, and . . . elation. All had gone well! He had moved into and out of the censor's presence like a wisp of smoke. Not even the companions could have overheard the whispered message. Why had Sun Qi and the others worried? Nothing could have been easier.

Smiling to himself, forgetting to twirl the wheel, Hong increased his pace and came to the Square Tower. Very tall, it faced the huge mound, covered by brick, which held the bodies of the Emperor and Empress. Somewhere beneath the

Square Tower lay the entrance to the tumulus, but its exact location was a closely guarded secret. Their burial chamber had been built of stone blocks carried on carts from Henan Province by sixteen hundred mules. Bricks lining the floor had come over the Grand Canal from Shandong. Now the royal corpses, rich furnishings, and gold utensils, along with toy servants made of wood, lay under tons of earth, hidden behind granite doors at the end of a concealed tunnel.

Hong was thinking of them down there, two people forever encased in thick stone and cold earth and unbroken silence, when he heard something behind him.

Turning, he faced three men wearing ordinary padded jackets and black trousers. Hong realized he was standing in a far corner of the tower, in shadow, the beads motionless in one hand and the prayer wheel motionless in the other.

"Who are you, boy?" one of the men asked gruffly.

"As you can see." To emphasize his point, Hong twirled the prayer wheel.

"Why would a young fellow like you become a monk so soon?" asked another with a smile. "They say as long as you forswear the world before dying, you'll gain merit."

"I put my trust in Buddha Amitabha." For emphasis he muttered the name soundlessly, quickly, repeatedly.

"What did he say to you?" asked the third.

Twirling the wheel, Hong said, "Buddha Amitabha, Buddha Amitabha. What do you mean? Who said what to me?"

"At the stele, the fat little man said something to you."

"Buddha Amitabha, no, he did not. Not to me. What little fat man? Buddha Amitabha, Buddha Amitabha."

One of the men turned away, but the other two kept studying the shaven-headed boy. One of them said, "Who founded the Pure Land?"

"Hui-yuan. He tells us if we try hard enough, we'll see Buddha Amitabha in visions."

"Come on," said the one who had reached the tower's entrance. "Let's go," he urged.

One of the other two shrugged and left, too. But the third stood there, regarding Hong with a doubtful look. "You don't have a Beijing accent. Where do you come from?"

"From God." Hong twirled the wheel rapidly. "We all do. We are put here to learn how to avoid suffering."

"What if I told you this: if you don't tell the truth, you'll have more suffering than you or any of you Buddhists ever dreamed possible."

"Buddha Amitabha will help me then."

This simple declaration had an effect on the skeptical agent, who, after sighing, turned and joined his companions.

Hong remained in the Square Tower a while longer, fearful of going outside and finding them awaiting him in the courtyard. But he couldn't stay here forever, so he took a deep breath and walked out. It was snowing lightly. A brisk wind was blowing the flakes almost horizontal to the cobblestones, sweeping them away like an invisible broom.

The Silk Robes were gone.

Now he twirled his wheel with enthusiasm. Had the name on his lips and the endless prayers protected him after all?

When finally he got home, having first discarded his religious paraphernalia, it was long past sunset. Chen leaped up from a chair in their room, calling out in astonishment, "What happened to your hair?"

"I lost a bet and shaved it off."

"I was worried about you," Chen said in exasperation. "So that's where you've been—flying kites!"

"And fighting them. That's the cause of this," he said, passing both hands over his bald head. "I lost. But that's hardly important. Tell me about the exam."

Two Brother described the questions.

"Overall," Hong said, "how do you think you did?"

Chen shrugged. "As usual."

"Then that's good news." Hong stared at his brother's frowning face. "So why do you seem troubled?"

"Do I look troubled?" Chen thought for a moment before

replying. "Well, I do feel troubled. I wanted to write an essay on a subject that they didn't give me."

Hong absorbed that remark slowly. "I'm not sure I understand. Does it matter what you want to write about?"

"No, of course not."

"Well, then, why . . ."

Chen sat down and stared gloomily at his feet. "I honestly don't know. But I do know I feel dissatisfied."

"I don't. From what you tell me, you wrote as usual and that means you wrote well."

A week later, after the President of the Board of Rites had verified the red-ink copies of the exam papers against the black-ink originals, the list of passing candidates was posted on a placard set up on a flower-bedecked platform erected in front of the Board of Rites in the Imperial City.

The name of the sixth-ranked man came first, making him "Head of the List."

Accompanying his brother, Hong shoved through the crowd and got them close enough for the taller Chen to study the list. "I'm not there," Chen said.

"This happened before," Hong told him reassuringly. "You wrote well."

Most of the unlisted candidates did not stay around for the eventual posting of the top five. But the brothers did. And when the President of the Board of Rites himself came with the List of Five, they pressed forward confidently.

Hong's prediction proved true: his brother had written well, indeed, wonderfully. The first-ranked man, called the First Metropolitan Graduate, was called Hui-yüan.

The second-ranked man was called Ya-kui, and beside this honorific was the name Lao Chen.

YA-KUI   LAO CHEN

Even Hong found it hard to believe. Later, when they were alone, he gripped his brother's arm and unloaded advice. "Listen to me," he said like someone fifty years older. "There's still the palace exam to go. You realize, don't you, it determines the final ranking."

"Yes," Chen said with a smile, "I realize that."

"So you can't rest yet, you can't let down your guard. With just a little extra effort, gege"—Hong's eyes widened as he made a wild conjecture—"you might even become Hui-yüan!"

Instead of the usual rain or snow at this time of year, dense clouds of reddish-yellow dust, carried by shrill winds from Central Asia, blew ceaselessly into the capital of Beijing. A powdery red substance whirled upward on fierce drafts of air and surged high overhead, then drifted down lightly to cover everything in sight. The air was so thick with it that the sun assumed the softly wavering glow of an ember. The light of midday possessed an eerie yellowish color, as if dredged up from river bottoms. The brothers saw Beijing through a veil of Gobi topsoil. Everyone wore a scarf over his face, covering it entirely save for bloodshot, watery eyes. Dust sifted into every crevice. It caused a gritty sensation in the throat that led to a hacking cough. The saffron-colored dust settled into food, bedding, and skin creases and left a shimmering film on tree trunks and the flanks of horses. It seemed as permeable as water, more insistent and remorseless than a flood spreading across a countryside. The appalled brothers hated it, and competed with each other in praising the weather and scenery of home.

If the yellow dust made them restless, so did the empty hours of waiting for the palace examination to begin. Chen had the best of it. Every day he went to the library, and though it was hard to study for the final test—only one general essay— nothing suited him better than quiet hours with books. The trio of immortals wasn't there. The gluttonous Zhongli had failed; according to the posted list, capricious Lu ranked forty-

seventh, and the imperious Cao eighty-fifth out of 122 municipal graduates.

Hong had little to do but wait for the second day of next month at noon. Every morning he went to a teahouse where Sun Qi would leave messages for him. None came. Aside from that, he took long walks through the city or lounged around the widow's mansion. Fufang made fun of his shaven head. "You look just like a novice," she told him and clapped her hand over her mouth to stop the laughter.

On his walks, when the yellow dust wasn't blowing too hard, Hong absorbed the sights and sounds of Beijing. He studied the disjointed gait of camels loaded with brick tea bound for Mongolia; gaunt willows in wintry parks; markets selling eggs pickled in lime and cakes in the shape of lotus leaves; cluttered shops displaying whirligigs, brassware, canvas shoes.

Once on a stroll he observed a terrible thing: public punishment, ordered by the Emperor, carried out in front of the Meridian Gate. An official was stripped of his robes and beaten with what they called whipping clubs—hard wood in rough sectional joints that snapped against the flesh. The official survived fifty strokes, but he would surely carry permanent scars on his thighs and hips. Completing the cruel sentence, two floggers then hoisted him on a canvas sheet and dumped him on the frozen ground outside the Imperial City. The official's family could take him home then. But any others, Hong learned, who looked after such a man and comforted him had their names taken by agents of the Red Depot and would later be summoned for questioning. When a man in the crowd began staring at him, Hong parted from it and hurried away.

He thought of what he had done at the Ming tombs. He had condemned a man to death on the second day of next month at noon. There was a saying he knew: "All that's done well is done without conscious thought." And another one: "A man should know without knowing how he knows." These Taoist ideas stood against the Confucian belief in reason, but they made a great deal of sense to Hong. Had he speculated on the chance of something going wrong and the consequence of failure, he would have approached the Ming tombs too weighed down by doubt and worry to carry out his assignment. But he had gone forward, following each moment to its conclusion, going on to the next, one two three one two three one two three. It was true: a man should know without knowing how he knows.

When Chen left for the palace examination, it was not at dawn but long after sunrise—this leisurely way of conducting the test was proof, if it were needed, that the final session would be different from the rest. He waved gaily to Three Brother and set out with his knapsack.

Hong sat on the stone bench in the courtyard. The yellow dust had finally disappeared, leaving the winter sky cloudless. Fufang came along and sat beside him.

"Does your brother go to the Forbidden City?" the girl asked.

"Yes, for the final test."

"You have a smart brother. But me"—Fufang grimaced—"I wouldn't want to go there."

"Why not?" Hong asked with interest. "I thought going to the Forbidden City was next to entering heaven."

"Men might think so, but not women." She offered him a sweet cake, which he took and began munching. Every year, Fufang explained, new girls were selected for the Emperor. They were nominated by the precincts, each having a quota to fill. Girls selected went through many rounds of screening and testing before they passed through the Meridian Gate and entered the Forbidden City. Once in, they remained there for the rest of their lives. "Yes, it's true," Fufang claimed. "If a girl doesn't catch the Emperor's eye, she might never even speak to him, much less share his bed. And so she'll never know a man in her whole lifetime."

Hong was shocked. Girls in his village never talked so openly about such matters unless the subject was limited to the mating practices of farm animals.

Fufang seemed oblivious of his unease. She explained that in their old age these palace women served as chambermaids

and broom sweepers. When they died, their remains were
cremated and buried in unmarked graves so their families
wouldn't be embarrassed because they had died virgins.

"I'm eligible for inspection," Fufang declared, tossing her
head. "Luckily the gods didn't bless me with too much beauty."

Hong glanced shyly at her. To his way of thinking, Fufang
was a pretty girl.

"Emperors are strange," she went on. "A girl didn't know
the song a Tang emperor wanted sung, so he sentenced her
to death. On the spot."

"Was it carried out?"

"In a way. From her hat they cut off a tassel as if it were her
head." Fufang giggled at the expression on Hong's face. "You
believe anything. You may have traveled, but you're still a
country boy."

"I'm not ashamed of it."

Fufang walked off a few paces, then turned. "If your brother
does well in the test, you can be sure a lot of people won't like
it. They don't want boys from the provinces coming here and
showing up the scholars of Beijing."

"Go away, go away," Hong told her angrily.

Meanwhile, Chen had arrived at the entrance to the Forbidden City. After a credentials check, he passed through the
massive Meridian Gate and entered the symbolic heart of his
country, along with other candidates arriving for the final test.

They were among the lucky few ever granted a look at this
famous half-mile square enclosed by crimson walls. Ahead,
across a long flat courtyard, rose the first of three audience
halls. Like the other two, the Hall of Supreme Harmony was
raised high above ground level on a tiered marble terrace. The
red-colored rectangular building was surrounded by carved
balustrades and supported by wooden columns.

Chen looked up at the tent-shaped roof, where ceramic
beasts crouched along the eaves. Their warm gold color was
enriched by sunlight and they seemed to be in buttery motion
against the blue sky. They were led by a little man riding a
rooster above brackets painted a glittering blue-green. Chen

stared as if he had never seen a roof before. The upswept corners made this one seem to float; yet the broad sides seemed to be crushed by the weight of their ceramic tiles. Studying the ornate roof, Chen let go of it visually one part at a time.

Someone touched his sleeve. It was the Immortal Lu Dongbin, who should be wearing a sword across his back and carrying a fly whisk so he could walk on clouds.

"As you go farther back," Lu explained, "the buildings get smaller. That's where Myriad Years and his palace women live. Out here it's all public display. What do you think of it?"

Chen shook his head as if words failed him in the presence of such magnificence.

"That evening at the Fengzeyuan Restaurant—we meant nothing wrong," Lu declared. "Even so, I wish to apologize for my companions and myself."

"That is most generous," Chen said guardedly.

"I also wish to congratulate you on being Ya-kui. A most singular honor."

"Thank you."

"It's more than likely you'll keep that ranking. The palace rarely changes anything. It's more a formality than a test. So," Lu concluded with a smile, "we can look forward to a long future together. I hope we'll be friends. Who knows? Perhaps we'll be colleagues in government service."

"Yes, thank you," Chen said coolly. He waited until Lu joined a few other candidates, then walked on by himself, past the Hall of Middle Harmony. The last of the three halls was where the palace examinations were held—the Hall of Protecting Harmony. Candidates were already climbing the marble steps, so Chen took his place in line. Inside, at long benches lit by rows of candles, the candidates sat with their writing materials. Assistants walked around, but without their usual suspicious glances. There would be no cribbing here, no cheating. Only one essay was required. After so many long and complicated tests, this seemed more like a celebration than an exam, so many candidates lounged around at ease, talking and laughing.

After Chen had found his assigned place, he sat down and laid out his ink stone, ink sticks, and brushes. Looking up, he saw the imperious Cao glaring at him from across the hall. But when their eyes met, the noble immortal lowered his.

Waiting for the test to begin, Chen decided to enjoy the pleasures of a distant visitor. He gazed at standing vases and rich tapestries and the high ceiling painted with hundreds of flying cranes. The great hall seemed cramped and stuffy; he preferred the soaring roofs outside. He would not like spending time here; his dislike of the Forbidden City surprised him.

After a roll of drumbeats and a loud rapid peal from bronze horns, the Ruler of Men, Myriad Years, Emperor of the Middle Kingdom, appeared from behind a large wooden screen. He wore tight sleeves and a sword almost too heavy to lift. An instant hush descended over the hall; then everyone knelt and kowtowed three times. Rising when everyone else did, Chen stared appraisingly at the only male allowed to sleep within the palace grounds. Battalions of attendants, wearing fur-lined robes with ear covers, hovered around the throne until Myriad Years was seated comfortably, one foot on a satin-covered stool, one hand thrust between his ample belly and jeweled belt. Finally he waved a pudgy ring-bedecked hand.

The Minister of Rites came forward with a gilt-edged scroll and with a deep kowtow presented it to the Emperor. In a high, wavering voice, Myriad Years began to read from it.

"For the municipal examination you wrote an essay on the question: What does 'good' mean in the social order? For your final essay write on the following question: What does 'good' mean to a prince who has the mandate of heaven?"

Handing the scroll back to the Minister of Rites, the Emperor settled against the throne and accepted a golden cup of piping-hot tea.

The minister signaled for the candidates to begin. Instantly the great hall was filled with the sound of ink sticks being rubbed against stone. It was like ocean waves breaking against the shore. Chen glanced around. Already some of the candidates were bent over, their brushes moving.

For a moment he couldn't look down at his paper.

Appalled, he felt the terrible images rushing in.

He was back in flood country, in the village where men carried pitchforks and a woman sat with her dying daughter.

Had he and Three Brother used good judgment then? What should they have done? Dragged the mother away? Killed the men who might otherwise kill the women?

When he dipped his brush into the thick black ink and held it above the answer sheet, he was already composing the first sentence of his essay: "Good is sometimes obscure and difficult to comprehend. To illustrate this truth, I will describe what happened to me and my brother on our way to Beijing." He wrote rapidly for some minutes.

Chen had hoped to feel good for having talked of his own experience. Staring down, however, he felt the characters written on the sheet were nearly meaningless. They might be chicken scratchings in mud or shadows in a forest glade. No thread of meaning bound them to him. They no longer belonged to him, no longer issued from his mind through his fingers onto paper. But why? Why? Confusion, guilt, sympathy had urged him to confess his feelings about that day, yet he was more dissatisfied than ever. Why?

He needn't search long for the reason: his Master would not approve of experience unattached to greater meaning. It was not enough to feel. The Confucian way was to bind one thing to another and to another and to another until everything came together in harmony.

Chen tore up the paper, the sound causing nearby candidates to snap their heads around and scowl.

He began again with the mandate of heaven. The ruler held a celestial license to rule as long as he ruled well, but if, through indifference or corruption, he failed to honor the covenant, someone would come along and overthrow him in the name of the people. In this sense all rebellions that succeeded were automatically justified. Chen argued against such a conclusion. He began by describing the good man of Confucian doctrine: honest, loyal, committed to the common welfare, possessed of a generous nature and respect for tradition. The good man operated from a belief in the reciprocity of behavior: Do to others as you would have them do to you. By this reasoning, a virtuous prince instilled virtue in his people. But the prince was also human and therefore flawed; not all of his decisions could be perfect or even good. (Here the scholar paused and saw himself in the village, unsure of what to do.) To the degree, however, that the prince strove for perfection, he was good and therefore a fit ruler. Confucius would say that such a prince was saved by his humanity. Some commentators insisted that the failures of a prince were the cause of disasters, flood, and famine. But this would be true, Chen argued, only if the ruler had consciously done wrong. Design and intention were everything when "good" was the issue. If no effort had been made to do wrong, wrong was not done to nature, nor was celestial harmony disturbed. Natural disasters were simply natural and not the consequence of a ruler's failings. "We are all human," Chen wrote in his conclusion, "from the highest to the lowest. This common bond can save both ruler and ruled and protect us all from celestial disharmony."

Looking at his work, Chen retreated from it far enough to judge its strength and weakness. A critic might argue that he had put too much stress on the "naturalness" of nature. That would take away from mankind's importance in the scheme of things. On the other hand, his emphasis on the ruler's imperfections, though bold, was not inconsistent with Confucian thought. He sat back and placed both hands on the bench, staring above the heads of other candidates bent over their work. Sweating from such an intense effort, Chen believed he had just written his finest essay. Without mentioning the flooded country or referring to himself, he had used his own experience to speak of a truth he had learned on the journey: flaws do not necessarily ruin a man, but persistence saves him.

Confucius would have approved.

———

Meanwhile, Hong had left the house and wandered into a downtown market, where shop owners sold caged birds and crickets. Regarding the insects with a critical eye, Hong was not impressed by them. They weren't as quick in their movements as his own back home. Someone came alongside him and muttered, "Not very impressive."

Hong stared at the sallow-faced little man, who responded to this openly inquiring look with a smile. "Where I come from," the man said in defense of his comment, "crickets are smaller, faster, stronger, and fiercer."

"Where is that, sir?" Hong asked.

The man held a garlic bulb. He peeled the husk from a clove and popped it into his mouth. "The province of Sichuan."

Hong cried out in surprise, exclaiming that he, too, was from there. With pride in a spectacular act of filial piety, the man told Hong that he'd come all this way to visit his aging parents. He lived in a village near Chengdu.

"Do you know the area west of Chengdu?" Hong asked.

"Of course."

"They had a plague of locusts there. Do you know about it?"

"I certainly do," the man acknowledged. "Very bad in some places. Terrible." He was peeling another clove of garlic. "The winds were so strong they scattered the locusts in strange ways. By that I mean one village was covered by insects, the next never saw any at all. In some places there was nothing to eat. An hour's walk away and people had stores enough to feed their starving neighbors. The gods had their fun all right." Tossing another clove into his mouth, he related harrowing stories of death from starvation, of people killing and eating family members, of whole villages wiped out. After a glance at the boy, he stopped talking. "You look sick," he told Hong. Whistling low, he added, "Forgive me. I talked too much about it."

"I want to hear."

"You don't know about your own village, is that it?"

Hong looked away, his lips trembling.

"Well, come, then. Let's sit and talk carefully. I need to know the exact location. Don't look so doubtful! Talk to me, tell me where your village is." After close questioning of Hong, the man said, "I know your village. It survived."

Hong shook his head. "Thank you, but you don't know it. The only way of knowing is to go there."

"I tell you I know it and I've been there, not many months ago. You have two Buddhist temples, one old and crumbling, the other new."

"Yes, go on," Hong said hopefully.

"A man named Tang has a stable there. I know it. I bought a horse from him."

"Old Tang's stable? Yes!"

Munching garlic, the man stared thoughtfully into the distance. "I was there maybe four months ago. I know that part. I went through your village and stopped to burn a joss stick at the temple. The priest was sleeping in the corner." He smiled. "A young fat man, as fat as a Buddha."

"Yes! That's the priest."

"Well, I know your village, and as I wish to live with myself, I'm not lying. Your people survived. Now then . . ." He placed one finger on his lips thoughtfully. "Another place southwest of there, it has a stream going straight across the main street, near the threshing square . . ."

"Yes, that village. I know the one you mean."

"Gone. Nothing but vultures sitting on the rooftops. Looters went through there, so the houses were cleaned out like a kitchen on New Year's Day." He shook his head. "There weren't even corpses. You see, when the vultures were done, the dogs cracked the bones and ate them." The man peeled another clove. Chewing a few times, he belched and said, "But your village survived. I know your village. Young fellow, I—" But the boy was already rushing away. The man chewed and watched and chewed some more. "I know that village," he mumbled under his breath. "It survived."

It took far less time for the palace exam to be posted than for any of the others.

Nailed to the Meridian Gate were the rankings. In the jostling crowd Hong yelled out and pointed.

HUI-YÜAN   LAO CHEN

People stared at the brothers as they walked arm in arm away from the Meridian Gate. "First Graduate," Hong announced joyously and bent over in an ostentatious bow. "I told you if you only tried . . . So you listened to me at last. All this time you resisted—but at last you listened. Look at the result!" After they walked in silence awhile, Hong stopped in his tracks and turned frowning to his brother. "I worried this time."

"Why?"

"Because of your talk about choosing your own subject. I was afraid you would write about something foolish."

"How could you think such a thing?" Chen asked with a laugh.

"Because when I'm sure of you, you do something else." He shook his head as if angry. "You're more of a crazy Taoist than you admit. Well, so am I. You passed and you passed first in all the land and you brought honor to Mother's memory, and so I'm happy if you are."

"I'm happy. I wrote an essay my Master would approve."

"Good. Let's go eat."

Presented Scholars received their Jin-shi degrees at a banquet in the Hall of Supreme Harmony. Benches had been cleared away and replaced by round mahogany tables. Graduates clustered to one side of a raised dais that dominated the hall. Civil service officials arrived, wearing fur-lined satin robes—red for Grade Four and up, blue for lower grades. Their ceremonial belts, studded with horn and jade and silver, glinted in the golden light cast by rows of chandeliers. The officials shuffled to and fro in blue slippers with white cotton soles, bowing to one another and exchanging pleasantries and discussing in low shocked tones the latest news.

That afternoon the Director of Palace Rites, Ni Fenglin, had been found beside a stream near the Temple of Heaven. He had been strangled with a black silk cord that was still around his neck. The python design worn on his jacket, authorized by the Emperor, had been ripped off. His five bodyguards all had their throats slit. Who was to blame for such a well-planned assassination? Theories blew through the hall like yellow dust.

The gossip subsided only with the grand entrance of the Emperor, who was accompanied by a glittering entourage. Each Presented Scholar was called forward by name, climbed the steps to the dais, and after a kowtow received his degree.

Lao Chen came last. Unlike the other graduates, who took their scrolls from the Minister of Rites, he got his directly from the Emperor, who muttered, "I read your essay. You're much younger than you write. Thank you for recognizing my flaws." The jowly face remained impassive, so Chen wasn't sure at first that he'd actually heard such a droll remark from Myriad Years, Ruler of the Middle Kingdom. To the beating of fans against palms in applause, Lao Chen of Sichuan, First Graduate, descended the dais and returned to his seat at the table of honor.

Then came the banquet. Chen wished for Hong to be there. It was the sort of thing that Three Brother would have liked. There were three waiters for every diner. Chen had only to take a sip of wine and a hand came out of nowhere with a golden flagon, pouring back an amount equal to what he'd drunk. Three Brother would have gorged himself on the forest of delicacies arrayed on the table—bolted them down greedily in spite of critical glances from other guests. The specialty was Beijing Duck: sautéed kidney and liver; deep-fried tongue; salt-fried pancreas; camphor-smoked brains; eggs braised in duck fat. And Hong's favorite black tea, Iron Buddha, was served in steaming potfuls. He should have been here, Chen thought, while picking at his own food.

When the banquet was over, the Emperor left immediately. Then everyone else left, observing the Chinese rule that once food was eaten, the table should be deserted. As Chen was leaving the hall, an elegant young man stood in his way.

It was Cao Guojiu, noble immortal, without his jade table that admitted him to the court for eternity. "Permit me a few moments, Peerless Sir," he began. His expression was earnest, his tone humble.

This lack of sarcasm astonished Chen.

"We're all thrilled," Cao continued, "by your success. That night at the restaurant after you left, we knew you were the man to beat for the first ranking."

"How did you know?"

"Your manner." Cao was struggling for words. "Something about you. It's difficult to say, but we knew."

"Your solicitation is most flattering," Chen said.

"Thank you. They say a wise man forgets old grudges."

"I neither am wise nor carry grudges."

"But you are very kind. We'll want you again for dinner. Will you please us by considering it?"

Over the shoulder of Cao Guojiu, he could see Lu beaming in the background. Without answering the question, Chen said, "Enough is usually more than most men have."

"Yes?" Cao smiled uncertainly.

"Put in another way," Chen continued, "who swallows quick can chew little."

"Yes, indeed. But I don't quite understand."

"Too much has happened to me recently. I'm only a poor scholar from a village in Sichuan, and yet everything good has fallen on me at once. I should go into seclusion, don't you think? At least for a while. Hide away and count my blessings and regain my humility. Don't you think?"

"Well . . ." Cao's mouth was trembling in confusion.

"When I return from such a retreat, perhaps you'll be so gracious as to renew your invitation. Would you be so kind?"

Cao smiled uneasily. "Yes, well, I'll do that. It would be my ... privilege." He walked away unsure if the country fellow had made a fool of him, had truly refused to see him and his companions, or had spoken the truth about having too much too soon. That evening in a teahouse, he would lean forward and say to the other two immortals, "He could become a threat to power in the capital. He speaks and smiles and sends you away unsure of what happened. He has the gift of saying nothing that he means."

When Chen left the Hall of Supreme Harmony, he walked under cold moonlight in the company of the Vice Minister of Public Works. Looking up at the stars, Chen vowed to himself never to stay in this place of dust storms and bitter cold and Mongolian winds and friendly enemies. What now? He had come a long way down this road, finding at the end of it nothing that he desired.

His rank predictably resulted in an immediate offer to join the Hanlin Academy. There, in magnificent surroundings, he'd be called upon to draft imperial proclamations, compile official histories, and in weekly sessions at the palace explain passages from the Classics to the Emperor and court. He met the Grand Secretaries who headed each of the halls of the palace; two offered him jobs. He met four of the executive ministers, three of whom suggested they see him for a talk about entering their respective ministries.

Each time Two Brother came back from an official interview, Hong asked him a reasonable question. "Do you want this post?"

"I don't know."

"What appeals to you?"

Chen shrugged. "I don't know."

This lack of resolve frustrated Hong. He had his own life to think of. The Lotus could not assign him anything for a while, not even as a messenger. The Silk Robes who saw him at the tomb could probably identify him, even with his hair grown out.

What should he do now? Eventually Two Brother would make a decision and enter an altogether new life. They never discussed it, but surely they must go different ways. Chen's ranking had thrust him into the forefront of Chinese society. Nothing could change that, not even Chen. Sooner or later he must surrender to the pressure of fame and accept the public life of a Confucian scholar.

That meant a new life for Lao Hong, too. He understood it with his typical clarity of mind. There was always home. He thought of his friends, especially Wujiang, and his sister and even his father. He recalled exactly the look of his cricket cages and the burial plot in the backyard. He walked down streets in memory and turned up lanes to wander through the surrounding fields. He flew kites and strolled along a stream where crawfish emerged in springtime. He thought of the layout of things—where houses were and the threshing square and old Tang's stable.

So did Chen. One night they spoke candidly of home.

"Do you miss it?" Hong asked.

"Last night," Chen said, "I lay awake a long time. In my mind I heard a poem by Li Po.

> *"Moonlight in front of my bed—*
> *I took it for frost on the ground!*
> *I lift my eyes to watch the mountain moon,*
> *lower them and dream of home."*

Chen sighed with such longing that Hong wondered if Two Brother was thinking of the girl Daiyun.

"Yes, I could go home," Chen said. "When you learned our village had survived, I felt overjoyed but sad, too."

"Why sad?"

"Throughout the journey I wondered if the people we loved were still there. When I learned they were, I no longer needed to see them. They were there; I was here. That was enough."

Hong waited for him to go on. When he didn't, Hong asked, "Do you think of her?"

"Yes, I do, I think of her. But differently now. The idea of her suffering and dying filled me with horror—and love. But well and happy, she doesn't come to mind."

"I see why you're sad. You don't really love her."

"I love the memory of her, and I'm glad she can have a happy life."

"So there's no reason for you to go home."

After another silence, Chen said, "Anyway, I couldn't go home. I owe the state for ranking first." He slapped his knee for emphasis. "I must serve the country."

"Yes, I know," Hong said with a touch of sarcasm; "your Confucian duty."

"But it's real," Chen claimed earnestly. "The higher the rank, the greater the obligation. My Master made that clear."

"I'm sure you have exact quotations."

"I have."

They were silent again. Then Two Brother described a new offer. This was for a district magistrate in the province of Jiangsu, not far from Shanghai. He'd be responsible for maintaining order, collecting taxes, overseeing education, and observing religious rituals. For these purposes he'd have a large yamen, with offices in the front and a private residence in the back. Clerks, runners, and secretaries would do his bidding. Guards would escort his sedan chair and carry a placard announcing his office. At night they'd light his way with swaying red lanterns. He'd preside at court behind a bench covered with red cloth stamped with his official seal. When he set punishment for an offense, he'd reach into a cylindrical holder and remove a number of bamboo spills to indicate the severity of the flogging. These he would throw on the floor so the miscreant could kneel and pick them all up, discovering how many strokes he was going to receive.

"Will you take this post?" Hong asked.

"Do you think I should?"

"If it suits you."

"Does it suit me? Be honest, didi."

"No."

"Why?"

"I can't see you throwing slivers of bamboo on the floor to show a man how many times he's going to be hit. I could do that. But you couldn't."

"Then what should I do?"

"I don't know. I'm sure your Master has words about patience. He has words about everything else."

Hong had lost his own patience. It wouldn't surprise him if Two Brother hung around Beijing for many months, unsure, lost in his thoughts, with his nose stuck resolutely in a book. Hong's natural inclination was to stay with Two Brother, nurture and watch over him until the future seemed clear. But it was time to send Chen on his way, alone. Having decided that, Hong turned to his own problem and solved it quickly.

At the teahouse he left a message for Sun Qi. Next day there was a message for him. Hong went to the Red Horsemen barracks and met the officer. When Hong revealed his decision to go south and join the army, Sun Qi was exasperated. "Why leave Beijing? You can do well in the capital. People always need a clever boy. And of course the Lotus has reason to appreciate your talents. I suspect there's no better young operative in all of China. We'd have work for you, and as for the army, I can get you admitted to the best military school in the country. By your twentieth birthday you'd be a captain. Your plan just isn't worthy of you, Lao Hong. Reconsider."

"No, sir," Hong replied. He spoke with such firmness that the Red Horseman said nothing. "I can't stay in Beijing if my brother does. He needs his independence."

Sun Qi laughed. "You talk as if he's your younger brother."

"In a way he is."

"Maybe he won't stay in Beijing."

"In any case, I want to be far away from him. Then I can't run to him when I worry about his welfare. He has to be on his own." He added, "And so do I."

"You're a very strange boy." Sun Qi regarded him solemnly.
"Come back tomorrow," he commanded, "without fail."

In the evening Lao Hong told his brother that he'd be leaving for the south within a week. Regional General Ma, Grand Defender of the Fifth Army Group, would honor the promise to help him with a military career.

"You'll make your life in the army?" Chen was appalled.

"I nearly ran down a hill and joined in a battle. My fate is to do that someday. I'm going, gege. You can't stop me."

Next day he met Sun Qi in the barracks. "Once a sworn brother, always a sworn brother," warned Sun Qi. "If ever you're needed and we call, you must come."

"I know that, and I will," Hong promised.

"Even if it means deserting your post."

"I know that, and I will."

"Facing execution as a traitor if you're caught."

"I know that."

"I know members of the Lotus who have had to leave China and never return. Who changed their names and now live in terror of being discovered. Who wander unknown across the earth. Can you be one of them?"

"If I must. I took a vow. It's more important than my life."

Looking into the boy's eyes, the Red Horseman nodded at last to show he was convinced. "Then go until you come again. But wait a moment." Sun Qi reached in his pocket and took out a small jade figure. It was a dragon, writhing through a web of clouds.

"A friend gave this to me. He made me promise to give it up someday. I've treasured it so long I wondered if the time would ever come when I'd give it up. But the time has come. Here." Sun Qi shoved it at the boy, who backed away and put his hands behind him. "Lao Hong," commanded the officer sharply. "Take it!"

So Hong did. Turning the jade figure, he stared at the lively green creature mounting forever through a tumultuous sky.

"These words go with it," Sun Qi said. He began to recite.

" 'The dragon comes to go. It comes from the clouds as a vision of the Buddha nature, the way, the undivided essence. Then back to the clouds it goes. And returns and goes and comes and goes. This dragon rises and falls in turbulence, fearless among the mysteries, beyond smoke or depths, forever and out of time.' That's what my friend told me when he gave it up. The dragon protects your honor. You have this protection when you need it. A day comes when someone else's need is greater. Then you give up the dragon with the same words." He repeated them until Hong knew them by heart.

"Lao Hong, you have proved yourself. You are truly a sworn brother," the Red Horseman said in farewell, turned, and walked away.

Chen had dinner with Censor Tang Wangai in the austere dining room of the Censorate. In his black high-collared robe, the paunchy little man reminded Chen of Gao Shi, the Deputy Examiner of Chengdu. Because Gao Shi had been kindly, the comparison put Chen at ease.

Appropriately for an agency of high standards, the Censorate offered meals of simplicity to guests. The courses were vegetarian and no wine was served.

Censor Tang Wangai talked first about the examination. Chen had learned that every official had a burning curiosity about a young scholar who ranked first. Initially, their questions about his way of thinking and his technique of writing made him nervous. But Chen learned to answer these questions simply— as if his answers were true. Actually, he had little sense of how he thought, and his technique in writing varied according to the test. But as the Master said, "A wise man adapts himself to circumstance, even as water shapes itself to the vessel holding it." Chen replied effortlessly, skillfully, patiently. He was ready to explain the whole history of his progress from district to palace examination.

So he was surprised when the censor abruptly talked of something else.

"It has come to my attention," Tang Wangai began, "that

your knowledge of the Classics is matched by your belief in them. That is indeed rare." He put up his hand to prevent a comment. "People are impressed by you. They believe in your belief." Now he paused, allowing Chen to thank him profusely, after which he broached a new subject.

"Surely you've heard of the Director of Palace Rites, Ni Feng-lin. A tragic and sad event," he declared without feeling. "The point is there has been a shift in alliances, in power, in . . . such things . . ." He waved his hand vaguely. "The point is the court has been changing. People are . . . coming and going. Do you understand?"

"Enough, Honorable Censor. Government is changing."

"The point is this. Wei Xi is coming to Beijing as the new Director of Palace Rites." Having let the young scholar absorb that news, the censor added, "So in Qufu there will be a position to fill. I'm talking about Vice Secretary of Rites there— in charge of the temple and tomb of Confucius. Do you follow?"

"Yes, Honorable Censor."

"Had you ranked lower, had you ranked even second, you would not be considered for such a significant post. Do you follow? No, I think you don't." Now the Censor was smiling. "We are offering the appointment to you. Because of your rank and your obvious devotion to the Teacher of Ten Thousand Generations."

As Hong finished packing, he turned to his brother. "When do you leave for Qufu?"

"Next month."

"Qufu suits you, gege. I can imagine you strolling around those gardens, stopping to look at pockmarked stones, holding a book in your hand, and the pines rustling and the stone animals standing near the graves. You'll be close to the source of your thinking. And you'll be close enough to Beijing to share in its decisions but far enough away so you don't have to eat dinner every night with immortals. I can see you in Qufu, walking in the pine forest and thinking of your Master, who'll be in the ground nearby. I can see it and I'm happy." He tied a cord around his knapsack. "But I'll miss you on the road. Remember all those hundreds of miles, never knowing what to expect next? We traveled well together."

"We did, Three Brother. Write me. Will you please write me often?"

"I depend on you to do most of the writing. But you'll always know where I am. Goodbye, gege."

"Goodbye, didi. Wait, didi." Chen embraced him. "Thank you for getting me here," said Two Brother in a trembling voice.

In the courtyard Fufang was waiting. She bowed slightly—a bow of reluctant respect—and raised her small mouth to Hong's ear. "You're as smart as your brother," she whispered.

Hong looked at the girl, wondering if the sudden odd rush of emotion was what Chen had once felt in the presence of Daiyun.

"Did you hear me?" the girl said, pouting. "I said, you're as smart as your brother."

Head cocked as if judging that possibility, Hong said, "Yes." He winked at her. "I know." Hoisting the knapsack, he went through the courtyard. Without looking back, Lao Hong leaned into a swirling gust of winter snow. He headed south, his eyes blinking rapidly as if snowflakes were in them.

"On the road," he said aloud as if Two Brother were beside him. Then he said, "Once more on the road."

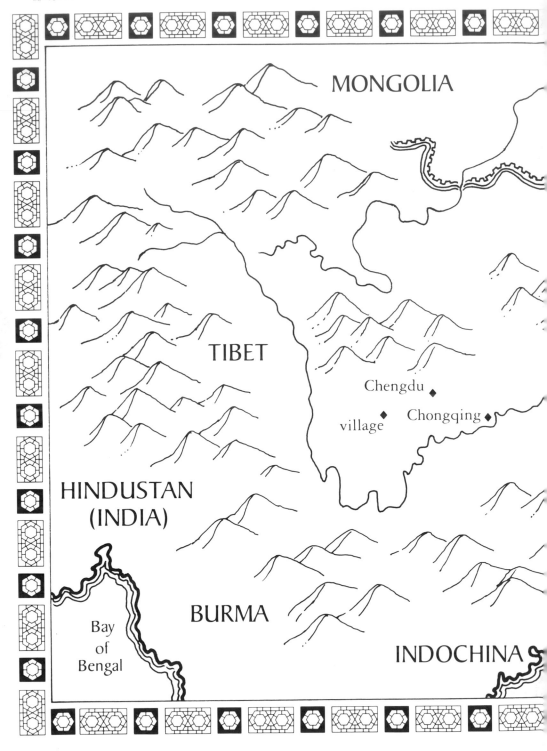

MONGOLIA

TIBET

Chengdu ◆

village ◆   Chongqing ◆

HINDUSTAN
(INDIA)

BURMA

Bay
of
Bengal

INDOCHINA